THE
GIRL
WHO
NEVER
CAME
BACK

BOOKS BY SUZANNE GOLDRING

My Name is Eva

Burning Island

The Girl Without a Name

The Shut-Away Sisters

The Girl with the Scarlet Ribbon

The Woman Outside the Walls

SUZANNE GOLDRING

THE
GIRL
WHO
NEVER
CAME
BACK

bookouture

Published by Bookouture in 2023

An imprint of Storyfire Ltd.
Carmelite House
50 Victoria Embankment
London EC4Y 0DZ

www.bookouture.com

ISBN: 978-1-83790-708-3
eBook ISBN: 978-1-83790-707-6

For loyal friends of many years, especially Sally.

A friend is a person with whom I may be sincere. Before him I may think aloud.

RALPH WALDO EMERSON, *ESSAYS*

SPECIAL OPERATIONS EXECUTIVE MANUAL

HOW TO BE AN AGENT IN OCCUPIED EUROPE

C. HOW TO DEFEND YOURSELF AGAINST SURVEILLANCE

3.b) If, on the other hand, you must carry out your secret work, you must first shake off the watchers. If there is more than one, you may have to do this piecemeal. You can nearly always drop all but one by taking a vehicle unexpectedly.

PROLOGUE

WHO'S WATCHING?

Sylvia slips the latest letter out from under the blotter on her desk and reads some of the words again:

How you could have abandoned my sister the way you did, I can't imagine. Can you live with yourself, knowing you didn't bring her home? You must have uncovered the truth at some point over the years, you selfish old witch. I demand to know what you found out.

She sighs, knowing what he says is true. She knows she must write the letter she has put off writing for so long; she can leave the rest of her affairs to Peggy, but not this. It wouldn't be fair and besides, Sylvia doesn't know how much longer she has left to her. There are days when she can't think straight, confusing the past with the present; days when she can barely hold a cup, let alone a pen. She knows Peggy has noticed too – she has seen the way she sometimes looks at her.

Sylvia looks over her shoulder; she has never been able to shake the habit, even after all these years. It is ingrained in her, the need for secrecy. It sounds like Peggy is busy in the kitchen.

She's humming, which hopefully means she is making soup and sandwiches for their lunch. The slightly sulphurous smell of hard-boiled eggs hangs in the air, hinting she will make Sylvia's favourite sandwiches with mayonnaise and cress. Yesterday they had fresh onion soup, followed by a round of ham and mustard on brown bread.

Dear Peggy, who has been Sylvia's close companion since they were children, now virtually her live-in carer. I couldn't do without her, Sylvia thinks. But that doesn't mean I can tell her the truth. I can't tell anyone what we did. I know we're allowed to these days, but how can you suddenly start to reveal everything when you've kept it bottled up inside all this time? How can I tell my dearest, oldest friend, such a trusting, sensible friend, that I always knew I was sending young women to their deaths? She'd never look at me in the same way again.

It's all here in the polished mahogany bureau. All the secrets. Files and photographs in the drawers. Sylvia kept a record of everything – all the fruitless searches, all the interviews. They're all here. She finds the one photo that she has studied more than any of the others. It's creased and dog-eared now after being handled so many times but the face in the picture is still fresh and young, so hopeful.

Sylvia remembers each one of her girls so clearly. All nervous and timid at first, wondering what they would be asked to do, but gaining confidence week by week with their Special Operations Executive agent training. She had checked on their progress at every stage, from their first assault course right up to the time when they were whisked away on a moonlit night. Of course, they were all advised of the risks, warned that capture could mean imprisonment and interrogation, told that the security of their friends depended on their ability to withstand discomfort. No, Sylvia tells herself, she never used the word 'discomfort', they weren't shielded from the reality of the situation. They were told they might well face pain, terrible pain, and would have to withhold information for as long as they could bear it.

How long did you last, my dear? she thinks, looking at the worn, tired photo. *I hope it wasn't too terrible.* But she suppresses the thought that she knows what really happened and very few people know the truth.

Sylvia glances at the window. There is no mist outside today. The sky is grey, not blue, so there is a clear view all around the cottage. She'd be able to see if anyone was watching. And Peggy is still humming, so now she can concentrate on this long-postponed task.

She glances over her shoulder again, then takes a sheet of creamy Croxley notepaper from the small pile in the right-hand pigeon hole and picks up her fountain pen, the one her boss, Harrington, had given her all those years ago. He was fond of trinkets, particularly gold ones. She never received one of the powder compacts from Asprey that he handed out so freely, but she was given this rather smart black pen with a gold nib and gold trimmings when their secret department ceased. She's used it for all her correspondence ever since. It's harder for her to grip than it used to be, harder for her to form the letters.

Sylvia curves her left arm around the paper, an old habit from school days, protecting it from prying eyes, if there ever were any. Her hand shakes and hovers over the page as she forms the letter in her mind. And then she begins to write, pausing occasionally to choose her words carefully. She will sign it, address it and seal it. But she won't post it. Here it will stay, for dear, trustworthy Peggy to deal with after Sylvia has gone.

ONE
ROSES ARE RED

We were all standing by the grave when it happened. Handfuls of earth had been scattered on her coffin and the words of the last hymn, 'I Vow to Thee My Country', were still echoing in my head. Sylvia had chosen it herself, of course, just as she'd chosen nearly everything that happened in our lives. She'd insisted on a plain order of service too. 'No photos, Peg,' she'd said. 'Far too vulgar.' She'd planned it all, the hymns, the flowers, the undertaker, all of it. Not quite so much towards the end though, when she was fading away in the hospice.

Barry was standing right next to me and gave me a nudge and said, 'Here, who's that lurking over there with that great dog? Not an old flame of hers, do you think?'

'Where?' I said, looking around just when I wanted to appear dignified, though any distraction from the tears and solemnity of the occasion was welcome, I can tell you.

'Over there,' he said, jerking his head towards the old yew tree. Meant to be the oldest in the country, that one is, propped up with a couple of timbers and a hollow in its trunk that local kids play in and pretend they're the witch of Little Bourne-Hardy.

Then I saw him, an old man somewhat stooped, leaning on a stick, long navy coat, black trilby, black scarf tucked round his neck. Well, it was bitterly cold that day, wind whipping from the north, down from the Pilgrims' Way, stripping the last leaves off the trees. I was wearing one of Sylvia's old coats. A grey one with a fur collar. I didn't think she'd mind and I felt she was with me when I put it on that morning. It still smelt of her perfume and she'd left her black suede gloves and a tissue, imprinted with her lipstick, tucked into the right-hand pocket.

The man was certainly watching the little crowd gathered around the grave; he seemed to be taking an interest. And then he turned away and was soon out of sight. A huge grey dog followed him, the sort Sylvia was always mad about. I didn't think dogs were allowed in the church graveyard.

I nearly forgot all about that man soon after, except when we went to look more closely at the flowers, because she'd said, hadn't she, that she didn't want wreaths, she wanted bouquets of flowers that could be taken to the hospice and the old people's home afterwards, there among the tasteful white chrysanths and lilies was a bunch of red roses. Red roses, I ask you, who sends red roses to a funeral? Valentine's Day maybe, but not a funeral.

The card attached to them didn't give much away. *For my dearest Little Swift, in memory of daring deeds, with love from Prinz and Charlie.* I'd never heard anyone calling her that, though she did have that little diamond brooch, shaped like a swallow or a swift, that I'd always wondered about. I quickly swiped the card and slipped it into my pocket. I don't think she'd have wanted anyone else to see it. She was private like that, like she had been all her life. 'Peg,' she'd say, just like she always did, even though I was Peggy to everyone else, 'Peg, you're the only one I trust. Always have, my darling, and always will.' And I'd say, 'That's all right, Sylvia, any time, dear.'

Peggy and Sylvia, Peg and Sylv, we were. 'What a pair,' my

old mum used to say. 'Always giggling, always up to no good.'
Well, of course we were. Us two were thick as thieves from the
time we first sat next to each other in Christchurch School, right
up to the time when Sylv got sent away. I remember thinking at
first it was because we'd played a trick on Mrs Jones and Mrs
Thompson, switching their milk bottles, so old Jonesy got the
gold top and her neighbour got her red, and we'd already nicked
the cream off the top. But no, it wasn't that, as Sylv said, it was
because, 'My aunt's left money for me to go away to school. So
Mother is going to be able to tour again with the repertory
company. They want her for Lady Macbeth.'

'What, a school where you stay and sleep?' I remember
asking, thinking it was bad enough to be in school all day, let
alone for weeks on end.

'It's called boarding school. I might be able to visit in the
holidays and I'll write, of course. Mother says it will teach me
how to be a lady.'

And that's how it started, I suppose. A lifelong friendship
kept alive with postcards and letters over the years and visits in
between. Every year, when we could, we'd see a show and eat at
an Italian restaurant in Soho that became our favourite. 'Meet
you at the Negroni?' was all we had to say and we both knew
where to go and which was our regular table. That one in the
corner, where we could whisper and giggle so no one but us
knew what was so funny. And we always ate the same food. It
didn't really change much over the years. A small carafe of
Barolo, melon with ham, lasagne and a green salad, followed by
what the owner called 'pudding', which was like a hefty great
trifle with layers of fruit, sponge, custard and cream, sliced up in
huge solid squares. We always left saying we weren't going to
eat for a week after that.

I'm going to miss Sylvia so much. Miss our meet-ups, miss
our girlish teasing, miss our confidences. The last couple of
years, spending more time at her side has nearly had me

climbing the walls, but it's also been rewarding, because I've come to understand her a little better and think about what our lives meant. So different, yet side by side we did what we had to do. I suppose some would say I was her carer, but I never thought of it that way. To me, she was always just my dear friend Sylvia. No regrets though.

Barry nudged me again. 'Want a lift back to the cottage?'

I nodded. Drinks were laid out before we left. That and nibbles. Nothing fancy but, again, just as she'd said she wanted it. There weren't many of us; members of the gardening club, a few she knew from church and Barry because he looked after the garden. Barry thought it would have been better to hold it in the pub, but she'd said, 'I want my farewell to be in the church and then at home, darling. That's where I want everyone to talk about me, so I can listen in,' she added with that famous wicked grin of hers. Charmed all the fellas, that smile did.

It's my home now, of course. She's left it to me. She told me that ages ago: 'There's no one else in my life, Peg. I'd like you to have it.' And I was very grateful at the time. It's what they call 'chocolate box' – all roses round the door and little windows with criss-cross panes. And a thatched cottage in the country-side is a darn sight more attractive than a dingy east London terrace, even if it does have a new kitchen. I've always loved visiting here and we used to take her wire-haired dachshund for walks over the surrounding fields when I first started coming. By then my dogs were long gone and anyway, her dachshund Fergus was never a dog for friends.

But that was when the cottage was looked after. The garden is still fairly tidy because Barry mows the lawns and trims the hedges. But he's not a big fan of weeding and the beds have got riddled with ground elder and groundsel. I used to pull a few weeds in the past, but I'm not so good bending down now, so I'd rather not risk a slip.

And as for the thatch, well, let's just say it's past its best. I think it had been done shortly before she first bought the place, but now there's thick pads of green moss growing all over the grey straw and the fixings and all sorts that hold it together are sticking out all over the place. She may have left me the cottage, but she hasn't left me the means to have it repaired, so sadly, I'll have to let it go. Last winter there was quite a leak above the staircase and she had to have the roof patched with corrugated iron. Looks terrible, but what could she do? Couldn't have rain streaming in for months on end.

We both saw a cottage being rethatched in another village once. It was quite a few years ago and I was all for taking the name of the thatchers. But Sylvia said she spoke to the owners later, who told her what a nightmare it was having it done. Straw all over the place, they said. 'I'm not picking straw out of my roses and aquilegia for months,' Sylv told me. 'It will see me out, I'm sure.' So it never was done. Pity that. I might have decided to stay on here if it wasn't for the state of the roof. Though to be honest, a cottage in the middle of nowhere, with other homes at least several hundred yards away, isn't perhaps the best place for an elderly woman to live. I've thought that a few times these last few months, when I've been here looking after Sylvia. There may be a regular grocery delivery, but everything else is a ten-minute drive away, even the pub.

So, there's nothing for it. Thatch Cottage, for that's its unoriginal name, will have to go. But first, I'll have to finish sorting out Sylvia's affairs. She was meant to have done it all before she went downhill. And I'll have to work out who this Prinz Charlie is. I'll start from the beginning, shall I?

TWO
LET'S SHOW 'EM, GIRLS!
OCTOBER 1941

'So, you think you can do it then, do you?' Harrington leant back in his swivel chair, sizing up Sylvia's reaction to his brief. He had just told her she would have the final responsibility for selecting women for a secret operation to send female agents into France.

'I'm confident I'm a good judge of character. I think I'll be able to pick suitable candidates with the right aptitude.'

'You'd better be! I'm not so sure about this development myself, but if we can't find enough good chaps, we're simply going to have to put up with the fairer sex.'

Sylvia seethed inwardly. If this was going to be his attitude, she'd have trouble controlling her temper. Women could be just as good as men, she was sure of it. But men often needed persuading of that. 'I promise you, any that don't come up to scratch will be weeded out early on, just as we do with the male recruits. So, you can be assured that I will only be prepared to send the very best.'

'Glad to hear it. We've got a remit for sabotage and subversion in this department. Churchill says he wants us to set Europe ablaze. Think your ladies will be up for that?' He swivelled some more, sizing her up and seeming to rest his eyes far too often on her lips and breasts.

Sylvia disliked him intensely, but if she was to make a success of the tremendous opportunity she'd been given, she was determined to overlook his patriarchal manner. She had wanted to make an important contribution to the war effort right from the start and after joining the Women's Auxiliary Air Force had been spotted for her excellent French and German. A recommendation for Special Operations had followed, resulting in her appointment as Harrington's assistant. And now it appeared she would have an even greater role to play in preparing female agents for missions in France.

'Of course, you do realise they'll have to undergo the same thorough training as the chaps. Think they'll be up to that?' Harrington lit another cigarette to add to the haze of smoke in his office.

Sylvia was already familiar with the rigorous programme to which agents were subjected. She had even sampled some of the courses herself. Recruits had to be fit and skilled if they were to stand a chance of surviving in occupied France. 'If we select the right candidates, I've no doubt they will cope very well,' she said, remaining calm despite her annoyance.

'Including all that stuff about silent killing techniques? Think they'll have the gumption for that as well?'

Sylvia's lips almost twitched into a smile. Did the man not realise just how beastly girls could be? Particularly those who had endured boarding school and the brutal swipes of hockey and lacrosse sticks? 'We'll ensure they cover everything, Sir. They'll be just as well equipped as their male counterparts and in many ways they'll have an advantage. The Germans aren't going to immediately suspect girls and women of being undercover agents.'

'Hmm, I suppose that's true. Attractive girls can get away

with a lot. Or do you think a pretty face will get too much attention? Would you be better off choosing the plainer ones?'

Really, Sylvia sighed inwardly. He was impossible. 'I think our recruits should be chosen and trained on the basis of their potential, not their looks. They could come from all walks of life. We might have debutantes or shop girls. The priority is their ability to think and react quickly, to learn and adapt. I think many women are able to do that perfectly even in their normal lives.'

'Very well, if you say so. How soon do you think we might have the first ones ready?'

Sylvia knew this question was coming. He was always so impatient, so keen to push ahead. It was one of his better qualities in many ways, but she wasn't going to be hurried. 'A small shortlist has already been compiled and they've had their preliminary interviews. I'll be seeing the first candidates next week, then we'll select those suitable for the initial training. I should think we'll have a few ready early next year.'

'Excellent,' he said, stubbing his cigarette out in the onyx ashtray and suddenly standing as an indication that the meeting was over. 'We'll see how you get on. If we can speed things up, it would be appreciated by our friends in high places.'

'We'll see what we can do. Some may be ready sooner than others, but I wouldn't like to cut corners. All our agents are valued personnel and we owe it to them to prepare them thoroughly as they'll be the ones risking their lives out there. We're all aware how dangerous this is going to be.'

'Quite right too. This is vital work. All the same, I've suggested your girls won't need to do as many practise jumps as the fellows. Three should be enough, I think.' He shook Sylvia's hand. 'Right, dismissed.'

Sylvia left Harrington's office rigid with fury. How dare he make that decision. What right had he to reduce the amount of training the girls would receive? Did he really not value the contribution they were going to make? She would have loved to share all of this with Peggy, her closest friend, but she couldn't divulge her top-secret work. It was all hush-hush and no one outside the department could ever know a thing.

She resolved then and there to make sure every single one of the girls she recruited was better than the men. They would show men like Harrington and anyone else who dismissed their worth that the 'fairer sex', as he so lightly described them, were the bravest and boldest players in this game called war.

THREE
POWDER MY NOSE

I was sorting through Sylvia's handbag the day after the funeral when I picked up her gold powder compact. I haven't used one in years, but she always did, always kept it in her bag. Lots of times, when we were out for lunch or tea, she'd suddenly snap it open and dab at her nose or check her lipstick wasn't smudged.

I flipped it open and, although the powder was nearly all gone, just a tiny rim of it all around the outer edge, I could still see her doing it. Sometimes she'd leave the table, or wherever we were sitting, and say, 'I'm just going to powder my nose, darling. Shan't be long.' You don't hear that euphemism much these days, just like when my old dad used to say he was going to see a man about a dog, when he meant he was popping to the gents' toilets. But Sylvia really did mean she was going to powder her nose. She might have spent a penny at the same time for all I know, but most times she was checking her face in the cloakroom mirror. I suppose because her looks had been her currency for most of her life, unlike mine. I got by on my wits and snarky remarks.

The pressed powder smelt of her, even though there was so little left. She may have used it in her last days at the hospice, for all I know, before she started to slip away. A blessing, that, really, that she drifted off into sleep and wasn't fighting it.

And then I thought, *well maybe I should start using face powder like Sylvia did, it's never too late, is it?* Such a lovely compact it was too, real gold with wavy engraving all over the lid in a pattern like watered silk. I decided to see if the powder came out, so I could buy a replacement, and that's when I found it. Underneath the powder refill was a slip of paper. Ever so thin it was. What we used to call airmail paper, almost like tissue. It was folded up and a name was scrawled in pencil on the underside when I turned it over. I thought it would say Sylvia, but it didn't. It was Phyllis.

That's odd, I thought. *Who's Phyllis when she's at home?* I'd never heard that name before. There was no writing anywhere else when I opened it out, so I folded it up again and tucked it back inside. I'd no idea why it was there. Maybe so someone knew the compact was hers?

I snapped it shut and, as I did that, something else came to mind. One time, goodness knows how long ago, when she'd finished checking her lipstick in the compact mirror and then clicked it shut, I must have said something about what a lovely thing it was and gosh, it must have been expensive, being real gold. Maybe I was angling to find out if it had been a gift from an old boyfriend or something. I can't really remember what brought it on. And she'd said, 'Oh darling, he gave them to all the girls. Must have bought a job lot some time.'

I didn't know what she meant then and I certainly don't now. She never said who He was, or the girls for that matter. Maybe He was a lover who gave them to all his conquests. The most I ever got was a cheap bottle of scent from any of mine. I'd always hoped for a bottle of Evening in Paris, just because I liked the name really. But all I ever got from my blokes was Yardley's Lavender or Devon Violets.

And it was Sylvia who finally bought me the scent I longed

for one Christmas. I'd given her a box of Bronnley Freesia soaps, which I'd thought was ever so sophisticated, and she gave me Evening in Paris. My heart did a little flip the minute I unwrapped the present and saw that dark blue box and the little blue bottle. 'I've always wanted this,' I said, opening the bottle and dabbing it on my wrists and behind my ears.

'I know you have, darling. And now you've got a whole bottle, all to yourself.' She was wearing Femme de Rochas of course, like she always did. That scent still lingers on everything of hers. It's faint in her handbag, stronger on her clothes, not much but still there, reminding me of her.

I huffed on the gold compact case and my warm breath clouded the shiny surface, so I polished it with my sleeve. I felt Sylv wouldn't approve of that. She was always one for doing things properly, but she's not here now, even though I seem to feel her all around me, commenting on everything I'm doing. 'Straighten the watercolours, would you, Peg? There's a dear,' she'd say when I was dusting and leaving her collection of pictures all skew-whiff.

Oh, the dusting. Never-ending it was. She used to have a cleaning lady – Sharon, I think it was. But by the time I was more or less a permanent fixture at the cottage she wasn't around any longer. Maybe Sylv thought she didn't need to pay someone else if I was there to help. I suggested getting a cleaner in again once, but she wouldn't have it. She said, 'I'm sure we can manage. I don't want strangers nosing around the cottage.'

And it wasn't just the dust that bothered me, it was the flipping cobwebs. I swear those spiders got to work every night, just to give me plenty to do the next day. Everywhere they were, spun from the oak beams to the mantelpiece and over to the tall dresser. They must have flung themselves from one spot to the other, spinning like mad as they went. And the problem with them is you can't always see the cobwebs. I'd think I'd brushed them all away, then the sun would come out and shine through the leaded windows and show up another dozen or more.

She had a window cleaner as well at one time, for the outside, not the insides. I started on those too, but those little diamond panes are so fiddly and besides I couldn't reach very well because of the wretched security grilles on every ground-floor window. You try wrapping your fingers in a duster and sticking them through a tiny space.

I mentioned it once or twice to Sylv and she said, 'Oh, what does it matter? Who's going to notice? I don't want anyone seeing in, anyway.' And soon after that she stopped having the window cleaner as well.

And I suggested taking the window bars away, saying, 'What do you need them for? You're not living in crime central like me back in London, you're in the middle of the countryside.'

But she said, 'I've learnt to look after myself, Peg. And the first rule is take precautions.'

Well, I suppose she was right to be careful, living alone for most of her life, while I lived in a terrace surrounded by other people, half of them petty criminals in any case. But I remember as well, one time, maybe soon after she moved to the cottage, when I questioned her choice. I said, 'Why'd you want to live in the middle of nowhere anyway?' The cottage looks out over fields front and back. You can see everywhere for miles and I must admit, it's a very beautiful view.

But she didn't say she'd chosen it for the view or for the lovely garden, she just said, 'So I can see if anyone's coming.' And she walked out of her sitting room into the garden and went and stood looking out over the hedge, which has always been kept at chest height but no more. She stood there gazing across the field, which was planted with potatoes that year, I seem to remember, as if she was expecting someone. Odd that, don't you think?

SPECIAL OPERATIONS EXECUTIVE
MANUAL

SURVEILLANCE

D. CONCLUSION

If you are being watched it is essential for you to be aware
of it.

FOUR
A FOGGY DAY

So, towards the end, there we were, two old ladies, alone in this isolated country cottage in the middle of nowhere. But I never felt uneasy. Compared to London, with all the shouting from neighbours, ambulance and police sirens, dog mess everywhere on the streets, drunks being sick on the doorstep, country life was all peace and quiet, I can tell you. Not completely silent though, as there's more noise than you might think, especially at night, what with all the foxes screaming, owls screeching and now and then a pheasant squawking as well. But I got quite used to those sounds and didn't find them at all alarming. Better than the drunken swearing and brawling round my way, I have to say.

We didn't have dogs in the cottage, not after Fergus had gone, nor any strong men nearby, but I never once felt frightened. While Sylv was another matter altogether. Jumpy? You can bet your life she was. A creaky door or the wind rattling a window and she'd leap up, as far as a very elderly lady with creaky legs can leap, saying, 'Did you hear that? What was it?'

And I'd have to leave my comfy armchair or whatever I was doing and peer out of the windows at the black night. It's pitch-dark out here in the countryside. No such thing as street lights round here and you can't see a blooming thing. Or I'd unlock the kitchen door with its two locks and two heavy bolts, switch on the outside lights and stare into the darkness, listening and wondering if that was footsteps I was hearing or just my tinnitus, which I have quite badly, by the way. Then I'd slam the door shut and call out the all-clear to her. That door really does slam shut with a great bang, like all her outside doors, as they're not only heavy wood, but reinforced with metal plates and grilles that criss-cross the glass too. Honestly, what was she expecting to happen?

A right pain it was when she decided to get a cat after Fergus had gone and wanted to put in a cat flap. I had to help her ask all around the village for someone to come and cut a hole in that metal with an angle grinder or whatever they call those things. Blasted noisy it was too, when the man was cutting through the plate. And then, blow me, once it was all fitted, she changed her mind. She never did get a cat. But it was handy for small deliveries. They could pop them through the flap if we were out and it couldn't fit through the letter box.

She was always at her jumpiest when it got foggy, which it often does out here. It's not that dense, dirty fog like we used to have all those years ago in London, when you couldn't see from one side of the road to the other, the sort that made you cough and made your hankie all black. No, it's more thick mist than fog, that builds up in the valley below us and floats right up to the cottage. Sometimes you can't see a thing past the hedge, when normally on a clear day you'd be able to see right across the fields and over to the Pilgrims' Way up there on the hills.

One time, years before I was at the cottage pretty much always, she phoned me, sounding panicky. 'You've got to come right away, Peg,' she said. 'I can't see past the privet. I don't know what might be out there.'

I talked her down that time. I couldn't rush straight to the station and get to her. I had Harry sick in bed with his chest. It was lung cancer and he didn't last all that much longer. And after that I was free to go to her whenever I liked. But that time and others, when she couldn't get a clear view out the windows and from the garden she was all on edge.

I never minded it when I was there on a foggy day. It was like being on an island surrounded by water, because the fog cut us off from the rest of the world. And on days like that, I remember her muttering something strange, which at first I could never make out, until one day when it was foggy yet again, I said, 'For goodness' sake, Sylv, what are you going on about? You're muttering away. Can't you speak clearly?'

'Nacked and naybel alas,' she said. 'It's like nacked and naybel alas here.'

'Knacked?' I said. 'What's that mean? Do you mean knackered?'

And of course I didn't have a clue what she was going on about. Maybe that's when I had the first inkling that she might be going a bit doolally. Shame that. She'd always been such a clever girl. Amazed me how she could memorise poems and recite them, word for word. Ever so good at maths and crosswords too. Did the *Daily Telegraph* cryptic right up to the end. Well, not quite, I suppose. There wasn't really any point in giving her the paper for the last few weeks. She sat there scribbling letters into the white squares and I looked a few times to see if she'd finished it but it was all total nonsense. She hadn't been writing in proper words at all, just jumbles of letters. Such a shame, she used to be so clever.

I found out what nacked and naybel alas meant later, when I mentioned it to Barry. The day had started out foggy, but was starting to clear a bit by the time he drove up in his old van to clear the leaves. There were loads on the paths, along with windfall apples that I hadn't had time to rescue and cook up, so

I was worried about Sylv turning her ankle and slipping over on the squashed fruit.

'How is she today?' he'd asked, jerking his head towards the house. I think he'd begun to notice she was quite often a bit funny. I'd just gone out to give him his usual tea with two sugars and a buttered bun – I always look after the help, it pays in the long run.

I shook my head and told him she doesn't like these foggy days. 'Keeps going on about nacked and naybel alas. No idea what on earth she's on about. But she'll be happier now you're here and when the fog has cleared a bit more. She really doesn't like not being able to see across the fields.'

'That's German, isn't it?'

'Is it? I didn't know she knew any German though I suppose she might have picked up a bit going out there for work over the years. What's it mean then?'

'Not sure. Something about night, but I don't know the other bit.' Barry frowned. 'Tell you what, I'll ask tonight down the pub. It's quiz night and there's some clever types in on a Thursday, they might know.'

'Don't let on where you heard it, will you? I don't want them thinking she's odd.'

He grinned, the gaps showing between his yellow teeth. 'Don't you worry. I'll say I overheard it somewhere.' He tapped his nose. 'Leave it with me.'

I didn't hear any more for another week and to be honest, I'd pretty much forgotten all about it. Once the fog cleared, we had some bright frosty days, sun and blue sky, with a clear view across the valley, and Sylvia seemed quite different altogether. But when Barry was back again to clear up yet more leaves, he said, 'I've got an answer for you. About that nacked thing you mentioned last week, when it was foggy.'

'Oh, what thing?' I said, not really remembering what we'd been talking about the week before.

'You said she was saying nacked and naybel alas. Well, the chaps I spoke to, they were the winning team down the pub that night. The Overlanders, they call themselves. They said was I sure that's what she'd said, because it sounded to them more like Nacht und Nebel Erlass. Here, look, they wrote it out for me.'

He dug into his trouser pocket and pulled out a scrap of paper along with a filthy old hankie. I think he'd been using it to wipe his windscreen. That or it had never been washed. I took a step back – I didn't want to get anywhere near that grubby, snotty rag. 'So, what's it mean then?'

'Well, I was right. I thought it sounded German. It means night and fog decree, like they've written down for me there.'

'I'm still no clearer,' I said. 'Is that supposed to mean something?'

'The team said it was an expression the Nazis used when they wanted prisoners to sort of get lost in the system. When they wanted them to disappear without trace, their names didn't get added to any of their records.'

'And why would they want to do that?'

'That's exactly what I asked. And one of the guys said, it was what often happened to foreign agents, during the war.'

'Spies, you mean? What's our Sylvia doing, talking about stuff to do with spies?'

Barry laughed, showing those terrible teeth again. 'Maybe she was one,' he said. 'Or she's been watching too many old black and white films.'

He went off laughing and I went in to make his tea. We'd run out of buns that week, so he had to make do with Rich Tea biscuits. That's all we'd got until the grocery order arrived. Quite how Sylv still managed to do it on her computer I don't know, but she was clever like that. Only I think the order was the same every week. We often got far too much milk and Cheddar cheese. I kept thinking I needed to get her to show me how to work it so we didn't keep overdoing it.

FIVE

LOOK IN THE MIRROR

SEPTEMBER 1942

But Sylvia knew all too well what the night and fog decree meant. She knew because she saw how it was employed to hide all traces of her lovely girls. Her girls, not theirs. How dare they try to cover up what they had done to her brave girls? And they weren't the only ones who didn't care, though her side at least allowed her to go in search of them after it all happened.

When she saw the fog rising in the evenings, like a misty veil swirling over the fields of stubble, she knew it would have wrapped the cottage in a thick blanket by morning. She watched it come, floating up from the valley, seeping from the very pores of the soil, until it was dense and impenetrable and she had no way of knowing who it might hide.

She remembered how all this first began, in that rather smart flat off Baker Street. It was early 1942 when recruitment really stepped up, but Sylvia had been involved from the very beginning, even before the occupation of Paris in October 1940. It gave her the shivers to think how it must have felt for the city's people to wake up to the sound of a strident Germanic voice announcing over loudspeakers that Paris was now occupied by German troops, their order imposed immediately, with an 8 p.m. curfew from that very first night. Sylvia was determined that London would never suffer a similar fate and had joined this secret organisation to undermine the German hold on France and help to win the war. Of course, she had her aunt's inheritance to thank for the opportunity. If she'd been sent to the local grammar school instead of the Royal Naval School, a select boarding school on the Surrey and Sussex border, she would never have been chosen for such secretive work.

She often wondered what the new recruits thought of her division's set-up, after their initial interviews in a dingy room somewhere in the stuffy grey and beige depths of the War Office. Once their credentials had been thoroughly checked by MI5, the young men and women proceeded to the next stage of recruitment and the girls came to the flat to be briefed by Sylvia. Compared to the drab surroundings of the Civil Service, the flat must have seemed positively luxurious. It had been decorated and furnished for a roving diplomat at some point in the 1930s and, in the fashion of the time, gleamed with chrome and mirror fittings. Sylvia held her interviews in the dining room, which boasted a mirrored cocktail cabinet, stripped of its liqueur glasses and shakers.

Sylvia had never been offered a cocktail at the office, but she had once checked whether the mirrors might conceal the ingredients for a White Lady, which she had first drunk in the American Bar at The Savoy hotel, encouraged, of course, by an American. To her disappointment, the cabinet contained nothing but files and stationery. And right now, she thought, she'd have happily settled for a Gin Fizz to perk her up as she waited for the next new recruit and reread their notes.

After a while, a buzz told her that her prospect was here and she called out, 'Come in.' The door opened cautiously and a slight young girl entered, her shoulders widened by the stiff khaki serge uniform all the female recruits were obliged to wear.

Assigning them to the First Aid Nursing Yeomanry gave them a respectable means of explaining their work to family and friends.

Really, Sylvia often thought, whoever came up with the title of this service and its acronym FANY must have had a sense of humour. Or maybe not, maybe it was one of the opinionated men she had to deal with on a daily basis who lightly dismissed the importance of the women she was preparing for such dangerous work. Ones like her boss, Harrington, who liked to charm these young girls and give them a gold powder compact from Asprey before they were sent off on their missions, telling them they could sell it or pawn it if they needed money in an emergency. He should have added use it as a bribe too, Sylvia thought, having heard his saccharine compliments too many times.

And this new girl had also just been treated to his patronising platitudes and was probably already thinking what a lucky girl she was to have received such a valuable parting gift. Little did she know he gave them to all the girls. Hovering in the doorway, this one gave a nervous smile, revealing the most perfect teeth framed by red lips. She was their youngest candidate so far, only nineteen years of age, so Sylvia was nearly old enough to be her mother.

'My dear Miss Lane,' Sylvia said, 'Please come in. I'll call you Phyllis if I may.' She stood to greet the newcomer, offering her hand. She knew that she made a good impression in her subtle, well-cut tweed suit and silk blouse, with a double row of pearls at her throat. Such a contrast to these girls in their newly acquired stiff uniforms, fitted at Lillywhites, but not made to measure by a proper tailor. Sylvia rarely bought off the peg and liked her clothes to fit her striking figure, a habit she'd acquired from her fashion-conscious mother, who always said, 'The way you dress goes before you, darling. Do remember that and take pride in your appearance.'

'Please do take a seat, Phyllis. We are so delighted that you are joining us. I am going to be arranging your training and will be able to answer all your questions.'

Phyllis sat down in front of the desk. 'I don't quite know what I'm going to be doing, Miss Benson. I've signed all the papers, but really I've no idea what I've got to keep secret.'

Of course you don't know what you'll be doing, Sylvia thought, *that's the whole point. Keep you in the dark and tell you only what you need to know.* Most of the recruits must have had some suspicion though; some had even already worked on resistance escape routes in France and all spoke French so well they could pass for natives. But this girl, this particular girl, seemed different from the others. Sylvia knew her department was becoming desperate for more agents, but they still had to be careful, they still had to prepare. This was not a cultural trip, nor a holiday, this was serious, this was war.

She studied Phyllis carefully. The girl was one of the prettiest they'd ever passed through to her. She had gold-flecked hazel eyes, creamy skin and dark-blonde, lustrous hair swooped into a net, tucked beneath her cap. Her hands fiddled nervously with the belt of her uniform and Sylvia thought she belonged in sumptuous evening silks and satins, not this rough serge. She carried a waft of Pond's Cold Cream about her, which Sylvia caught despite her own lingering hint of Femme de Rochas.

'You'll start at one of our preliminary training centres first, probably the one near Guildford,' she said. 'Then if all goes well, we might be sending you on to one of our other special places – all here in this country, of course.'

Phyllis frowned, then said, 'And France, you'll want me to go to France, won't you? That's why you want me, isn't it, because of my French?'

'Your excellent language skills are of immense interest to us. You are a great asset.' Sylvia was relieved to see a slight look of pride pass over the young face. 'We don't undertake recruitment lightly. We can only afford to train the very best.'

Now a smile was lightening Phyllis's face and Sylvia knew she had captured her. The girl's confidence would grow at every stage and she would become fearless. Cautious, but utterly brave, like the others Sylvia had sent on their way before her. She felt pride in Yvonne, who had been a better shot than any of the men at the Wanborough training centre, while Violette and Vera could load any kind of gun in the dark, simply by feel. In some ways women were much more intuitive and skilled than the men, Sylvia thought.

'But what am I going to be able to tell my mother?' Phyllis asked.

Sylvia knew this question was coming. She familiarised herself with every recruit's family history before they even walked through that door. She knew about their education, their previous jobs, their friends and their relatives. Sometimes they were shop girls, some were from well-connected families, others had already joined the Women's Auxiliary Air Force. But just about every single one of them wanted to know what they might be allowed to say to their nearest and dearest. If they didn't, it raised a question in Sylvia's mind about both familial and national loyalties. You have to feel this war is worth fighting for the sake of those you love, she always thought.

'You can tell her that you are doing extremely important war work and that you might be going away for a while,' she said. 'She'll soon get used to the idea that you are making yourself useful.'

Phyllis broke into a broad, happy smile, which Sylvia thought should have been noted as one of her assets; a beautiful smile could get a girl out of trouble sometimes. 'Thank you so much,' she said. 'I feel much better about it all now. And will I see you again at any point?'

'All the way through, my dear. I'll keep checking in on you

at every stage. Rest assured, I won't let them send you off until I'm completely sure you're quite ready.'

Smiling again, Phyllis said, 'That's so good to know. It makes me feel much more confident, knowing a woman is involved and not just the men. I feel you understand so much better.'

'That's why I'm here, dear. To make sure you succeed. Girls like you are vital to our operation and we will take great care of you.'

October 1942

Dear Miss Benson,

My big sister Phyllis said if we had any worries while she was away, we could write to you as you would know where she was and would send our letters on to her. I know she is very clever, but she is still my sister and I will always worry about her, especially as my two older brothers are also away from home now, training with the RAF. My mother is widowed, so at present I have to be the man of the house.

Phyllis said you would make sure she will be all right. Please take good care of her. She is the best big sister a boy could ever have.

Yours sincerely,

Humphrey Lane

SIX

A NICE DAY OUT

There was one day – oh, ages after I'd started living here – when Sylvia got the idea into her head that we should go out for the day. She kept saying she wanted to go to the forest. I remember saying, 'But you've got your hair appointment this morning. We haven't time to do that and go off for a drive as well.'

'But I have to go there today. I have to check how they're all getting on.'

I'd no idea what she was going on about, but just to keep her quiet, I said, 'Well maybe once your hair's done, we could take a bit of a drive. We could go for lunch at that nice little place near Alresford that you like.'

'No, I have to go to the New Forest. It's vital that I go today!'

She was getting all hot and bothered, so I said I was going to make her morning coffee and I went off into the kitchen. By that stage, she couldn't go anywhere without me or someone else to drive her, so I thought she'd calm down in a bit and forget all about it. She was definitely getting vaguer and didn't remember everything, which confused her even more.

And I didn't know why she'd suddenly got a bee in her bonnet about the New Forest. I mean it wasn't as if it was one of our regular places for a day out, though we'd been there from time to time, usually to catch the rhododendrons at their best in Exbury Gardens in April and May. They've got a wonderful collection, well worth seeing. There's a lovely café there too, but it was a bit of a drive and too far to suddenly decide to go on the spur of the moment.

I always made the coffee just the way she liked it. Real ground coffee with hot milk. I'm not all that fussed myself, I think a jar of instant is fine, but Sylvia always insisted that was how it had to be done. And I had to bring it through to what she called the drawing room – it's a fancy name for the front room to my way of thinking – on a tray, using the little gold cafetière and the matching willow-pattern china. She insisted on what she called 'coffee sugar' too. I'd never seen anything like it till I visited her for the first time. Little coloured sugar crystals, blue, pink, yellow and green, like fairy dust in a silver bowl with a special spoon shaped like a little trowel. I don't know where she got these notions from, but I think it's got something to do with her mother being on the stage. I reckon she picked up all these fancy ideas when she stayed with her on tour.

But I never said anything, I just got on and did it. Oh, and we had to have two posh biscuits each too. We ran out one time and I could only find the Rich Tea, but she was happier the next morning as I popped down to Waitrose specially and got the dark chocolate ginger thins she liked best.

'Here we are,' I said, as I carefully put the tray down on the side table. It's one of those papier mâché trays with a curved gilded edge and a painting of a bowl of fruit. 'We've got plenty of time before we have to go out.' I didn't mention the blessed forest again as I rather hoped she'd forgotten all about it.

'Ooh, lovely,' she said. 'Ginger thins, my favourite. We must make sure they're always on our grocery order.'

'That would be a good idea. I had to go out specially to get these for you.'

'Did you, darling? You're such an angel, looking after me so well. What would I do without you?'

At this point she always touched me lightly on the wrist with her jewelled, manicured hand and smiled her sweet smile. She'd never given up the habit of having her nails done and that was another thing we had regular appointments for. Nails, hair, dentist, optician, doctor not so much; all of them I drove her to, uncomplaining.

I remember looking at my own nails as I plunged the coffee and poured. They're always short, the cuticles are pushed back and they're clean. I'm quite happy with that, as my hands have to work hard and I'd fret if I was chipping my polish.

'If you showed me how to do the grocery order I could make sure it was always up to date,' I said. 'I probably notice more than you do when we're going to run out of things.'

It wasn't the first time she'd given me a wary look. 'I'm quite capable of ordering the shopping. Besides, darling, you don't know how to use a computer.' She sniffed, then sipped her coffee.

It's true I didn't know how, but I was sure I could learn. It wasn't like I hadn't learnt to do lots of difficult things in my life. How else did I cope with all that machinery at the factory during the war? And since Harry'd gone, I'd taken over all the jobs that he used to do, bless him. Once he wasn't around any more I became a dab hand at painting and decorating, mending things and using an electric drill as well. It wasn't for her to look down her nose at me and think I couldn't learn quickly.

I thought she just didn't want me going in what she called her 'study'. It's only small, little more than a space carved out at the bottom of the stairs, but it's where she'd got all her files and papers. Her computer is on the desk, but much of her filing is all over the floor. I'd offered several times in recent years to help her clear up, but she always waved me away, saying, 'I know just where everything is, darling. There's no need for you to touch a thing.'

I suppose she did know what she was doing after all the secretarial work she did for years. It must be like second nature when you've spent that long typing and filing. I've got no need for lots of papers. The ones that matter are all stuffed into one long envelope in my dressing-table drawer underneath my smalls. All the certificates, birth, marriage and death – hatch, match and dispatch, as they say – along with the wills Harry and I signed years ago. There's my christening certificate too, proving I've been baptised, so I can go through the Pearly Gates when the time comes. That's the only kind of passport I've got because I've never felt the need to go abroad, unlike Sylvia, who had to travel with her job. I wouldn't like the heat or funny food, so I'm better off here. Bournemouth always suited me and Harry. Lovely walks along the front and listening to the band in the gardens. We had some lovely holidays there.

But what am I rambling on about? As I was saying, that particular day it was time to get Sylvia off to the hairdresser's. I'd hoped she'd have forgotten all about the forest by then. I thought while she had her shampoo and set, I'd see what I could pick up in Sainsbury's – they always reduce a few things at the end of the week.

'Come on, Sylvia, time to go,' I said. 'Can't be late.'

'Where are we going?' she said. 'I was thinking of going somewhere, wasn't I? Give me a minute and I'll try to remember.'

Oh dear, I thought. *I'd better get her going before she goes off on one again.*

SPECIAL OPERATIONS EXECUTIVE MANUAL

8. Rumours

b. Placing a Rumour

The rumour must be placed in the direction of the group who are intended to hear it. The rumour should be whispered only once by the original 'rumour-monger'. The 'rumour-monger' should choose 'fertile' ground for his rumour (e.g. hairdresser, dentist, barmaid, prostitute, queue outside a shop etc.).

SEVEN
DOWN IN THE WOODS
NOVEMBER 1942

Sylvia loved her frequent trips down to the New Forest. She knew exactly what her new girls faced in their training, because she'd insisted on going through it herself.

'You don't have to go to all that trouble, Benson,' Harrington had said when she first told him of her intention. 'Just send them off and have done with it. Leave it to the professionals.'

'No, I want to see it all for myself. These are very special young girls. I want to have a complete understanding of what we're subjecting them to.'

'Next, you'll be telling me you want to be dropped off in France as well, I suppose. No chance of that. Some of the chaps are pretty peeved that we're sending women out there in the first place. Bomber Harris has made his views very clear. He doesn't think his pilots' training and their planes should be wasted on any agents, particularly not the women.'

Sylvia ignored him. This disregard for her girls was deeply irritating. As the war progressed, more men were away in the services, so there was no choice but to recruit women for her division, as well as in many areas previously handled by men. Women were working in engineering, on farms, canals and even felling trees in forests, so they could certainly learn how to secretly deliver and transmit messages abroad.

'Whatever you might think,' Sylvia said, glaring at Harrington sitting at his desk and swivelling in his leather chair, 'I'm glad I went ahead with the training and I'm going to visit the centres regularly to see how they are treating my girls. They're precious creatures; tough, all of them, but they need to be handled with care.'

'Oh, very well then, off you go. I can see you won't be satisfied until you've reassured yourself that they aren't ruining their nails.' He gave her a dismissive wave of his languid hand and returned to his papers.

It was a relief to escape Harrington's company and the stuffy offices in London, even though bombs were no longer a daily threat, to drive down to the New Forest to the training centre hidden away in the dense woodland. It was one of several such centres based on large country estates requisitioned for the task of preparing agents for missions, acquiring the Special Operations Executive division the soubriquet 'the Stately 'Omes of England'.

Her pass was checked by the guards at the gate as she turned off the road lined with trees dressed with the golden and scarlet leaves of autumn. Her face was familiar to them, but they were thorough as always.

As she progressed down the drive towards the main house, she wound down the window to breathe in the scent of the forest floor, where mushrooms were sprouting between the roots of trees. Only two months had passed since Phyllis had first sat nervously in Sylvia's London office in her stiff uniform. She had been drilled, interviewed and equipped, sent to the wilds of Scotland to survive the moors, taught to handle guns, knives and radios, and now she was nearing the final stage.

When Sylvia parked alongside the Bedford trucks used to ferry trainees around the estate, she could hear distant shouts and the drone of a Lysander plane. That meant they were practising in the dropping zone. She tightened the belt of her Burberry mac and tied a silk scarf over her head. The air was damp and she had to protect her recently curled hair. Salons were still open but you never knew when a hairdresser might suddenly close down after those early bombing raids in London.

She began walking towards the area of open ground where candidates were trained to land after jumping at a great height from the plane, just in time to see one floating down and executing a perfect roll across the grass, feet first. A quick scramble to upright, a rapid pull on the parachute, then the silk was bundled to one side to hide the evidence of this clandestine arrival. Was that Phyllis in that jumping suit, commonly known as a striptease suit, or was that a man she was watching?

Sylvia couldn't quite tell at this distance and was concentrating so hard that she jumped when she felt a poke in the back.

'Got you there, didn't I?'

She turned towards the gruff voice of the tall man sticking the stem of his pipe between her shoulder blades. 'Bloody hell, Fergus, you gave me a fright there. Where'd you come from?' They had developed a healthy mutual respect for each other after she'd proved herself on his Highland assault course.

'I watched you turn up. Knew you'd be down sooner or later to see your latest find.'

'How's Phyllis doing? I've high hopes for her, you know.'

'You have for all of them. They're all fine gels. But you may be right, she could be the best of the bunch.'

'Was that her just now? I couldn't tell from this distance.'

'No, she's back in with Big Al. She hasn't quite got the hang of it yet.'

'You and your ex-cons. She's bright though, she'll catch on soon enough.'

'She'd better! You never know when picking a lock might save your life.' He pulled a tobacco pouch from an inner pocket of his Barbour jacket and began packing the bowl of his pipe. 'Big Al's my top man for locks and Little Al's my best safe-cracker.'

Sylvia smiled to herself. This motley crew of servicemen and felons were the men to whom she had entrusted her girls and she knew they were in safe hands. 'Has she struggled with anything else?'

Fergus sucked his pipe as he struggled to light it in the damp air. 'Rabbits. She didn't like snaring and gutting the rabbit. But she ate it all right in the end. It wasn't cooked through, but she survived.'

'I'd like to see her when it's convenient.'

He checked his watch. 'They'll break for lunch in about half an hour. You can chat to her then.'

'I hope Mrs Searle is still here, with her famous rabbit pie?'

'Surly Searle is still here but I'm pretty sure the pie today will be pigeon. They've nabbed quite a few recently.'

'That will do nicely. This country air is giving me an appetite.' She glanced back at the dropping ground; the men were packing away the parachutes to use again. 'I might have a wander around if we've time before lunch.'

'I've got something to show you,' Fergus said with a wink. 'I think you'll enjoy this. Come with me.'

He turned towards the arch in the high yew hedge and they made their way across the formal garden, laid out in squares edged with clipped box and lavender. Each section was planted with pruned roses, some still bearing the last flowers of the year, clinging on for dear life and looking rather the worse for it. Sylvia thought that the gardens must be among the few in

Britain still growing flowering plants when everywhere else they'd been sacrificed for vegetables.

Fergus led the way to a low arched doorway in the corner of a mossy courtyard at the back of the main house. He opened the creaking door and went down the stone steps into a large, vaulted cellar. 'It's perfect for our purposes, down here. Used to be his Lordship's wine cellar, but I think all the best stuff has found a new home.'

Sylvia could hear women laughing in the distance, coarse shrieks reminiscent of street market traders. The air was cool, but had a damp, rather ripe smell, like mature cheese. She could see a few dusty bottles languishing on their sides on racks, but the main area of interest was the long bench in the centre, underneath bright arc lights. Two women appeared to be stuffing and then sewing furry grey bundles and, as she and Fergus grew closer, she could see they were handling dead rats with long tails.

Fergus noted her look of disgust and laughed. 'Don't look like that. You needn't worry, I haven't got your precious young ladies doing this kind of work. Meet Doris and Muriel, our expert bombmakers.'

The women cackled and one of them held up her rat, waggling its long, muscular tail.

'I don't understand what you're doing here,' Sylvia said.

'We're experimenting,' Fergus said. 'The rats are filled with plastic explosives. We've also done mice, horseshit, fake pebbles and booby-trapped torches.'

'You're not expecting my girls to stick one of those rats in their bag, I hope!'

'No, don't you worry. This is the sort of thing we'll use if the Germans invade. We've got to be ready and we've got to be devious.'

Sylvia pulled a face. 'This sounds rather like the ungentlemanly warfare strategy some of the chaps have been talking about. But what about the rules?'

'What do the Germans care for rules? You've heard what they're doing to anyone helping the resistance in France. Women, children, innocent farmers, anyone and everyone shoved into barns and set alight. This is turning out to be a very nasty war, Sylvia. It's no holds barred from now on.'

As they left, the two women stuffing another couple of dead rats in the foetid atmosphere of the cellar, Sylvia couldn't help asking herself if it was right to send young girls out into this murky conflict. Firing guns on the open battlefield was one thing, but underhand tactics were entirely different, and she wondered if any of them could be truly prepared for what awaited them.

EIGHT
A PENNY WORTH
LONDON 1919

The first time I ever saw Sylvia was when she came into my parents' shop on her own to buy some sweets. Ever so pretty she was, with long blonde hair down her back, tied with a white silky bow on the top. Like all the girls at that time, she wore a loose smock dress, with a pinafore over it that buttoned down the back. But her dress was perfectly clean and her black stockings didn't have darned holes, like mine always did.

She looked clean, rosy and fresh and I longed to stroke her shining hair. I wasn't allowed to wear mine loose, because Mother said I'd be bound to pick up nits. So, mine was always scraped back into tight plaits that hung behind each ear. When my hair was brushed out, it had rippling waves and I could pretend I was a mermaid for a while until the curl dropped out and it was all dead straight again.

'Please may I have a penny-worth of pear drops,' she'd said, putting her coin on the counter. I was meant to be sweeping the back room, but I could see her through the doorway. With the sunlight coming behind her through the shop's front windows and door, her head had a golden haze all around it, where the light caught her hair, making her look like she was wearing an angel's halo.

I couldn't stop staring at her, until Father bumped into me from behind, carrying through a crate of apples. 'Mind out, Peg,' he shouted and that was when she noticed me and smiled. It was a shy smile, not like the ones she later on gave the men and boys when she wanted something, but I knew it meant we would be friends.

Once Mother had given her the sweets in a little twist of paper, she left the shop, but she turned to look at me and smile as she went through the door. And then she looked again through the window outside and waved. 'Get a move on, Peg,' Mother said crossly. 'That floor won't sweep itself if you just stand around gawping all day.'

I started sweeping again, but couldn't stop myself saying, 'I wasn't really gawping, I was just wondering who she was.'

'She's moved in to number fourteen Roll Gardens with her mother. Hoity-toity woman by all accounts. Theatrical type, I've heard. I expect she'll end up at the school when you all go back. And no, I don't know her name. You'll have to wait and find out, won't you?'

School was due to restart after the summer and to be honest, I was quite glad. The days had been long and boring and I hadn't been allowed out on my own very much, other than to run errands. 'There's been too many unsavoury types roaming the streets since it all ended,' Mother kept complaining, referring to the unemployed soldiers who'd come home after the Great War. So I was kept occupied helping in the shop, looking after the little ones and folding up the washing when it was dry. The shop wasn't so bad because we sold almost everything: sweets, tobacco, groceries and some fruit and vegetables. But my little brothers and sisters were always squabbling and needing their noses wiped, so I got very impatient with them.

When school started in September, that was when I saw

Sylvia again. Her hair was still long and well-brushed, her pinafore was clean and pressed, unlike mine. She hung back as the girls skipped in through the archway marked 'Girls' and the boys roared in through the archway labelled 'Boys'. I thought she looked lost and shy, so I spoke to her. 'You're new here, aren't you?'

She nodded, but didn't speak.

'What's your name?'

And then she did speak. 'I'm Sylvia,' she said. 'And you're Peg. I heard your father saying your name.'

Sylvia, I thought. *What a lovely name, all silvery and shiny, just like her.* 'Would you like to sit with me?'

She nodded again and so that is how it all really began. How we became friends and how I was with her till the end, when I held her hand as she closed her eyes for the last time.

Later that very first day in school, after we'd put up with chanting the nine times table and written out the Lord's Prayer ten times on our slates, I asked her, 'Why haven't you been back to the shop for more sweets?'

She shook her head, her silky hair falling forward in little ringlets around her cheeks. 'Mother doesn't approve. She says they will rot my teeth and spoil my looks. She wants me to join her on the stage when I'm old enough.'

'No more sweets? What, never?'

'She won't let me have any money to buy them.'

'What if I got you some?'

Her face brightened as she looked directly at me. 'Are you allowed to take them? Won't your parents be cross?'

'I can take broken ones and there's always a few spilling out when we empty them into the jars. What's your favourite?'

'Pear drops. Then sherbet lemons. What's yours?'

'Aniseed balls,' I said, adding, 'and gobstoppers,' because I knew it sounded a little crude and would make her laugh, which it did. 'I'll bring some sweets in my pocket tomorrow and give them to you at playtime.'

It became our little joke from there on. If she ever looked a bit miz, even in later years, I'd say, 'Fancy a gobstopper?' It worked every time and she'd always say, 'I'd rather have a pear drop, darling,' and then we'd both always laugh.

They never did spoil her looks, those sweets. Not when we were at school, nor later. What did spoil her was that darned boarding school. When she first came back in the Christmas holidays, early 1920s it must have been, her skin was pasty and spotty, her hair greasy and she'd got quite podgy. And she wasn't really the type, because she'd always been slender, but it was just all that stodgy food they gave them there to fill them up. Not healthy greens or any kind of fruit, just potatoes, suet puddings and bread, she told me. She went for the sweeties that holiday, I can tell you.

And the next time she came back, for Easter it must have been, her hair was all cut off. I nearly burst into tears when I saw her. 'Why'd you have all your lovely hair cut short?' I remember saying, trying not to show how upset I was.

She just shrugged. 'School rules. One of the girls had nits, so they aren't allowing any long, loose hair now.'

'But couldn't you have put it in plaits, like I've got?' Without thinking, I instinctively put my right hand to one of my plaits, feeling the ropey cord of hair on my shoulder.

She shrugged again. 'Mother says it's probably just as well. It's not the fashion any more, short hair is all the thing now.' She shook her head and the silky hair fell back into place like a shining helmet. 'Besides, it's so much easier to look after.'

I cut my plaits off that night with Mother's big dressmaking scissors. Snip went the first one, snap the second. Mother didn't know till morning and covered her mouth with her hand when she saw me. 'Whatever have you done to yourself, Peg? You look a fright, really you do.'

I had looked in the mirror over the washstand in the room I shared with my little sisters, but I'd only seen my haircut from the front, of course. 'It's all the fashion,' I said. 'I want to look like my friend Sylvia.'

'That's all very well, but she's had hers cut properly by someone who knew what they were doing. You look like you've been through a hedge backwards. You can't go out looking like that, you'll be a laughing stock. Here, eat your breakfast and then I'll sort you out.' She plonked a bowl of porridge in front of me and turned back to the stove to make Father's bacon and eggs. My little brothers and sisters sat spooning their porridge too, wide-eyed with shock at the way I looked.

After I'd finished eating, she made me sit with an old apron over my shoulders while she trimmed my hair at the back and around my ears, all the while muttering about what a mess I'd made of my lovely hair and how she'd see if she could sell my plaits to a wigmaker. She combed some of my hair forward over my forehead and snipped away above my eyebrows and as she finished, I could feel the cold scissors tickling the back of my neck.

By the time she was done, I felt even more lightheaded and there was a pile of hair on the floor. She brushed my neck with her hand and I could feel hairs prickling me all the way down my back, where they'd slipped down my dress. 'Now you can sweep all that up and put it on the compost heap,' she said. 'Maybe the birds will take some for their nests.'

I rather liked that thought, a robin or a chaffinch weaving my hair into their nest, and I was quite happy until I looked into the mirror again. I hadn't realised how short she'd cut it. The fringe was so high on my forehead I looked like a Kewpie doll, all startled and stupid. I cried a bit then for sure, more than I nearly had over Sylvia's hair.

And when Sylvia saw me later, she burst out laughing. 'Who did that to you?'

'I cut off my plaits last night and Mother insisted she could do a better job.'

'Poor little Peg.' She pulled a sad face. 'It'll grow back though. It won't look like that forever.' She held out her hand. 'Still friends?'

I nodded and it felt strange because there was no hair to weigh me down. I felt lightheaded and free and suddenly decided I liked this new short hair after all. I grabbed both her hands and we twirled round shrieking. When we stopped, breathless, she said, 'Fancy a gobstopper?' and we just kept on laughing.

NINE
JAM ROLY-POLY
MARCH 1943

Sylvia couldn't help thinking how much Phyllis had changed since she had first arrived as a timid girl at the London office. She looked sturdier than she had done then and livelier too. The months of hard training, the slogging over Scottish moors, had strengthened her muscles and coloured her complexion, but she was still beautiful.

'Have you been enjoying yourself?' Sylvia said as she greeted her protégée in the oak-panelled hallway of the New Forest training centre.

'Every single minute,' Phyllis said. 'Well, apart from the business with the rabbits, that is. But I could do that now, if I had to.'

'You may never have to. You'll largely be based in Paris. I doubt there'll be many opportunities for snaring and skinning rabbits there.'

Both women laughed at the thought.

'And how have you found it doing the sessions on silent killing?'

Phyllis laughed again. 'Not always so silent unfortunately! Apparently, I breathe too heavily when I'm creeping up on someone and I hesitate when I'm meant to do a swift garrotte. I'm rather hoping I'll never have to do it.'

'Let's hope not. But at least you now have the skills if you ever needed to.'

'Barney says everyone can do it if they're in a fix. He says don't even think about them as people. Try to think it's a wasp or a fly that has to be swatted.'

'Good advice, I should think,' Sylvia said, picturing Barney, another of the ex-convicts Fergus had recruited, a thin, weaselly fellow with a sly face. She wasn't sure what he'd been sentenced for, but assumed he'd probably not been caught for all of his crimes.

'And now I'm starving. All this stuff gives me a huge appetite. I'm hoping I'll still fit into my uniform.'

'Well, you won't have to worry about that much longer. You won't be taking that with you and you should be flying out in May.'

'So soon?' Was that fear or excitement etched on her face? 'I can't wait.'

She was excited, but steady, Sylvia decided. Definitely ready to go. 'Let's talk some more over lunch,' she said. 'I hear it's pigeon pie again today.'

They strolled through to the vaulted dining hall, where staff were chattering and gathering beneath the enormous chandeliers, queuing like hungry schoolchildren for their lunch. They were all being accommodated in this grand country mansion, which had been requisitioned for the exclusive purpose of training secret agents, but there were no butlers, servants or chambermaids to care for them as there would have been in its heyday.

Everyone took a plate and waited patiently in line for their portion of pie, greens and potatoes, then found a free seat at one of the many tables that filled the hall. Senior officers tended to group together, but Sylvia wanted to sit alone with Phyllis and hear more about her experiences.

'I'm so lucky, because I've got such a lovely room in the main house,' Phyllis said, as they sat down at a small table. 'Some of the others are in an annexe alongside, but I'm up on the top floor and have a view right across the landing drop and the forest. I was told it was originally the servants' attic rooms up there, but I don't mind. I think it's simply lovely.'

'I'm pleased for you,' Sylvia said. 'Who knows where you'll be living in a few weeks' time, so make the most of it.' The support staff were mostly billeted in Nissen huts and converted stables in the grounds. She was sure that would not have impressed Phyllis quite so much.

'I'm so looking forward to getting back to Paris. It seems ages since I was there.' Phyllis was half-French and had finished her education in the city only weeks before the Germans arrived.

'They've scheduled regular conversation classes here for you as well, I hope? Just to make sure you're completely up to scratch?'

'Absolutely. They're lots of fun. A few of us are doing them and we have songs and a great time. It's a bit like another finishing school in many ways. I mean, who'd have thought I'd be doing this kind of thing when I left Paris? My mother couldn't think beyond me finding a suitable man to marry and here I am, jumping out of planes, learning to pick locks, slit throats and gut rabbits!'

'Well, I'm sure you'll do your mother proud. It must be hard not being able to tell your family what you are up to.' Sylvia discreetly removed a piece of shot from her mouth with a genteel gesture. At least the pigeon could not have been hung for long, as the flesh had not darkened and fouled around the entry point.

'One day, when it's all over, I'd love to be able to tell her about this. She'd be awfully shocked.' Phyllis had nearly cleaned her plate. She looked at the section of burnt piecrust Sylvia had pushed to one side. 'If you don't want that bit, I'll finish it off for you,' she said, pointing to the fragment.

'Go ahead, probably good for you to learn to eat up every scrap. You never know when you might be desperate.' Sylvia hoped her girl would eat well in France, but knew that she might well have to rely on contacts for food. 'I hope your mother wasn't too worried when you told her you were going to be away for a while.'

'She'd like to know more details, but she accepts that I have work to do and trusts me. It's my brothers who are the problem, particularly the youngest. Humphrey's the baby of the family, but he's got it into his head that he is my protector, since my father died last year. The two older ones are away with the RAF and I suppose he feels left out. He was trying to ask me loads of difficult questions when I last saw him. He says if anything happens to me, he will take his revenge. He's so sweet, it's as if he's just like some medieval knight, defending my honour.'

'I hope you didn't feel tempted to tell him where you're going?'

'Of course not. I know we can't give our families a clue as to what's going on.' Phyllis smiled and waved her hands around at the grandeur of the dining hall. 'Such a shame I couldn't have him visit me here. He'd absolutely love it all, this wonderful house and the beautiful grounds. Oh, and he'd love all the training too. Probably want to have a go at it himself.'

'Very *Boy's Own*, isn't it? And to think that at first they were very reluctant to take girls through the same rigorous programme they've used for the men.' Sylvia laughed. 'Funny how you girls have turned out to be just as good as, if not better than them. And you have the advantage of not being on the Germans' radar. They see women as all Kinder, Küche and Kirche, not crafty radio operators and killing machines!'

'I love that! We're going to really surprise them, aren't we? Show them that women can do a man's work after all! It's happening everywhere now, isn't it? Girls are working as land girls on farms, they're cutting down trees and working in the factories. And you know what? They're all loving it. I think that though this war is terrible, especially coming so soon after the last one, it's going to change the way men think about women and give women a different view of their futures. There's simply nothing we can't do. We aren't just wives and mothers now, we have exciting opportunities ahead of us.'

Phyllis was pink with enthusiasm, her eyes sparkled and she seemed to be relishing this chance to launch herself into danger. Sylvia was filled with admiration for this vigorous young girl, about to have the adventure of her life, and with an appetite for solid food to match. 'Have you got room for the steamed jam roly-poly and custard after that huge portion of pie?'

'Have I ever! I need fuel. I've got another radio session this afternoon. I need to feed my brain.'

'Let's both get a helping and then if there's time, perhaps you can show me round the gardens.'

'If we gobble it up at top speed, I can do better than that. I can take you across to the chapel. It's the other side of the meadow, where all the sheep are. They've got the sweetest little lambs at the moment. Let's do that.'

After finishing their pudding in a few swift spoonfuls, they left the dining hall to set out across the grassy field, treading carefully to avoid tripping over the wiry tussocks and skirting the sheep droppings. Ewes called to their offspring as they approached and Sylvia could see why Phyllis so enjoyed this walk. Here was everything she was going to fight to protect. The English countryside under a cloudless spring sky.

And when they reached the chapel at the far side, Phyllis opened the studded arched door with a creak, saying, 'I come here sometimes for a little bit of peace and to think.' She led the way into the cool interior, scented with dust and old prayer books.

'It's lovely,' Sylvia said, taking in the linen-fold panels of oak that lined the stalls. She took a seat in one of the pews and Phyllis did the same on the opposite side of the aisle.

Shafts of sunlight streamed through the stained-glass windows, casting glints of ruby and sapphire gems across the flagstoned floor. It was still and silent apart from the distant bleating of the sheep and their lambs.

Sylvia was about to say she should be leaving and returning to London, but when she glanced across at Phyllis, she had to stop herself. The girl's head was bent and her hands were clasped in her lap. Sylvia was struck by her composure and, though she was not used to praying herself, she closed her eyes for a moment, then prayed as she had not done since her school-days that Phyllis would be 'delivered from evil' and return safely home.

SPECIAL OPERATIONS EXECUTIVE MANUAL

FIELDCRAFT

1.c) Remember, village dogs can give away your presence; approach them upwind.

TEN

MARKING THE WAY

It was Sylvia who first noticed the little signs. Well, she was bound to, wasn't she? Always alert she was, forever asking me why that white van went past the cottage twice, why the paperboy was late and so on. Any change in her routine and she got a bit jumpy.

It all happened one afternoon back in the summer when we were doing our regular walk, because it's good to keep moving, especially as you get older. We used to walk a lot when she had her dog Fergus and there was an incentive: he was always jumping up and down to go out, desperate to go down the lane, sniffing for rabbits. An eager dog is a great encouragement to get off your backside. But even after he was gone, it was still good to get the exercise.

'Come on, Sylv,' I used to say. 'Let's go for our constitutional. Get those old bones moving.' And she'd grumble as she pushed herself out of her armchair. I think she found it harder than I did because she spent more time sitting, while I was always sweeping the floor, doing a bit of hoovering or hanging out the washing. Always on the go, I am.

Anyway, we started doing our usual circuit of down the lane

and back across the fields and hadn't gone far along the track across the field at the back of the cottage when all of a sudden Sylvia gasped, grabbed my arm and pointed. 'What's that?' she said, showing me a white circle on the footpath. 'Who did that?'

I stared at it and couldn't work it out. It looked like it had been done with talcum powder or flour. But I couldn't think what it meant. Then a little further on, where the path nears the lane, there was another one and then a little yellow paper triangle, stuck into the ground with a short stick.

Sylvia was holding onto my arm so tight I thought she'd cut off the circulation, really I did, she was gripping me so hard. And as we walked where we usually went, we kept coming across more yellow triangles and signs made with white powder. Some were circles and some were arrows. 'It's a message,' Sylvia muttered. 'I don't like it at all. Who's done this?'

'It's probably something to do with the farm,' I said. 'Some kind of sign for the tractor to follow or you know, like when they send a man in to clear the footpath.'

'No,' she said. 'It's not right. I saw a man out here the other day. He was walking this way with a clipboard.' She dropped my arm and stood looking wildly all around her. There was no one else near us. We were the only ones out walking that afternoon. Sometimes we came across other neighbours and villagers doing a longer walk with their dogs, but that particular day, there was no one else in sight.

'Where are they?' She was breathing quickly and looking about and I thought, *she's scared, she's really scared.*

'Let's go back, Sylv,' I said. 'We've walked far enough. I expect you're tired now.'

'I'm not tired,' she said. 'I'm putting a stop to this right this minute.' And she started walking back the way we'd come, scrubbing over the white trails with her stick and knocking over the yellow arrows. 'There,' she said. 'That should put them off the track.'

I'd no idea what she was thinking, so I just went along with it, hoping the farmer wouldn't suddenly turn up and tick us off for mucking up his plans or whatever. She did that all the way round our walk and we even found several of the arrows and signs quite near the cottage too, but she didn't miss a single one. Some of the arrows she pulled off the sticks and tore up, others she just stamped on.

'I'll make us our tea right away,' I said, when we got back, hoping she'd be calmer once we were home. 'It's a lovely afternoon, so I'll bring it outside.' I got her to sit in one of her old green Lloyd Loom chairs in the garden under the apple tree, while I set the tray. I threw a yellow and white checked cloth over the outside table too, just to make it seem special, then brought it all out. I'd made cucumber sandwiches that day and we had a fresh Victoria sandwich, which I'd made that morning with raspberry jam I'd bought at the village summer fete. They'd had a cake stall there too, but we'd eaten all the coffee and walnut I'd bought there in two days flat, it was that good.

We were just sitting down and starting to enjoy ourselves when a man in a vest and shorts with a number on his chest came running along the lane. He looked a bit puffed, to be honest, but then it was quite hot that particular day. And he was soon followed by another man dressed the same way and then a woman. Though she wasn't in shorts, she was wearing a T-shirt and leggings. And they all had numbers pinned on them.

We watched them for a bit because they didn't run past us, they stopped at the bottom of the steps that go up into the field opposite to join the footpath. And they all seemed to be quite puzzled. They slowed down, stood there looking around them and then they started scratching their heads.

I said to Sylvia, 'They look like they're lost,' and I went across to speak to them over the front hedge. As I did that, about another half a dozen runners all came staggering down the lane to join them, all looking very hot and bothered. 'Do you know where you're going?' I called across to them.

'There's no markings,' one of them said. 'Our trail has vanished. We should be following the signs all the way.'

I looked over my shoulder at Sylvia and thought she looked mischievous. She had that naughty little smile on her lips. But she didn't comment, she just kept on nibbling her cake and sipping her tea.

'We're the North Hampshire Harriers,' one of the other runners said. 'We're running cross-country, following a trail that was laid out for us yesterday.'

'How interesting,' I said. 'And now you can't find any more of your signs? Oh dear, I expect it's kids. Or badgers maybe. They cause of lot of damage in gardens round here.'

And just then one of the other runners, who'd raced right across the field at the front to the far side, yelled out, saying he'd found the next arrow, and then they were all off again, all huffing and puffing. I think some of them shouldn't have been doing such a long run in that hot weather. It couldn't have been doing them any good.

'Did you hear that, Sylv?' I said as I returned to the tea table. 'They were all meant to be following those markers you messed up earlier this afternoon. What do you have to say for yourself?'

'Load of nonsense,' she muttered, dabbing her finger in the crumbs on her plate. 'They can't fool me. It's just an excuse to nose around.'

ELEVEN
A PINCH OF SALT
APRIL 1943

'I don't think I'm really very good at this, Miss Benson.' Phyllis hobbled into the dining room in muddy dungarees after a morning's training under the supervision of one of the men recruited by Fergus.

'Oh, have they been putting you through your paces in fieldcraft? You'll probably never need it once you've buried your parachute and been picked up by your contact. You'll be in towns and cities and on trains, mostly. Very rarely out in the field.' Sylvia was amused by her young recruit's tangled hair and smudged cheeks.

'That's true, but I've still got to pass every part of our course. There was a man called Smudge Smith in charge of us this morning. He's vicious!'

Not as brutal as the Bosch if you're caught, Sylvia thought. 'I'm sure he's doing his best. He doesn't want you picked up minutes after you've hit the ground, now does he?'

'No, you're right,' Phyllis said, gulping her tea as if she'd been deprived of food and drink for days. 'But I find some of the instructions utterly baffling. Like the one about approaching village dogs upwind. I mean, will there always be a wind? And if there isn't, will they still know I'm there and bark at me?'

Sylvia laughed, 'Oh, they've been handing out the Special Operations Executive Manual, have they? Well, you don't have to memorise every single line of it. Just take it with a pinch of salt and use your common sense. That will probably do you more good than trying to remember all the rules.' Copies of the closely typed instructions were handed out to all SOE trainees in a little Gestetner duplicated booklet, entitled *How to be an Agent in Occupied Europe*. Quite ironic, Sylvia thought, that a slender rulebook that might help to defeat the Germans was duplicated on a machine invented by a Jewish company.

'Well, thank goodness for that,' Phyllis said, topping up her cup of tea. 'Some of the instructions are quite beyond me. I mean, there's one about going on surveillance that I can't understand at all. Well, I think I can. I think it means make sure you spend a penny before you begin your stakeout, as you might not be able to move for hours.'

'Oh, I know the one,' Sylvia said, laughing so much she nearly choked on the seed cake she was eating. 'It says something about the watcher should relieve himself, with reference to the Duke of Wellington!'

'Exactly! What on earth has the Duke of Wellington got to do with it, I'd like to know? I mean, as my old nanny always used to say, if you've got the chance to visit the lavatory before a journey you should go while you've got the chance, but other than that, I've simply no idea!'

'I hope you didn't feel peeved that the manual is peppered with references to the opposite sex?' Sylvia had tried to get a draft copy of the manual amended, but as usual, the department's male cohort wouldn't listen to her advice.

'Well, I did notice that, of course. Not a single reference to the hard work we girls will be doing. Are they ignoring us and the risks we'll be taking?' Phyllis looked indignant, and rightly so.

Sylvia thought of the opposition she'd faced trying to recruit women for active service in the first place, despite the fact that they could often slip undercover more easily than men. But she was determined she wouldn't undermine Phyllis's confidence at this late stage and said, 'No, that's just a civil service slip-up. Not a reflection at all on their appreciation of the important work you'll be doing, along with a number of other women.' How foolish the hierarchy was, overlooking such an important detail. The last thing she wanted now was for Phyllis, or any other woman she'd recruited, for that matter, to feel that their contribution didn't count. She'd have to have words again with Harrington when she returned to London.

'And I mean, I know I'm not an authority on these things, but some of the instructions sound quite ridiculous. A few of us have had great fun going through the manual and pulling out the ones that are blindingly obvious, then reading them out in stuffy voices. They sound just like a maiden aunt wrote them out in longhand first, before they were typed up. There's one that goes something like, *Surveillance is the keeping of someone under observation without his knowledge*. How could it ever be anything else?'

Sylvia couldn't help smiling, even though she knew that the manual had been written in good faith and was intended to be helpful. 'I'm glad to hear that it amuses you and you seem to be in such good spirits.'

'Oh, and finally, my favourite is the one about how to keep up appearances if we get arrested and are in prison. It says we should always appear clean and neat and ends by suggesting we keep doing some P.T.! Isn't that simply hilarious?'

'Mmm, I seem to remember noticing that one.' Sylvia thought someone like Harrington would have added that last point. Typical of him. As if combing your hair and touching your toes could make a world of difference in a dangerous situation. If he'd ever been persuaded to rewrite the manual and make it more appropriate for her female recruits, he'd have added some ridiculous comment about wearing lipstick and powdering their noses with their gold compacts at all times, probably.

'I do hope silly things like this aren't putting you off,' she said, smiling at Phyllis, who was now tucking into a plate of fish paste sandwiches.

'Mmm, no.' Phyllis tried to speak with her mouth full and it was a moment before she could talk properly. 'We're all sensible enough to realise that some dogsbody who's never going to do any of these things is just trying to be terribly efficient.'

'They're doing their best but sometimes it does seem a little like overkill. However, I think if you focus on the advice given to you directly by the experienced men who are training you then you can't go far wrong. They all know far more about the circumstances you're likely to encounter than some clerk typing out instructions in Whitehall.'

'Oh, they're all marvellous men, Miss Benson. I just love them all. And the stories they tell. Goodness, my mother would have a fit if she knew I was consorting with hardened criminals! But how on earth would we have learnt how to start stolen cars or pick locks without their instruction?'

'They certainly know their stuff. And it is quite amusing to think that this war is being fought not just by trained soldiers but by old lags, as they are called.'

'What wouldn't I give to be able to tell my brother all about this. He'd love to do all the things I'm being trained to do. I know I'm not allowed to tell him, but he'd think it was such a grand adventure.'

'You may never be able to tell him, my dear. You're going to be under oath, remember, for a very long time, even once this war is over.'

'Yes, that's rather a shame. It would be such fun to go home and talk about all our daring exploits. And I know I wasn't meant to give my family any hints whatsoever about what I might be doing, but I couldn't resist telling Humphrey that I'd met you and you'd convinced me I could do this. I just couldn't stop myself telling him how marvellous you were and how you gave me the strength to take part.'

Sylvia heard the words, but she was staring at her plate. A few crumbs were left and she dabbed at them with her finger. Humphrey knew her name because it was on the address that the family could write to. She hoped he wouldn't blame her if the extravagant gold powder compact, the closely typed manual and even the tuition from the ex-convicts couldn't save his sister's life and bring her safely home.

April 1943

Dear Miss Benson,

My mother doesn't know about me writing to you. I don't want to worry her, but I do think it is very hard on mothers that they can't know what is happening to their sons and daughters. I think you should change the rules and allow mothers to write to their children and receive letters in return. If you were a mother you would realise how hard it is and how she worries so about Phyllis.

I also haven't told my mother that you are the person who persuaded Phyllis to do this work we can't know anything about. My sister could have volunteered to do something much safer, such as learning to drive officers around in this country. I know we are all facing danger every day during this war, but I shall blame you if anything ever happens to my wonderful sister.

Yours sincerely,

Humphrey Lane

TWELVE
ONLY ON PRESCRIPTION

I'm sure I can't be the only one with a habit of hoarding useful things. With me it's always been elastic bands, especially those nice thick brown ones postmen use for bundles of letters. I've got a whole ball of rubber bands in my kitchen drawer, wrapped around each other into a tight wad, so I can just peel one off whenever I need it. I'm one for envelopes too, especially those ones with a clear window. You can use them again.

But with Sylvia, it was pills – well, all kinds of medication really. I know, because one day when I'd been trying to find a sticking plaster in her bathroom, I said to her, 'Sylv, why don't you let me sort out your medicine cupboard? There's loads of stuff in there that's way past its best and probably isn't going to do you any good now.'

'What sort of things? They might still be useful.' She lowered her head and gave me a suspicious look, over the top of that day's paper. She only looked at the obituaries and the crossword, but she still insisted on having it.

'Old cough mixture? There's a couple of bottles with hardly anything left in them and they're all sticky and crusty round the tops. I'm sure they won't be any good now.'

'Oh, well all right, those can go out.'

'And you've got all these out-of-date antibiotics and allergy tablets too. I'd better chuck those away as well.' I showed her the whole clutch of pills and boxes I was holding.

'Let me see,' she said, holding out her hand.

So, like a twit, I handed her the packs to check – and blow me, she only went and stuffed them in her handbag.

'No, Sylv, they're not to keep. They're really old, they won't be any good now.'

'You never know,' she muttered.

'No, really. They've got to be thrown out. They might even be bad for you now, they're so old.'

She snapped her handbag shut and held it tight on her lap. She was sitting in her armchair near the fire, I remember, staring into the fireplace. I hadn't yet lit the fire that day, but had laid it ready for later, with a firelighter tucked into the twists of paper and kindling to get it all going. In the autumn and winter we always had a fire and I usually lit it at teatime.

'Hand them over to me now, dear, and I'll get rid of them. You don't want to take any of those nasty old pills. They might even make you ill.' I held out my hands towards her, assuming she was just being temperamental, but she clutched the bag to her chest and lowered her chin, so I could see there was no way I was going to get it away from her.

'Oh, please yourself,' I said. I didn't have time for her sulks. They were getting worse by that point, I think. 'But please don't go taking them while I'm staying here. I don't want to have to clear up after you if you end up making yourself sick.' And I walked off to finish making us lunch. I'd had to find a plaster because I'd cut my finger slicing cucumber for our salmon and cucumber sandwiches.

As I turned away, I could hear her muttering. She might even have been swearing at me behind my back. She did that sometimes, but I couldn't resist turning round and saying, 'What's that? I didn't quite hear you.'

'Poor dears. They took away their pills.'

'Who did? What are you talking about?'

'My lovely girls,' she almost whispered.

It was very difficult to hear her. I was wearing hearing aids by then, but when she didn't speak up, I still found it hard to catch every word she said. 'You'll have to repeat that, Sylv, I can't quite hear you.'

'Girls. My girls. They had no way of stopping it.'

She was always talking about her girls. I'd no idea what that was all about. She hadn't got children and there weren't any nieces that I knew of. Maybe she meant people who used to work in her office. I didn't know. I thought she was getting worse.

'They took away their pills. Shouldn't have done that.'

'I'm going to make lunch,' I said. I couldn't hang about all day waiting for her to talk sense, I had to get on.

I went back into the kitchen and finished making the sandwiches, taking off the crusts and cutting them into triangles just the way she likes. I put a bit of fresh parsley on the serving plate, like they do in posh hotels, then I took our plates and napkins into the dining room. We always ate in there, even if it was just a sarnie or a bowl of soup. So much nicer to sit down properly and take your time over a meal, however small and simple. Teatime was different. We always sat in the garden when it was fine in summer and by the fire in the sitting room the rest of the time.

'Sylvia dear,' I called out, popping my head through the doorway, 'lunch is ready. Do you want to wash your hands first?'

She got up rather shakily from her chair and tottered through to the downstairs cloakroom. And as she walked away from me, I realised she'd left her handbag on the floor. I quickly opened it, grabbed the pills and threw them at the back of the fire, behind the logs. I immediately struck a match and lit the firelighter I'd tucked into the kindling and it caught straight away. I wasn't going to have the fire till we'd sat down in the evening with a little glass of sherry before dinner, as we were going out for tea that day, but it was too good an opportunity to miss, so I had to do it then and there.

By the time I'd made the coffee after we'd eaten our sandwiches, I could tell she'd forgotten all about those darn pills. She was rabbiting on about the plates of sandwiches she used to have at The Ritz with afternoon tea. I let her go on, even when she said she wanted full afternoon tea at the cottage from now on. I thought by the time we'd been for a drive and she'd had a bit of Victoria sandwich she wouldn't remember what she'd been going on about before lunch.

THIRTEEN
FOR A TIGHT SPOT
APRIL 1943

Shortly before Phyllis was sent off on her mission, Sylvia went to see her again in the training centre hidden away in the New Forest. It was a spring day full of primroses, birds nesting and a feeling of hope when she drove along the fresh green avenues of trees. *Surely nothing bad could happen on a day like this*, she thought.

But her task that day depressed her. It always did, seeing these lively young girls, so full of beauty and energy, being asked to consider what they should do if they were cornered. She spotted Phyllis almost immediately, wearing a smart dark red dress with a white belt, lounging on the lawn in the warm sunshine with a young man. They were drinking lemonade and sharing quarters of apple, the white flesh rimmed with red peel, rather like Phyllis's smile.

It almost made Sylvia want to tell her that she hadn't passed the course with flying colours, so she couldn't go, so she wouldn't be sent into the dragon's lair after all. This is exactly what a girl of her age should be doing, she thought: laughing, flirting and charming young men. Of course she should be tempting handsome men to fling their arms round her, not track her down and interrogate her with terrifying threats.

Yet Sylvia took a deep breath and steeled herself to proceed. She stepped forward with a cheery wave, saying, 'What a lovely day for a picnic on the lawn! May I join you?'

'Miss Benson, how lovely to see you,' Phyllis said, jumping to her feet as the young man beside her also stood up. 'I didn't know you were coming here today. May I introduce Michal? He's from Poland.'

Sylvia shook his hand, thinking how very handsome he was. From his uniform she guessed he was one of a number of Polish airmen who had managed to escape their country and join forces with the British.

'Eagle Owl?' she asked him, with a lift of the eyebrow. She knew that a special team had been thrown together under this name to defend Britain's historic cities after the German reaction to the bombing of Lübeck.

'Ja,' he said with a nod. 'We are the Baedeker boys now. We have to save your wonderful cathedrals.'

Sylvia held up her hand. 'No need to say any more. You've got a difficult and dangerous job to do.' Since the destruction of one of Germany's most beautiful cities, and further RAF bombing of other historic sites, Hitler had ordered the targeting of Britain's most picturesque landmarks, as listed in Baedeker, the famous guidebook for German tourists. Exeter, Bath and Canterbury had all suffered the previous year and Coventry Cathedral had been destroyed in 1940.

'I will leave you both now,' he said, shaking hands with them in turn. 'Good luck, whatever you are doing in this damnable war.'

They watched him leave, Sylvia hoping he survived his missions, unlike many of the young RAF Spitfire pilots, who had an average life expectancy of six weeks once they took command of a fighter plane. She glanced at Phyllis, whose cheeks were still flushed from this enjoyable encounter with such a handsome, eligible man.

'I'm so sorry to have to interrupt your lovely afternoon,' Sylvia said. 'There's a little bit of business I need to discuss with you.'

'We can go in for tea if you like,' Phyllis said, standing up and brushing down the skirt of her dress. 'It's probably just jam sandwiches, but they may have a cake on offer, if we're lucky.'

They strolled towards the dining room, Sylvia thinking how fortunate they were to be based in the countryside, surrounded by productive farms and resourceful farmers' wives. If there was no jam left over from the autumn harvests, there might be apple butter, or at the very least someone might have laid in a stock of Marmite. Her London diet had recently become very dull, unless she was lucky enough to dine with Campbell at The Savoy.

Once they had collected their cups of tea and sandwiches, Phyllis led the way towards an empty table for two, saying, 'We should find it quiet enough over here in this corner.'

They sat down and Sylvia decided they should eat before she tackled the matter on her mind. She took a bite of the triangular sandwich and was pleased to find it contained a sprinkling of peppery watercress, probably the first of the year, picked that morning from the sparkling chalk streams that ran through Hampshire.

'So, what did you want to see me about?' Phyllis didn't seem at all apprehensive, Sylvia thought. Probably still buoyed up by her recent flirtation with the Polish airman. And why not? She might not be able to relax and enjoy male company for some time to come. Once she embarked on her mission in France, it would be unwise for her to let down her guard and allow herself to socialise freely. Although many young people, including her, were recklessly throwing aside the social mores of yesteryear and snatching whatever opportunity there was for passionate love in the midst of conflict.

Sylvia hesitated for a moment, then said, 'You know that we've tried to prepare you for every eventuality on your course?'

Phyllis laughed, then said, 'Oh I know I shouldn't find it funny, but when they pounced on us in the middle of the night, pretending to be German interrogators, it was just so hilarious! I went along with it because it wasn't at all scary. But one of the other girls told them in no uncertain terms to buzz off and let her go back to sleep!'

Sylvia couldn't help smiling at her reaction, but said, 'Of course we can't replicate the exact circumstances of an interrogation during training, but we do try to help you think about the very worst that could happen. I don't want to overemphasise the possibility, but it's a very risky job indeed, being an agent in the field.'

Phyllis looked more serious. 'I know that. We all do. But we don't want to keep thinking about it.'

Sylvia tried to give her a reassuring smile, but found it hard to do so in light of the information she had to deliver. 'Now I know you've been coached in resisting pressure, but you really won't know, until you are up against it, how you are going to react to intimidation, discomfort and even, let's face it, physical duress.'

'Of course we don't know. None of us can really know but we all hope that we can stay strong and remain loyal to our country. We don't want to risk other lives as well as our own.'

'Quite right. There's a tremendous amount at stake. You're just one tiny but valuable part of a whole network of people risking their lives to resist the Germans. Some of them, like you, are trained, some are ordinary citizens with families, children even, who may suffer terribly as a result of reprisals. I don't think the Germans can be depended on to act honourably if they are thwarted. They are very fond of brutal punishments and won't hesitate to wipe out a whole family or even an entire village in response to any act of resistance or sabotage.' Sylvia sipped her tea and tried to judge Phyllis's mood.

'We've all heard about it, Miss Benson. And we all know that we have to try our best to withhold information and not compromise our colleagues. Luckily, as I understand it, we won't know everyone in our network, only those with whom we are in immediate contact.'

'Of course, but if they can drag even one name out of you that will lead them to others. Each time a link in the chain breaks, the next one will come under attack.'

'But we know all this. So, what else is there to be done?' Phyllis finished her cup of tea and took the last bite of her sandwich.

'My dear, if you are unfortunate enough to be arrested and find yourself unable to withstand interrogation, you will have only two options. You can try to escape or you can supply false information. However, that option comes with its own risks. The reprisals for you and your associates could be even greater if your inquisitors realised they had been misled, so that is not ideal.'

'But there's another option, as well, isn't there? And I think that's what you're here to talk about. I'm right, aren't I?' Phyllis was calm and clear-eyed, looking at Sylvia with a steady gaze.

'Yes, my dear. Do you wish to be supplied with the option of an exit? Do you want to carry a cyanide pill on your person? You will have to make sure it is safely hidden, not just so you can retrieve it if necessary, but also to avoid the possibility of it falling into innocent hands.'

'I was expecting this and I've already given it some thought. Where do you suggest I hide it?' Phyllis looked excited, as if this was a drama and she was the star.

'We will supply you with more than one pill. They can be secreted in a button attached to an item of clothing that you might wear all the time perhaps, like a coat or a jacket. We can also stitch them into hems or cuffs. Or one could be concealed in a pen top. You don't wear glasses, do you? We've had some success inserting them into spectacle frames.'

'I'm going to be representing a cosmetics company, aren't I? That's my cover? So, I've already decided I'll put one beneath my lipstick. I can carefully slip the lipstick out of the case and pop the capsule underneath. It will be quite safe, as long as they let me keep my lipstick.' She flashed her stunning smile.

Sylvia was relieved that Phyllis seemed so matter of fact about the subject. 'They might well let you have your lipstick, if they like the look of you, my dear. We'll arrange the capsules before you finally leave.'

'And I've just two more questions, Miss Benson. If I decide that the time really has come, if I realise I can't hold on any longer and I go ahead and swallow the poison, how long will it take to kill me? And will it be painful?'

'It's almost instant, my dear, and you won't feel a thing,' Sylvia said with a blank face, thinking, how the hell do I know? I've been told it's swift, but in those seconds would one feel agonising spasms, gut-wrenching pain?

She laid her hand over Phyllis's, adding, 'It's only to be used as a last resort if you think you will break under the pressure. A quick exit.' But she couldn't help thinking, but only if the Germans haven't already confiscated your one chance of escape.

SPECIAL OPERATIONS EXECUTIVE MANUAL

SELECTION OF DROPPING POINTS AND ARRANGEMENTS FOR THE RECEPTION OF AGENTS AND STORES BY AIR

2. Weather must be favourable. Usually bright moonlight. Average night available: Five or six on either side of full moon, making eleven or thirteen in all. Operation can, in favourable circumstances, be carried out without moon, but some very reliable landmark, such as a large lake, is necessary.

FOURTEEN
GIVE ME THE MOONLIGHT

Sometimes when Sylv was a bit down in the dumps, which happened more and more often towards the end, she'd sit staring out the window. It's a lovely view of the valley of course, but I don't think she was admiring the scenery. There's nothing to see there but fields and the hills in the distance, and she'd sit there for ages. Not always in silence though. Quite often she'd hum under her breath, or sing a few words I could just about catch.

I can almost hear her again now. One of the songs she sang most often was 'I Want to Buy a Paper Doll I Can Call My Own'. I always recognised the tune straight away even though she couldn't manage all the words. It was one of those songs we listened to all the time towards the end of the war. And when she was like that I knew she was thinking about those times, back then.

Months would go by without us seeing each other in those days. She was in an office somewhere, doing God knows what. Filing, she always said. 'I did an awful lot of filing.' And I was underground, literally underground. It was the new part of the

Central Line and they'd moved the whole Plessey factory down into the tunnels that ended at Gants Hill. Bloody marvellous when you think of it, all of us down there making important bits and pieces for machinery, munitions and whatever.

I'd no idea what on earth I was making, I just knew it was vital to the war effort. And it was safer than working in my mum and dad's shop above ground, I can tell you. That survived all the bombings, though we had a couple of near misses, but I was quite glad to be safe down there in the factory, doing my bit.

Sometimes, when Sylv was in one of her moods, when even me saying, 'Fancy a gobstopper?' couldn't shake her out of it, I'd try making her laugh with my Gracie Fields' impression. She was ever so popular in our day. So, I'd give Sylv my version of the Thing-Ummy-Bob song that Gracie sang. You know, the one about making bits and bobs that are going to win the war. Us factory girls all loved that song because it seemed like it had been written just for girls like us and we sang it a lot of the time while we were working down there. I mean, like in the song, we didn't know what on earth we were all making, we just knew our work was important. Well, they wouldn't have moved a whole bloomin' factory down there if they didn't think it was vital, would they? The old factory got bombed in 1940, I think, when the Blitz really got going and, as the tube line was built but not yet open, they had the brilliant idea of moving the whole shebang down there.

It was great for me because I could walk to work from home and go straight down into the factory at Gants Hill station. Miles long it was, with a little railway inside to ferry parts backwards and forwards. Important visitors used the train as well when they came sometimes to see what we were up to. Might have been more help if they'd let us ride it to get to the toilets though. You had to run a mile if you wanted to spend a penny. I used to go at the start of my shift as the toilets were near the entrance and I was always bursting by the time I finished for the day.

Looking back on it, I sometimes think I may have had a better war than Sylvia. My work may have been boring, making the same widget thingy day in, day out, but us girls knew how to have a right laugh while we worked. I can't imagine filing being that much fun, can you? We were nearly all women down there, a couple of thousand of us altogether. And we had a canteen, so they looked after us pretty well with regular breaks.

I remember one time I hummed a bit of that Gracie Fields' tune when Sylvia was having one of her off-days, staring out of the window, and she turned round to look at me. 'What's that noise?' she said. 'That dreadful woman. Never could stand her.'

I didn't think anything was going to cheer her up that day. She'd gone right back in on herself. I guessed it was because of the full moon. She was always a bit funny when the moon was really bright. I caught her a few times staring out of her bedroom window at the moon. She used to stand there muttering to herself. One time I'm sure I heard her say, 'It's a good clear night for flying,' and another time something like, 'The Lysanders should go out tonight.' *Who's Lysander when he's at home?* I remember thinking.

She always refused to draw her curtains at night, so the moonlight came right inside her bedroom when the moon was full. So many times I offered to pull her curtains for her, because I like my room to be really dark to get me off to sleep, but then she'd say, 'No, don't do that, Peg. We watched them on a moonlit night. I saw them go and some didn't come back.'

What on earth she was on about, I've no idea. Yes, the moonlight is lovely and out here in the countryside with no street lamps it really does light up the garden at night. I'd never really noticed the moonlight until I came to live in the country. You're not aware of it in town with all the glaring street lights, but out here, where it's pitch-black, it makes everything silvery and every shade of grey you can think of. But in the winter, I always think it means a frost and that meant I'd have to scrape the car off if she wanted anything in the morning. Maybe I've never been an old romantic like her.

FIFTEEN
BY THE LIGHT OF THE SILVERY MOON
MAY 1943

Sylvia always went to see them off. She'd taken care of them this far, interviewed them, sent them on challenging courses, her brave girls – of course she had to be with them right up to the very last minute.

She no longer bothered reminding Harrington that she was going. He didn't see the point. 'There's staff there trained to sort them out. You don't need to trouble yourself,' he'd said the first time she went. So she took no notice of him. For her it was important and it might be the last time she'd ever see them alive.

It was always such a lovely drive down to Tangmere airfield, very close to the Sussex coast. In the summer months she drove her girls there in an open-top car, past the billowing hills of the South Downs, dotted with sheep and lambs. Sylvia always wished there was time to stop and gather primroses, bluebells or cowslips, or whichever wild flower was blooming at that particular moment, but they pressed on until they arrived at the modest brick and flint cottage tucked away behind the thick, high hedges, so passing villagers were hardly aware of the secret arrivals. Indoors, two burly RAF flight sergeants took charge of the catering, rustling up mixed grills and full breakfasts for pilots and agents departing and arriving.

Two or three agents were usually dropped into France on each flight, but the one Sylvia particularly remembered was the last time she ever saw Phyllis. Her protégée was so calm and cheerful when she collected her from Bignor Manor a few miles away, where agents gathered to await the moment of their final departure.

'It's been just like a summer holiday staying here,' Phyllis said. 'We even had salad for lunch today. Lovely new potatoes, with boiled ham and hard-boiled eggs. So fresh too. I collected them myself from the hens outside in their run.'

Sylvia was glad Phyllis was relaxed and thought the peacefulness of Bignor, with the hens scratching and murmuring contentedly in their dusty run suited her. 'And did Mrs Bertram check your clothes and luggage for you?' Sylvia knew that the Bignor Manor housekeeper would have done a thorough job of looking for labels and obviously English items, as well as slipping cyanide capsules into hems and cuffs.

'Of course,' Phyllis said. 'I'm all ready to go. But I forgot to ask her to post this birthday card to my brother. Could you do it for me? You will remember, won't you?'

'Don't worry about it. I'll keep in touch with your family the whole time you're away.' Little did Sylvia know that would end up being for much longer than she could ever have imagined. She also had several pre-written letters that she could send to Phyllis's family for reassurance and would find herself using them all in the months to come. 'And once we've had supper at the cottage, I'll need to go over a couple of things, just you and me in the sitting room.'

Sylvia and Phyllis joined a small group of pilots and agents in the cottage dining room, which was furnished with two trestle tables. The room had once been used as a chapel by the station's Roman Catholic chaplain and the walls were inscribed with Roman numerals representing the stations of the cross. It was eerily appropriate, Sylvia thought, that Phyllis and other agents should be prepared for their departure among such symbols. But she hoped it did not signify that they too were moving towards their final destination and an exceptionally cruel death.

After eating only a small portion of the famously generous mixed grill, served by the two capable sergeants, whom Phyllis teased and nicknamed the Marx Brothers, Sylvia took her aside to the room next door. As they sat in the lumpy sagging armchairs, draped in green linen loose covers, either side of the fireplace that blazed in colder months, Sylvia said, 'I just need to double-check all your belongings and make sure nothing will seem out of place if you end up in the wrong hands.' She knew that the clothes Phyllis was wearing had already been inspected before she dressed for her departure, but she still looked through her pockets and handbag, slipping in a pack of French cigarettes for cover.

'I haven't done anything wrong, have I?' Phyllis was always so eager to please, so keen to be top of the class.

'No, not at all. But it's so easy for the wrong kind of label or button to slip through at the last minute. You wouldn't believe how often it happens. So many things have *Made in England* labels tucked away on them somewhere. Men's hats are the worst. We usually have to confiscate those, much to their annoyance.'

Phyllis found this highly amusing. 'Oh dear, does that mean they have to go bare-headed?'

'Sometimes, but Mrs Bertram can usually lay her hands on a substitute. Mind you, they might have to make do with a battered old cap instead of a smart trilby from Lock's.'

'Oh no! You're not going to have to remove some of my things and send me away with some awful old clothes, are you?'

'No, my dear, I can't see anything wrong with your packing

at all. Now, it's time you changed into your jumping suit and it's a good idea to have some ready cash tucked into your pocket. You need to have your hands free when you jump.'

Phyllis's eyes registered this reminder of the action she would be taking in the next few hours. 'Of course. I remember being told that.' She patted her jacket pocket and took out the gold powder compact Harrington had given to her, before she left London. 'I was going to take this as well, for good luck. But it's worth a bit, so I'd rather not, in case I lose it. Will you look after it for me?'

'Of course I will. And don't worry, you'll do well, my dear,' Sylvia said, thinking the girl was going to need a lot more than a powdered nose to survive her mission and, gold compact or not, she needed all the luck she could get. A resistance cell in the Auvergne had recently been broken, meaning that particular network was unravelling fast. Phyllis would certainly need her wits about her when she travelled as a cosmetics company sales-woman, allowing her to move between cities by train overnight.

Three agents were going off to France that evening. As they were driven to the airfield in an army station wagon the two men were quiet, smoking nervously with shaking hands. But Sylvia noticed that Phyllis was totally composed, making polite conversation. The bright moon was already picking out the hedges and grassy verges along the way and although the hour was late the countryside wasn't completely dark, it was like a black and white film in varying tones of grey, black and silver.

The wagon drew up alongside the Lysander planes on the airstrip and they all jumped down, then hauled out their various bags and equipment. Phyllis was the most encumbered as she had not only a case but the heavy radio she was delivering.

Sylvia wished each of them a smooth flight and a safe land-ing, ending with Phyllis. 'My dear,' she said, 'you are about to undertake a vital task. I wish you every success in your mission.'

'Thank you, Miss Benson. Your support has given me such

confidence. I'm so grateful to you. My brother would be reassured to know that I've been working with the most marvellous woman.' Phyllis shook Sylvia's hand, then climbed up the flimsy ladder attached to the side of the aircraft.

Sylvia stayed watching while the little plane scooted down the runway and took off into the clear sky. As it circled above her and headed towards France it passed in front of the full moon, a little black bird silhouetted against that bright circle of light. 'Good luck,' she whispered. 'May God be on your side.'

Returning to the cottage after the agents and their pilot had left, Sylvia experienced a painful feeling of emptiness. Two other pilots had turned up to have a late supper and were in good spirits, but she wasn't in the mood for their kind of black humour that night. She knew their jokes were part of their way of brushing off danger and sometimes she joined in their off-duty sessions of banter and bluster. Some of the boastful comments they tossed around were recorded in a logbook kept in the cottage and were a source of much amusement. Lines such as, 'Until you've done bomber ops, you don't know what ops are'.

She understood their attitude, of course; these pilots were risking their own lives as well as those of the agents they were ferrying. A couple of them had already survived being shot down in their Spitfires and captured, and had escaped to take up what they considered to be safer missions flying the Lysanders. But that night the joshing between young men nicknamed 'Bunny' and 'Sticky' didn't appeal to her and Sylvia left them to their jollity and drove back to Bignor.

'I think I'll turn in,' she said to Mrs Bertram as soon as she arrived. 'It's been a long day.' The housekeeper always kept the beds freshly made for whoever was staying overnight. Upstairs in the sparse room she'd been allocated, Sylvia sat on the hard bed, wondering if she'd be able to sleep. She always felt low after sending her girls off to heaven knew what. They should be met by their contacts after landing, they were bright, well trained and resourceful, but everyone knew that the consequences if they were ever caught were disastrous. She could not bear to think of those bright young faces being beaten or worse.

She then remembered the gold compact she had slipped into her pocket. Flipping it open, she lifted the soft, brushed cotton pad, backed with pink satin. It carried the lightest scent of vanilla and she could tell that the pressed powder had already been used a little. Perhaps Phyllis had even powdered her nose one last time, before she gave Sylvia the compact for safe keeping. It amused her to think that Harrington thought this gift was almost an addition to her girls' essential equipment and she felt a wry smile twitch her mouth. Tearing a blank strip from the airmail letter tucked in her handbag, she wrote Phyllis's name in pencil and slipped the paper inside the compact, then snapped it shut.

She felt the weight of expectation would never lift from her heart, so she switched off the bedside light and went to the window. As she pulled the curtains and the blackout blind aside, pools of silver light fell onto the candlewick bedspread and carpet.

Sylvia looked up at the full moon. It was at its height and she knew that by now the plane would have dispatched its precious cargo and her lovely girl would either be in the hands of their French counterparts or the Germans.

June 1943

Dear Miss Benson,

Mother says she has written to you several times asking for news of Phyllis, but you never have any. So, I've decided to write to you again myself to ask if you know when my sister will be coming home. My older brothers keep saying we shall hear in due course, but I think as you were responsible for her you must know something.

Please let us know at the earliest opportunity when Phyllis will return.

Yours sincerely,

Humphrey Lane

SIXTEEN
FEMININE INTUITION
OCTOBER 1943

It was the men who were the problem, Sylvia always thought. Oh, there were plenty of courageous men and men of integrity, but there were so many who thought they were the ones who knew best, who thought they had all the answers and that women were there just to make their job more efficient. No wonder Sylvia always said she did 'a lot of filing' at her wartime post.

She once said to Harrington, when they were double-checking whether an agent's cover had blown, 'I know you'll tell me not to use my feminine intuition, but I think if Maurice was really the one still freely transmitting, he wouldn't have used his safety words.' Every agent had an agreed phrase for use only in extreme circumstances and Maurice had incorporated his into his latest messages.

'Don't make a scene. The rest of the network is still functioning. We're still in operation,' Harrington said, turning back to his paperwork. 'On your way out, tell Jean I could do with a fresh cup of tea.'

Sylvia seethed, but handed on the request to Jean, a brunette with neat buffed nails and a well-deserved reputation for detail. Sylvia hadn't seen their agent's messages herself, it had been Jean who'd spotted it and reported it to Harrington first, then to Sylvia when he hadn't reacted with any sense of urgency. 'You know how important it is that they use their code messages only for emergencies,' Jean had said. 'I'm sure there's a problem, but he won't listen. Maurice has slipped in his special message, "can we have goose for Christmas", in all his transmissions. It's extremely irregular.'

'Let me know what else you pick up, if anything,' Sylvia said. 'If Maurice has been caught, the Germans might try to make him continue transmitting. I agree it doesn't sound right. And we've got too many valuable agents out there now. We have to be vigilant. Damn Harrington for being so pig-headed.'

She felt like screaming, but she restrained herself and marched back to her desk, no longer in the glamorous diplomat's apartment but in the drabber surroundings of another office in Baker Street. A drearier environment than the swanky flat in which she had first recruited her girls, it was full of Civil Service protocol with not a mirrored cocktail cabinet in sight.

A day or so later, Jean knocked on Sylvia's office door. 'May I come in?' She looked over her shoulder as if she was desperate to hide.

'Yes, whatever is it? You look like you don't want to be seen coming in here. Close the door, quick, and sit down. I'll switch on my Do Not Disturb sign.' Sylvia pressed the button that lit up in the corridor, indicating she was concentrating on papers, a phone call or a conversation.

'Thanks, I've only got a few minutes. I said I had a headache and needed to get an aspirin. He won't miss me for a while.' Jean sounded breathless, not from rushing but from nerves.

'What's happened? Has another code word slipped through?'

'Yes, it has, and I knew you'd want to know straight away.' She fiddled with her engagement ring, turning it round and round.

'I want to know everything. He thinks he's so damn clever. All this "need to know basis" he insists on. But these are my people he's playing games with and I care deeply what happens to them. So what have you found out now?'

Jean bit her lip and took a deep breath. 'It's happened again.'

'Maurice, again?'

'No. Another one. Called Simone. And I know she's one of yours.'

Sylvia gasped. Simone was the operational name for Phyllis. 'Oh no, please no! He's got to find out if she's safe.'

'I know. But he says he's not going to.'

'Not going to? But why ever not?' Sylvia could not conceal her impatience. She pushed back her chair and began pacing backwards and forwards.

'He says it's the perfect opportunity to beat the Germans at their own game. He says it's a chance to double-cross them.'

'What on earth does he mean by that?'

'He's having a meeting with Steele-Smythe. They're talking about using this as a breakthrough to feed the Germans misinformation. They want the Jerries to think London hasn't realised their agent is compromised, so they can pull the wool over their eyes.'

'Of course he is. He raised this once before. I said he could not in all conscience do it if it meant putting agents' lives at risk. He promised me it would only ever be a last resort.'

Sylvia stared at the framed photograph of King George, on the wall facing her desk. It was standard issue in all the offices, a reminder that they were fighting for king and country. She thought of her last meeting with Phyllis, how plucky she was and how she had grown in confidence from the timid girl she'd first interviewed. 'They might be forcing her to make the transmissions herself. In which case, she's still alive.'

She spun round to face Jean. 'Has he said anything else about her messages? Do they still think it's her? Please tell me it is.'

Sylvia could tell from the way Jean's eyes flickered that she had more to say. 'I wasn't in the room, but I could hear them talking. I'm afraid I listened outside, with my ear close to the door. I'm sorry.'

'No, don't be sorry. I'm glad you did. What did you learn? I need to know.'

'I heard him say *they're pretty sure it's not her fist. It's close, but it's not her* and then he said, *but we don't need to let them know we've cottoned on.*'

'Damn him. He's loving this, isn't he? A chance for him to play stupid games and tell the Germans what he wants them to hear.' Sylvia's heart was thumping, not with fear but with anger. Every agent had their own distinctive transmission style, the so-called 'fist', and if this wasn't Phyllis, what had happened to her?

'But does that mean there's a chance Simone is still alive then?' Jean clasped her hands under her chin. The girl had a good heart and knew she was breaking the department's rules about not sharing information.

'I certainly hope so. The Germans have generally had a degree of respect for our female personnel so far. So, I hope she is being well treated.'

'But they'll want to find out exactly what she knows, won't they? So, what does that mean for her?' Jean's eyes were filling with tears and Sylvia knew she had to reassure her. She couldn't send the girl back to Harrington and his co-conspirator looking an emotional wreck. Tears in the corridor would be a disaster.

'Look, you've done your bit by coming to see me. You're not to worry about it any more. But if you hear anything else, let me know.' Sylvia stepped round her and opened the door. 'Get back before he wonders why you're taking so long.'

'Yes, I'd better,' Jean said, quickly wiping her eyes with a delicate lace-edged handkerchief. 'He wanted me to bring them tea and biscuits on my way back.' She slipped out of the door.

'Say you had to wait for the urn to heat up,' Sylvia said as she left.

She closed the door and returned to her desk. Sitting down, she realised her hands were trembling. Maybe she was the one in need of hot sweet tea. Bloody Harrington and his cunning cronies, all eager to be oh so clever and get one over on the Germans. They didn't think about the flesh-and-blood agents they had dispatched, they were just thinking about the complex charades they could play from a safe distance. Harrington was probably already instructing his London operator to transmit false information about favoured landing spots for a possible invasion force.

Sylvia sat with her head in her hands, trying to calm herself. Her thoughts were racing ahead to what might be happening to Phyllis now. She might still be transmitting under the direction of the Germans. If that was the case, she could have slipped in her code to alert London to a breach in security. Or she might be transmitting and reinforcing her predicament by consciously changing her fist, her operating style, to let her colleagues know she was compromised.

What was more likely? Was Phyllis now a prisoner? Was she being well treated? Sylvia closed her eyes. Horrific reports had filtered back to London. The Gestapo was merciless in its search for information. Dear sweet Phyllis, so determined, so courageous, might well be incapable of transmitting any more. Her hands might be so badly hurt, she would be unable to tap out a message.

Sylvia took a deep breath. She was convinced that Phyllis would be pushed hard, pushed to breaking point, to spill everything she knew about London, the training, the other agents, the entire network. In this instance Harrington was right about 'need to know'; the less each segment and division knew about the whole operation, the less they could reveal. But in the meantime, her agent would be cajoled, persuaded, then finally physically tortured, until her mind had been emptied of every fact. How was the slight, delicate figure of Phyllis going to be able to withstand that?

SPECIAL OPERATIONS EXECUTIVE MANUAL

INTERROGATIONS

2. INTERROGATION METHODS

2b) During Interrogation

iv) Prisoner may be wholly or partly stripped sometimes in the presence of members of the opposite sex.

SEVENTEEN

BOYS IN THE CLUB

OCTOBER 1943

Sylvia decided she had to stop Harrington's game right away. She had to insist that whatever was happening to Phyllis, the Germans should be encouraged to believe that their ruse was no longer working and that she was no use to them. At least then, Phyllis stood a chance. She would still be a prisoner, but if they thought she had no more information to give them, she might survive.

Sylvia marched down the corridor to Harrington's office. Jean looked up as she threw open the outer door. 'You can't go in there,' she said. 'He's still in that meeting.'

Putting a finger to her lips, Sylvia shook her head and pushed his door open. Two heads swivelled round as she entered, one with greasy strands of grey hair plastered across his pate in a pathetic attempt to conceal his obvious baldness, the other with a thick blond mane, which he swept back with his hand. Campbell Steele-Smythe was handsome and knew it. He'd made a play for Sylvia at one point and she had fallen for his charms. She'd regretted that later, but knew he might still be open to flattery.

'Gosh, Campbell, will you forgive me for barging in like

this? I didn't realise you were here. What are you two up to?'
She threw him a dazzling smile, knowing it would distract him.

'Here to see you of course. We've nearly finished, haven't
we?' Campbell turned his handsome profile to the frowning
Harrington. 'Why don't we all meet up later for a drink at the
club? Set us up for the evening now the nights are drawing in.'

'That sounds lovely,' Sylvia said, forcing herself to smile. 'It
would be good to catch up with you and hear all the latest
news.'

Campbell saluted them both. 'Shall we say six o'clock?'

'Perfect,' Sylvia said as he left. Swiftly turning to Harrington, she said, 'Right, where's Simone? Where's my girl Phyllis?'

Harrington gave an embarrassed cough and began shuffling
the papers on his blotter.

Sylvia leant on the edge of his desk and slammed her hand
on top of his files. 'Don't ask how I know, but I do. If she's in
trouble, I want it stopped right this minute. You've no right to
play your petty games with my girls.'

'I don't know what you're talking about. We might have
encountered a slight problem and we were just working out the
best way forward for the present.'

'The best way forward is to protect my girls. And I hear that
Phyllis is at risk because you are thoroughly enjoying your
stupid machinations. Why don't you just drop all the pretence
and tell me the truth? Is she safe or isn't she?'

Harrington took a deep breath and reached for his gold
cigarette case. Sylvia found his liking for expensive accessories
distasteful, but maybe it was a gift from his heiress wife. He
took his time lighting one, drew on it, blew the smoke towards
her and said, 'A special favourite of yours, is she?'

Sylvia took a step back. 'She's one of our best. And she's our
youngest.'

'You seem particularly upset about this girl.' He raised an
eyebrow.

'I'm not upset, I'm furious. These are people, Harrington, not pawns for you to play games with.'

He studied her, then drawled, 'You've got to admit there's a certain advantage in letting the other side think we've haven't spotted their switch.'

'So, you're now admitting that Phyllis is no longer transmitting herself? That they've got their hands on her radio now?'

He appeared to be considering his reply, his mouth twisting, before saying, 'It looks rather like it.'

'And what are they doing to her in the meantime? Where are they holding her? Do you know? Do you even care?'

'We may know more in due course. But right now, we're more concerned with how we can take advantage of this opportunity. Our enemy is desperate for any hints they can pick up about our plans for the invasion. We can use this development if we're clever. If she's as bright as you claim, your girl would understand that only too well.'

Sylvia gritted her teeth. Of course it was an opportunity, she could see that. But at what cost? 'We have a duty of care as well, you know. Phyllis is only just twenty years of age. She's our youngest recruit and one of our most brilliant. She may be young, but she showed herself to be incredibly tough when she was put through her paces. That means she will resist all attempts to get her to talk. You know what that means, don't you?'

Harrington took his time stubbing his cigarette out in the onyx ashtray on his desk. He'd smoked barely half of it. 'All our chaps knew what they were signing up for. One of the hazards of the job, I'd say.'

'How you can be so damn casual about this, I don't know. You've met with those who've managed to return, haven't you? I know you have. So you know exactly what the Gestapo are capable of. They don't care how they break a man, or a woman, for that matter. Have you ever seen the feet of someone who's been in their custody? Looked at their mangled toes?'

He closed his eyes and sighed. 'Benson, you're being rather emotional about all this. Take a detached view. This is a nasty war, there will inevitably be casualties. It's not pretty, I know, but sometimes we have to take steps that cause losses for the greater gain.'

Sylvia took a breath and paused. 'I understand that, of course I do. But think of the girl whose life you are risking. She knew the stakes were high, but she deserves our respect and our help, not to be a piece in the board game you're playing. She's worth more than that.'

'I beg to disagree. She is worth more to us right now than she was before. We'll continue double-crossing them as long as they're falling for it.'

'This is disgusting. So underhand and devious. That beautiful, brave girl shouldn't be subject to your whims.'

He smiled to himself, swivelled his leather chair to the left and to the right, then said, 'It's so touching to see how much you miss her. Was she very special to you?'

Sylvia couldn't stop herself gulping. His patronising tone made the back of her neck crawl as she anticipated his next words.

'I've often wondered why you haven't found another chap to take you on since your fiancé threw you over. Maybe you just weren't his type.'

'I don't know what you are thinking, but I know I'm in the right here. All our agents are very special and are working in extremely high-risk situations.'

'But some are more special than others, is that it? Is that your problem?'

His quizzical eyebrow infuriated her even more and she felt her fists clenching and her shoulders tensing. 'I'd be standing up for any of them in this situation. They're all valuable and important to our work.'

'Hmm, I see. You have my sympathy. I find a detached attitude is more helpful than a close relationship with colleagues, at all levels. You might do well to remember that.'

Sylvia could stand it no longer. She turned on her heel and marched out of his office. This time she didn't slam the door, she left it wide open. He didn't deserve her respect and she needed that drink.

EIGHTEEN

HANKY PANKY IN THE SAVOY

OCTOBER 1943

'Gin and It? That's still your tipple, if I remember correctly.' Campbell was appraising her, she could tell, as he raised his hand to summon the barman.

She had met him on the steps of the club, but clutched his hand and said, 'I'm escaping Harrington. Can we go to The Savoy instead? I've had quite enough of him for one day and can't bear to be stuck with him any longer.'

'Your wish is my command, dearest. Let's walk along the Embankment.' He offered her his arm, which she willingly took, feeling her nerves abating as they strolled in the late-afternoon sunshine glinting on the waters of the great Thames.

They walked in silence for a while and Sylvia thought how they might once have made an ideal couple, romantically linked, as she watched the boats on the water. It struck her that the permanence of this mighty river was reassuring; nature continued in force, despite the bombardment of the city.

'Penny for them,' he said, inclining his head slightly to look into her eyes.

'Tell me honestly what you really think of Harrington's

plan. And don't hold back, please. The girl in question is one of my protégées.'

'Aah, I see, she's one of yours. That makes it personal.' He cleared his throat. 'To be frank, I can't see this little scheme of his lasting more than a day or so.' He squeezed her hand holding his arm. 'Why don't we talk about it properly over that drink?'

Sylvia gave his hand a pat to assure him she was in agreement. She was prepared to do more than that if it meant she would get the result she wanted.

Once they were seated in a secluded corner of the American Bar with their drinks, Campbell said, 'The trouble is, the Germans are sure to guess sooner or later that their messages don't contain the right security check, so then they'll realise we've been stringing them along.' He'd put his arm along the back of the velvet seat, leaning in close to her so their voices couldn't be overheard. It was instinctive for them to adhere to the 'careless talk costs lives' edict at this stage of the game.

'That's exactly what I think. And if my agent never gave them the right check in the first place, once they've cottoned on to that, they're likely to make her life very unpleasant.'

'Afraid so. That's the way they like to play it.' He toyed with the olive in his Martini.

'She was meant to start her messages *Dear Mother*, if all was well,' Sylvia said, 'but change that to *Dear Humphrey* if she was caught.'

'I know. Harrington told me. Her transmissions switched to using Humphrey about three weeks ago.'

Sylvia gasped with shock. 'He's known for as long as that?'

'Apparently so. But his boys only started slipping the false information through in the last four or five days.'

'He's known all that time and let this link continue?' She took a gulp of her drink, and then a second.

'Another for you? Seems you needed that one.' Campbell clicked his fingers and signalled they would have the same again. While they were waiting, he ran his finger down the long menu of cocktails offered by this famous bar. 'Look, what do you say to trying one of the specials Eddie, the barman here, has concocted in honour of each of the armed services? How do you fancy an Eight Bells or a New Contemptible?'

'I think I'd better stick to what I know, Campbell. Pity we can't tell Eddie all about us and SOE and get him to make us a special.'

'We're far too hush-hush for that, but what do you think he'd put in a top-secret mix and what would he call it?'

'Silent Killer, perhaps?' Sylvia laughed.

'Oh yes. A mix of every lethal spirit he can lay his hands on?'

It felt good to talk nonsense with Campbell, but Sylvia was there to get answers. She needed the anaesthesia of alcohol, but told herself to take the next drink slowly. 'I understand that there had also been another agent, a man, Maurice, who was also allowed to carry on despite signalling he'd been picked up.'

'Yes, it seems that didn't last very long. His messages suddenly ceased altogether.'

'Any clues where he is now?'

'We believe he was moved to the prison in Fresnes. They may do the same with your girl, once they decide they've got enough out of her. It's a pretty nasty place, by all accounts.'

'I'm rather afraid they're not going to get anything out of her at all,' Sylvia said. 'And they won't like that, will they?'

'Good, is she?'

'One of my best. She may look fragile, but she's tough as anything. Beat the men on the Scottish moors section. She'll hold out for ever if she can.'

'Good for her. I mean, good for her network, but she may pay a terrible price for holding out.'

'That's what I'm afraid of. But what can we do?' Sylvia

leant her head on Campbell's shoulder, letting him feel her weariness and desperation.

His hand dropped from the back of their seat to her shoulders and then to the back of her neck, stroking the skin above the clasp of her double row of pearls. 'I can have another word with Harrington if you like. If you really want me to.'

She lifted her head to look into his intensely green eyes. 'Please, would you? What will you say?'

'I'll convince him that there's nothing more to be gained.'

'How are you going to do that?'

Campbell smiled and put his index finger on her lips. 'A little bird told me what he's been up to. His wife wouldn't like it.'

Sylvia couldn't help laughing. 'What, stuffy old Harrington, up to no good? Whatever next?'

Campbell laughed with her. 'Seems he's not so stuffy after all, but his wife's the money, so he'll back off, I'm sure.'

'And what exactly are you going to get him to do?'

'I'll say the next message has to tell the Bosch that we've spotted their little game and that we're shutting off the line.'

'But they may still hold her and try to make her talk.'

'They've had long enough already. They'll want to put all their effort into bagging another transmitter if they can. So, they'll dispense with her.'

'What do you mean dispense? You don't mean shoot her?'

'Who knows? They may hang on to her as a piece in the puzzle. They may lock her up somewhere.'

'Poor Phyllis. I wish we could get her out of there.'

'No can do, I'm afraid. This is the best option. If she's lucky, it won't be too awful.'

'It certainly won't be The Savoy,' she said with a sad sigh.

His hand returned to stroking her neck. 'Another drink here or shall we go somewhere quieter? Did you know they do a cocktail here called a Hanky Panky?' He gave her a mischievous grin.

'Let's go somewhere quieter,' Sylvia murmured. She felt the need for company and wanted to ensure that he would fulfil his promise. 'I'm really very grateful to you,' and she gave his thigh a discreet little squeeze.

SPECIAL OPERATIONS EXECUTIVE MANUAL

INTERROGATIONS

5. COUNTER-MEASURES

v) Always try to appear clean, neat and, if possible, well dressed. Do a little P.T. regularly.

NINETEEN
THE TROUBLE WITH MEN

'I blame the men,' Sylvia often said. I didn't really know which men she meant, but I always encouraged her to say what she thought. I mean, I blamed the men too. After all, it wasn't wives and mothers who started that awful war, was it? And it was women and children who suffered the most in the end, as far as I can see.

When I was in the factory, stamping out whatever widget or gasket they asked of me, I didn't ever complain now, did I? Soulless, repetitive work it was too, hour after hour, the same darn thing. And what thanks did us girls get? Old Bert Lugg, the foreman, would try to get a feel whenever he came round to look over our work. All of us talked about it and laughed about how we were going to get our own back on him one day.

Joanie, one of my friends there, said she was going to elbow him next time he tried it on. A sharp dig in the ribs when she jerked the lever on her machine. I said I'd rather he got a sharp you-know-what in the wotsits. But we all had to behave as best we could, because he was in charge and we were just the girls on the production line.

He'd come and stand behind us, lean forward to see how many thingys we'd made that morning, and you could feel him pressing himself up against your backside. Horrible he was, with his smell of cheap hair oil and pickled onions. He had stinky pipe-smoker's breath as well. One time he put his arm round me and I swear his fingers crept round my back and I could feel him groping and trying to get a feel of my Bristol. I stood back on his foot that time – that soon put a stop to it.

I told Joanie what he'd done and she said, 'When he was pressed up against your thigh, did you think that was a spanner in his pocket, or was he just pleased to see you?' That made me giggle, because he did have a habit of pressing himself too close and something hard always dug into me from under his dust-coat. 'Oh, Joanie,' I said, 'you don't mean his willy? Don't be so disgusting.' But she said it was him that was disgusting.

Then Joanie told all the other girls and it turned out I wasn't the only one. He was pawing all of us with his grubby mitts whenever he got the chance. He thought because he was the supervisor he could do what he liked and we'd never complain.

It was hard for all of us girls, because most of us had never done factory work like this before. We might have been used to hard work in shops, and charring, but not this kind of tedious, relentless, repetitive work. We knew we'd had a lot to learn and that gave him an excuse to poke in his nose and his creepy, dirty fingers. But he should have been looking after us, not touching us up. We were the ones getting our hands filthy, breaking our nails, standing there hour after hour banging out all those important widgets and things.

Anyway, once we'd started comparing notes about how often he'd had a grope, I think that's when we all decided we needed to teach him a lesson. So, one night after our shift, we rushed up to the exit, ahead of him. It was pitch-dark of course, there were no street lights because of the blackout. Luckily, there was a moon that night or we'd have had real trouble seeing. We'd all agreed we were going to wear our darkest clothes that night and cover our faces with scarves and we weren't going to say a word, but hold our breath and stay completely quiet.

When he came out of the tunnel entrance, we were lurking nearby and began to follow him home. We knew he didn't live far away, just the other side of Clayhall Park, not far from the factory, and we knew he always went back to his house by going down the alleyway at the back and in through the garden. One of the girls had followed him a couple of nights because she lived nearby and she told us that's what he always did.

We split up into two groups and entered the alleyway from either end, so we could grab him before he reached his back gate. Two of us got him from behind and Joanie threw a rope round his chest and tied him up. But before she tied his legs together, we pulled his trousers off him. He looked so pathetic, lying on the ground, his white baggy pants and skinny legs all grey in the dim light. We had to stop ourselves laughing. Then we half dragged him to the end of the alley and out to the street and tied him to a lamppost with a placard strung around his neck. Joanie had made it and I couldn't read it in the dark as there were no street lights. So, once we'd run off, I said, 'What did you write on that notice?'

She burst out laughing and couldn't stop, so we all had to support her till we got to the Green Man and bought her a shandy. 'I wrote on it, *Why Don't Women Like Me?*' she said, collapsing again. Well, we all knew that George Formby song, because it was ever so popular. But we were a bit puzzled, till she added, 'And beneath that I wrote, *because you can't keep your hands to yourself*!'

Well, that did it. We all got the giggles. It was shandies all round then and how we laughed and sang a verse or two of that song too. But I have to admit that later that night, when I got into my bed and thought about what we'd done, I felt a bit bad. I don't know if the others had noticed, but I had. As we walked away from him after tying him up, I saw that he'd wet his underpants. I didn't feel too happy about that.

The next day he didn't come in till late. He looked a bit sheepish too. But he stopped his antics for a while. Not for good, but if he ever came too close we all started humming that George Formby song and he'd end up walking away. He couldn't pin anything on us, certainly not on a whole workforce of girls whose jobs were vital to the war effort, now could he?

But somehow I don't think that's the sort of man Sylv has come across. Where she worked, she'd have been dealing with gentlemen, wouldn't she? But then even gents can get a bit free with their hands sometimes, can't they? So, no, I don't think she had that kind of problem with the men in her life. Not that I know everything of course, apart from the fact that she'd never married or even been engaged, as far as I know. I'm sure she'd had admirers, but I don't know all the ins and outs. I've often asked myself why there was never anyone special in her life. She was always so attractive, she must have stirred up feelings among some of the men she met.

I sometimes wondered if something had happened at some point to put her off men altogether. She often said things like, 'They lied. They all did. It was one big lie.' I didn't know if she meant a boyfriend had let her down at some point, been unfaithful to her, perhaps. I'd try to egg her on to say more, but she'd just shake her head and look cross, then sad. Then she'd mutter about her 'lost girls' and how they were sacrificed.

It all sounded a bit Hammer Horror to me, but then I never worked in an office in London, I just did my bit in the factory in the war and then carried on with them for years afterwards when they moved out of the Underground. They were a good company to work for and as me and Harry didn't ever have kids in the end, I didn't have to stay home. I don't think I could ever have done with being just a housewife after being a working girl getting a good wage all those years. I mean, I kept the house clean and cooked and all that, but I don't think that would have been enough for me without kiddies as well. So, I was glad I stayed a working girl with a bit of money for myself.

TWENTY

THE BIG LIE
NOVEMBER 1943

How could any of them be trusted? Despite Campbell's assurances that he would do his best to put pressure on Harrington, Sylvia knew she couldn't be certain he would achieve a successful result or even want to. It seemed to her that everyone had a score to settle. All of them were playing games within the hierarchy and their secret agents were no more than pawns for them to move around, as and when they pleased.

That morning, Sylvia sat slumped at her desk with her head in her hands, wondering if there was anything else she could do to save Phyllis. In some ways, she realised, prolonging the illusion that HQ believed she was still alive and well, transmitting her messages, was some kind of protection in itself. While they all continued to play this game, she was useful to the Germans and, even if she was being ill-treated, so as long as they thought she could still supply them with more information, she was not going to be executed.

But what did Sylvia really wish for her courageous girl? A swift end, a bullet to the back of the neck, was preferable to the long, drawn-out agony of beatings and starvation. And would that poor girl, even now, be thinking about popping that cyanide pill into her mouth and biting the capsule? Maybe Mrs Bertram's habit of stitching the poison into a cuff or a hem had been too obvious. Once the Germans had discovered one such hidden pill, they were bound to check for others. Or perhaps Phyllis had stuck to her original plan of hiding it beneath her lipstick. Sylvia hoped she still had it with her, but knew that her personal belongings might well have been confiscated, leaving Phyllis with no option but to think about blabbing everything she knew or escaping.

Sylvia stood up from her desk and began pacing her office. If Campbell's move to put pressure on Harrington didn't work, maybe she and Jean, his secretary, could talk some sense into him. They were both convinced the network connected to Phyllis was now blown, so there was no point in prolonging the pretence. She resolved to speak with him again immediately. Churchill was putting pressure on their division to send more agents into France ahead of D-Day, but if the networks were compromised they'd effectively be training agents to be sacrificial lambs. These carefully selected, skilled and brave men and women would be met by Germans posing as French resistance the moment they landed.

As she approached Harrington's office, Jean stopped typing and sighed. 'You'd better wait a moment. He's got Campbell in with him.'

'Good. I'm pleased to hear that. Has he been in there very long?'

Jean glanced at the clock on the wall opposite her desk. 'Nearly twenty minutes. And I don't think they've nowhere finished their argy-bargy yet.'

Sylvia smiled. 'I hope Campbell's getting somewhere with him then.' She sat down in a chair to wait and then heard the rattle of the tea trolley coming along the corridor. 'Oh, perfect timing. I'm parched.'

'There's ginger biscuits today too,' Jean said as the trolley rolled to a stop by her office.

'No more than one each now, young ladies,' the tea lady said with a wink. 'I know you girls and your sweet tooth.'

'Is it Camp coffee again today?' Sylvia said. 'I'm dying for a cup of real coffee.'

'You'd better find yourself an American boyfriend then,' the tea lady said. 'They seem to have no end of luxuries, those lucky fellas. In the meantime, you'll have to make do like the rest of us.'

'Two Camp coffees then,' Jean said.

The girls pulled faces at each other as they sipped from their cups, once the trolley had rattled away round the rest of the department. 'At least it's better than the tea,' Sylvia said. 'That's been stewing for at least an hour by the time it gets round to us.'

Just as she was about to dunk her biscuit in the bitter ersatz coffee, the door to the main office opened and Campbell charged out. He began heading off down the corridor, then realised that Sylvia was sitting there. He turned back towards her and shouted, 'He won't listen. It's all gone belly up but he still won't see sense.'

Sylvia was tempted to run after him, but just then Harrington came to the door. His face was red and furious. 'Oh, for goodness' sake. Not you as well,' he said. 'Well, come on, let's get it over with.' He returned to his desk and she followed.

'Have you been having a row with Campbell?'

'Hardly. The man's simply impossible.' He took a cigarette from his gold case and tried to light it. His hands were shaking. 'Damn it. And what do you want?'

'Right now, I'd like to know what's upset you so much. Want to tell me?'

He rolled his eyes and took an exaggerated pull of his cigarette.

'You can tell me yourself or I'll ask Campbell.' Sylvia shrugged. 'It's entirely up to you.'

'We've had a slight disagreement. Nothing more. It all comes down to interpretation.'

'Of what exactly?'

He waved his hand to indicate that the matter was vague but complicated. 'The latest messages. I want to wait a little longer, that's all. He doesn't agree.'

'Does this involve my girl? Is this to do with Phyllis?' He didn't answer, but just kept smoking and looking thoughtful. 'Well, is it?'

'We're concerned about the whole set-up,' he snapped. 'Not just your blessed pet girl.' He stood up and stubbed out his cigarette in the onyx ashtray. 'Now if you don't mind, I've got an important meeting with the minister.' He pushed past her with a file under his arm.

Sylvia was open-mouthed at his rudeness. That did it, she thought. She wasn't relying on him for information. She'd find Campbell and work on him till he told her everything. There was no way she was waiting for Harrington to weaken.

As she left his office, she said, 'Jean, how long do you think he'll be gone?'

Jean consulted the diary. 'At least a couple of hours, I should think. I take it that didn't go well.'

'No, it bloody well didn't. I'm going off to find Campbell. Any idea where he might have gone?'

Jean scoffed. 'The mood he was in when he stormed out, I'd say he was desperate for a drink. Pub round the corner probably.'

'Right, well if anyone asks for me, tell them I've popped out for aspirin.' Sylvia turned on her heel and marched back to her office, collected her handbag and coat, then left the building.

. . .

It was a relief in many ways to leave the stuffy atmosphere of the office. Even though the streets were dusty and littered with debris, the sun was shining and she could glimpse the trees of Regent's Park tempting her. There might be a war on still, but families who hadn't fled to the countryside were outside airing babies in prams while older children were sailing boats on the pond, feeding the ducks and kicking the crisp, fallen autumn leaves.

Sylvia so longed for normal life to return in full, with everyone free to work and play as they pleased. Her days centred on her department, her lost girls and drinks with lonely men. She no longer even had a family to run home to, not that Mother had offered her many homely comforts in the last years of her life as she declined through tuberculosis exacerbated by heavy smoking.

Campbell wasn't in the first pub Sylvia tried, but she was in luck when she walked into The Clarence, glittering with engraved mirrors and polished brass, its moulded ceiling burnished a dark shade of amber by pipe and cigarette smoke. This early in the day there was less of a fug, but the place still had a sour smell of stale beer and fag ends. There were few customers and in place of the usual rumble of conversation she could hear only the soft ticking of the pub's huge collection of chiming clocks. The last time she'd had a drink here with Campbell they'd placed bets on which clock would strike the hour first. She'd won, of course, having chosen a black marble French ormolu mantel clock.

'Aah, there you are at last,' she said, spotting him slumped over the bar, clutching a Scotch. 'I thought I was going to have to go round all the pubs in the area before I'd find you.'

'You know me all too well,' he said. 'You having one yourself?'

'Better not. Bit too early in the day for me.' She noticed his glass was almost empty. 'I'll buy you another though.'

He didn't say no, but slid off his stool and sauntered over to an empty corner. 'We'd best sit where we can talk in private.'

Sitting down with Campbell's second Scotch and a lemonade for herself, Sylvia launched right in. 'You may as well tell me everything. That Harrington is stubborn as they come.'

'Too right,' Campbell muttered in a mournful tone. 'He's trying to avoid facing the inevitable conclusion, despite the evidence before him.'

'Tell me, what's the latest?'

'The whole of the Paris network is blown. Just about everyone has been rounded up. Might even all be shot by now.'

'But there are some left further afield, surely?'

'Very possibly. But his refusal to believe the signs that they'd been arrested in the first place is the real problem. We should have shut them off at the first hint they were compromised.'

'That's exactly what I've been saying all along. Why on earth doesn't he listen?' Sylvia rolled her eyes in exasperation.

'And to cap it all, the Germans are now laughing at us. That's what's making Harrington so bloody-minded. He feels utterly humiliated and doesn't want to admit his colossal bloody mistake.'

'How do you mean, they're laughing?'

Campbell snorted and knocked back his drink in one gulp. 'Can you believe, my love, that the Germans actually radioed us, thanking us for all the supplies they've now got their hands on? They just couldn't resist crowing about getting one over on us.'

'You mean they've been in on our plans for ages and just helped themselves?'

'Exactly. Harrington's seen the messages. Thanks for the armaments, they said, and thanks too for telling us all about your intentions. You've been most helpful, yours sincerely, Siegfried, or words to that effect.'

'No wonder he's utterly furious. He's surely got to accept his little game is over now, hasn't he?'

'Absolutely. No more playing silly buggers with our agents, no more so-called clever double-crossing. It hasn't been so damned clever after all, has it? In fact, it's blown up right in his face.'

Sylvia drew a deep breath. 'Thanks to his stupid games, he's effectively given the Germans everything. Our agents, our codes, our supplies, every damn thing. And on top of that, we have no way of helping our people out there.'

'They're at the mercy of the Bosch, my love.'

'Oh hell, Campbell, I think I need that drink after all.' Sylvia put her head in her hands with a sigh, as the first clock chimed twelve and the other twenty or so followed a split second behind in a badly timed orchestration of hell's bells.

15 May 1945

Dear Miss Benson,

Surely you have some news of my sister, now the war has ended? We are desperate to hear from you or her as soon as possible. We cannot believe that we still don't know how she has been these last couple of years and are very anxious.

Please contact us as soon as you are able to tell us when she will return to her loving family. My eldest brother did not survive and my other brother was badly injured when his plane was shot down so my mother is beside herself with worry about Phyllis. You must make every effort to get in touch with her, as she would never have taken this dangerous position without your encouragement.

Yours sincerely,

Humphrey Lane

TWENTY-ONE
ON YOUR TOES

Ages ago it was, I noticed Sylvia was limping. I know we all get a bit creaky with our joints as we get on, but she really wasn't walking properly. 'Whatever's the matter with you?' I said. 'You got a stone or something in your shoe?'

'My foot's a bit sore,' she said. 'Don't make a fuss. It'll soon pass off.'

But it didn't, did it? It was a week or more before I could get her to take her shoes off and let me have a look. Well, I was horrified. Not only did she have a nasty bunion on the side of both of her big toes, but her toenails were a fright! The one on the big toe had cut a huge hole in her tights. 'What were you thinking?' I said. 'Your toenails need cutting.'

'I can't do it any more,' she said. 'I can't quite reach.'

'Well, then I'll do it for you. You can't carry on like this, you'll ruin your feet.'

'No, no,' she said, struggling to put her shoes back on. 'I'll do it. I don't like other people touching my feet.'

There was no telling her, as usual. But I kept an eye on her and a day or so later, when she was hobbling again, I said, 'Oh, really, Sylvia! You're being silly. You've got to get your feet sorted out. You'll end up a cripple, carrying on like this.'

She didn't like that, I could tell. She sort of gave this kind of huffy snort she does when she's offended. 'I'll do them myself after my bath if you don't mind.'

'All right. Please yourself.'

Well, I knew she wouldn't. I didn't even know when she'd last had a bath. By then, I'm not sure she could even get in or out of it. I mean, I've been finding it a bit of a struggle myself these days, but I'm determined to carry on as long as I can, because a shower isn't the same, is it? I love lying back in the bath with bubbles all around me. I have to pull myself up using the taps as well, mind. Sylvia's bathroom has got handles either side of the bath, so that was a help, but, as I say, I don't think she was even using the bath by that stage. I'm pretty sure I heard the shower going every other day though.

So, after that latest confrontation I thought, well, we'll just have to see, shall we? I let it go for a day or so and, as I didn't hear the bath running or draining, one morning soon after that, I said, 'So, have you managed to have a bath and cut your toenails?'

She hadn't even put shoes on that day, just these sloppy old sheepskin slippers, so I knew her feet must have been hurting her. I waited till she'd sat down for breakfast, poured her a cup of tea, then said, 'Come on, Sylv, admit it. You can't cut your toenails yourself, now, can you? You're going to have to let me help you. I can do it while you sit in your armchair.'

She sipped her tea, took a spoonful of marmalade for her toast and then, while she was spreading it, she said, 'Oh, if I must. After I've had my breakfast, darling. At least let me do that.'

Well of course I was going to let her finish her breakfast. It didn't take all that long. She only ever had tea, toast and marmalade. Always the expensive stuff. No Sainsbury's Taste the Difference for her, it always had to be Tiptree or Frank Cooper's.

I knew it wasn't going to be easy dealing with her, but I was quite prepared for the challenge. I'd done it for my Harry when it got too hard for him to manage so I wasn't going to be put off. I filled the washing-up bowl with warm soapy water to help soften the nails, laid down a clean towel on the carpet and got out another one to dry her feet afterwards. I'd found some nail clippers as well as nail scissors and had talcum powder standing by to make her feel comfortable afterwards.

It was always Johnson's baby powder for Sylvia, because she refused to use toiletries that clashed with her Femme de Rochas perfume, which she's worn for years and years. She once said to me, after a lady walked past us in Sainsbury's, 'Why would you want to smell like a French tart?' It was quite strong, I must admit, a bit like coconut or something similar.

So, no highly scented talcum or deodorant for Sylv. She only ever used unperfumed Mum roll-on. Me, I don't mind a bit of artificial scent under my arms, but then I'm also not precious about what I dab behind my ears, unlike her.

But that particular day, I never imagined how impossible it would turn out to be dealing with her feet. I could see they were bad, all thick and yellow, ridged and curling, more like claws than healthy toenails. But the terrible thing was, I simply couldn't cut them, they were that hard. And not only was it an impossible job and I felt dreadful about not being able to do it for her, but oh my goodness, the terrible fuss she made! You've never heard the like.

It started as soon as I lifted her first foot from the water. 'Oh, I don't like it!' She gave a little squeal, which became more of a scream when I tried to cut the first nail.

'It's no good if you keep fidgeting about and screaming,' I said. 'I'm sure I can do it if you keep still.'

'No, I can't. I hate the thought.' She put her hands over her eyes.

'Well, let me try with the other one. Maybe that's not as bad.'

But when I lifted her left foot she yelled, jerked her foot back and kicked the bowl at the same time. Water went everywhere! I was soaked, the carpet was soaked and Sylvia was crying.

'Now look what you've done,' I said. 'If you won't let me help you, there's no two ways about it, you'll have to see a chiropodist.'

That started her off again. Another bout of screaming and tears. And words too. Odd words, I couldn't understand. 'Poor girls, their poor toes... I can't bear it.'

I'm afraid I was a bit impatient with her that day but it was only for her own good. In the end I made that appointment, but I had to go in with her and hold her hand throughout the whole thing. That poor chiropodist, he didn't know what had hit him. He was ever so gentle, but she made such an awful scene.

She was okay about it in the end after a couple more sessions, went in on her own she did, but that first time she made a right old fuss. No, it was more than that. I'd say she was terrified. Had some idea in her head that it was going to hurt her. I don't where she got those ideas from. But we got her sorted out in the end and then she could walk properly again.

SPECIAL OPERATIONS EXECUTIVE
MANUAL

DISPOSAL OF PARACHUTE

CONCLUSION

Finally, see that shoes are clean – although you may have been given a second pair.

TWENTY-TWO
DOWN ON HER HEELS
SEPTEMBER 1945

She met her at Euston. Yvonne, one of Sylvia's first agents, had been flown back from France all the way up to Scotland, then had to catch the night train down to London.

Sylvia guessed straight away that it was her because of the way she was walking. There, among the stream of bustling people disembarking from the train, all rushing for the Underground, buses and taxis, was a hunched woman, stumbling, hobbling along the platform. Yvonne was walking on her heels.

With a sickening feeling in her heart, Sylvia could guess what had happened to her. She didn't want to think about it, but she was going to force herself to face every horrific detail for the sake of Phyllis. Still no word, no messages, no letters, no intelligence. And those who had survived were returning with horror stories of their ill-treatment.

Sylvia had been waiting at Bignor Manor in Sussex for news. She knew one of her girls would be returning that night and expected that light flimsy aircraft to land at Tangmere, only a few miles away near the Sussex coast. She'd been passing the time that evening in the Bignor kitchen with Mrs Bertram when the call came through that her girl had been dropped off in Scotland on the only available flight.

'Poor lass will have to catch the overnight train,' Mrs Bertram said, piercing another of the sloes that filled the bowl in her lap, then dropping it into a container at her feet. The bushes surrounding Tangmere Cottage were smothered with sloe berries that year, predicting a hard winter, the housekeeper said. The dusky blue fruits were plump but so hard they had to prick them all over, to ensure they absorbed the alcohol that transformed them into Mrs B's famous sloe gin. She had served nips on frosty nights to all departing and returning pilots and agents and, although the war was over, the habit was hard to break.

After receiving the message, Sylvia selected another of the purple-black fruit with its misty bloom. 'I'm looking forward to greeting Yvonne, but I'm afraid she may have bad news too.'

'You won't know till you get there,' Mrs Bertram said, stabbing another berry.

But Sylvia thought she did know, and as she waited for Yvonne to clear the barrier, running forward to help the incapacitated girl with her case, she hoped there might be some elements to her story that would help her trace Phyllis. Sylvia held out her hand, ashamed of her purple fingertips. The sloe berry juice had left a vivid mark on both her and Mrs Bertram.

'Sorry about the state of my hands,' she said, realising that Yvonne had also seen the inky stain. But she knew it was nothing compared to the indelible stains that had been left on her girl. 'Let me carry your case for you and please take my arm, if that helps.'

Yvonne gave her a weak smile. Her thin face was etched with tiredness and bluish shadows circled her hollow eyes. 'Thank you. Sorry I'm being so pathetic.'

Pathetic? Sylvia felt a stab of guilt. How could this poor injured girl say that after her ordeal, which had ended with imprisonment in Dachau? 'Don't even mention it. We'll take a taxi. Do you feel up to being debriefed this morning?'

'Of course. Let's get it over and done with.'

'They're expecting you, so once that's all done you can rest.'

Sylvia walked her charge slowly to the taxi rank, as slowly as if she was escorting an elderly lady, unsteady on her feet. The loose shoes she'd been given didn't help much either. Men's shoes, to avoid putting pressure on her toes, Sylvia assumed. Every few steps Yvonne hesitated and their pace halted. When she had to put her weight on her foot to step up into the taxi she winced and gave a barely audible gasp.

It was clear that she was still in great pain, even though she had been treated by the Red Cross and had spent a while in a military hospital before her return. As the taxi wound its way through the London streets, Sylvia decided there and then that she shouldn't subject this battered woman to an immediate official debriefing. Yvonne needed to be handled with care so Sylvia took the unprecedented step of deciding to whisk her away to her flat, where she could rest and talk without the strictures and formality of the usual interview in a bare soulless office.

In the cab, Sylvia said, 'Actually I've changed my mind about the interview. You've had such a long tiring journey. We'll have a chat at my place first. You must be worn out. Better that you rest, have a bath and I'll give you supper. You can stay the night as well if you're happy about that, then we'll start the usual routine tomorrow.'

Yvonne visibly relaxed. 'A bath would be lovely. And I barely slept on the train. Thank you so much.'

Sylvia smiled. 'One day won't make a jot of difference. I'll let the office know you were too tired and they can question you as much as they like tomorrow. I sometimes think these chaps don't appreciate the restorative powers of a hot bath with scented bath salts and fresh towels.'

The quiet little voice beside her told her she was right. 'Thank you. I feel as if I'll never be really clean again after that dreadful camp.'

Sylvia patted her knee. 'Don't worry. Once you've soaked in warm water and washed your hair you'll feel so much stronger. And while you have your bath and rest, I'll work out what we're having for lunch.'

Later, much later, Yvonne sat on Sylvia's sofa wrapped in a cream candlewick dressing gown, wearing soft sheepskin slippers. Her hair was still damp and she was pink and powdered like a baby.

They ate scrambled eggs and smoked salmon with buttered toast on their knees and Sylvia uncorked her last bottle of Moselle, thinking it would help Yvonne relax. 'Do you think you feel up to talking about what happened now?' She leant back in her armchair opposite the sofa, crossing her legs.

Yvonne took a gulp of the cool wine and seemed to reflect, as if wondering where to start. 'It's not a pleasant story,' she said, 'but I realise you have to know all the details.'

'You can tell me as much or as little as you want. You'll be expected to go over the whole story again once they've got you in the office.'

'Then I'll see if I can carry on, once I've started.' Yvonne stared into her glass and took a moment to compose herself. 'It wasn't too bad at first. They were almost gentlemanly in Avenue Foch in Paris.'

'So I've heard,' Sylvia murmured.

'But once they realised I wasn't going to yield to gentle persuasion, it got rather nasty.'

'In Paris, or later?'

'Avenue Foch was just intimidation, followed by slaps and punches. That was nothing. But when I was transferred to

Fresnes, that was when they really started applying the pressure.'

'Go on, you don't have to spare me the details.'

'They beat me up a bit to start with.' Yvonne opened her mouth and pointed to a gap on the right where her dog-tooth should have been. 'I was lucky not to lose more teeth. Plenty of others did.'

She sipped some more of her wine, then looked up and over Sylvia's head at the egg and dart cornice running between the wall and the ceiling, as if she was revisiting her view of that time. 'It was being able to look out of the window that saved me, you know. If they hadn't made me face the window, I couldn't have done it. Through the glass, I could see trees in leaf and I thought of life, of fresh growth, and imagined I was a sapling that would grow strong, despite the battering from however many storms.'

'And what did they do then?'

Yvonne turned back to direct her gaze fully at Sylvia's face. 'They burned my back with a red-hot poker. It was agony, but I told myself it was the sun beating down on fresh grass.'

Sylvia felt a sickening shiver run down her own back. How had this young woman been able to deal with such pain? Was it like when she'd entered the freezing water of the open-air swimming pool at her austere boarding school, telling herself that if her feet could cope, the rest of her would too? 'And did you say anything after that awful treatment? Anything at all?'

'Of course. Every time they did that, I spoke. I always said I have nothing to say. Then after a while, they'd send me back to my cell to reflect.' Yvonne gave a weak laugh. 'Oh, I reflected all right. It just made me more determined. I knew I'd never give them what they wanted. My friends, the network... I couldn't sacrifice any of them.'

'You were so very brave. Not everyone could hold out the way you did.'

'But I had to. I did it for my friends and also for Henri. I loved him and had to protect him.' Yvonne's eyes filled with tears.

'And did you save him? Did he survive?'

Yvonne nodded and took a deep breath. 'He did. We are engaged. He says we will marry as soon as I am well enough.'

'And you will be soon, won't you?'

Yvonne laughed more enthusiastically. 'I hope so. But I said I won't marry him until I am strong enough to walk down the aisle on the arm of my father and back again on the arm of my husband.' She slipped her feet out of the soft, comforting slippers. 'See? They ripped out my toenails, one by one, with pliers!'

Sylvia had already guessed that this had happened. It was a favourite SS ploy. She forced herself to look at Yvonne's feet and not feel sick. Although the toes had been mutilated more than a year ago, they still hadn't healed completely. They were red, raw and scabbed.

'But it was worth it. It meant I could save Henri and he and I will be able to have a life together. We managed to beat them and one day, we will marry and have children.'

'And you will soon be his wife and walk down the aisle.' Sylvia gulped her wine, steeling herself to ask the next question. 'You were lucky they didn't shoot you after that. You were sent to Dachau next, weren't you?'

Yvonne grimaced. 'Unfortunately, yes. I was dumped in a truck and driven to the station with some other prisoners.'

Sylvia's ears pricked up. 'With other women?'

'There was four of us altogether. Not at first. One of them joined us at Karlsruhe. None of us identified ourselves, other than first names, so I suspected that the other three were in a similar position to me. They too looked as if they had been roughly treated, but at least they were able to walk. I could only crawl by that stage, so the girls had to hold me up when we left the train.'

'Did you get any idea who the other women were?'

Yvonne shook her head. 'They were young and they spoke French, but I think one of them was English. There was something about the way she talked – she said her name was Simone.'

Sylvia felt a tingle at the back of her neck. 'Let me show you a photo,' she said, standing up and reaching for the briefcase containing the file on her girls.

'Here, look at this,' she said, holding out the studio portrait of Phyllis. 'Do you think this could have been the girl you met? Her name is Phyllis.'

Yvonne studied the picture, tilting her head. 'I think it might have been. Yes, I'm pretty sure it was her. But I think I heard the guards saying she was a dangerous prisoner. She looked very different by the time I met her, of course – she'd been badly knocked about.'

Sylvia stared at the photo in her hand of Phyllis, a smiling, poised young woman with styled dark-blonde hair, painted lips and bright eyes. 'I can imagine,' she said. 'I wonder what it was about her that they didn't like.'

Later, Sylvia boiled the kettle for tea. The wine had helped Yvonne to feel at ease, but she needed clarity from her now. Returning to the sitting room, she was pleased to see that Yvonne had slipped her damaged feet back into the cosy sheepskin slippers. She didn't want to have to keep looking at those mangled toes. Placing a cup of tea on the little table at her side, Sylvia said, 'Do you feel you can carry on for a bit?'

'I'm fine.' Yvonne yawned. 'A bit sleepy, but I can keep going. I tried so hard not to say a word for so long, it's a relief to talk openly to someone, especially now I know it might be of use.'

'Phyllis was one of ours, just like you. And she was our youngest recruit. I wondered at first if we should have sent her, she was so very young. But she excelled in every way during her training and we were desperate for more good operators on the ground at that time. She kept us in touch for several months, despite having to move her base a number of times.'

'I saw her again now and then after we arrived at Dachau. She wasn't kept with us. We were pushed into a small cell together on our own, but she was somewhere else.'

'You said you heard them saying she was dangerous? I wonder what they meant.'

'She looked as if she could be defiant,' Yvonne said. 'She still had quite a spark in her eyes. And I'm sure I heard her tell a guard to keep his hands off her when we arrived and climbed out of the truck. I had to be helped out, of course, with my feet being in such a state, but she didn't want anyone assisting her.'

'And when you saw her again, how did she seem?'

'I'm afraid to say she didn't look at all well. I believe she was being kept in solitary confinement. I heard there were some particularly small cells where it wasn't even possible to stand up. I expect she was in one of those. We were all expecting to be put to work somehow; we'd joked on the journey that we'd be peeling mounds of potatoes. But the truth is we were lucky to get the peelings, let alone the potatoes. We were sent out to work in the fields, but I wasn't much use.'

'I assume the food was appalling there?'

'Thin soup and bread, that's all. But I don't know about your Simone, I mean Phyllis. She didn't come out to work with us, she stayed in her cell, so we only saw her occasionally. She looked very thin and she was badly bruised too.'

'Do you mean fresh bruising on top of the injuries she already had?'

'I rather think so. But at least she could walk!' Yvonne looked down at her sorry feet, safely tucked inside the soft comfort of the slippers. 'I don't know why she was singled out like that.'

Sylvia sighed, 'Nor do I. It would seem she irritated them more than the rest of you, perhaps.'

'One of the Gauleiters, Schäfer, his name was, shouted and pushed her. We all heard him shouting at her in her cell. But I should think he had to take her somewhere else if he was beating her, because the cell was such a cramped space.'

'How inconvenient for him,' Sylvia said under her breath, making a mental note of the name.

'And I remember that the next time I saw her, she wasn't just bruised, there were sores on her arms too. They looked exactly like cigarette burns to me. I'd seen similar in Fresnes.'

'Can you describe this guard for me?' Sylvia struggled to stay calm on hearing of this fresh cruelty.

Yvonne frowned as she thought back. 'He was typically Aryan and broad-shouldered. I remember that. Not particularly tall, but hefty. Yes, he was quite solid. He'd have been capable of packing a nasty punch and a kick.'

'Sounds the type to enjoy his work. I wonder sometimes if they recruited men and women with a penchant for violence or if they trained them to be vicious? Astonishing how we're continuing to hear of so many malicious acts of cruelty, far beyond our imagination.'

'There was nothing for Schäfer to gain by hitting her,' Yvonne said. 'She no longer had anything to give. He did it because he was bored and because no one stopped him.'

'She was only a slip of a girl,' Sylvia said. 'Phyllis was no more than five feet two. And with little food, she'd have weighed barely anything. Hardly a challenge for a brute like him. I shall look forward to meeting him one day.'

SPECIAL OPERATIONS EXECUTIVE
MANUAL

INDIVIDUAL SECURITY

1. INTRODUCTION

Security must be the first consideration of the agent.

TWENTY-THREE
SUCH AN HONOUR

Quite a while back – oh, long before I came to stay at Thatch Cottage more or less all the time – Sylvia phoned me in a panic one day. 'I need you to come down right away, Peg, darling. I've simply got to have you here by my side on Wednesday.'

'I can't come till Thursday,' I said, 'because Wednesday is the day I always go to my Pilates class.' You can laugh, but it's what's kept me in fine fiddle. Without it, I wouldn't be able to touch my toes and I'd almost certainly be worrying about leaks at awkward moments. Keeps your pelvic floor in good nick, it does.

'No, no, I'm serious, Peg. I really do need you. It has to be Wednesday. A journalist is coming to see me.'

Well, I was completely thrown by that. 'Whatever for?'

'I'll tell you when I see you, darling. Now, you will come, won't you? She's going to be here at eleven in the morning.'

'I'd better come the night before,' I said. 'Then you can explain everything before she arrives.' You see, I was thinking about the traffic, because I still drove down there in those days. I had to stop eventually because the North Circular was such a nightmare. I thought it would get better when the M25 opened, but that's hardly any improvement.

When I arrived at the cottage, Sylvia seemed to have calmed down and she said we'd have tea in the drawing room. She'd laid out the tray herself and there was a coffee and walnut cake, which she knows is my favourite. We sat down and had our tea, but she didn't say a word about the state she was in earlier, so eventually I thought I couldn't hang around all day waiting and I had to say, 'Well, aren't you going to tell me what this is all about?'

She put down her teacup and sat back in her chair with her hands in her lap. 'You must have you seen the honours list in the newspapers?'

'No, Sylv, you know I hardly ever read the papers. I get the *Daily Mirror* and the *Ilford Recorder* and that's enough for me. But what's the papers got to do with you getting all in a flap?'

'I've been awarded an OBE.' She sat there with a very smug smile on her face, expecting me to congratulate her, but I knew she must have known for ages before the honours were announced in the papers. They don't exactly spring them on you out of the blue, do they? Everyone knows that. They have to check you'll accept it for a start.

'And how long have you known about all this, may I ask?'

'Oh, I was notified quite some time ago and then they confirmed it. You must have seen the news. The Birthday Honours were listed in all the papers.'

'Well, I didn't see it, as a matter of fact. Didn't think I'd ever know anyone who'd get one of those things. So, is that why this journalist wants to see you?'

'Yes, she's going to interview me tomorrow morning.'

'Whatever for? Why are you getting an OBE?'

'For my war work, Peg darling.'

I must admit I was flabbergasted. I couldn't think what she'd done to deserve this. 'But you've always said you just did a lot of filing in the war.'

'Yes, well I had to say that. I wasn't allowed to say any more. But it was rather important filing.'

And in that moment, looking at her with that very satisfied smile on her face, I knew she'd never told me the truth. Because by then we all knew that lots of secret things had happened during the war. I mean, even I wasn't meant to talk about what I did down in the Underground station at Gants Hill. I told my parents of course, so they wouldn't worry about me. But they would never have talked and anyway, what they could make of me saying I make a thingummyjig and I don't know what it's for? None of us knew what our little bits actually were or what they'd be used for, so we couldn't really spill the beans if we could only say it's a widget or a cog, could we? Hardly a state secret that, is it? But all I could say to Sylvia was, 'Well, what kind of filing exactly?'

'It was a little bit more than filing, actually, darling. I sent girls off to France. Trained them and sent them to work with the resistance.' And her smile fell away and she showed me what she really felt. 'But some of them never came back.'

I could see she was pained by this and I reached across for her hand. 'In that case, you did really important work, Sylv. Far more important than I ever did. How wonderful!'

She lowered her head and a tear or two began to roll down her cheek. 'They were such brave girls, Peg. But I sent them off and terrible things happened to them. Some of them were badly hurt by those awful Nazis and some of them died.'

'But that wasn't your fault, Sylv. We all lost friends in the war. We all had to do our bit, didn't we?'

She sniffed and managed to brighten up, nodding her head. 'We did. And they knew about the risks, they always knew they'd be in danger. But my girls were so young, Peg.'

'And is this why you're getting this honour and why this

journalist is coming here to talk to you?'

'Yes, but I suppose it's more because of what happened afterwards.'

She was being so mysterious that I was getting rather impatient and couldn't stop myself blurting out, 'Then tell me! How can I help you if you don't tell me everything?'

'No need to be so tetchy, darling. I wasn't allowed to say anything for years and years. But afterwards, I tried to find out what had happened to the missing ones. I knew they were dead by then, of course, but I needed to know what had happened to them.'

'Oh, I'm sorry to snap, Sylv. I want to help, of course I do.'

'And that's what this journalist really wants to talk to me about. My long hopeless search for the missing girls. Trying to find some answers after it all happened.'

'And you're allowed to do that?'

'Oh yes, I'm allowed, but I'm not sure I want to.'

'But if that's part of the reason why you're getting the honour, don't you want people to understand what it's for?'

She shrugged. 'I suppose so. But I don't want people knowing about me and where I live and so on. That's why I want you to be there, darling. To stop me saying too much and to make sure she understands that I'm very private and I'd like to keep it that way.'

I must have pulled a face at that point, because she curtly said, 'Well, what's the problem?'

'Nothing, dear. I just don't really know why you're being so sensitive. You should be proud of your war work and getting this honour.'

'Oh, you wouldn't understand. You've never had to deal with top-secret affairs.'

I ignored that snide remark. 'Well, who is this journalist anyway? If it's only the local paper, I don't think you need to be feeling so cagey.'

She lifted an eyebrow to warn me. 'As a matter of fact, it's the *Sunday Times* colour magazine. And they're sending a photographer as well. You'll have to help me decide what to wear.'

Aah, I thought. So that's what it's really all about. She needed me to approve her outfit, help her decide how much jewellery to wear and so on. 'You could wear your nice pale-blue two-piece with the silk blouse. That really suits you.'

'With my pearls perhaps?'

'Yes, they go well. Oh, and maybe your little brooch. That little bird one. Looks like a swallow or a swift. Are they diamonds, or just marcasite?'

Her face stiffened. 'Diamonds, of course. No, not that one. I wouldn't want anyone to think I was worth targeting.'

'Please yourself.' I cut another slice of cake for myself. I didn't need to wait for her to offer me a piece and it was very good. I think she must have popped out for once, down to the posh farm shop that sold all kinds of gourmet and organic foods. She was still driving at that stage. Not very often, just to the church and the village. She had a little white Wolseley Hornet to nip around in. Nice it was, with leather seats and a walnut dashboard. I thought the farm shop was a rip-off, but Sylv thought it was exclusive. Well, it's all right if you can afford it, I suppose.

'Perhaps we should save some of this cake for your journalist tomorrow,' I said, thinking I didn't want to have to go running around to the shop as well as helping Sylv get ready. 'And do you want me to sit in with you for the interview?'

'That probably won't be necessary but it would be nice if you could open the door when they arrive and show them in, then make coffee for us.'

Honestly, I nearly choked on that blessed cake. She was starting to treat me like staff. If this was how things were going to carry on, I thought I might not rush to her side in future – I'd leave her to sort herself out.

'Of course,' Sylvia added, 'I don't yet know when the investiture will take place.'

'The wotsit?'

'The investiture, darling. When they actually give me the honour. They hold them at various times during the year, rather than all at once. I expect I'll receive a proper invitation at some point.'

'I suppose they don't want a big queue building up,' I said. 'They can't have people keeling over and wanting to go to the loo.'

'Really, Peg, do you always have to lower the tone? And there I was, thinking you might like to accompany me.'

'What? Go with you? Do you really mean it? Buckingham Palace? The Queen?'

'Yes, all of that. It's not always the Queen though, darling. I might have to make do with one of the others. But you can only come if you promise me you'll behave yourself. I can't have any silliness, it's too important.'

'I'd love to go, Sylv. I'll be on my best behaviour.' I gave a sort of two-fingered salute, like Scouts and Guides do. 'I promise I will do my best—'

'Stop that, you didn't even join the Guides.' She was pretending to be cross, but I could see a giggle was trying to burst out of her pursed lips and frown.

'We'll take a quarter each of gobstoppers and pear drops and offer them to whoever does the business,' I said. And that did it. The dam burst and she couldn't stop laughing.

The next day I did exactly as she asked. I opened the door to the journalist and her photographer, showed them through to the sitting room, made coffee, served cake on a fancy plate with a doily and kept my distance. But as for all that nonsense about me being there to stop her saying too much, well, I can tell you, she hardly said anything worth saying to them. I know because, although I wasn't sitting in there with them, I could hear it all quite clearly from the kitchen. I heard every word because I was careful to keep very quiet while I peeled potatoes for our dinner. I couldn't boil the kettle again because it makes too much noise, so I just quietly did my peeling and listened.

I could hardly believe it when Sylvia suddenly said, 'I'm sorry, I can't do this any more.' My ears really pricked up then and I heard the journalist saying, 'Just take your time, Miss Benson. I appreciate that this must be very difficult for you, going back over your heartbreaking search.'

Then Sylvia said, 'I wasn't the only one involved. We were following orders and it was all so secret.'

Afterwards, when her visitors had left and I'd seen them off at the door, I went in to check on Sylvia. She was hunched in her armchair, staring at her clasped hands. Her face was pale, despite the touch of powder, rouge and lipstick. 'Are you all right?' I said.

She was quiet for a moment, then she said, 'I shouldn't have done that. I don't want them to find me. The children of the dead...'

'Don't worry, Sylv. I'll stay with you when the article comes out. You'll soon forget all about it.' Though to tell the truth I didn't really understand what she was worried about. But I didn't want to upset her, because I was really looking forward to going to Buckingham Palace with her.

'I'll never forget them,' she said. 'I can't. I see their faces every day. They were so young. So bright and optimistic.' Then she dabbed at her eyes with her hankie.

She never cried normally, so I knew she'd got upset. 'You've had a tiring morning,' I said. 'Tell you what, let's have a treat. I'll bring you a sherry before lunch. That'll perk you up no end.'

June 1982

Dear Miss Benson,

Are you still Miss Benson in real life, or did you marry? Maybe you now have grandchildren as well as children, opportunities my dear sister could never experience because you were all too keen to sacrifice her. And it was all for nothing. Your agents did little to end the war. I've known that for a long time. It was all in vain, wasn't it?

I read the interview in the Sunday Times with great interest. You managed to make it sound as if you had gone to tremendous lengths to find all your missing agents and they thought you were quite wonderful. But you never found Phyllis, did you? You never found my darling sister! How could you have stopped looking?

I thought the article and the photo made you seem very noble. I examined your picture with great interest, noting the pearls, the coiffed hair, the painted nails and the lipstick. You've done very well for yourself, haven't you? I wish the same could be said of my sister, whose fate we still don't know! I bet she'd love to be like you, well-dressed, well preserved, living in comfort. Where is it you live? They gave very few clues, didn't they? Was that deliberate? Did you refuse to let them say where you live? I expect, given your former occupation, you have learnt how to hide yourself. You are certainly very hard to find, but there were a few clues in the article. I thought the view through your window looked like arable fields and you mentioned seclusion and also said it was handy for London. That's not going to be Scotland or deepest Wales, is it? So my guess is southern England. Have no fear, I will find you one of these days. I won't stop.

Yours sincerely,

Humphrey Lane

TWENTY-FOUR
FRENCH LEAVE
OCTOBER 1945

Sylvia had only participated to some degree in the celebrations when everyone knew for certain that the war had finally ended, in May that year. Although she didn't splash in the fountains in Trafalgar Square, kiss a sailor in public nor link arms with the riotous crowds in a conga dance around Nelson's Column, she and her colleagues had a quiet toast to victory.

Harrington gave a pompous little speech boasting that his department's work had helped to shorten the war, but she couldn't bear to listen to him. She sipped the champagne they'd hoarded in anticipation of victory or failure and stood at the office window surveying the bomb damage along most of Baker Street, which their building had been lucky to escape, although windows had been shattered a couple of times.

She wanted to celebrate, but how could she when she didn't know the fate of some of her lovely girls? So brave, so confident, so well trained, but silent now for months. Some had returned after hair-raising escapades, a few had been caught and then released. And after learning about the terrible conditions in which some had been imprisoned, she couldn't reassure herself with that old adage, 'no news is good news'. In this instance, no news could well mean that they were no more and she owed it to them and to their families to discover exactly what had happened to them. *If they are still alive,* she told herself, *then I desperately want to find them and bring them home. And if they've died, I have to know how and when, not as a final note on their file, but so I know the end of their story.*

Sylvia's sense of victory felt bittersweet. While her colleagues laughed and cheered, she could not overcome her misgivings. By the October of 1945, she decided she could wait no longer: she was determined to go in search of her missing girls. Reports had reached her that three of her agents might have ended their days in Dachau, but she still had no final news on Phyllis, who she believed might also have perished in that terrible place.

'We have a duty to uncover the truth,' she told Harrington when she confronted him in his office. 'We recruited those brave young women and told them we would always look after them. We can't forget about them now.'

'As you wish,' he said with a nonchalant shake of the head. 'But I don't really see why you feel you have to go yourself. There's plenty of help out there, Red Cross, United Nations Refugee Resettlement and so on. If they're still alive, one of those is bound to turn them up sooner or later if our chaps don't come across them first.'

He toyed with the gold cigarette lighter he'd acquired recently, reminding Sylvia of his lavish gesture in presenting her girls with those expensive but useless powder compacts. A fat lot of help they'd been, when it finally came down to it.

'Don't you feel the slightest bit guilty?' Sylvia struggled to keep her emotions under control. 'You do know that Phyllis was our youngest recruit. She was just twenty years old when we lost contact with her.'

Harrington's cold eyes stared at her, his mouth twisting into a wry smile. 'It wasn't me who decided she was up to the job.

You sent her off for training, you passed her fit to go. If anyone should feel guilty, I'd say it should be you. But then I don't assign blame. We did what we had to do, to the best of our ability, based on the intelligence we received.'

'I don't know how you can be so uncaring.' Sylvia was furious, but knew it was best to keep her temper in check if she was to obtain the clearance she needed for her search. 'There are thousands of displaced people out there and thousands recovering from the most appalling ill-treatment. The agencies you've mentioned, however well-meaning, simply don't have the time to go searching for our personnel. It would be like the proverbial needle in a haystack. I believe we have a duty of care and so I am going to start my search where she was probably first detained, in Paris at Avenue Foch.'

That made him sit up and pay attention, she thought with some satisfaction as he raised a quizzical eyebrow at the mention of the Gestapo's French headquarters. Avenue Foch was the first place in which the agents in that part of France were held for questioning and in many cases brutal interrogation. One returning agent, Sebastian Roberts, said he had been well treated and had even been allowed to order books for his legal studies during his imprisonment. But another had heard reports of drowning in iced water and the enthusiastic deployment of a horse-whip by a young German called Peter Pierre.

'Very well then, you can go, but keep me up to date at every stage. I want to know how that damned place became so very well-informed about our entire operation here. Seems there was nothing they didn't know.' Reports had come back to London of Avenue Foch having an entire chart of their section's staff and responsibilities, as well as many of the agents and networks. Someone must have talked at one point and at length.

. . .

Travelling by boat train from Victoria station reminded Sylvia of schoolgirl trips with her classmates. Businessmen studied *The Times* and anxious families clutched baskets of food for their deprived relatives. On the cross-Channel steamer to Boulogne, all the porters and stewards wore service ribbons pinned to their uniforms, reminding passengers of their wartime roles. The train rattled away from the bomb-damaged French quayside, slowing down to cross recently repaired bridges with an exhalation of steam like a sigh of relief, echoed by the passengers as their journey to Paris continued without incident.

When she stepped out of the taxi at the end of her journey, Sylvia thought what an elegant address the Germans had chosen for their horrific deeds. Number 84 was but one building in a terrace of five-storey villas situated on this wide residential boulevard overlooking an avenue of horse chestnuts and lime trees, now beginning to shed their leaves. The houses on either side had also been commandeered by the Germans for their efficient administration during their time in Paris, in which Parisians mockingly renamed the street 'Avenue Boche'. But others, she knew, had dubbed it The Street of Horrors, because of its chilling reputation. Standartenführer Helmut Knochen, commander of security in Paris, who had arranged the deportation of Jews from the city to concentration camps, had settled himself comfortably in offices on the third floor. But the top floor had been adapted to provide cells for the prisoners and rooms for the vilest torture.

Sylvia had first visited the villa late in the summer of 1944, soon after Paris had been liberated, when she and her colleagues based themselves in the Hotel Cecil to liaise with returning agents. She had gone to number 84 to see the offices of Sturmbannführer Hans Kieffer, who had been responsible for the arrest, interrogation and, in some cases, execution of both agents and members of the resistance. Stepping into the grand salon where he had presided, she had been astounded by the glittering crystal chandeliers and gilded Louis XV furniture, upholstered in silken gold brocade.

'You didn't stint yourself, Kieffer,' she muttered, looking up at the ceiling and then out of the arched windows opening onto wrought-iron balconies. But in stark contrast to this luxurious opulence, upstairs on the very top floor she saw the slogans and dates inscribed on the walls by beaten prisoners, along with splatters of their lifeblood. Tracing them with the tip of her finger, she felt sick. She took a deep breath, shaking off the disgust she felt at the evil aura that oozed from every surface of these cells.

'One day, I will meet you, Kieffer,' she vowed under her breath. 'You know what happened to my beautiful girls and my lovely Phyllis.' She'd learnt that after their arrests they had been processed and interrogated here before being moved to the filthy prison of Fresnes, south of Paris. What happened next was proving hard to trace and it soon became evident that four of her girls, including Phyllis, had disappeared into the darkness of the Nacht und Nebel ploy, the neverland of night and fog, in which names were not registered and prisoners were moved around in secret.

'They tried to make you disappear, to cover up their treatment of you, but I won't forget any of you,' Sylvia vowed. 'Your bravery and your names must be remembered. I will find you in the end.'

On her second visit to Avenue Foch, she went straight to the cells where prisoners had been held. She stooped to examine the walls again, running her hands over the cool, creamy plaster, which was flaking here and there where the inscriptions had been inscribed with a prisoner's desperation. *Did you try to make your mark, here, my dear?* she wondered as she tried to note every scratched and scribbled line.

Were these scratched lines a clue as to her girl's next destination? But she had no idea which cell had held Phyllis or any of her girls. There were initials, dates, patriotic slogans such as Vive la France and Rule Britannia, but no clear directions that could hint at their fate. She knew by then that further brutality had occurred when prisoners were transferred to the prison at Fresnes – that's where the worst of the interrogation was likely to have occurred.

Sylvia closed her eyes as she pressed her hands over the graffiti on the cell walls, willing them to tell her what they had seen here. *I will find you*, she vowed, *I will devote myself to finding answers*. Her department had closed down and locked away its files. But no matter; she had her own way of storing the information she needed to continue her search. And the key facts were all stored indelibly in her head.

TWENTY-FIVE

MERRY CHRISTMAS

I know people often say that Christmas is just for children, but I have to say that I've always enjoyed every minute of that time of year even though me and Harry didn't ever have any kids. I suppose we thought it might happen one day, but it never did. And before we knew it, the moment had passed. So, we consoled ourselves by saying at least we weren't woken up at the crack of dawn by little ones tearing open their stockings and making themselves sick, stuffing too much chocolate as well as marzipan off the Christmas cake. And we'd go up West to see all the Christmas lights and the shop window displays, especially Selfridges. We always liked doing that.

But we still enjoyed getting together with Harry's family, my brothers and sisters and all the nieces and nephews. One year we'd have dinner at one of our sisters' and then another year it would be my turn. And I never minded the extra work, even though we had to borrow more chairs so everyone could sit down. We'd pull out the flaps on the extending dining table and fit everyone round it, bumping each other's elbows as we ate our turkey and pigs in blankets. There was hardly room to move, there wasn't, and when I brought the plates in from the kitchen I had to stand at one end of the table and pass them along.

And then we had games. Oh, we loved all the games, just like it was back at my mum and dad's when I was young. Musical chairs, the Hokey Cokey, blind man's buff... you name it, we played it. One time, years back, Sylvia came to my house on Boxing Day, that was before she was sent away to that school, and she taught us all how to play charades. I suppose it was because of her theatrical background, with her mum being an actress and that. She was very good at it – very good at acting things out, she was. Her way of doing Charlie Chaplin's walk had us all in stitches and my mum had to excuse herself because she said she'd wet her knickers if she laughed any more.

So, I don't know when Sylvia stopped enjoying Christmas and all the different events leading up to it. She didn't even ever have any Christmas cards arriving at the cottage. There'd be the odd bit of post in December, but I never remember her receiving any cards. Odd that, I always thought, because back at my place in London the post came through thick and fast in the run-up to Christmas. And not just relatives either, there were cards from neighbours, people I knew from my days at Plesseys, all sorts really. But there was Sylv in her lonely cottage in the middle of nowhere, with not a single card to wish her a Happy Christmas, apart from mine.

I tried to make it up to her, of course, especially once I was there pretty much full-time. Then I'd get back to my place in January to a pile of post on my doormat, on top of all that had arrived before I left to be with Sylv.

I suppose years before, while she was still working, there must have been parties and things she got invited to, but she never talked much about Christmas office dos. I always had loads going on. Not just with the family, but all the time I was still working at Plesseys, they looked after us really well and there was always a big works do with a proper dinner and dance with a band. And every year there was a party for kiddies too and even though I didn't have any of my own, I'd take my nieces and nephews along just to enjoy seeing them stuff their faces with fairy cakes, sausage rolls and jelly. And for the Father Christmas, of course – they always had one of the managers dressed up like that. Scared half the kids, he did, and made them cry. But it was such a laugh.

Maybe with Sylvia, it was being out in the country as well that was different. Not being surrounded by big shops belting out Christmas music, it's much more traditional out here. More like the Christmases you see pictured on Christmas cards and in films, with twinkly lights, holly and snow. And I like all that stuff, so every year I'd say to Sylv, 'There's lots of Christmassy things happening in the village, look. Why don't we go to everything?'

She'd grumble a bit about going out, but I think she must have enjoyed some of it. The season started with the most beautiful candlelit Advent service in the local church, with a proper choir singing. Quite magical it was, even though half the songs they sang were in Latin and you couldn't understand a blessed word. They must have been professional, they were that good. Then a week or so later it would be the church Christmas fair. They spelt it 'fayre' on the posters, just to make it look more quaint and traditional, I suppose. I liked going to that because it was a chance to buy some really good home-made marmalade and chutney, because you've got to have a nice chutney to go with all the cold meat on Boxing Day, haven't you?

I always thought all these lovely events would get Sylv in the mood for Christmas, but she still seemed to find it a struggle. One year I took her into the nearest town to see their Christmas lights being switched on by someone from *EastEnders*, a couple of years after it first started, though I forget who it was now. I thought it was a lovely evening, with lots of people milling around with their children, a sleigh on the back of a lorry

belting out carols and stalls doing mulled wine and roast chestnuts. But Sylvia moaned about standing around in the cold,
even though we'd both wrapped up well and were wearing thick
socks inside our fur-lined ankle boots.

She cheered up a bit with a glass of that mulled wine
though. And I remember when we got home, she said, 'Have we
got any warm wine here, darling?'

I said, 'You mean mulled wine? We'd need red wine for that
but I'll get some next time I'm out, or you can put it on your
delivery order.'

'Glühwein,' she said. 'You can make glühwein with white
wine. We had it in Baden-Baden and when we met Schäfer…'

'Who's that, dear?' I didn't know that name. Never heard it
before.'

'Oh, never mind, Peg. What have we got to drink?'

'Sherry, Sylv, we've always got sherry. You know how you
like your sherry. I'll light the fire and then I'll bring it over.'

She sat down in her armchair by the fire, just like she was a
child waiting for a special treat, and when I returned with our
glasses she said, 'People today haven't got a clue what it was like
then…'

'When's that, Sylv? When we were young, do you mean?'

'During the war and after. There was no Christmas for
years then. My poor girls. How did they ever cope…?'

Her voice drifted off and I knew she was going somewhere
else, like she often did. She was stroking the diamond brooch in
the shape of a swift that she always wore at this time of year. I'd
asked her once if it had been a present and all she'd said was, 'It
was in my Christmas stocking once a long time ago.' I could tell
she was very fond of it, so I've always thought it was a special
gift from an old boyfriend.

'But we had some good times in the old days, didn't we,
Sylv? We knew how to enjoy ourselves back then. We didn't

need to spend a fortune on expensive presents and decorations. We made paper chains for decorations, remember?'

But I could see she wasn't remembering the simple ways we celebrated. She was drifting away into the past, like she seemed to more and more as time went on. It really bothered me that she couldn't be happy – she just wanted to dwell on something to do with 'her girls' all the time.

I always tried to shake her out of it and I think that time I said, 'Mulled wine tomorrow, eh, Sylvia? And I'll make mince pies. You know how you always say my mince pies are better than shop-bought ones.'

We clinked glasses and as she sipped, she seemed to cheer up a bit. Oh dear, I remember thinking, was alcohol going to be the only thing to make her happy in her old age?

December 1945

Dear Miss Benson,

I am writing to you again because my mother is beside herself with worry as this will be the fourth Christmas that my sister Phyllis has been absent from her family, if we include the year when she was away doing her training. One year of absence Mother says she could understand, since we all knew that Phyllis was doing important war work, but four years is too much for any of us to bear.

This is a time of year when all families long to be together, to be reunited. Now that the war has been over for months, it is not unreasonable for us to long to see our dear Phyllis again. Surely you can understand that.

For my mother's sake and for all our sakes, please make a great effort to find my sister and bring her back to her family. We fully understand that Europe is still in turmoil in the aftermath of that terrible war, but we will not give up hope that she will come back to us, if not this Christmas, then certainly the next.

Yours sincerely,

Humphrey Lane

TWENTY-SIX
IN THE WRONG PLACE
CHRISTMAS EVE 1945

Was it going to be like this for the rest of her life? Sylvia wondered. It was several months on from the end of the war and she still felt as if she was in the wrong place. While others celebrated and acted as if life was once again full of promise, she could only think about what she could have done, should have done and failed to do.

She had first experienced that feeling of emptiness when news broke that the war was finally over. While crowds thronged the streets of London, cheering and dancing, even kissing total strangers in public, her colleagues popped bottles of hoarded champagne and talked of the important part they had played in the victory. But she could only think about the failures and the deaths. Where were the young men and girls who had bravely played their part but paid the highest price? What could she tell the families still waiting to hear about the fate of their daughters and sisters?

Even years later, her failure to establish the precise facts about their ends hit her hardest when frivolity was on everyone's lips. Such as the clamour of excitement that surrounded the launch of the Christian Dior 'New Look' collection in 1947.

Barely two years after the constant scrimping and saving of dress materials, the remodelling of garments and the ingrained, puritanical need to make do and mend, extravagant full skirts were swirling and prancing in the streets of Paris and London. How could she rejoice in such extravagance when her dear, brave girls had been reduced to filthy rags?

And in the summer of 1951 when a rash of gaudy exhibitions and fanciful events exploded in London and other cities during the Festival of Britain, how could she find any peace in among the thousands flocking to see the Festival Pleasure Gardens in Battersea on the banks of the Thames? Were fairground frolics really able to paint over drab grey post-war Britain and persuade the population that prosperity and enjoyment had returned?

It certainly couldn't boost Sylvia's spirits when she still felt she should return to the most likely scenes of her girls' deaths. No, she thought, she would only feel she was in the right place once she had answered all the questions that still plagued her and she knew what had happened to Phyllis. She was fairly certain now that three of her girls had perished after some time in Dachau and that Phyllis had probably also been imprisoned there. But was that where she too had died? Until Sylvia knew for sure, whenever she heard laughter and gossip, wherever she saw unnecessary extravagance, she knew she was in the wrong place.

Christmas was also a time when Sylvia found it hard to feel she was in the right place. She couldn't help thinking of the desperate families she had met soon after the war's end in the devastated towns of Germany, filled not just with displaced people from Poland and Hungary, but with homeless Germans too. Picking their way through the rubble, stinking with the fumes from leaking sewage pipes, mothers struggled to find food for their children day by day, let alone presents at Christmas.

In the many refugee resettlement camps, men dragged fir

trees, freshly cut from the nearby forests, trying to give their families their first proper Christmas in years. Sylvia visited some, hoping that perhaps among the traumatised, weakened patients, lying in their hospital wards, she might recognise one of the young women she had encouraged to risk their lives in the service of their country. And in the buildings that sheltered the refugees, she was struck time and again by how the occupants were determined to celebrate, finding carp for their Christmas Eve feast and distilling vodka from flour, potatoes or turnips.

She found herself questioning the meaning of the festivities surrounding this holiday as she approached the first peacetime Christmas for six years. Eight months after peace had been declared, she found herself unable to join her colleagues in celebrating. A number of them had linked arms and trooped off to the nearby pub decked out with limp paper chains and Chinese lanterns, singing carols.

But what is the point of all this, Sylvia found herself thinking, alone in the abandoned office that Christmas Eve, *when I still don't know the fate of all my girls? Could Phyllis be recovering with the help of the Red Cross in a hospital somewhere? Like her brother, I cannot rest easy until I know what has happened to her. She's been missing since the autumn of 1943. Poor girl, no Christmas celebrations for her for at least two years, three if we don't find her soon.*

During their time in prison, that first Christmas after their arrest, maintaining the pretence that they were French, were my girls tempted to sing a traditional French carol like 'Il Est Né' or did they hope their German guards would not realise if they were humming an English song such as 'God Rest Ye Merry Gentlemen'? Sylvia almost laughed, thinking that Phyllis especially would have enjoyed teasing the Germans and pretending that she was singing an old French peasant tune. It would have been just like her to sing 'Away in a Manger' in a language that was not her own. Or perhaps all the girls, if they were locked up in neighbouring cells, would tap out the rhythm to 'The Twelve Days of Christmas' and sing to each other through damp, graffiti-riddled walls to give each other courage?

Sylvia sighed and slammed her desk drawer shut that first Christmas Eve in 1945. Enough, enough. The Germans and British might have sung to each other across the barbed wire of the trenches in the first war, but she'd heard very few encouraging tales from this last one. Many of her colleagues had left the office early, taking cabs to parties and trains to the country. She was alone and she stepped out into the damp cold of the London streets, pulling up the collar of her coat and wishing she was wearing warm boots and not court shoes. But she was on her way to meet Campbell, who had promised to cheer her up. She tucked her chin into her scarf, her breath misty in the chill air. At least blackouts were a thing of the past now and the street lamps glowed with ethereal haloes in the gloom.

She hummed as she walked at a brisk pace towards Claridge's. 'Silent Night' was a universal Christmas song, wasn't it? Perhaps that was what the girls had chosen to sing in their seasonal imprisonment? In which case, their guards would have recognised the tune and might have contributed their own familiar words. And maybe for a brief moment there would have been unity and harmony to comfort the girls until the song ended and the horror resumed again. *I'll share that thought with Campbell*, she decided, *before I forget, before we have too many Martinis or Gimlets or Hanky Pankies.*

When she entered the Champagne Bar he was waiting for her, lounging in a corner with an empty glass. She slipped out of her coat and kissed his cheek. He grasped her hand and held it to his lips. 'Come and cuddle up,' he said. 'You're frozen.'

She snuggled close to him and sighed. 'You're making me feel better already.'

'It's not just the cold, is it, my darling?'

She sighed. 'I'm sure I can't be the only one lacking in

Christmas spirit. I simply can't find it in me at all this year. And I feel guilty that I can't be joyful after the years of hardship.'

'Same here, my love. Though I don't think I've felt the spirit for years. Not since boarding school.'

'Oh, Campbell, I'm so sorry. What a miserable pair we are! Everyone else is warbling carols and scoffing mince pies and here we are with not an ounce of Christmas cheer between us.'

'No plans, my love?' He gave her ear the lightest of kisses.

'The best plan I've come up with is to burrow my head under the blankets and wait for it all to be over and done with. I just can't find it in me to celebrate when I still don't know for sure about my poor dear girls. I just can't, Campbell.'

'And I can't face Scotland and my grim family. And up there it doesn't stop after one day, I can tell you. Out on the ruddy freezing moors till well after New Year. Sodding stags, bloody haggis, effing Highland reels, non-stop.'

'What are you going to do then?'

'Pretty much the same as you.' He signalled to the bar that they were ready to order drinks and a waiter in a white jacket glided over to their corner.

When he'd gone, Campbell said, 'Perhaps we could bury ourselves under the blankets together. What do you say?'

Sylvia giggled. Dear Campbell, always so ready to take her into his bed. And she was always so ready to accept. He was so... so welcoming and rewarding. 'Where do you suggest? My flat is freezing cold and there's hardly any food and drink there. Nothing to keep us going for a couple of days.'

'Mine's in the same state of affairs. Not cold, but no supplies apart from whisky. So, I've already made other plans.' He stroked her back as their drinks were brought across to their table. They toasted each other in silence, then he said, 'What about staying here with me? I've already got a room. A very nice room. With plenty of blankets. I was planning to drink the place dry, but it might be better for me if you stayed here to keep me sober.'

He could always make her laugh. 'You are impossible! Were you planning this all along? And what if I said no?'

He shrugged. 'Then I'd be all alone under my blankets. And very, very sad and very, very drunk. What do you say?'

Sylvia sipped her gin. 'I might have to nip back to my flat first to let Father Christmas know where I'll be staying. But if you can arrange dinner and dancing as well as blankets, I think the answer would be yes.'

He squeezed her hand. 'There's a Christmas stocking waiting for you already.' He fished in his coat pocket and brought out a tiny parcel, wrapped in gold paper, tied with red ribbon, dangling on the end of one finger.

She gave him a playful slap on the hand. 'So, you knew I'd agree? How could you?'

'I know you all too well, my darling. Happy Christmas.'

And Sylvia thought that perhaps for once, just this once, she was in the right place. Maybe not for long, but at least while it was Christmas.

SPECIAL OPERATIONS EXECUTIVE MANUAL

5. COUNTERMEASURES

a) During the detention

vii) Do not express personal affection or interest in anybody.

TWENTY-SEVEN

NOT SO CUNNING
JANUARY 1946

Why would a hunted Nazi, one as intelligent as Kieffer, hide himself away in plain sight? That was the first question running through Sylvia's mind when she heard that the former inter-rogator of Avenue Foch had been caught doing a menial job in a hotel at a ski resort in Bavaria.

What a comedown, from the opulent chandeliers and gilded furnishings of his wartime eminence in the elegant town house in Paris to skulking as a caretaker, changing light bulbs and emptying bins, Sylvia thought. And now he wasn't even in his modest accommodation at the hotel, he was waiting for her in a clean but sparse prison cell, where he was awaiting trial, the only relief a photograph of a young woman, possibly his daughter, on his desk. Were family ties why he hadn't left the country, like many of his accomplices in crime?

Sylvia had noticed the picture immediately. It reminded her of Phyllis as she was before she left on her mission: fresh-faced, joyful and alive. 'Do you keep that picture to remind you of the young lives you destroyed?' she asked him without a trace of humour.

He glanced at the image and frowned. 'That's my daughter, I don't understand what you're saying.'

'Oh, you don't remember the lovely girls we sent over to France? The girls you imprisoned and then dispatched from Paris?'

His eyes betrayed him. 'We were only doing our duty. They were not harmed during their time in my care.'

'That's as may be, but they weren't cared for or treated with respect once they left Avenue Foch, were they?'

He shook his head. 'I merely followed orders. I never gave any instructions about their treatment once they had left my section. I didn't even know where they were sent.'

For a man who had once had the power to decide the fate of highly trained British intelligence officers during his time in charge of the German headquarters in Paris, Kieffer did not impress. When Sylvia had first entered his cell, she had seen a shrunken, unshaven, unkempt failure, afraid he would be hanged, whose first words to her were, 'Can you please arrange for me to have a proper shower and a shave? And I wish to have a suit for my trial, please.'

Sylvia sat before him and placed her file on the table. 'I will see what I can do,' she said. 'But first I'd like to ask you some questions about your time in Avenue Foch in Paris.' She knew he had stayed there until just before D-Day and the city's liberation in the August of 1944. She suspected he might hold the key to the whereabouts of Phyllis and although she had long ago resigned herself to the knowledge that her other missing girls had probably met their fate in Dachau, she wasn't yet fully satisfied that Phyllis had ended her days there.

'I will help you if I possibly can,' he said, visibly relaxing when he realised she wasn't going to interrogate him about the charges against him. He had not been indicted for his involvement with her agents, but for arranging the execution of a group of six SAS soldiers, who as uniformed men should have been held as prisoners of war. He had ordered they should be stripped of their uniforms and dressed in civilian clothes, and then had them all shot.

Sylvia spread out four photos of her missing girl, tapping the best one, a portrait of her not in uniform. At the time of her arrest, when Kieffer would have met her, she was wearing civilian clothing. 'This girl, do you recognise her?'

He picked up the picture and studied it, then looked up at Sylvia. 'She's very beautiful. Is she related to you? There seems to be a likeness.'

Sylvia was indifferent to his clumsy attempt at flattery. 'No, she was one of our agents. She was working for us in Paris. We know you held her at Avenue Foch for a time.'

'She's very young, isn't she? Were they all that young?'

'Stop playing for time if you want me to help you. I'm sure you remember her.'

He nodded and smiled. 'She was very good. Very strong. You chose well.'

'What happened to her?'

'She still hasn't come back to you yet?'

'We know she was in your hands for a time. I want to know what went on while she was with you and after she left your premises.'

His eyes seemed to grow distant, as if he was either trying to remember or concocting the answer she would like the most. 'Once your people left us at Avenue Foch, they usually went off to Fresnes and then to Karlsruhe.'

Sylvia felt a shiver run down her neck, the neck that Campbell had kissed again only two days previously before her flight to Germany. Both prisons had a reputation for extremely harsh treatment. 'But while she was in your care, how was she treated?'

'I was always very considerate,' Kieffer said with a sympathetic smile. 'My clients may have had their freedom curtailed, but they were always accommodated in relative comfort and well fed.'

'You didn't order intense interrogation resulting in physical duress? In other words, torture?' Sylvia delivered her question in an icy tone. She was determined not to show any sign of emotion.

'I never ordered torture. Nor did I ever witness any.'

'Let's not split hairs here, Kieffer. You may not have been personally involved in any torture, but is that what happened in Paris? Did you allow my girl to be questioned by your henchmen?'

She saw how he swallowed before he said, 'Some members of staff could perhaps be a little heavy-handed.'

'Why was that? Maybe because you suggested they might succeed in getting more information if they beat up your prisoners?'

He looked down as if he was a little ashamed. 'She tried to escape, you know.'

Sylvia felt a slight thrill of pride for her brave girl. Plucky Phyllis. Of course she'd have tried to break out. 'And I suppose you felt you had to punish her for that?'

'I wouldn't call it punishment exactly. Her attempt forced us to consider her status. It meant she had to be classified as a dangerous prisoner. She had to be watched carefully.'

Sylvia thought about what he'd said. Did that mean solitary confinement or restrictions on her movement? Or did it really mean punishment, despite his denials? He was a clever manipulator; he had been a respected policeman before taking up his wartime position. He knew how to control people. And yet he had ended up working as a shabby janitor in a run-down ski resort, trying to restore its reputation after the years of war. He was a fallen man.

She decided to try another tactic and softened her voice, just as he probably did in those early interviews with prisoners who'd been trained to give evasive answers and resist pressure to tell the truth. 'I'm not surprised she tried to escape. She was always wilful. But I'm sure you did your best for her. What did you think of her?'

He smiled. 'She reminded me a little of my daughter.' He looked across to the framed photo of a blonde-haired, laughing girl in her teens. 'I couldn't see much of Hildegard during my time in Paris but I always took a gift for my daughter when I was able to get home. Your girl had the same kind of bold spirit that I saw in my Hildegard.'

So, I was right, Sylvia thought. *That was why he didn't run far.* Perhaps she could use this weakness to push for more information. 'Phyllis was very young, you know,' she said. 'Our youngest agent, in fact. She was nineteen when she started training and when we lost track of her, she was only twenty.'

'The same age as my daughter now.' His eyes were filling with tears.

After giving him a moment to dwell on this, Sylvia said, 'I am well aware that she may no longer be alive, but I am determined to find out what happened to her, however awful.'

She waited for him to respond, but he seemed to be wallowing in his distress, which was beginning to make her despise his weakness. Here in this prison he was being well-treated; she knew for a fact that it was most unlikely that Phyllis would have been as comfortable as he was once she had been reclassified as a dangerous prisoner. 'I owe it to her family and those who had worked with her,' she added. 'They all deserve to know her fate.'

He hung his head and fumbled in his pocket, bringing out a large, rather grubby handkerchief, which he used to blow his nose very noisily, taking his time.

'If you want me to help you,' she said, 'I am going to need a little more information. You have told me nothing of value so far.'

He finished wiping his nose and scrunched the cloth in his clenched hands. 'I authorised her transfer to Fresnes. You will have to pick up the trail there.'

'So, she was still alive when she left Avenue Foch? Was she in good health or had your men got their hands on her by then?'

'She was in one piece, as you say. There may have been a few bruises, but I think that resulted from her trying to escape. She had tried to jump out of a window. She was pulled back and may have fallen on the floor. We didn't provide safety mats or cushions for our prisoners.' He allowed himself the merest hint of a smirk.

'I see. Then I doubt you can help me any further. I will have to turn to the records held in Fresnes and question any personnel connected with her imprisonment there.'

He looked at her as if he was eager to be more helpful, to ensure his requests were fulfilled. 'I doubt very much that she would have been held there for long. Probably no more than a couple of weeks. I expect she was then sent on to Karlsruhe.'

'I'll start with Fresnes, all the same. I like to be thorough.' Sylvia stood and slipped the photo of Phyllis back into her file. She turned away, not wanting to shake the hand he held out pathetically. 'You know that some of my trained agents, educated women who deserved to be treated better, ended up at Dachau?'

She could see the shock register in his eyes, but he composed himself sufficiently to plead with her. 'You'll still pass on my request? For a proper shower, shave and a suit?'

She didn't answer, but as she left the cell the thump of the heavy door closing had a finality about it. When she reached the end of the corridor the guard on duty threw back his shoulders, ready to salute. She didn't look him in the eye as she passed, but gave him a clear instruction: 'Don't give him anything. No shave, no shower, no suit. Let him stew.'

SPECIAL OPERATIONS EXECUTIVE MANUAL

C. MOVEMENT

iii. At night if you meet a motorcar or a bicycle, hide.

v. Be careful on market-days, or if there has been trouble.

TWENTY-EIGHT
ESCAPE ARTIST

Quite a few years ago, before Sylvia became less mobile, she didn't half give me a fright one day. I'd had to pop out to Sainsbury's, because, although they'd delivered as usual the day before, they hadn't given us everything that was on the list. Sylvia's very particular about her sherry and as we like to have a glass every evening I had to go out to get the Tío Pepe Amontillado. I thought I'd get a few other bits while I was at it as well as it makes a change to wander around a real shop instead of just unpacking bags brought into the cottage. When I'm in my own home I do all my shopping every day, as and when I need it, in the little Tesco Express just down the road, but out here in the middle of nowhere we haven't got a shop nearby you can walk to, we're not even in a village.

In the end I must have been gone for nearly two hours because I treated myself to a coffee in their little café. I always liked having morning coffee with Sylvia, but it's not the same as having a coffee made for you by a nice young man, is it? And I fancied one of those frothy coffees with chocolate on the top. I allowed myself a chocolate brownie too as we never had those for tea at the cottage.

I'd left Sylvia going through some papers at her desk and muttering about her girls again so I expected her to still be sitting there when I got back. When I got indoors, I called out to her, 'Sylv, I'm back now. Shall I make you a nice coffee?' I knew she wouldn't have bothered to make one for herself and I thought it wouldn't hurt me to have another one after I'd been out and got her sherry and some other bits and pieces.

There was no reply, but I didn't think anything of it at first. *She must be involved in whatever*, I thought. So, I carried on making the coffee as usual and carried the tray through to the front room. I peered into the little office area and she wasn't there, so I called up the stairs, 'Sylvia, are you up there?'

There was still no reply, so I called again. Then I thought perhaps she was pottering around in the garden, planning things for Barry to do next time he was there. She did that sometimes, getting ideas about what she wanted pruned, moved or planted. One autumn, she had him dig over a whole bed so it could be filled with tulip bulbs. That was a good idea of hers as they gave us a marvellous show in the spring and I'd enjoyed helping her choose them from the catalogue. All pale pink and deep purple, almost black they were. She did tell me their names, but I can't remember them now.

So, I went outside into the back garden and walked around, calling her name. It's a lovely garden, full of shrubs and things, though I couldn't tell you what half of them are. And because you can't see all of it at once, the garden seems bigger than it really is. There's little corners tucked away, hidden by different bushes and so on. It was a lovely spring day, almost warm enough to sit outside if you kept your coat on. The blue tits had eaten all the peanuts in the bird feeder and I told myself I'd better remember to fill it up before the end of the day – Sylvia always loved watching the birds flitting about through the window.

But once I'd gone all round the whole garden, even down as

far as the messy part where the compost heap is, I still couldn't find her, so I began to feel uneasy. It wasn't like she'd have popped out to see a neighbour, because all the neighbours are half a mile away. *This is daft, Peg*, I told myself. *She's here somewhere and she's just playing silly buggers. You haven't checked upstairs yet. You'd better do that before you decide you've got to call 999.*

So, I nipped back inside and went up the stairs towards her room, calling her name again. Because the cottage was once two smaller ones, there's two staircases. One goes to Sylvia's room and the other end goes straight up to my room. And when I got to the landing at the top of the stairs, I saw that her bedroom door was shut and as I stood there, I could have sworn I heard a little bump or a scraping sound. It could have been the birds, of course and there's always mice getting into the attic too. They go and pop their clogs every now and then and we get the most terrible smell hanging around for weeks on end until they finally disappear. You can't believe what a stink one little mouse can make. I always go around spraying furniture polish and air freshener to cover up the smell, but Sylvia likes to light one of those scented candles. I like them too, but I think it's a lot of money to burn when a quick squirt of polish and an open window can do the job just as well in half the time.

Her bedroom door was usually always wide open after she'd dressed in the mornings and I was about to turn the handle when I thought I'd better knock first, just in case. Well, I knocked and I still couldn't get a reply and I began to feel quite shaken, thinking she might have had a funny turn. So then I decided I had to go in no matter what and I turned the handle, but the door wouldn't open. *That's funny*, I thought, *it's not normally stiff*. I tried again and it just wouldn't budge. Somehow it had got stuck. I couldn't understand it. I mean, it's not like it's an outside door that gets wet and warps. So I tried giving it a real shove and then it dawned on me that it wasn't stuck at all, it was locked or bolted from the inside.

I bent down and peered through the keyhole and could see straight away that the key was in the lock. And that's when I began to get really worried. Why had she locked herself in there? And then I remembered all that funny business with the pills and suddenly had this awful thought that she might have taken an overdose and been lying there on the bed, passing away, all while I was stuffing my face in Sainsbury's cafe.

But I didn't want to call for an ambulance unless I was sure, so I thought, *come on, Peg, you've got to get that door open. You're going to have to pick that lock.* It wasn't Barry's day for the garden otherwise I'd have called him in and got him to barge the door down. And although it's not something I readily admit to, I do know how to pick a lock. My old dad showed me how to do it years ago. You never know when it might come in handy, he said. You just need a Kirby grip, or a fine skewer will do the trick. I never asked whether he'd picked many locks in his time, but he was full of surprises like that, my old dad.

I was sure I had some hairgrips in my room, so I ran back down the stairs and up the ones on the other side of the cottage. And when I'd reached the top of the other stairs, I was surprised to see that my bedroom door was shut as well. And that was strange, because I never close it after I've been back to make my bed and tidy up.

Then I opened the door and to my horror, there was Sylvia, standing on my bed on one foot, trying to climb out the little window on the side of the cottage! 'Whatever do you think you're doing?' I shouted, rushing over to her and grasping her round her hips. She'd already got most of her top half out of the window.

'No, let me go. I've got to escape. I can do it, I know I still can.' Her free hand was trying to push my hands away, but she wasn't very strong by then and I was soon able to pull her back down onto the bed.

'What on earth are you up to?' I said as I was really cross with her for worrying me so much, like a mum scolding her kid for running across the road without looking.

'You should have let me try,' she said. 'I was seeing if I could still do it.'

'Still do what? Throw yourself out the window and kill yourself? Whatever were you thinking?'

Her eyes widened and she looked frightened. 'You don't understand, Peg. They might find me one day.'

'Who might find you? And who'd want to anyway? You didn't half give me a terrible fright just then! And if you had managed to get out of the window, how were you going to get down again? You'd have fallen off the roof, you silly girl.'

'Aah,' she said, 'but that part of the roof slopes down to the ground. I can slide down, I've done it before.'

I realised she was right, of course. That section of the thatched roof does slope and it stops about two or three feet above the garden path, so in theory she could have slid down to ground level. But whether she'd have got caught on the wire netting that covers the thatch, or landed in the prickly plants that grow down there, I don't know. It just sounded half-cocked to me.

'Let me get you off the bed and take you downstairs,' I said. 'I was just coming in here to find a grip to pick the lock on your bedroom door. What did you have to go and lock it for?'

I began to rummage on the dressing table for a hairpin and that's when I saw that there were things all over the floor next to the little cupboard built into the wall between the two bedrooms. 'What's been going on in here, Sylvia?' I turned round and saw she had an impish smile on her face.

She tapped the side of her nose. 'Aha! You don't know about my secret passage, do you?'

'Your secret what?'

'Secret passage.' She slid off the bed, pushing herself upright with the help of the bedside cabinet, making the little table lamp wobble about. I had to grab it to stop it falling over – there was enough mess all over the floor without that smashing to smithereens as well.

She took a couple of steps across the tiny bedroom and pointed to the low cupboard door, set into the thick inner wall between the two halves of the cottage. Then she bent down stiffly and unbolted it.

I'd never had any reason to use that cupboard, but I knew it was like what my old mum called a 'glory hole', where she put all the things we didn't use every day. It's the same in my London house, the cupboard under the stairs, where I keep the Ewbank carpet sweeper and old tins of paint. But everything Sylvia had in that cupboard was all over the floor – a rolled-up sleeping bag, a little suitcase and what looked like hiking boots, though I can't remember her ever hiking anywhere. The whole cupboard was empty on both sides, from my room to hers, and I could see right through to the back of the matching cupboard door that was in Sylvia's bedroom.

'See,' she said, 'it's my secret passage, my escape tunnel. I'll unlock the door now.'

She lowered herself to her hands and knees and crawled halfway through, unbolted the cupboard door at the far end, which was locked on the inside, then crawled out into her bedroom.

I heard her unlock her bedroom door and go downstairs but I was stunned and simply stood there looking at the wreckage on the floor, wondering if I should put it all back again. I'd never known that the cupboards were connected, but I could see how they formed a sort of crawlspace that ran along one side of the big chimney in the middle of the cottage. Both the bedrooms still had their fireplaces and chimney breasts, but we never lit fires upstairs, just the one downstairs in the sitting room. After a minute I put all the junk back in the cupboard and went downstairs. Sylvia had got there before me and had poured herself a cup of coffee. She sipped it and looked at me over the rim of the cup with a frown: 'It's gone quite cold,' she said.

SPECIAL OPERATIONS EXECUTIVE MANUAL

RULES

G) PLANNING FOR EMERGENCY

iv. Plans must be laid for eventual flight if he comes under grave suspicion, and a suitable hide-out prepared.

TWENTY-NINE
I MUST BE GETTING OLD

Not so long ago I could do it easily, Sylvia thought. *I must be getting old at last. When I was younger and nimbler, I could shin up drainpipes and down them too. But maybe not now.*

Her training had taught her to always look for an escape route, just as it had with Phyllis. Clever girl, trying to get out of a bathroom window in Avenue Foch, though she'd paid a price for that, according to Kieffer.

Didn't their handbook say *always prepare for flight*? So, Sylvia had done just that wherever she was, always checking out fire escapes in hotels, back stairs in country houses, alleyways and windows elsewhere. And when she'd moved to her thatched cottage she'd thought carefully about her exit route, in case she'd ever need it.

Never let them corner you, her instructor Fergus always said. *If you can't get out quick, find a way to delay them.* In her compact but comfortable London flat she had always thought she could be trapped. The creaking lift with its clanking iron grille signalled the arrival of visitors, but to get out of the flat itself she had to leave through the front door. There was a fire exit, but she couldn't reach it without running across the landing past the noisy lift. That had always bothered her, though she'd often thought a stealthy intruder wouldn't take the lift; they'd creep up the stairs in silence, hiding in the dark corners the watery lights didn't quite reach.

What she needed, she'd always told herself, was to live where strangers would be conspicuous, where she could see Him coming and where she could hide in a trice. She'd considered a little terraced house in one of the more genteel parts of London, even rented one for a time, but it wasn't perfect. Too many pedestrians passed her door, too many neighbours would notice her coming and going and might be inclined to be helpful to visitors of a respectable appearance. Even if she varied her habits and sometimes entered the house from the cinder-strewn alleyway that ran behind all the back gardens, her movements might become obvious.

But London was where she'd needed to be for so many years and she just had to be extra careful. Her best protection was extreme tidiness, so she would always be able to tell if her home had been searched in her absence. An almost invisible strand of black cotton across the garden path, a strategic dusting of ash on a book, or a tuft of fluff on the edge of a drawer, all tips recommended in the Special Operations Executive Manual. But what good did it do her girls once they were up against it? It was no protection against treachery, confession under duress and efficient surveillance.

I have to be on my guard, Sylvia always told herself. *It is my responsibility to protect myself. At least I know my enemy.* Out there in France, they couldn't always spot them. It could be a neighbour, or the friendly baker, or the old waiter in the corner café. Anyone might turn informer for money or out of fear. One girl was betrayed by a jealous woman in her network, afraid that her own boyfriend was drawn to this attractive, secretive incomer.

Once Sylvia no longer needed to work in London, she

began searching for her ideal bolt-hole. The thatched cottage appealed because she could see for miles all around the place. By then, she no longer had to work long hours in an office, she was free to do as she wished. And she thought she'd feel safe, hidden away in the countryside.

Peggy was the only person who had known her from before. Peg, the friend she'd trust with her life. Sylvia didn't tell any former work colleagues where she was going to live. She wanted to be anonymous, quiet, surrounded by ordinary villagers who grew dahlias, entered the flower and vegetable show, rang church bells and gathered produce for the harvest festival. Among these people she could enjoy her garden, her dog and Peg's regular visits.

But as old habits die hard, her first task when she moved to the cottage was to plan her escape route. She'd already spotted a possibility when the estate agent had taken her to view the empty property, previously only used as a weekend retreat for a London banker. 'It's very peaceful here,' the agent said, 'and although it's very isolated, there's the local gamekeeper living at the end of the lane, so you can feel quite secure. He's in charge of the estate's pheasant shoots and is hot on security round here.'

A man with a gun, Sylvia had thought. *I like that. I'll befriend him and ask him to keep an eye out for strangers. Let him think I might be nervous, living on my own. I won't let him know about the gun under my bed, of course. But maybe I could keep my hand in if there are regular shoots in the area. Clay pigeons, real pigeons, pheasants, rabbits... I'll take a shot at all of them if it means I can still be a hotshot when I need to.*

'And although it might feel like the back of beyond,' the agent continued, 'you're only a ten-minute drive from a main-line station and can be in London in just over an hour. And you've got all the normal high street shops in the nearest town, less than fifteen minutes away.'

I don't care about trains or shops, Sylvia thought. *I just care that I can see anyone coming from every window in the house. And that sloping roof, ending less than three feet above the ground on its western side, could be just what I need, as well as the secret crawlspace between the two halves of the upper floor.*

Once the purchase was completed, Sylvia camped out in the cottage for a couple of nights before the removal company arrived with the contents of her flat. She didn't really have a choice, she thought. She didn't like the idea of the hefty men knowing she was going to live here alone, but she told herself she'd tip them well and trust they'd respect her privacy. She told them she was a writer and needed peace and quiet in which to work.

Yet again, her fieldcraft came in handy while she waited for the cottage to be fully furnished. All she needed was a camp bed, a washbag and a change of clothes. The stove was electric, there was running water and the immersion heater meant she could have a bath. She had also arrived armed with some heavy bolts and chains, screws and basic tools. The previous owner had left lined curtains hanging in the sitting room and the main bedroom, but Sylvia preferred to keep them open, so she could hear and see any disturbance at all times. The private security man former colleagues had recommended was booked to install the window grilles and metal door panels a few days later. He could be relied on never to tell he had recently made an isolated cottage totally secure for a retired member of the Secret Service.

On that first day, after unrolling her canvas camp bed and inserting the steel frame and legs, Sylvia examined the bedroom doors. They were made of sturdy pine planks, with a thick cross-strut. The low doors either end of the crawlspace were strong too, with frames that could take the large bolt trappings she'd bought. The cottage could have been tailor-made for her, she thought, screwing the heavy bolts in place. She could seal the entrance to the first bedroom, crawl through her escape tunnel, bolt the far doors and wriggle out of the window, then down the thatched slope.

It worked well the first time she tried it, thinking of how Phyllis had attempted to climb out of that window in Paris. If that girl could attempt an escape when she was under guard, terrified and probably exhausted, then Sylvia could certainly do so in calmer circumstances.

The drop down to the garden path from the sloping roof was easy, but it was squeezing herself through the narrow casement that was the main problem. Year after year, she retested her escape route and slowly but surely, that window became harder to negotiate. She watched her diet, she walked the dog, she swam length after length at a local sports centre, but somehow, without her even noticing it, her hips and waist thickened, making the manoeuvre tighter and more difficult with the passing of time.

Phyllis had been a mere slip of a girl when she tried to slide through that bathroom window in Avenue Foch and you, Sylvia, she told herself, you are nothing but a silly old fool. You'll never be able to escape.

THIRTY
REMEMBRANCE

Me and Sylvia didn't go to the village church all that often. I think she might have gone more frequently when she first moved to the cottage, just to get to know the locals, but in later years it was only high days and holidays, as they say. But she was always insistent about going there for Remembrance Sunday. I didn't mind that, because it's always such a special service and very touching when you hear the names read out for both the Great Wars and realise that whole families with the same name were lost in each of them, especially in a small village like this one. It brings a tear to my eye every time, it truly does.

Mind you, I never once saw Sylv reaching for a hankie. She's a stiff-upper-lip kind of a girl, though I often heard her muttering things like, 'Such a terrible sacrifice, terrible losing them.' I don't know who she thought she was talking about though. She didn't have any brothers or male cousins that I knew of. And I lost my young uncle and my Harry lost his brother, so if anyone had cause to be sad it was us. But then Sylv's always been a bit of a drama queen. I guess she got it from her mother, being on the stage and all that.

We usually made sure we bought our poppies for Remembrance at least two weeks before the actual day. I always thought I must still have one lying around on a coat or on my dressing table from the year before, but I could never find one in time. So, when me and Sylv went out to the shops in late October we always felt obliged to buy them all over again. I mean, you feel a bit guilty when you see a dear old man in a mac and a black beret with an eyepatch, shaking a tin out in the cold and everyone else is wearing their poppy from the end of October. I've usually lost mine again by the time Remembrance Sunday comes round, but then I think I was always out and about a bit more often than Sylvia, wearing my mac one day and my warm coat the next. Trouble is, the poppies don't stay on, even if you do try and pin them.

Oh yes, that was it, Sylvia and the pin. It only happened the once, as far as I can remember, but it was all very strange. November eleventh actually fell on a Sunday that year and we were both getting ready to go to the service. The church usually holds its regular morning service at half past nine, but for Remembrance it's always a bit later, at ten, so everyone can gather around the war memorial afterwards for the special two-minute silence at eleven o'clock, followed by the laying of the wreaths and that.

Luckily that year it was a fine day. It was very cold and bright, one of those lovely, chilly, late-autumn days with a clear blue sky. I don't think we'd yet had a frost that morning, but it was near enough to freezing. So, I said to Sylv, 'I think we should wear our warm winter coats, don't you?' We'd had mild weather up to then, but standing around outside in the cold I thought we'd soon freeze if we didn't wrap up well. Neither of us had worn our proper winter coats so far that year, we'd managed with just our macs or a light jacket, so I said I'd nip upstairs and get them out of the coat cupboard on the landing. They're too thick and bulky to keep downstairs on the coat pegs near the front door and anyway it's best to shut them away with mothballs.

When I came down, with both our coats over my arm, smelling of camphor, which always reminds me of my nan's house, Sylv was sitting at the dining table, hunched over a bit of paper, her mac sort of scrunched up on her lap. She'd taken her poppy off her raincoat, ready to pin it on her warm winter coat, but she appeared to be doing something with the pin off her poppy.

'Here we are, I've got your coat for you,' I said, hanging it over the back of one of the dining chairs. 'Is there a problem with your poppy?'

She muttered something, which I couldn't quite hear. 'What's that?' I said. 'You'll have to speak up. I keep telling you I'm going deaf.'

'I'm trying to see how she did it,' Sylvia mumbled.

'Well, whatever it is, we ought to get a move on. You know how difficult it is to park if we're late getting there.' The church has hardly any parking nearby and for big services they usually open up the field opposite, but I don't really like going in that as it's often muddy and I'm always worried the car is going to get bogged down. That happened one very wet summer, would you believe, when we visited an open garden in another village. Middle of summer and I had to be pushed out of the field where all the cars were parked by some nice helpful men. The wheels were spinning and they got splattered with mud and grass all over their trousers.

'She did drawings with her own blood,' Sylvia said.

I caught that all right. 'That sounds horrible. Who'd ever want to do a thing like that?'

'No ink, no pens, no paint. That's all she had.'

She was still bent over her bit of paper, not moving, and I looked at my watch again. 'Come on, we've got to go. There'll be no spaces left if we don't hurry up.' Then I took a closer look at what she was doing. I'd assumed she was having trouble unpinning her poppy, but that wasn't it at all. It turned out she was tracing the pin across the paper, leaving a thin red trail. Then I realised her thumb was dripping blood all over the table.

'What the hell are you doing, Sylv? We haven't got time to mess about and you're going to hurt yourself if you carry on like this.' I grabbed a paper serviette from the basket we keep on the dresser and wrapped it round her hand. The blood seeped through straight away and I could see it was going to take more than a bit of flimsy tissue to sort her out.

'Stay right there,' I said, 'and don't move, while I run and get a plaster.' I was about to dash up to the bathroom when I thought I'd better grab that pin off her first. She was still holding it in her right hand and was about to do more of her bloody scrawling.

I took the pin with me while I found the box of plasters and hurried back down to her. And by then, she was pressing her thumb on the paper, leaving bloody prints all over it.

'Oh for goodness' sake,' I said, because I was near to losing my patience with her. 'You're not exactly helping, are you?' I wiped her thumb with another paper serviette so it was dry, then quickly wrapped it with two long plasters, just to be on the safe side.

'I don't know what you were thinking of,' I said, 'but you've made a fine old mess here.' I wiped the table down last of all and luckily the blood hadn't left a mark because it's veneered mahogany and I'd polished it only a day or so before, when I was dusting the dining room.

'Now come on. Put your coat on and we'll get going.' Then I realised I'd gone and left the pin for her poppy in the bathroom, so I had to give her the pin from mine and stick my poppy through my buttonhole and hope it didn't drop out halfway through the service. Honestly, I remember I was beginning to feel quite breathless by then with all the dashing about.

I steered Sylvia out the back door, hoping there wasn't going to be any more nonsense before we got to the church. I didn't like it if people gave her a strange look when she was having one of her off-days. I mean, she may have seemed a bit peculiar around that time, but she was still my old friend Sylvia inside.

'Drawings were no help at all,' she muttered as I helped her do up her seatbelt in the car. 'She should have written. I'd have known more about what had happened if she'd written.'

SPECIAL OPERATIONS EXECUTIVE MANUAL

3. HOW TO REPORT

vi. Accuracy. It goes without saying that an agent must never invent, never exaggerate, never quote as facts things for which there is only hearsay evidence.

THIRTY-ONE

THE WARDRESS'S STORY

For the last leg of her journey to Karlsruhe, Sylvia transferred to an American jeep, driven by a healthy young GI with straight white teeth. She had begun to think she would never reach her destination. Roads and rail links were still in a terrible state of repair as the city near the border with France had been badly bombed towards the end of the war.

Bumping over the frozen potholes in the road on the edge of the Black Forest, she had to ask herself if this whole search was going to be a wild goose chase as life in post-war Germany was still so chaotic. It was going to take the country a long time to repair the damage and now most of Europe was experiencing the worst winter in years. Both sides of the road were blanketed with pristine white snow, concealing who knew how many craters and corpses. If only, she thought, the destruction and horrors of the war could all be wiped out like this with a fresh, clean canvas.

'How are your supplies managing to get through now?' she asked her boyish driver from the American Military Base in Karlsruhe.

'We're all doing fine, ma'am. The locals are trying their

damndest – excuse me ma'am – to clear up the damage still. But I reckon it's gonna take a whole lot longer to get it back to the way it was.'

'I understand it was heavily bombarded by the Allies. And I gather it was quite a beautiful city before the war.'

'All life was beautiful back then, ma'am. But the Germans brought it on themselves.'

Sylvia smiled to herself at his simple philosophy. So true, she thought. And look what they had done to those around them. Millions dead, thousands scarred for life. And for what? She glanced away from the rutted road to the darkly forested mountains set against a backdrop of the most brilliant blue sky, reminding herself that there was still much beauty to be admired in this country of culture as well as cruelty.

'But we're trying to round 'em all up,' he continued. 'Our boys and some of the local vigilantes too.'

'What's that? Vigilantes?' Her ears pricked up at the word. 'You mean unauthorised gangs?'

'Sorry, ma'am. Not exactly. But we know that there are still Nazis out there who must be made to account for their actions. There's a group round here calling themselves the Magnet Men, on their trail. We kind of give them a hand whenever we can. Any leads we can't follow up, we pass on to them.'

'What an odd name. I wonder what it means.'

He laughed. 'They've earned that name because they say they can find a needle in a haystack. They've gotten themselves quite a reputation, ma'am.'

Sylvia liked the sound of this and resolved to meet this group if she could. Retribution where appropriate was very much on her agenda.

As they entered the city some time later, the jeep steering around ruins and piled debris, they passed groups of women and old men clearing rubble in the streets, stacking bricks and tiles for rebuilding the city. It was clear little progress had been made so far and the air was filled with the foul stench of sewage seeping from shattered drains.

They found the prison in a different location to the address she had originally been given. The old women's prison had been bombed and that section had been combined with the men's quarters on another site. 'I guess this must be it,' her driver said, dropping her as near to the entrance as he could, despite the rubble barring the path.

Sylvia was relieved to leave the odour of the streets and enter clean white corridors perfumed with the strong scent of disinfectant. Fräulein Braun, a gaunt woman of fifty or so dressed in a faded blue uniform, welcomed her into her neat office. As soon as they were sitting down either side of the desk, Sylvia explained her mission and laid out the portrait photographs of the four girls she was trying to trace. 'Do you recognise any of them? I believe these three were sent on to Dachau, but' – she tapped the photo of Phyllis – 'I'm not yet sure what happened to this girl.'

The wardress of Karlsruhe's women's prison immediately said, 'Yes, I remember all of them. They arrived here together. I think they may have been held at Fresnes. We didn't normally have that kind of prisoner here. Common criminals yes, but not political prisoners. That's what I assumed they must be, but no explanation was ever given. It was most irregular.'

She shook her head, with its thin, tight bun of grey hair, clearly irritated by the thought that her prison's regime had been misused. 'They sent them to us here and then seemed to forget all about them. I wasn't told what they'd done or how long they were going to be with us. It wasn't our normal procedure and after a while I had to complain about it.'

Sylvia could tell that Fraülein Braun was still aggrieved by those who had taken advantage of her professional services. 'But surely you were told the names of all the prisoners sent to you?' She wanted to establish for certain which of her agents had been sent there and whether Phyllis was in fact one of them.

'Normally I had full details – names, crimes and sentences. For these women I was given names, but no other information about them at all. They spoke French, but I was not sure that was their nationality. I was just told they were being held under what we called protective custody. It meant they couldn't have contact with any of the regular prisoners. They couldn't work or eat with the others here. We even had to arrange a separate exercise period for them.'

'So did that mean that no one, apart from you and the guards directly responsible for them, knew they who were?'

'Exactly. And it meant a lot more work for us, keeping them apart from the other prisoners. And I distinctly remember that we were very overcrowded at that time. They should never have been sent here. After three weeks, I had to complain to the prison governor. He said he would have to check with the authorities concerned.'

'Did you ever hear the name Phyllis mentioned?'

'No, I don't think so. There was a Simone, I know that. I remember her especially, because she was so pretty.' She pointed to the smiling photo of Phyllis. 'Though I don't remember her hair being so light. It was dark, yes, I'm sure she had dark hair.'

Sylvia tried to stay calm on hearing the alias that had been assigned to Phyllis for her mission. Perhaps she had dyed her hair to throw watchers off the scent. 'And how did they appear to you when they arrived here? Were they in good health?' Sylvia longed to know that the girls had not been ill-treated at Avenue Foch or Fresnes.

'They all looked quite well, considering the nature of their journey here. They were much smarter than our usual intake. All in decent clothes, with styled hair, like they'd just walked in off the streets of Paris. And that Simone had a bow in her hair as well.'

Fraülein Braun frowned, recalling the appearance of the four girls. 'She was a lot thinner than the others though. And I thought when she arrived that her face was bruised. But other than that, they all looked fairly well.' She raised an eyebrow as she added, 'Here, we have always been firm but fair. We do not ill-treat our inmates like some prisons do.'

'And how were they kept occupied while they were in your care?'

Fraülein Braun shook her head. 'There was nothing for them to do here. Normally our female prisoners can work in the laundry and the prison garden. Not these girls though.'

'They were just locked in their cells all day?'

'Apart from their exercise period, they were. But two of them liked to sew. I gave them uniforms to patch and mend. That kept them occupied.'

'Weren't you worried about them handling needles?'

'Oh, they had to be counted and handed back at the end of every session. I'm very careful like that.'

Sylvia could tell from her neat manner that she was careful, this methodical woman, unmarried, still responsible for prisoners. 'And is there anything else you can tell me?'

Fraülein Braun appeared to be thinking about her charges of three years before. 'Simone also liked doing embroidery. I let her work on a dress for my niece, she was very clever.' And then, feeling in the pocket of her uniform, she pulled out a ladies' handkerchief, with the motif of a daisy worked in chain stitch in each corner. 'She did this for me too. Pretty, isn't it?'

Sylvia examined the dainty design stitched in white and yellow silk thread. She imagined how the highly trained and resourceful Phyllis must have been itching to attack her guards with her needle and make her escape. But instead, she must have realised that any attempt would have been futile and resigned herself to passing the time with stitching to maintain her composure.

'There seemed to be a bond between them, these four girls. They were all united in some way,' Fraülein Braun said. 'We were also short on rations most of that time, so they were always hungry and often talked about what they'd like to be eating. They weren't really starving, but they were hungry.'

It reminded Sylvia of Phyllis's hearty appetite during her training in the New Forest and how she had demolished her pigeon pie so rapidly. She hoped her hungry girl had never truly starved during her periods of incarceration.

'And one of the girls liked to draw as well. I couldn't give them pens or pencils because the prisoners might have tried to get messages out of the building. But she would prick her finger and draw in blood with her needle. Look here, I have one of her pictures.'

Fraülein Braun opened her desk drawer and took out a flimsy sheet of paper with a sepia-tinted sketch of four girls. A name was written underneath each figure, followed by an initial in brackets. And one figure, labelled Simone, had a 'P' beneath it. Her hair was tied back with a ribbon, just as Braun had described. The girl was looking up at a tiny high barred window. Was this a depiction of their cell?

Sylvia absorbed the scene. Her four girls. And one of them appeared to be Phyllis. Were they all in good spirits when this was drawn? 'This is all very helpful. And after you'd complained to your governor about their status, did a transfer order come through?'

'Not straight away. It took quite a few more weeks. I had them here for more than two months altogether. I got to know them and liked them all. They definitely weren't common criminals, they were far better than that.'

'And what did the order say? Can you remember?'

'They were to be transferred to Pforzheim, which was much more appropriate, if they were what I thought they were.'

'Why do you say that?'

'Because Pforzheim is for political prisoners, of course. Whatever their crime, they shouldn't have been sent here. This prison is for thieves and prostitutes, not educated, well-bred young women.'

Sylvia considered this new information. She was going to have to investigate the prison records, if they still existed, at Pforzheim. And she already knew that particular prison had a reputation for a harsh regime. Phyllis and the other girls would never have been given any opportunities to sew there; certainly not fine embroidery on delicate white handkerchiefs.

SPECIAL OPERATIONS EXECUTIVE MANUAL

KNOW YOUR ENEMY

3. REGULATIONS

B. Residence

viii) Do not stay in one place too long.

THIRTY-TWO
MAKING HAY

Once I started spending a lot more time in Sylvia's cottage, one of the things that really surprised me was how much there was to learn about the countryside. You can't help it, you see, because it's all around you.

You think it's peaceful out there, but there's so many sounds as well. Not that I can hear all of them with my ears. I've never heard the nightingale that everyone says sings high above the fields in the summer and I certainly never heard the bell-ringers in the church across the fields, though Sylv swore it was clear as anything.

And it's not just green fields out here with cows and sheep, oh no. One moment there's a tractor digging up potatoes, spurting them out of a funnel into a truck that follows behind. Then before you know it, another tractor turns up to start ploughing and the field is sown with what the local farmer calls winter wheat. And then when that's all cut down and taken away, sometimes the field fills up with hundreds of sheep for a week or so. It never stops, really it doesn't. You don't see that sort of thing on the streets of London. The nearest you get to the changing seasons is leaves littering your doorstep and kids throwing eggs at your front door for Halloween, little tykes.

And I couldn't help noticing how, now and then, the different farming jobs out here seemed to affect Sylvia's mood. She was very odd about the sheep. Kept muttering that she couldn't see the shayfer. Goodness knows what that was all about. And take harvest time, for example, and by that I mostly mean haymaking and cutting the corn. I never knew before I came out here what was hay and what was straw, but I certainly do now. Hay's for eating and straw's for bedding, so now you know. The field opposite the cottage is always grown for hay and the one round the back chops and changes; sometimes it's potatoes, then it's bright yellow rapeseed, and then the next year it's back to wheat again. Once the wheat has been harvested, that's when they come back again to cut all the stalks and bundle them up and that's the straw.

Anyway, the hay always set Sylvia off again. I don't mean sneezing and that, although all the cutting and cropping creates almighty clouds of dust and we have to shut all the windows when they're harvesting in the field. No, I mean it made her have one of her funny turns. She always started muttering about haystacks, needles and magnets.

And I remember saying to her, 'That's in the olden days, Sylv. Farmers don't do haystacks no more.' It's clever stuff these days, you see, and we'd sit out on her front lawn in our garden chairs and watch the farm machinery circling the field. One tractor is in charge of cutting the grass, then another comes and turns it. They let it dry out for a day or so, then they come back again and one of the machines bundles up the dry grass into what they call bales. Then another one follows behind, wrapping them up in black plastic and stacking them, just like a pile of kiddies' building bricks. There's no haystacks in the fields these days.

I remember them of course, from the few times in the past

when Harry and me drove out from London to Epping or Hain-ault Forest. In the middle of summer we'd go past the fields and see the haystacks dotted around. But the way they deal with the hay these days is much quicker and much more efficient. Farmers used to burn off the stubble in the fields as well in those days, but that's not allowed any more. Quite right too. It would be far too risky having the field next to a thatched cottage set on fire, sending sparks onto the roof and smoke everywhere.

But Sylv still went on about haystacks. 'Look,' I said, 'they don't do stacks of hay no more. They do stacks of bales. You don't know what you're talking about.'

'The magnet men. Lovely men they were, could find a needle in a haystack.'

'Well, yes,' I said. 'I expect in the old days the farms employed lots of men to turn the hay by hand and pile it up. Must have taken ages. I suppose your cottage was lived in by some of those men, eh, Sylv?'

'No. Not here.' She frowned. 'In Baden-Baden.' Then she'd shake her head and I could tell I'd lost her again. She'd go into one of her dark moods where she hardly spoke for hours and just stared out of the window while it was still light.

'Barden what?' I said. 'Do you mean the garden? The garden's going to be fine.' And then, if the farm was in the middle of cutting the hay or the straw, we might both end up running indoors because the other thing that happens during harvest is the rats and mice. All over the lane quite often, running away from the machines, poor things. All over the garden too. I used to feel sorry for them, but Sylvia would set the dog on them, when she still had one. She was very practical like that.

Fergus caught quite a few rats in his time. I suppose a dachshund is good for ratting, though I'd always thought they were meant to be badger dogs. Sylvia always said he was named after a good friend of hers from years back. She never said who though. But he's long gone. The dog that is, I don't know about the friend. So, when the farm boys were out cutting, we either ran for it or kept out of the way of the vermin. Though Sylvia wasn't averse to giving them a thwack with one of her walking sticks.

Her favourite one she called a knobkerrie or something like that. It's a shortish stick with a heavy, knobbly bulb at the end. She usually got them with one hit. I'm not a squeamish sort, scared of mice and that, like my old mum was, but it did surprise me how someone as dainty and feminine as Sylvia had no problem whatsoever dealing with vermin. Must have been her boarding school upbringing, I suppose.

I saw her deal with mice that got in the house too. It happens quite a lot when you live in the countryside in an old cottage. I was all for getting a cat but as Sylv got older, she said it might trip us up, so better not. She didn't use the knob stick thing with the mice though. No, she had another method for them. Because they were so small, she said. If she knew a mouse had got into the kitchen and especially into the pantry, she used a humane trap. But what she did next wasn't what I'd call humane though. Once she'd caught the little bugger, she'd empty the trap into a plastic carrier bag, tie it up, then smash the bag against the brick wall outside. Bash its brains out, like. I had to bury those in the garden. She'd never let me throw the bag in with the general rubbish. 'Oh darling, whatever would the dustmen think if they found a pulverised mouse in our dustbin?' she'd say. I just thought what the heck? They're never going to stop and check through our rubbish, are they?

But it did bother me how she'd get in a tizz about the hay. She'd be muttering away, saying things like, 'Dear boys, true to their word... Could find a needle in a haystack... they certainly did... but should I have let them... was that the right thing to do?'

And she'd also got it into her head that one of our neigh-

bour's dogs was involved in the hay as well. I could never get to
the bottom of it. They weren't exactly neighbours, not like in
London where we're all next door to each other, cheek by jowl
as they say, but it was someone we often passed in the car on our
way out to the local shops or somewhere. It was on the edge of
the nearest village and we'd often see this little old man walking
a Great Dane. Beautiful pale-grey dog, but Sylvia was obsessed
with it. I'm not sure why, when she'd loved her little wire-haired
dachshund Fergus, who would have barely reached this
monster's ankles.

But every time we saw this man out with his huge dog, Sylv
would say, 'Stop the car, Peg, stop the car,' and I'd have to slow
right down. Then she'd wind down the window and poke her
head right out and call, 'Prince, here, boy. Here, Prince. Have
you found the needle in the haystack today?'

Of course the dog never responded, other than to lift his
head for a second, because his name wasn't Prince, was it? I
can't remember how many times his poor owner had to say, 'His
name is Hamlet, like the cigar.' But she never remembered. And
then as we drove away, she'd say, 'The magnet men liked dogs.
Helped them find the needles in the haystacks. I wish I'd had a
big dog like that.'

And I'd say, 'What, in your tiny little cottage? You've got to
be joking!' And I'd keep driving and she'd start humming and
I'd realise she was singing 'Some Day My Prince Will Come'.
Oh, she always made me laugh, she did. Drove me mad, but
made me laugh at the same time.

Sylvia thought she could enjoy wallowing in the warm thermal waters of the hotel's spa for ever. Baden-Baden's water was famed for its healing and cleansing powers. Dipping her head into the depths of the baths, she felt grime and distress washing away from her hair and from her brain. After the mud and devastation of Karlsruhe and the dismal walls of its disinfected prison, she wanted to feel clean.

But, she told herself, she wasn't here for pleasure, luxurious though the facilities were. She was here to seek out members of the Magnet Men group and maybe test their claim they could find a needle in a haystack. This assorted crew of mostly German and Austrian exiles, a number of whom were Jewish, had dedicated themselves to rooting out Nazi war crime suspects who at the end of the war had scurried away to prearranged burrows and hidden themselves, hoping no one would ever come looking for them.

On her first night here she had wandered into the hotel bar, wondering whether she really wanted to drink alone, and a member of the group had introduced himself. Exceptionally tall and blond, he reminded her of Campbell. He also stood out because he was accompanied by a loping Great Dane, the colour of grey watered silk. 'Charles Muller,' he said. 'And this is my constant companion, Prinz. May I buy you a drink?'

'Sylvia Benson,' she said, offering her hand to Prinz's soft velvety muzzle by way of introduction. 'A gin and tonic would be lovely, if that's possible.' She was glad she had decided to wear her uniform, even though it was normal to dress for dinner in the evening, as it immediately conveyed her authority and purpose. She'd had the blue-grey Squadron Officer WAAF uniform tailored to flatter her slim figure.

'Are you here with the French war crimes lot or the British liaison team?' Charles asked in excellent, very slightly accented English.

'Neither, actually. I represent a section of British intelligence. I'm on the trail of some of our missing female agents.'

'Then I must introduce you to some of the men I'm currently working with. They could well come across information you may find useful.'

They moved across to a corner table with buttoned seats upholstered in burgundy plush and were joined by one of the Englishmen who were part of the team. 'David Peterson, pleased to meet you,' he said, shaking her hand. Prinz wagged his tail enthusiastically, clearly pleased to see a familiar face. 'Good boy,' David said, stroking the dog's wrinkled forehead. 'I hope you've terrified more of those bad boys today.'

Sylvia's raised eyebrow prompted him to explain. 'We all think that the reason for Charles here's enormous success in getting information out of suspects is down to the fact that he never goes anywhere without this brute.' David laughed and patted the dog again, adding, 'You scare the pants off them, don't you? It's all down to you, isn't it, boy?'

'Plus, my skill in asking the right questions,' Charles added with a smile. 'I know exactly how to put on the pressure without resorting to threats. Besides, Prinz would pine if he wasn't by my side the whole time.'

'And that's why Charlie hasn't settled down yet, either,' David said, raising an eyebrow and grinning. 'No woman is going to accept a canine companion in the bedroom.'

'Oh, I don't know,' Sylvia said. 'Some might prefer the dog to the man.' She stretched out her hand to the creature's soft muzzle for him to lick.

When the group's laughter had subsided, Charles said, 'So how can we help you? Do you have a name?'

She shook her head. 'Not yet. I think I need to find whoever was in charge at Pforzheim when my agents went missing. But that might not be the end of the trail.'

'Do you suspect foul play?' David downed his drink and clicked his fingers for replacements.

'I doubt there's going to be a happy ending. I don't think I'm likely to find that they are still languishing in a hospital or have lost their memories, if that's the alternative. I've more or less traced the outcome for all but this one girl. I'm pretty sure she was with three others who went to Dachau. I think they ended their lives there. Our agents weren't treated as prisoners of war, because they weren't in uniform. But I've always felt I owed it to their families to establish what actually happened to them, that's all.' She had finished her drink too and was longing for a refill.

'When do you think they may have been sent to Pforzheim?' Charles looked as if he was searching his memory for information.

'Some time during the winter of '43. But I don't know for sure and I don't how long they may have stayed there.'

'Hmm, that girl we talked to last week, Hilde Keitel, I think her name was.' David turned to Charles for confirmation. 'Wasn't she held in Pforzheim around that time?'

Charles frowned, then nodded. 'I think she was. Maybe

she'd be worth talking to. She's very willing to help. Poor girl was locked up for a mild joke about the damned regime. Heavy price to pay for a bit of loose talk.'

'They came down like a ton of bricks on anyone who spoke out; even a throwaway remark could result in an arrest,' David said. 'That's how the bullying bastards got their way. No one dared to oppose them.'

'I'd like to meet her if I could,' Sylvia said. 'She may not have come across my girl, but she might have some useful information about how they treated prisoners there.'

'Have you got any photos of your girl? You could ask her if she remembers her then.' Charles flipped open a silver cigarette case and offered one to Sylvia.

She declined his offer with a shake of her head. 'Yes, I've several pictures of her, in both uniform and civilian dress.' She pulled an envelope out of her bag and fanned the photos out on the table in front of the two men.

'What a lovely young lady,' David said, leaning forward to take a closer look.

'Especially in this picture,' Charles said, picking up the photograph of Phyllis. 'She has a real film star quality to her. That should make her memorable enough.'

'All my agents were chosen for their language skills and their loyalty,' Sylvia said a little tetchily. Really, men always talked about appearance first. 'They were all immensely brave and I hate to think what may have happened to them.' She retrieved the photos and returned them to her bag, pausing for a second to linger over the picture of Phyllis that had provoked those compliments, shaking her head. 'She was my best girl. Such a waste.'

'I'm so sorry. But you should brace yourself for the worst.' David suddenly looked a little tired as he paused and looked across the bar filled with British, American and French personnel, all enjoying themselves as if they were having a grand holiday in this elegant hotel. 'I'm hoping I can forget the horror stories when I finally get back home.'

Sylvia detected a little world-weariness in his tone. What had he uncovered in his investigations? Identifying and accusing those guilty of war crimes couldn't be a pleasant task. No wonder the staff involved in the work flocked to hotels like this one in Baden-Baden for recreation and maybe for glamorous company. The French war crimes team had been first on the scene, soon after the end of the war, and had chosen the luxurious hotel near Karlsruhe as their base, then organised a variety of entertainment for all stationed there, including a casino, horse shows and hunting. Better that though, she thought, than the way the French troops had behaved when they first occupied the zone. Their reputation for rape was nearly as bad as that which had preceded the arrival of the much-feared Russians.

'Why don't we all go through for dinner?' Charles said, standing up and offering Sylvia his arm. 'We can continue our conversation over a bottle or two of Gewürztraminer. It's particularly good with the schnitzel.'

Sylvia accepted his invitation. She was rather glad not to have to dine alone. If she'd found herself at a table for one, she'd have stuck her nose into her copy of Daphne du Maurier's *Rebecca* to take her mind back to the English countryside, far away from this post-war apocalypse.

As they strolled into the dining hall, glittering with chandeliers, sparkling with glasses and silver on every table, she half wished she had changed for dinner after all. She had travelled light, but her black wool crepe frock would have set off her creamy skin beautifully. *Stop it now, Sylvia*, she told herself. *This isn't wartime any longer, you no longer have a duty to comfort every handsome soldier as if you might both die tomorrow. The days of eat, drink and make merry, for tomorrow we die, have gone*. But those were the days, she thought. It was a different age, different morals for a while.

Charles gallantly pulled out a chair for her to sit down and David joined them. 'Where's Prinz?' Sylvia said, noticing that the long, loping body and mournful eyes no longer accompanied the group.

'He knows where to find dinner at this time of night,' Charles said. 'Besides, he'd drool all over my shoes if he stayed here – that's the trouble with a soft-mouthed hound.'

Sylvia noticed that despite his excellent English, he pronounced hound with a hard 'd' as if he was restraining himself from using the German *'hund'*. It was a tiny hint to remind her that this was his world, his homeland. What must a man born and raised in this country feel about his fellow countrymen? Shame, horror or confusion? Had he tried to object or had he left and attempted to help the opposers?

Her thoughts must have been written on her face, for Charles suddenly said, 'I know what you're thinking. Everyone asks me the same question. Where did I spend the war? Well, the answer is prison, Poland and free France but not necessarily in that order. And before that, I attended school and then university in your country.'

'We'll be here all night if he has to tell you the whole story,' David said, looking up from the menu. 'Just tell Sylvia the bit about skiing out of Poland with the Polish airmen and save the rest for another time.'

Sylvia laughed. This was obviously going to be an entertaining evening. She was enjoying their company and felt very much at ease with these two Nazi hunters. 'But I also want to hear a little about your work, especially your successes. Have you landed any big fish? Any names I might have heard of?'

The two men looked at each other, both with the same quizzical expression. David spoke first. 'We're all in agreement that we want to see justice done, aren't we? And it's admirable that the war crimes trials were held so soon after the end of the war, but some of our men feel that the punishment didn't always fit the crime.'

Sylvia was puzzled. Like everyone else, she had followed the outcome of the trials closely. 'You mean you think the sentences were too light in some cases?'

'Most of them were, considering what terrible deeds they had committed,' Charles said. 'Those who were condemned to hang certainly deserved it. But why give a man a prison sentence of only five years when he's participated in the deaths of hundreds or thousands?'

'But the trials were well run, weren't they, by able prosecutors?'

'They were overwhelmed by the sheer scale of the horror,' David said. 'Wanting to show the world they could exact justice and at the same time clear up the mess. But they did their best and now we're sweeping up the rest of them.'

'So, you're having some luck? You're still finding Nazis you can prosecute?'

Charles cleared his throat. 'Gathering evidence is difficult and time-consuming, but if we can confirm identities and facts, we can ensure results.'

'And then you pass your findings on to the proper authorities to undertake formal prosecution and sentencing?' Sylvia was finding it hard to concentrate on studying the menu while they were talking.

'Some of the time...' David said, snapping the red leather wine list shut so the silken tassel swung above the white tablecloth.

'What do you mean, some of the time?' She was starting to tingle with excitement.

'He means sometimes we pass the details on to other... um... authorities... those with a vested interest, shall we say?' Charles signalled to the waiter that they were all ready for him to take their order. 'The legal system is all well and good, but it can take a little too long for some of the victims. Sometimes we all want to see a just result sooner rather than later.'

Sylvia murmured the name of her chosen dish, but all the while she was thinking, *these are very dangerous men. They are playing the system and adopting a civilised front, but at the same time they are just like a Wild West posse, heading out to get their man by any means possible to face rough justice. I'm glad I've found the Magnet Men. These are the sort of men who will help me track down my girl and bring whoever harmed her to justice.*

3. REGULATIONS

B. Residence

vii) Brothel. Possibly for one night in an emergency, but strict
supervision and possible informers.

THIRTY-FOUR

THE MORNING AFTER

'Is that Prinz trying to wake you up?' Sylvia turned her head towards the door of Charles's bedroom and yawned. A weak dawn light crept between the curtains, but it wasn't that which had woken her, it was the scratching outside.

She slipped out of bed, picking up Charles's shirt off the carpet to cover herself as she opened the door. The silky grey head looked up at her and she fondled his velvet ears. 'Come on in, boy,' she said and he ambled across to the far side of the bed and laid his head on his master's pillow, nudging the sleeping figure's cheek with his wet nose until he woke.

'Go away, you brute,' Charles grumbled, fondly patting his dog's head. 'I'm not ready to take you out yet.'

'Does he need to go outside?' Sylvia was half-dressed and had finished knotting her regulation tie. 'I can take him out for you if you like. It might look better if we don't go down to breakfast at the same time.'

'Please do,' Charles groaned. 'He knows where to go, you won't need a lead. When he's done his business, tell him to go to the kitchen. He'll find his own breakfast.'

What a wonderfully obedient, clever dog, Sylvia thought as she and Prinz strolled down the grand staircase and out across the marble floor of the foyer, the tapping of her shoes accompanying the clicking of his claws. She pushed open the glass doors and shivered as the icy air shocked her skin. Standing on the steps at the front of the hotel, she half wished she was wearing the woollen coat that was part of her uniform. The morning was bright but frosty and the pink light of dawn was touching the glittering rime on the grass and trees surrounding the hotel.

As she followed Prinz, her footsteps crunching along the gravel paths threaded through the grounds, Sylvia was reminded of the walk she and Charles had taken after dinner last night in the moonlight. Cocktails, wine and good food had worked their spell and her resolve had melted by the time they were holding hands and then kissing in the dark.

Sorry, Campbell, she thought. It was too good an opportunity to pass up. A lonely woman sometimes needs company too. They were much alike, he and she, and she suspected Charles was also of a similar frame of mind. Risky work created a threshold that made it easy to ignore convention. Wartime and the constant threats of the Blitz had made her a more daring person than she might ever have been in peacetime. *I don't think I'll ever settle down now*, she thought. *How could I be a housewife, a mother, confined to domesticity, after all I've seen and done?*

She watched Prinz crouch at the base of a tree, then cock his leg against the bark and finish with a vigorous scratch of the frozen grass, as if he was clearing up his toilette. 'Here, boy,' she called and he trotted over, looking for all the world like a long-limbed pony, which she would have loved as a child. She stroked his ears as he gazed into her eyes. *Maybe it's dogs for me*, she thought, *not children. Dogs from now on. I'll turn into one of those crazy dog breeders in my old age.*

She turned back towards the hotel. 'Come on, breakfast for both of us.' At these words Prinz broke into a gallop, skidded to a halt on the gravel in a spray of tiny stones, then waited for her to catch up with him.

'Go on,' she said. 'Go find breakfast.' He stared at her for a second and then he was off, bounding across the paths and grass and round to the back of the hotel.

Sylvia walked as far as the corner of the building to see if he had found the kitchen and saw him taking a sausage from the hand of one of the cooks. She immediately realised that she too was feeling hungry and went straight inside.

She couldn't see either of the men from last night in the dining room, humming with hungry personnel and the clatter of cutlery. But this time she wanted to be alone, to sit quietly and think about the next stage of her search. She found a small corner table and sat down, taking her notebook out of her satchel. While she waited for her order to be taken, she scribbled down what she remembered of the previous evening's conversation.

Over dinner David and Charles had been discreet, alluding to collaborators but not really giving away any details. But later, after she and Charles had enjoyed each other's company in a more intimate fashion, she'd said, 'Tell me more about your friends. The ones who deliver justice.' Was that partly why she had gone to bed with him? To persuade him to reveal his secrets? Maybe she'd had an ulterior motive, but she'd been very happy in his arms that night.

'It's not to be repeated,' he'd said, nuzzling her neck. 'If we think the evidence is a little too flimsy to stand up in court, or the witness is not too clear on exact dates, we can hand the case on for further investigation.'

'Who to? Other official authorities?'

He laughed. 'Hardly. *Juden* usually. Jews with a score to settle. If they satisfy themselves that a Nazi worked in a camp or if the suspect was a *kapo*, they're happy to deal with it.'

'But don't you have to account for someone disappearing?

Aren't you responsible for what might happen? There must be something to record your involvement.' She wasn't going to blame him for dispensing unofficial justice, she just wanted to know the facts.

'The evidence disappears along with the suspect. If we don't file a report, who's going to know?'

'And what do you think happens to them once you've handed them over to your associates?'

'I don't ask. We usually alert our contacts, tell the suspect they're free to go and that's the end of it, as far as we're concerned. If they happen to have an accident round the corner on their way home, or maybe later that night, it's nothing to do with us, is it?'

'But you must have some idea of what happens?'

He lay back on the pillows and reached for his cigarettes. Taking one and slowly lighting it, then putting it to his lips, he said, 'I can guess. Look around you. The woods are dark and deep, there's miles of impenetrable forest. A person could get lost and never be found again.'

'So you think they kill them and dump the bodies out there?' She pictured the Schwarzwald, the mountainsides coated with dark trees, the vast acres of forested hillside stretching into the distance, and knew that he was probably right. The bodies would never be discovered and who would be concerned, anyway? Anyone who suspected their neighbour was a war criminal would probably decide it was better to pretend they knew nothing.

'Go out in the countryside on any night of the year, find a quiet road and the chances are you'll hear a gunshot or two,' he said. 'Could be a hunter after deer or perhaps vermin. Who knows and who's going to ask?'

'I suppose compared to what some of them may have done to the wretched prisoners in their care, a quick shot in the head is nothing.' Sylvia was beginning to feel that this form of justice maybe had its merits.

'Who said it was quick? And who said it was just a shot?' Charles breathed smoke through his nostrils like an impatient dragon. 'It depends who takes them away. You know in the early days, when the Allies were liberating the camps and uncovering the hell that littered those places, a lot of us turned a blind eye if the remaining prisoners wanted to turn on their guards. We thought why not? You were the ones who suffered, not us. If you've got the strength to tear them apart, go ahead. Do whatever you like.'

Sylvia held her breath, wondering just how bloody that might be, then Charles went on: 'In one of those hellholes, the ovens were lit and they stripped a guard, tied him to a gantry and shoved him in. They'd turned into animals. But who could blame them after the terrible cruelty they and their families had suffered?'

He was quiet then. Stubbing his cigarette out in the ashtray on the bedside table, he closed his eyes and was soon snoring. But Sylvia couldn't sleep. If she found out the truth about the fate of her best girl, Phyllis, if she identified individuals who had caused her harm or had killed her, how would she feel? Would she turn to the Magnet Men for help or would she take pleasure in exacting justice for herself?

January 1946

Dear Miss Benson,

I understand you have been tracing the missing agents involved in your secret operations during the war and are being successful on many counts, but you have failed where my sister is concerned. How hard have you and your colleagues really tried to discover her fate? You can't have made much of an effort and surely, now the war crimes trials have been widely reported, there must be much more information available.

My family and I believe that certain agents may not have been supported as much as their relatives could have expected and I would like to ask you some questions. I will call your office to make an appointment to see you if I may.

It won't be long before I have to sign on to do my National Service and I very much hope to be sent to Germany so I can continue searching for my sister. After that I hope to study modern languages, including German, and will spend part of my third year in Germany. If you have not had any luck by then, perhaps I will be able to uncover more details about my wonderful sister and why you failed her and her entire family.

Yours sincerely,

Humphrey Lane

THIRTY-FIVE
DON'T LAUGH
JANUARY 1946

A day later, Sylvia returned to Karlsruhe to interview Hilde Keitel, the former inmate of Pforzheim Prison who David and Charles had mentioned. 'She feels she was very hard done by,' David said, handing her an address. 'She really didn't deserve a prison sentence and is doing her best to get her own back on them now by helping us as much as she can. She's expecting you, so you should find her at home.'

Sylvia was sympathetic but said, 'I'll get her to tell me her side of the story first.' She wanted to be sure Hilde's account was going to be reliable.

She walked the ruined streets, dodging the ruts and holding her breath whenever the smell was particularly bad, until she found the right place. It was a rooming house, accommodating a number of those whose homes had been destroyed.

When she knocked at the door, a timid young woman peered out. Her pale face and amber eyes reminded Sylvia of a pallid lemur she had once seen in London Zoo. She couldn't have been more than in her late twenties, certainly not much older than Sylvia's lost agents. They went to Hilde's cramped room with its single bed.

The accommodation was extremely neat, the once-white sheet crisply turned over the grey blankets, and Sylvia could see the girl was trying hard to rebuild a shattered life after surviving the terrible conditions of the prison. 'Tell me about it,' she said, sitting down on the only chair in the drab room while Hilde seated herself on the bed. 'Tell me what happened when you were arrested.'

Twisting a grey handkerchief in tiny hands, her bitten nails another sign of her distress, Hilde said, 'I hadn't done anything wrong. It wasn't really even a crime. I was only having fun in the park when my boyfriend and I were out for a walk. I made a joke about Hitler. That was all I ever did.'

'And that was enough to get you into serious trouble?'

She hung her head. 'A woman overheard me and reported what I'd said to the Gestapo. They came to get me a day later. And then I was sent to prison.'

'Pforzheim? You were imprisoned there? When was this?'

'Nineteen forty-four. Early in the spring, the beginning of April.'

Sylvia scribbled the date in her notebook. 'Can you recall any of the other female prisoners there at that time?'

Hilde nodded. 'I particularly remember the ones in cells either side of me. They were all young women, around my age, I think. I got the impression they were all French. I recognised the language because I had learnt it and my boyfriend was French.'

At this point, Sylvia thought she should display her photos. Leaning over, she spread them out on the bedspread, right next to where Hilde was sitting. 'Do you think you saw any of these girls?' Phyllis and the other girls Sylvia was sure had perished in Dachau all smiled at Hilde from the glossy prints.

Hilde picked the four photographs up one by one, studying them with a solemn expression. After a couple of minutes she said, 'I think all of them were there at the same time as me. But this one,' she pointed to the picture of Phyllis, 'looked different to how she does in this picture. Her hair was dark, not blonde. Though I think it wasn't her natural colour because her roots were much lighter.' With her hands Hilde indicated a wide parting in her own hair.

Clever Phyllis, Sylvia thought, further confirmation that her girl could have dyed her hair before she was imprisoned. Maybe she'd had to disguise herself and go into hiding to avoid capture. 'And do you remember anything else about her?'

'Yes, she wasn't in the cell with the others. I'm sure she was locked up on her own and she never came out for exercise. The other girls were always made to walk around the yard every afternoon.'

'Why was that, do you think?'

Hilde bit her lip and frowned. 'I'm not sure, but I believe that girl was chained up.'

Sylvia's heart sank. Her courageous girl, in chains? How could they? It must have been so uncomfortable for her, unable to move freely. 'But why would they do that? Why was she treated differently to the other three?'

'I overheard the girls talking once. They said she was considered to be dangerous, because she had tried to escape. I think I heard them call her Simone.'

Oh, Phyllis, you brave, spirited girl, Sylvia thought. *But what a price you paid for your recklessness*. 'She was brave, but she could hardly be called dangerous,' she said.

'None of us were. They classified us as political prisoners. None of us were a real threat to them. They just couldn't allow anyone to think for themselves or speak their own mind.' Hilde's voice was bitter, recalling her time there.

'And how was that particular girl treated otherwise? Did you notice anything?'

Hilde frowned again. 'I don't think she was given much food. I can't be sure, because I couldn't see her. I saw the others when we exercised outside in the yard, but she was never allowed out.'

'You mean you think she was starved?'

'I don't know, but messages were scratched on our food tins.' Hilde made a little scribbling action with her right hand, as if she was writing. 'We all had to hand our tins back after we'd eaten and then when it was mealtime, food was dished out and given to us in our cells. So, we might each have had a different tin every time. I don't know for sure if it was her, but more than once I saw the words, *I am hungry*, and *I am lonely*.'

Sylvia looked down at her notes. She felt such pain hearing this, feeling such sorrow for the distress of all the prisoners, but most of all for Phyllis. 'This was a very harsh prison,' she said after a moment's pause to regain her composure. 'You were all being punished severely.'

'What had she done to deserve it?' Hilde asked.

'She was just serving her country,' Sylvia said. 'She was extremely loyal and very brave.'

'And another thing,' Hilde said, 'those girls tapped on their tins and on the walls. The guards sometimes came and shouted at them and took the tins away. They were sending messages, weren't they? Talking to each other and to your so-called dangerous prisoner?'

Sylvia smiled. 'Yes, it sounds like they must have been communicating with each other in Morse code. Clever girls, good for them. The guards probably wouldn't have known what they were saying.' But, she thought, Phyllis would have known and their messages would have been such a comfort to her in her isolation.

'And more than once, I think the girl who was always alone was beaten by one of the guards when they stopped the messages they were sending each other. They seemed to really dislike her.'

Sylvia shook her head and made another note in her book.

Phyllis must have known she was going to receive more ill-treatment if she tried to talk to the other girls. She admired her defiant bravery, wondering at the same time why it was so inflammatory.

'I often wondered what those girls might have done,' Hilde said. 'It occurred to me that they might have been spies for the Allies. Is that what they were?'

Sylvia pursed her lips. She'd never be able to tell her. The secret was locked away inside her. 'I really couldn't say. All I can tell you is that Simone's real name was Phyllis and those girls shouldn't have been there. They were all very brave.'

'And I think some of them were shot one day while I was there. We were all locked in our cells, but I heard the guards taking the prisoners next to me away. Then after a while we heard three shots outside. Nothing was said, but I'm sure I heard crying from Simone's cell, I mean Phyllis, so I knew she was still there.'

A tear trickled down Hilde's cheek. 'None of us deserved to be treated so badly. The Nazis were evil.' She had wrung the life out of her handkerchief and now needed it to mop her tears as she wiped away the trail. Then she held her chin up defiantly. 'I'm not sorry I made that joke about Hitler. I hated him and all of his followers with my whole being.'

Sylvia smiled at her. Hilde was just one of many victims. Another brave girl, trying her hardest to find a way forward. Of course, she was not terribly damaged like those who had suffered in the concentration camps, but she had suffered wounds nevertheless, and all because of the arrogance of those who thought they knew best.

SPECIAL OPERATIONS EXECUTIVE MANUAL

INTERROGATION METHODS

During Interrogation

ii) Prisoner seated on uncomfortable chair. Not allowed to eat, drink or smoke while examiners indulge in all three.

THIRTY-SIX

THE OLD GUARD

Sylvia ducked to enter the tiny white cell at the end of the corridor in Pforzheim Prison. Is this where they chained Phyllis? A feeble, frightened young girl, treated as a dangerous prisoner? If Phyllis had been fully restrained, she might not have been able to stand to look out of the barred window, set high up in the wall. She couldn't have seen other women walking around the quadrangle; the only human beings she'd have met would have been her jailers.

Sylvia peered up at the window and could see nothing but a fragment of blue sky and a wisp of white cloud. How isolated Phyllis must have felt, on her own in this bare, damp cell with nothing to keep her occupied. But maybe she had caught fragments of chatter and singing from the exercise yard or from other cells, reminding her that she was not the only one here. It comforted her to think that Phyllis might have seen the messages scratched into the mess tins and recognised the tapping of Morse code. She hoped that had been of some solace to her brave girl. 'We all sent words of help, hoping some would reach her,' Hilde had said. 'We told her, you are not alone.'

Sylvia ran her fingers across the surface of the cell walls, hoping for a name or a sign of defiance scratched into the plaster, but maybe any ounce of energy Phyllis might have still had was saved for communicating with her neighbouring prisoners. 'We had messages back from her,' Hilde had said. 'She said she was English and we heard the guards say that she was a parachutist. We thought that meant she was very brave and daring.'

Oh, but she was, Sylvia thought. *And you dear girls surely helped her endure her time here. But sometimes it must have backfired too.* 'We sang so she could hear us,' Hilde had said. 'Mostly songs of liberation, but one day we sang news that we'd overheard from other prisoners and the guards about how the war was going very badly for Germany. But then we heard the guard go into Simone's cell and hit her. We heard her crying out. There was one particular guard who liked to beat her and we could hear him shouting.'

Beat her? What had she done to deserve a beating, other than listen to the singing of other female prisoners and maybe respond to the chorus? But Phyllis had been classified as dangerous and, if her jailers were feeling unnerved by the failures of their troops, they might well have taken out their frustration and anger on this slip of a girl, who had tried her best to help the French resistance and scupper the Reich's military progress.

Sylvia edged out of the grim cell, barely large enough for the bed and bucket that were all it contained, and turned back to the corridor. Like all the prisons she had visited so far, the predominant smells were of cabbage, disinfectant and human sweat.

She returned to the prison office with questions for the current governor. 'We have the records from the period you are interested in,' he said, passing a file across his desk. 'It shows that there was correspondence about this prisoner with the Gestapo in Karlsruhe.'

She scanned the page he indicated. Her German was good

enough to understand the statement, but she asked him to summarise and he said, 'It appears that the governor here at the time thought the measures being requested for this particular prisoner were unnecessarily harsh. On her arrival he had her chains removed, but he was then told they should be replaced. He went on to suggest that a looser chain, attached to one hand and the bed, would be sufficient to restrain her. That would have allowed the prisoner some degree of movement. He also asked if she might be allowed to exercise, even if this had to be taken in solitude. But all of his requests were denied.'

'Do you know why they were so keen to restrict her in this way?'

'It was not unusual for spirited prisoners, particularly the defiant ones, to receive such treatment.'

Oh, Phyllis, oh you dear girl, plucky and courageous to the end, thought Sylvia. *But you paid a heavy price for resisting.*

'And also,' the governor continued, 'it appears that she was held under the Nacht und Nebel edict on poor rations, because she was dangerous.'

Sylvia let that sink in but shook her head to indicate her disgust at a system that took every opportunity to weaken an already frail young woman. 'And then what happened to her? Did she stay here or go elsewhere?'

'There are no further entries on the register. We know that some prisoners were taken away and shot in the woods nearby, but their names were recorded. Your girl's name is not among them.' He showed her the list. The three agents she thought had died in Dachau were identified by their code names, Paulette, Louise, Solange; but no Simone, so no Phyllis.

So much for the legendary German efficiency, thought Sylvia. But then another question occurred to her: 'Do you have records of the wardens who were on duty during this period, who might have guarded the cell concerned and had close contact with this prisoner?'

And with little hesitation, the governor ran his fingers down further lists of staff. 'During those particular months, the rota was shared by Helmut Kopkow and Johann Boemelburg.'

'Male jailers assigned to cover a female division?'

'It was not that unusual at that time.'

'And are they still employed here?' *Tell me*, she thought, *tell me that the men who were on duty, the men who chained and beat my girl are still alive and that I can meet them face to face. I want to see and hear their reaction when I confront them.*

'One of them is still with us and the other has recently retired, but I can find you an address for him. Would you like to meet Boemelburg today? His shift doesn't start until later.'

'I'd very much like to speak to both of them. I'll return to speak to Boemelburg just before he starts and in the meantime I'll go and see Kopkow, if you can tell me where I might find him.'

Leaving the governor's office, Sylvia wondered how easily she would locate her man. The city of Pforzheim was another of those heavily bombed by the RAF in the spring of 1945. It was targeted because its watchmaking trade had been diverted into the making of precision instruments designed for the war effort. More than 80 per cent of the city's buildings had been destroyed and three-quarters of the population had been rehoused in temporary accommodation. Once again, Sylvia felt pity for the ordinary citizen whose life had been so hugely disrupted by the destruction of war. They'd suffered the loss of homes, businesses and livelihoods. What had been the point of destroying the previously relatively comfortable way of life for the German people?

Passing yet more gangs of workers, as before mostly women and older men, pressed into service piling rubble, sorting bricks to be reused, she felt that industry in Germany would resurrect itself more quickly than in Britain, which had been drained of energy as well as economics by the war effort. After walking for twenty minutes, she thought she had found the refugee centre she was looking for, a home for older, retired residents. Huts were clustered around a hall that may once have been part of a church and which now served as some kind of soup kitchen, if the smells of onion and cabbage were an accurate indication.

'I am here to see Herr Kopkow,' she said to the elderly woman acting as a concierge at the door. She was bundled into a ragged coat tied around with a grubby shawl.

The woman jerked her head over her shoulder towards a group of men playing cards at a table with rusted metal legs. 'The one in the middle. Wearing the greatcoat.'

Sylvia thought they all looked like old soldiers, but ones from the war before, not the most recent conflict. One man wore an army cap and another, to his right, had a sheepskin helmet with earflaps, which wasn't standard German army issue but could have been Russian.

'Herr Kopkow?' She spoke as she approached the card players.

Sly, bloodshot eyes looked up at her below bushy white eyebrows. 'Who wants to know?'

'Your former employer, the prison governor, sent me to find you.'

Kopkow slammed his cards down on the table and scooped up his winnings, a handful of cigarettes. 'What's he bleating about now?'

'He thinks you might be able to help me. I'm enquiring about a former prisoner. Can we go somewhere and talk?' She pulled a bottle of schnapps from her coat pocket, but kept hold of it, noting the glint in his eye.

He stood, his chair scraping back on the tiled floor with a harsh screech, and waved his arm at a corner of the hall, where there was a free bench. With a shuffling limp, he led the way and sat down, indicating that Sylvia should sit beside him. She poured a little of the alcohol into a tin mug she'd picked up and handed it to him.

'You English or American?'

'English. But I'm being assisted by the American division. We're all working together.'

'Hmm, you know all this is your fault.' He jerked his head of greasy grey strands to indicate the ruined city outside.

Sylvia forced herself to ignore his remark. 'I'm trying to establish what happened to one of our people. I'm pretty certain she was held at Pforzheim in the autumn of 1943.'

'She? You're saying it was a woman?' He knocked back the schnapps in one gulp and wiped his mouth with the back of his hand, then held out the mug for another tot.

Sylvia thought she detected an unpleasant glimmer in his eyes. 'I'm trying to trace a very young woman. She was little more than a girl, I've got photos.' She poured another shot and screwed the bottle tight.

He grinned, revealing blackened teeth beneath his nicotine-stained moustache. 'Let's have 'em then.' His hand reached for the prints Sylvia took from her satchel. 'Pretty girl,' he said, shuffling the photos as if they were playing cards. 'Very nice.'

Sylvia felt her skin crawl as his filthy fingers, his long yellow nails ringed with dirt, touched Phyllis's features. They traced her lips, stroked her hair and hovered over her breasts. She longed to snatch the images back from him, but tried to restrain herself. 'Do you recognise her? Was she in your care?'

'Not like this she wasn't. She was still a little beauty, but she wasn't half so fancy as this while she was with us.'

'Do you mean she was being ill-treated?'

'We had orders and we followed them. That's all.' He slid the photographs back onto Sylvia's lap, his filthy hand slowly stroking the skirt of her uniform as he did so.

'Why was that?' She shifted her knee away from his fingers and ignored the mug he'd emptied again.

'The powers-that-be told us she was dangerous. That means being extra careful.' He chuckled. 'Feisty little thing, though, she was. Needed taking down a peg or two.'

Sylvia tried to stop herself shuddering at his words. 'Did she receive the same treatment as other prisoners at that time?'

'You do-gooders, you all think prison's a holiday. It ain't. It's there to teach 'em a lesson.'

'But tell me how she was treated.'

'She had to be restrained. We were told she might try to escape again so we had to keep her chained up.'

'And what else? Anything you can remember?' Sylvia felt sickened by his casual attitude to her girl's imprisonment, but she maintained an even tone of voice, determined not to give any hint of her distaste for him and his account.

'She had to stay in her cell most of the time. And she was on short rations too.'

'Why was that? Was it another form of punishment?'

'You don't know a bloody thing, do you?' He laughed out loud. 'We like them docile, the tricky ones. The weaker they are, the less trouble they become. We can't have strong prisoners breaking out and beating us up.'

Sylvia took all this in. *Of course you didn't want them well-fed*, she thought, *you liked to have cowed and weakened prisoners. But Phyllis was only ever a delicate young girl, even when she was at her strongest and in full health. She could never have been a threat to strong men like you.* 'But she couldn't have hurt you or escaped if she was chained all the time, could she? So why did you think she amounted to a threat?'

'I can't say that I did, especially. But someone clearly did. Otherwise we wouldn't have had those orders, would we?'

'Did she ever mix with the other prisoners? Or exercise?'

'She went out a few times, but then she got bold. Tried talking to other inmates and sending messages. So, we had to put a stop to that.' He held out the mug in his filthy fingers, so

Sylvia gave him another drop of schnapps. He tossed it back in one gulp, giving a satisfied gasp.

'We? You mean you stopped her?'

'I knew she had to be stopped, but Johann usually dealt with difficult customers like her. He knows what to do with anyone who gets mouthy.'

'And you don't?'

'It's better for me that I don't. I might lose my temper, see?' He gave a crafty wink that made Sylvia shudder.

'Johann? Do you mean Boemelburg? The warden who is still employed at the prison?'

'That's him. Tell him he owes me. He hasn't yet paid me what he owes from our last game of cards.' Kopkow stood, a sure sign that this interview was over. 'And now if you'll excuse me, I must get back to my friends. I can feel a winning streak today.' He slammed the empty mug down on the bench between them.

He limped away to rejoin his cronies and Sylvia heard coarse laughter and saw heads turn as she walked out of the foetid hall, fogged with the steam of cabbage soup and cigarette smoke. Was Kopkow passing the buck, hinting that his colleague was the one who was not averse to beating prisoners, or was he just covering himself? She didn't trust his story, but she knew where to find him if she had to return.

SPECIAL OPERATIONS EXECUTIVE
MANUAL

3. TYPES OF INTERROGATORS

Second Interrogator puts clear, concise, sharp questions. If results are unsatisfactory, prisoner may be 'beaten up'.

THIRTY-SEVEN
AN EYE FOR AN EYE
JANUARY 1946

Sylvia timed her second visit to the prison so she'd arrive just before Johann Boemelburg was due to start his shift. She waited in the entrance hall, where she'd already asked the guard on duty to alert her when he arrived. But she wasn't expecting a strong, young man, who might well have spent his war on the front instead of in a prison. It was only when he turned to face her that she realised why he hadn't been sent off on active service. His face was badly scarred and as he stared at her, she realised that he was blind in one milky eye. Was this an early injury from fighting in the war, or something else?

'I've been told that the governor wishes me to speak with you,' he said. 'I am permitted to do so for fifteen minutes and no more. Then I must start my shift. We may sit in the visitors' room for now.' He led the way down the corridor from the entrance to a room with a few tables and pairs of chairs. He pulled out a chair for himself with a clatter, but didn't show any respect for Sylvia by offering her a seat.

She ignored his rudeness and settled herself down with her notebook and envelope of photos placed on the table before her. 'I'm here to get some information about a prisoner who was in this prison for a few months, I believe, from October 1943. There is a record of her being sent to Pforzheim, but little about her time here or her whereabouts after that. I've been told that you were one of the guards on duty here during that time.'

'Do you have a name for me?'

'At that time, she was using an alias: Simone.' Was that a flicker of acknowledgement in his eyes? Sylvia wondered. 'I doubt that she would have admitted to any other name.'

'She was one of your spies then?'

'She was doing her duty for her country, just like you and many of your fellow countrymen. She should have been treated as a prisoner of war.'

'If she had been able to prove that she had been conscripted, then she would have been treated as such.' Boemelburg looked smug, bearing a self-satisfied half-smile.

'Maybe these will jog your memory.' Sylvia fanned out the photographs that his older colleague had pawed at only an hour or so before. But Boemelburg didn't touch them. He kept his arms folded and barely glanced at the pictures. 'Does she look familiar?'

He slowly shook his head. 'I can't say she does. But maybe she wasn't looking quite so pretty and well-groomed by the time they sent her to us. Some of the Gestapo, you know...'

'She was transferred here by the Gestapo in Karlsruhe. I gather that she was deemed to be a dangerous prisoner.'

'Oh well then,' he shook his head, 'if they thought that and had got their hands on her first, who knows what kind of a state she might have been in by the time she got here.'

'The prison records indicate that you were in charge of her at that time. You and Kopkow. He's already told me that she wasn't treated as well as the other prisoners, not that any of them were living a life of comfort here.'

'Kopkow, eh? I'm glad my old friend's been helpful. I can't say I remember much about that time. There was a war going on, you know. Rations were in short supply, we were managing as best we could.'

'Including depriving a poor young girl of her fair share of food? Is that what you call managing?'

Boemelburg shrugged. 'I couldn't say. We were all having a tough time back then.'

'And what did you do if a prisoner answered you back? Especially if that prisoner was female? Did that make you more inclined to treat them badly?' She knew she had caught him there, because he couldn't resist the ghost of a smile curling the corners of his mouth.

'We don't get paid here to put up with insubordination. It's a tough enough job as it is, without prisoners being insolent and difficult.'

'And what would you do if one of them was?'

'I might have let them know who was boss.' He looked down at his watch and Sylvia could tell he was itching for this interview to end.

'Is that how you lost the sight in your eye? I take it that wasn't on the front line.'

He clenched his teeth and she could see his fists flexing. 'I didn't... I wasn't... But she asked for it.'

So, it was caused by a woman, Sylvia thought. He failed to make the grade because of a woman, who'd fought back. And a spirited girl, determined to stand up to him, wouldn't have pleased him, would she? Had she flung boiling water or hot fat at him to protect herself? That would have made him angry. Sylvia hoped the girl responsible hadn't suffered more as a result.

'Do you happen to remember if anyone might have had to remonstrate with my girl, with Simone?' She tapped the photo of Phyllis, just to remind him who she was.

Again, that faint smile lit up his face, confirming that she was on the right track. 'I don't particularly remember. But of course, from time to time everyone in authority has to show them who's boss. You can't have a riot in a place like this.'

'And can singing be classed as rioting?'

He looked so smug, so pleased with himself. 'We might have had to put a stop to it. That sort of thing could unsettle the other prisoners.'

'And how would you stop it?'

'We'd speak to the prisoners concerned and make it clear that we wouldn't tolerate it.'

'By speaking to them, or by denying them rations and beating them up? Which was it?'

'Well, it really all depends now, doesn't it? If someone is obstinate and persists, we might have to get a bit tough with them.'

'A big, strong man like you would have to get tough with a frightened young girl?' Sylvia glanced at his fists, twitching while he clenched them on the table between them.

'Girls and women can be just as difficult as men.' Boemelburg stood up, looking at his watch. 'Well, you've had long enough. I've got to be on duty now, I won't be popular with my staff if I linger.'

Sylvia watched the broad-shouldered figure march down the corridor. He would have made a fine SS officer if it hadn't been for his injury and she guessed he knew that. But could his resentment have led him to overstep the mark or was rough treatment the order of the day at that time during the war? She decided she needed to speak to the governor once more before she left the prison.

His secretary ushered her into his office. He closed the file on his desk. 'How can I help you, Fräulein Benson? Were my two men not forthcoming?'

'They've been most helpful, thank you. But I just wondered whether you have a policy here on the degree to which prisoners, male and female, can be punished.'

'Hmm, I think I know what you are asking. During those years, this was a very harsh place. Not so much now, of course. We are much more enlightened.'

'Kopkow said he wouldn't ever hit a prisoner, because he might lose his temper. But what about Boemelburg?'

The governor gave a slight cough and then turned to another file on his desk. 'I have to admit that he can be somewhat heavy-handed. I have his record here. There have been a few incidents in the past.'

'Where he's gone too far?'

A nod told Sylvia that she was right in her assumption.

'Has anyone ever been in hospital as a result of his involvement?'

'Yes, and I'm afraid there's more. One inmate during that time died, after Boemelburg dealt with him rather too severely.'

'And what about the women? Did he punish them too?'

'Not to the same extent, but yes, he did. He isn't assigned to the women's wing any more.'

'But you've already confirmed that he was guarding women during the time my girl was here? So might he have beaten her as well?'

'Our records show that he did. More than once.'

Sylvia felt sick knowing that strong, well-built man, fuelled by resentment over his injury from a girlfriend, had hit dear Phyllis, a slight, weakened, vulnerable girl. She could never have stood up to him. 'Please tell me he didn't kill her too, did he?'

'No, he never went that far. It wouldn't have been fatal.'

A wave of relief filled Sylvia's heart. 'So, what did happen to her? Where did she end up if she didn't die here?'

'I'm sorry, but there is no record of what happened next. I know her cell was allocated to a new prisoner, so she must have left this prison and been taken elsewhere, but I have no information on her destination. That was the way with the Nacht und Nebel prisoners. They disappeared into the system.'

But the system was so efficient in so many ways, thought Sylvia. *There must be a record somewhere. She couldn't have vanished into thin air and fog, could she?*

THIRTY-EIGHT

SCARE HIS PANTS OFF

'What do you think, Prinz? Want to give a nasty man a great big bite?' Sylvia fondled the dog's soft, floppy ears as she lay on Charles's bed. The Great Dane nuzzled her neck. He was almost as seductive as Charles. Prinz was the gentlest dog she had ever known. Only his slobbering jowls and heavy paws with their huge claws were capable of causing harm.

'Bite, did you say? You want him to bite someone?' Charles yawned. It was late in the evening and all three of them were tired after an exhausting day of searching and questioning.

'I'm pretty sure I've found a guard who gave Phyllis a very bad time in Pforzheim Prison. He's on record as having beaten her. And it wasn't the first time he'd ill-treated prisoners. One even died from his ill-treatment.'

'You've got a name? Want me to talk to him?'

'He's a smug bastard and he hates women. So damn sure of himself. I'd like Prinz to pin him down and bite his balls off.'

'Not Prinz's style, I'm afraid. He might drown them in sticky drool, but that's the worst he can manage. He's about as far as you can get from those fierce German Shepherds the Nazis were so fond of using.' Charles propped himself up on one elbow and stretched out the other arm to pat his handsome dog.

'Well, I'm afraid drowning him in doggy saliva isn't going to be enough for me,' Sylvia said. 'And I feel sure he has some idea where Phyllis went next. There's nothing on record, but if she'd been executed while she was still at the prison, the governor assured me that there'd be something on file.'

'But she was meant to disappear, wasn't she? What do they call it?'

'Nacht und Nebel Erlass. Like they never existed. She was meant to melt away into the misty darkness. But I can't just let her vanish, I have to know for sure.'

'Then maybe Prinz and I will have to have a word with this chap.' Charles slapped Prinz's rump and the dog's muscular tail wagged vigorously. 'That's his best weapon. That hefty tail can inflict some spectacular bruises on legs. I'm glad he wasn't docked.'

'Can you really do that? Have words with him, I mean?'

'Of course I can. I have a remit to question all suspects linked to war crimes. That covers anyone and everyone. If I have reason to think someone might have information or has behaved improperly themselves, I can haul them in for questioning.'

Sylvia threw her arms round Charles and kissed him, then hugged Prinz as well. 'Thank you. Both of you. Scare the pants off him, please.'

'I'm looking forward to it already. Now, let's give Prinz a quick late-night stroll, then get back up here so you can tell me again how grateful you are.'

Two days later, as Sylvia returned to the hotel after a day of double-checking the records at Karlsruhe, she spotted Charles sitting in the bar with David, Prinz spread out full-length at their feet like a pile of grey velvet. Charles waved to her and she went straight across to their table. Both men were freshly shaved and looked pleased with their day.

'I've had an interesting day with your friend,' Charles said. 'You're going to need a drink to hear the details.'

'I'm desperate to hear all about it but let me dash upstairs and change first. I feel as if I've been thoroughly impregnated with the disgusting odours of that wretched prison. All cabbage, Dettol and perspiration. I shan't be long.'

Sylvia was quick. After a speedy wash, she slipped into her one decent frock, brushed her hair, reapplied Red Velvet lipstick, a generous gift from a very kind American she'd befriended, and allowed herself a small spray of Femme de Rochas. Feeling fresher, she sauntered into the bar to join the men, hoping for positive news.

'So,' she said, smoothing her wool crepe skirt as she sat down and took a sip of the gin and tonic that was already waiting for her, 'Did you get much out of him?'

'I found out he's a damn coward,' Charles said. 'It wouldn't at all surprise me if he'd provoked that girlfriend of his into maiming him so he couldn't enlist. He had a pretty cushy war out here until the bombs dropped.'

'Oh, surely not,' Sylvia said. 'Who'd risk losing their sight to stay out of the war?'

'Men have done as much in the past,' David said. 'It's astonishing what some people will subject themselves to if they don't want to see action.'

'Well, he's not exactly averse to a fight,' Charles said. 'But only on his terms.'

'Meaning?' Sylvia sipped slowly. She wanted a clear head for this, even though she was dying to knock the drink back after her tiring day.

'He's a bully as well as a coward. He won't risk getting hurt himself but he likes to hurt others. And I'm sorry to say that he has admitted to beating up your girl.'

Sylvia took a deep breath. 'How badly? Did he say?'

'Not in so many words, but he was rather fond of employing a whip and a cane. Never his fists. Though the toe of his boot might have come into play a few times as well.'

Sylvia felt a little sick and took a big gulp of her drink. She was going to need another very soon at this rate. 'I expected as much. He's a sadistic brute. Poor Phyllis. She'd have had the most terrible bruises, maybe fractures too.'

'Sadly, I expect that was the case.'

'And did he say anything about where she went or if she even ever left the prison?'

'He claimed he knew nothing about her final destination. All he could tell me was that she left with some other prisoners one day. He didn't know exactly where they were going but it was usually back to Karlsruhe.'

'I didn't find anything there today.' Sylvia sighed. 'It's looking like a dead end. I was given a lead to Dachau a few months ago, but that's not going to be easy to unravel.'

'I didn't like your man one bit,' Charles said with a shake of his head. 'Nor did Prinz.' He bent to give his dog a comforting pat, at which Prinz raised his head for a moment to look enquiringly at his master, then dropped it again to rest on his giant outstretched paws. 'By the time we'd finished, he was utterly pathetic. Crying and saying they'd been overworked at the prison and had struggled to maintain discipline.'

'That's no excuse,' Sylvia said. 'I doubt that any of the prisoners were rioting. And Phyllis was chained up as well. She could hardly have done anything to cause trouble.'

'Aah, but she troubled him, you see. Her defiance, her insolence – that's what got under his skin. He couldn't take it.'

'So, he hit her. He hit a young, weak and frightened woman. What are you going to do next?' Sylvia finished her drink and when David reached for her glass with an enquiring look, she nodded.

'I think there's enough evidence to charge him,' Charles said. 'I doubt he'd get a heavy sentence, but it would be enough to upset him. It would certainly give him a fright.'

'Or we could take him out for a drive in the forest,' added David. 'It's up to you, Sylvia. He's your man.'

She thought about the self-satisfied man she had interviewed. She certainly wanted him to suffer, but she didn't want it over and done with quickly. 'Charge him then. The longer he's scared about the outcome, the better. A walk in the forest would be far too quick for the likes of him. I want him utterly terrified for as long as possible.'

'Consider it done then,' said Charles as a second round of drinks arrived. He lifted his glass and the other two did the same. 'Here's to scaring our man shitless.'

SPECIAL OPERATIONS EXECUTIVE MANUAL
INDIVIDUAL SECURITY

1. INTRODUCTION

c) The agent must, therefore, remember that, like primitive men in the jungle, he has only his alertness, initiative and observation to help him.

He has to look after himself but we can prepare him for this by training.

THIRTY-NINE

MORE SHERRY, DEAR?

That business with Sylvia trying to climb out the window really bothered me. I'm sure I couldn't have managed it, even though I'm much more spry than she was then, so she must have been really determined to crawl through those cupboards and haul herself halfway out that window. She could have ended up killing herself, or at the very least found she'd got a nasty break, which we all know is not a good idea at our age. Even a little slip indoors can mean a broken hip and a stay in hospital, let alone falling off a roof. That could have spelt the beginning of the end.

I kept thinking about why she felt the need to do it in the first place. What did she mean when she said, 'They might find me'? That woman was a mystery to me, really she was. All that stuff I didn't know about her time in the war and then this nonsense about escaping. So, one evening when we were sitting down by the fire, soon after all that funny business, I said, 'Whatever were you worrying about the other day when you locked your bedroom door and crawled through that passage into my room? Who did you think might want to find you? Is there something I ought to know?'

And it was odd, because she didn't look impish, the way she had when she'd told me about her secret tunnel; this time she looked really frightened. Her eyes widened and I swear she started taking little breaths and looking around her as if someone might peer through the window at any moment or come and bang on the front door. We were sitting in our fireside armchairs with our evening sherry, so I thought she'd be feeling relaxed and ready to talk, but she was definitely nervous.

So, I thought I shouldn't say any more about it. I just took a sip from my glass and offered her the little silver dish of cashews. We both think they're much nicer than ordinary salted peanuts. We used to both like pistachios, but Sylvia kept grumbling about what a fiddle it was to open the shells and the ready-shelled ones are so expensive, and unsalted, so we decided we'd rather have cashews instead.

She took a couple of nuts and popped them in her mouth and then, before I knew it, she'd started coughing. She managed to control herself long enough to put her glass down on the tray, but she was beginning to choke, so I leapt up and began patting her quite hard on the back. I was wondering if I was going to have to do that special first aid thing, grabbing her round her middle, and I wasn't sure if I knew how to do that properly, but she gasped and coughed a bit more and managed to wheeze out a few words: 'I'm all right now, you can stop all that fussing.'

Fussing, I thought, *trying to stop you killing yourself, more like*. And right then I just couldn't stop myself snapping back at her: 'I'm not fussing, Sylvia, I'm caring for you! First, you go and try to throw yourself out of the window upstairs and now you're choking to death. I'm not obliged to live here half the time and look after you, am I? I'm here because I care about you and you are my oldest friend!'

She sipped the remainder of her sherry and said, 'There's no need to get so snappy, darling. I wasn't throwing myself out of the window, as you put it, I was checking that I could still escape if I had to. I hadn't tried it for a while and I just wanted to see if I could still do it.'

'But what on earth for? If there was a fire, you'd hear the smoke alarms first and we'd call for help. And if it got really bad, well, we'd run outside and I'd turn on the hoses. You don't really need to go crawling on your hands and knees and jumping out of windows, do you, dear?'

'You have no idea, Peg, in your safe little suburban life of nobodies. Absolutely no idea at all.' She rolled her eyes at me as if I knew nothing about her world, when we both knew that we'd been close friends all these years.

'What do you mean, no idea? If you don't tell me things, then of course I can't understand what's bothering you. But we've known each other for ever, Sylv, and I can only know as much as you tell me. If you insist on keeping things to yourself, how can I possibly have any idea what else might be worrying you?'

I knocked back my sherry in one gulp and decided I needed a top-up. We only usually had one glass each in the evening, but she was annoying me that much that night. 'I'm having another. Do you want one?'

She handed me her glass. 'If you're having one, darling, I will.' And she turned her face away and gazed into the fire, which was at that stage where the flames had died down but all the wood was glowing red-hot with the embers.

I topped up both our glasses in the kitchen, took a deep breath and walked back in feeling a bit calmer. To be honest, I'd sipped from my glass even before I went back to her and then topped it up again, so I was feeling quite merry by then.

'Here you are,' I said, handing her the glass. 'Supper will be ready soon.' We were having a shepherd's pie I'd made earlier. I'd popped it in the oven with a ready-made cauliflower cheese from Sainsbury's, so it was a quick and easy meal to make.

'Lovely, darling. Cin-cin.' She saluted me with her little glass. They weren't matching glasses. I don't think she still had any fully matching sets. It was all two of this, three of that and so on. The same with her china, all mismatched cups and saucers, but very pretty ones all the same and good quality. My house is like that too, though most of my stuff came from church jumble sales. It happens over the years and you get to the point of thinking what's the point in buying a whole new tea set when these few cups and so on will see me out?

So, she held up her crystal glass with the chunky-cut stem and I did the same with mine that had a gold rim. We always used the same glasses for our sherry. She was cut-glass, of course she was, and I was cheap and gaudy, naturally. 'They might find me one day,' she murmured.

Oh God, not this again, I thought. But all I said was, 'What's that?'

'I wouldn't be hard to find. So, you never know when they might come.'

'Are you on about this again? Who are we talking about?'

'The children of the dead. Or their brothers.'

I was quite lost by then. No idea. So, I thought I'd just play along with her to stop her worrying about whatever it was that was bothering her. To be honest, I thought her mind was playing games and it wasn't anything serious.

Later that night, once we'd had supper, we watched a bit of TV. Sylvia always insisted on seeing *EastEnders* and then *The Royle Family*. She said both programmes had such marvellous characters and she hooted with laughter over the one about the family. Personally, I couldn't see anything funny about those people who were no better than they should have been, being so crude and horrible to each other. But that's what she liked and it was her house and her TV after all, so we watched what she chose. I wasn't really concentrating on the programme because I kept thinking about what she'd said. And even after I'd cleared up in the kitchen and gone to bed that night, my mind was still going round and round. I couldn't concentrate on the articles in *Woman's Own* at all and I ended up turning the light out early. I just kept thinking about the way she'd locked her bedroom door, bolted the cupboard door from the inside and crawled through to my room.

I got out of bed, turned the light on again and took a good look at the cupboard set into the thickness of the chimney breast between our rooms. It didn't have a bolt on the inside, only the outside. That meant that after crawling through the passage from Sylvia's room, someone could shut that little door and stop anyone following them. And my bedroom door didn't have a bolt or a lock, so that could always be opened and then they could run down the stairs and out of the cottage. Or slide out through the window, like she'd been trying to do.

All of those locks and bolts had been deliberately added at some time. It was as if she had always intended that crawlspace to be an escape route. But why? She could have gone down the second set of stairs outside my room. She didn't have to try to climb out of the window.

But then I began to think about the rest of the security around the cottage. The grilles on all the downstairs windows, which always drove me up the wall whenever I tried cleaning them. The heavy bolts and metal plates on all the outside doors and the Chubb locks. None of those were part of the original farmworkers' cottages. They'd have left their doors unlocked at all times of day and night, probably, and never come to any harm. No, all of that high-security stuff had been added, presumably by Sylvia when she moved here years ago.

I'd asked her once why she didn't have an alarm system because I'd have thought that would have been the best solution. I don't have one in London, but I've thought about it often

enough with the number of break-ins around our neigh-
bourhood.

Sylvia said, 'Oh, I used to have one, but they're hopeless in a
thatched cottage like this. No use at all. There are too many
spiders. They set off the alarm so often I got sick and tired of it. I
couldn't expect the local police to keep coming out to catch
spiders! So, I had it disabled. Besides, it scared me half to death
every time it went off. You try thinking there's an intruder in the
middle of the night, stuck out here in the middle of nowhere.
So, I thought I'd rather not have that thing shrieking at me.
Anyway, I'm too far away from neighbours to get immediate
help. No one could hear it for miles! And the police were never
that quick in any case. I'd have been dead in my bed before they
got here, half the time. I'd be better off firing a shot to scare
them off if there really was a break-in.'

I nearly said something then. I wouldn't have put it past
Sylvia to have a gun hidden away somewhere – she was
surprising like that. But I think she then started rambling on
about something else and I forgot all about it.

And you know, the more I thought about Sylvia and how
jumpy she was, the more I began to think that she was just very
afraid of burglars. I suppose a thatched cottage in the middle of
nowhere is always going to be a target and any number of
people might guess she'd got some valuable bits and pieces in
the place. There's all these Staffordshire china figures, some
good mirrors and quite a few lovely paintings. She'd got a fair bit
of jewellery too. There's that little diamond bird brooch and
some pieces she said were her mother's – a heavy gold chain
necklace and a gold bracelet, among others. Lucky her. I've got
a couple of bits that belonged to my mother, but I reckon they
all came from Woolworth's. Still, I've kept them all the same, as
they remind me of her. I can remember her wearing the little
white crescent moon clip-on earrings.

But if it was burglars that was making her paranoid, she

wouldn't have kept saying 'they' would find her, would she? And what was all this stuff about the children of the dead? She was a mystery, that woman, she really was. Maybe I'll never know what she was really thinking. But back then I decided I'd do my best to stop her climbing out of any more windows, that was for sure.

FORTY

WHERE IS MY SISTER?

JANUARY 1947

It was a simple letter that started it. A letter asking to see her, asking questions about Phyllis, made her feel afraid. Dear Phyllis, the one agent Sylvia had been unable to trace. Or rather, she thought she had traced her, but the result was so awful she preferred not to think about it, nor tell anyone what she had uncovered.

The first time she received such a letter was soon after Phyllis departed on her mission. It was from her brother, the brother Phyllis had been so keen should receive a birthday card from her just before she left British soil. Sylvia had posted the card, as she'd promised, and as she'd done for all her agents' families, gave a London office address as a point of contact. Not the actual address where she and Harrington and the others worked of course, that would have been madness, but effectively a Poste Restante somewhere in the bowels of the War Office.

She received such letters from time to time from all of her girls' relatives. Mothers and fathers mostly, sisters sometimes, brothers less so. During those frantic months of training and preparation for their missions, she normally sent off at least one of the pre-written letters before her recruits finally flew. *All is well, I am well, do not worry*; they all said more or less the same and continued to do so throughout their time away from home, maintaining the myth that they were not in danger and would return safely as soon as the mission was accomplished.

But the girls could not receive letters from their families while they were abroad and this caused some of their relatives a degree of consternation. Some mothers wrote to her constantly asking for news, until Sylvia ran out of her stock of short notes and had to reply herself, trying to reassure them. But once the war was over, once the troops, the refugees and the lost ones began to pick themselves up and find their way back, everyone expected the return of all the agents as well.

It took time to trace these brave souls and she was not successful in helping all of them find their way home. Phyllis was one of them. It was the greatest sadness of Sylvia's life, how that bright, beautiful girl didn't make it back. But she never expected that she would be blamed for the disappearance of any of her agents and certainly not for Phyllis. Most of the families and friends of her brave girls accepted the consequences of war, understood that sadly there would always be casualties. After all, she had done her best to prepare her recruits, equip them for the missions, and she could not be blamed for the final outcome. Or could she? One person seemed to think she was culpable, one person wrote to her directly, via the War Office, and said:

Dear Miss Benson,

I know you did your best to trace all the agents involved in your secret operations during the war and were successful on many counts. However, it has come to my attention that certain agents may not have been supported as much as their families could have expected and I would like to ask you some questions.

Yours sincerely,

Humphrey Lane

She wasn't prepared to be interrogated by Phyllis's brother and she certainly didn't have answers she was comfortable giving him. And soon after her latest trip to Germany, to see what crumbs of information might still be scattered among the former camp and prison guards, he had turned up one morning when she arrived at her new quarters at the War Office. Her old department had closed and evacuated its former premises in late 1946, but she had continued her search into the beginning of 1947. On her return to the UK in the middle of January, the country was blasted by the most severe snows and freezing temperatures ever known. In Wales, half the sheep died from lack of food and the intense cold.

London and the rest of the country was snowbound for seven weeks, but Sylvia still trudged into the office from her flat in Pimlico. That particular day she had just arrived and had pulled off her cold, wet sheepskin-lined boots, hanging her damp stockings on the back of a chair in front of the radiator to dry. Once she was tucked behind her desk, she slipped into a pair of black court shoes, hoping no one would notice her bare, goose-bumped legs and feet purple with cold.

She was just wondering how long her feet would take to thaw out when the phone on her desk gave a shrill jangle. 'Young man called Humphrey Lane here to see you,' the front desk porter said. 'Says he's the brother of Phyllis, so you'll know why he's here.'

Sylvia sighed, thinking damn it, she shouldn't have mentioned her recent trip to Germany in her last brief note to him. 'Can you bring him straight through?' Despite the obvious disapproval in the porter's voice, she couldn't parade the corridors in bare legs. He wouldn't have approved of that either. She'd sweet-talk him later and see if she couldn't find a bag of his favourite confectionery, humbugs.

When her visitor arrived, she was surprised to see that he looked even younger than she'd expected. His cheeks were nipped pink by the icy air, and smooth, apart from a slight shadow on his upper lip and chin. From the style of handwriting and the tone of his letters, she'd thought he'd be a little older, but he could have only been about seventeen or eighteen and was clearly Phyllis's baby brother. She thought back to the birthday card she had posted on his sister's behalf and guessed that Phyllis had been a very fond big sister.

'You shouldn't have come all this way in such awful weather,' Sylvia said, shaking his hand, icy cold even though he'd been wearing thick woollen gloves.

He sat down, saying, 'Oh, I was already staying with friends in London. I got stuck here with the last snowstorm after I'd come up for my university interview. I'm hoping to secure a place before I do my National Service. I'm due to go away in the spring with the army.' He unwound the long dark-green muffler tucked round his neck. It looked home-made, knitted perhaps by an adoring mother – or his doting sister.

'A very sensible plan. And where do you hope you'll be sent once you start your stint?'

'Germany, of course. That's why I've chosen the army. And if you haven't had any luck by then, I was hoping I might continue the search for my sister.'

Sylvia studied this serious, sincere boy. She could tell he really meant what he said, but she knew he wouldn't have any more luck than she'd had and he certainly didn't have her influence and contacts. But all she could say was, 'That's most commendable. I share your concern.'

'I've got to know what's happened, Miss Benson. Even if she isn't still alive, I want to find out. Did you manage to learn any more on your last visit?'

'Nothing significant, I'm afraid to say.' Sylvia maintained eye contact with him, hoping her expression didn't betray her feelings. His eyes were hazel, with gold flecks, exactly the same as Phyllis's. 'I made contact with a lot of organisations out there as there's still a slim chance we could find her. She could be ill, incapacitated in some way, or even have amnesia. It's not unknown for that to happen in such troubled circumstances, even after such a long time.'

'So do you mean other people are searching for her too?'

'We've made sure the various agencies have information about her. If one of them comes across a person who is evidently English and in need of assistance, they will check descriptions of missing personnel as a first port of call.' Sylvia laid her clasped hands on her desk blotter, striking what she thought was a sincere and sympathetic pose.

'So, there is still a chance she could be found? I really hope we will know more before I have to go away. My mother isn't well and it would be a great comfort to her if there was some good news.'

What could Sylvia tell him at that time? That she already knew the most likely outcome, that he wouldn't be pleased to hear what she had to tell him? She couldn't bear to do anything other than continue to give him and his family hope. 'If I hear anything definite, I can assure you I will be in touch. You must let me know where I can find you once you have signed up.' She then stood up and put out her hand, signalling that their interview was now at an end.

But he stayed sitting down for a second longer, before he slowly rose, not taking her outstretched hand. 'You know she told me, before she first went away, that she would never have agreed to work for your department if it hadn't been for you.

She said she felt confident that she could do it, all because of you.'

He must have detected Sylvia's surprise that Phyllis had said as much from her expression, because he added, 'Oh, you needn't worry. She was never specific, she didn't betray any of your so-called secrets.'

They shook hands now and he held Sylvia's rather more firmly than was comfortable. 'She went away because of you so I and my whole family consider that you are responsible, whatever happened to her in the end.'

Sylvia smiled. There was nothing else she could do or say. 'Goodbye, Mr Lane. Thank you for taking the trouble to come here today.' She wasn't going to see him out; she stayed put behind her desk, to conceal her stockingless legs.

She doubted that she would ever have good news for him; and her next trip to Germany might bring confirmation of the worst kind. This was the only time she'd ever seen Humphrey Lane, but the conviction with which he spoke disturbed her.

FORTY-ONE

THE GATES OF HELL

Once she had escaped the badly bombed ruins of Munich, Sylvia could breathe the clean air of the surrounding Bavarian countryside. Green fields dotted with grazing cattle, snow-topped mountains in the distance and a blue sky scudding with white clouds were a refreshing contrast to the stench of shattered sewage pipes and the sight of downtrodden citizens sorting salvageable bricks in the streets.

She had been about to travel alone to Dachau when a young woman staying at the same hotel overheard her checking train times with the receptionist. 'I can give you a ride if you like. You'd have to walk from the station at the other end,' she said in an American accent, offering her hand as she introduced herself. 'Molly Green, war correspondent. I'm going out there again myself. May as well go today.'

Sylvia was glad of the company as well as the lift. She hadn't been looking forward to going to the notorious concentration camp, but felt compelled to see for herself the last place where Phyllis might have been alive. She knew she was pinning all her hopes on the account Yvonne, her crippled agent, had given her over a year ago, but this might not be the end of the trail.

Sylvia had been unable to shake the feeling that it was her duty to follow in Phyllis's footsteps, though the cliché hardly seemed appropriate, she thought wryly. Had Phyllis still been capable of walking or had her feet been mutilated like Yvonne's? And what could Sylvia hope to discover by making the effort to go to every prison where Phyllis had been held?

Avenue Foch, Fresnes, Karlsruhe, Pforzheim. Each of them conjured nightmare visions of how brutally Phyllis had been treated. Sylvia had been to them all and still didn't have a final answer. She suspected the worst. How could it be otherwise? If the poor girl hadn't died from a beating or a shot in the neck, she had probably succumbed to the rigours of starvation, cold and disease, as thousands of others had.

Harrington had been dismissive of her efforts, just as he had been every single time she had expressed her concern about their female agents. 'Don't be ridiculous, Benson. You're not going to find any clues after all this time. If she was still alive, one of the relief agencies would have come across her by now. But go on. Go if you must. I can see you won't be satisfied until you've laid your pet girl to rest.'

Pet girl. How dare he? Sylvia hated his insinuating voice. Phyllis wasn't her pet, she was the youngest and the best. And she mattered. Harrington's dismissive tone rankled with her and made her even more determined to discover the truth.

'This will be my second visit,' Molly Green said as they set off in an American jeep borrowed from the occupying forces. 'But I'm here mostly to write a feature on what the ordinary Germans knew of these awful camps.'

'From what I've heard, they didn't really know very much,' Sylvia said, noticing the fringes of green sprouting between the rail tracks that led to the camp. Nature was restoring the damage, even if the people hadn't yet recovered. 'When

Himmler set the place up, he said it was a camp for political prisoners. And I think many normal Germans believed that.'

'But how could they not have known what was really happening? I mean, the townsfolk nearby must have smelt the stench and seen the smoke, surely?'

'Maybe they guessed what was going on, but didn't want to see.' Sylvia thought this girl's response was all too simplistic and added, 'I've read some of the comments made by your Colonel Quinn after the camp was liberated. He recorded his interviews with local residents and they all said, "Was könnten wir tun?" You know what that means, don't you? What could they do? You've got to realise that these were people who were totally dominated by a criminal government. Anyone objecting to their system could easily have found themselves in one of those camps.'

'I guess I hadn't thought about it quite like that,' Molly said. 'And I so want to get it right for my editor. I'm such a fan of Martha Gellhorn. Did you know that she came here, the day after it was liberated in April of that year? What a woman! She and Lee Miller are real trailblazers for girls like me.'

'I read the Gellhorn report. She certainly didn't try to shield her readers from the shocking truth of what she saw here.'

'Do you remember that line she wrote, something like how she saw skeletons sitting in the sun, searching themselves for lice?'

Sylvia remembered it only too well. A terrible image captured by a fearless woman. Could one of those poor creatures have actually been Phyllis? She shuddered, picturing that beautiful young face grown thin, with hollow cheeks and eyes, her feminine curves wasted away. Though more likely, by that time, she'd have been hidden beneath a pile of skeletal limbs; or her body had already been reduced to ash.

As they drew closer to the camp, Molly said, 'It's not as shocking now as when our guys first discovered it. They said the smell as they approached was a clear sign something was really amiss. But they had no idea what a hellhole this would turn out to be.'

Two years after that frightful discovery, the air was clean, now the place had been cleared of corpses, starving survivors and the stench of decay. But, Sylvia asked herself, what if there was still a clue somewhere in Dachau? As far as she knew, it was probably the last place where Phyllis had drawn breath. If this was the end of the trail, then she had to enter the camp too.

She felt as if she almost knew all about this place of terror already. News of the horrific crimes perpetrated in Nazi concentration camps had shocked the free world since the summer of 1944, when Majdanek was liberated by Soviet troops. At each step of the Allies' advance, fresh atrocities were uncovered, revealing how this evil system of destruction was planned, controlled and orchestrated. But there was also proof that the fleeing Nazis had made unsuccessful attempts to destroy evidence of their crimes, burning corpses and forcing weakened prisoners to embark on futile death marches.

In those circumstances, what chance was there that she would find any record of Phyllis's fate? She might have been one of those who had been sent on a final trek to her death, or she might have succumbed to typhus, her body thrown into a furnace, or a deep pit dug by other prisoners. *But I have to look,* Sylvia vowed. *I cannot fail her. I must see the place where she may have last been alive for myself.*

The jeep drew close to the site of this notorious camp. Ahead of them, set in an archway in the perimeter buildings, high wrought-iron gates barred the entrance. In their centre, a smaller gate, adorned with the chilling phrase so familiar from pictures of Auschwitz: *Arbeit Macht Frei.*

Molly parked the vehicle nearby and the two women stepped through the gate, beneath those ominous words. Only death could set the camp's prisoners free, not the punishing work they were forced to undertake on a starvation diet. An early butterfly hovered among the weeds struggling to grow in the pathway and a warm sun was shining. Was life returning to this place of death? But Sylvia was only aware of the ice-cold grimness of this cruel prison where, strangely, there was no bird-song. The only sounds were their steady footsteps as they proceeded around the hollow, silent buildings. She felt the ghosts of the thousands who had perished here, reaching out to her with skeletal fingers, begging her to tell their story too.

'No wonder Hitler committed suicide the day after this camp was liberated,' Sylvia said. 'The full horror of his crumbling empire was exposed with each terrible discovery.'

'I guess he knew the whole world would be pointing the finger at him,' added Molly. 'Commander Eisenhower came to see it for himself a few days later. Said he felt he had to bear witness to the awful things that had happened here.'

The solid barracks built as an SS training centre by slave labour still stood and so did the ramshackle huts where prisoners had been crammed in their hundreds into tiers of bunks with thin straw mattresses. 'This was their first concentration camp, wasn't it? And they used it as a model for all the others.' Sylvia's face twisted in disgust. 'Deliberate, cold evil.'

'And not so very efficient either towards the end.' Molly pointed towards the empty trucks still standing witness at the end of the railway line. 'Our boys came across those cattle boxes first. Forty of them, crammed with rotting dead bodies. Piled up like cordwood, one guy said. Three thousand prisoners from Buchenwald, who were meant to get here in a matter of days, but instead it took three weeks. Half of them died on the way.'

'And just before the end they marched thousands of dying prisoners from here to Tegernsee. The road must have been littered with bodies.' Sylvia shook her head in despair. 'What on earth were they thinking?'

'Have you been to any of the other concentration camps?'

Molly was taking pictures of the empty huts and grounds with a large camera, just like Lee Miller, whose graphic photographs were making her name.

'No, I just wanted to see this one – I have a special interest in it.'

'May I ask why you're here?'

Sylvia turned to look at Molly. There was no reason not to tell her. The girl was older than Phyllis would have been by maybe five years or more. She was athletic, blonde and confident in her simple white blouse and practical fawn slacks. A slick of red lipstick framed her perfect teeth. She was clearly modelling herself on her war correspondent heroine, the famous Martha Gellhorn. 'A girl who worked for my department was held here.'

'Gee, that's awful. Was she a prisoner of war?'

'Technically yes, but she wasn't in uniform, so they didn't treat her as such. They said she was a dangerous spy and treated her very badly at every stage of her imprisonment. She was so young, even younger than you.'

'I'm real sorry to hear that. Did she get out okay?'

'I rather fear not. I know she was held here, but I don't know whether she ever left.' Sylvia shook her head in despair, turned away and started walking towards the crematoria, so Molly couldn't see the tears threatening to fall or capture her distress with her camera. Of course it was hopeless. Any personnel documents still remaining had been removed after the camp's liberation. She would have to look elsewhere for information about the guard Yvonne suspected had brutally beaten Phyllis.

She took a deep breath to calm herself and instinctively reached for the gold powder compact in her pocket. She had been using the compact for some time now, ever since she had begun to feel resigned to Phyllis's inevitable death. *Will I ever know what happened to you, my dear?* she asked herself, checking her face in the mirror and dabbing the corners of her eyes with a clean handkerchief.

She dabbed her nose with the same powder that Phyllis had briefly used before her moonlit departure. *Dear girl, you don't mind, do you? If you ever come back, I'll happily replace the powder and the puff.* She snapped the case shut and slid it back into her pocket, her hand stroking the engraved surface, as if she could communicate with Phyllis through transference of ownership.

Sylvia looked around the site again. How could she have ever thought she would find any evidence here that Phyllis had been held in this awful place? Her girl's spirited defiance had consigned her to the neverland of Nacht und Nebel Erlass. There would be no record of her ever having been here. This was a place only for ghosts.

SPECIAL OPERATIONS EXECUTIVE MANUAL

3. SECURITY PRECAUTIONS

h) Preparations should be made for destroying incriminating evidence that is too dangerous to conceal.

FORTY-TWO

GOOD HEALTH

'I guess you're going to need a real drink after our trip today,' Molly said as they met in the hotel bar, that evening back in Munich. 'Tell you what, I'll get the barman to make us Martinis.'

Sylvia didn't want to completely forget the impact the visit to the concentration camp had made on her, but she welcomed the cushion of alcohol more than usual. And Molly's breezy company was most helpful. Although Dachau had been emptied of horror two years previously, she had felt its past, relaying in her mind the photographs of truly terrible scenes taken at the time of liberation. And while she'd not been able to uncover any more evidence about the fate of her girl, she was satisfied that she had done all she could. And she had visited the last place where Phyllis might have been alive.

'He already knew how to make them,' Molly said with a triumphant smile, returning from the bar. 'Said all the Americans have had him shaking and stirring Martinis ever since they arrived the year the war ended.'

They clinked glasses and sipped, then Molly said, 'Did it help you any, going out there today?'

Sylvia sighed. 'Oh, a little, I suppose. I don't have any more leads, but at least I've explored every avenue I can so far.'

'What was she like, your agent?'

'I can show you. I've got her photograph here.' Sylvia pulled a picture of Phyllis from her bag. 'I carry it everywhere with me, just in case I think I've stumbled on another possible witness.'

Molly gazed at the print, which was becoming a little more creased and dog-eared every time Sylvia produced it. 'Gee, she's a beauty. And brave too, I guess, if she was doing undercover work.'

'Extremely. But I've begun to think that it was her bold spirit that was her downfall. Maybe if she hadn't been so defiant, she might have survived.'

'But you can't know that. Dachau was brutal but it was also rife with disease. It wasn't just the cruelty and lack of provisions that killed there. People got real sick.'

'You're right. But I really don't expect to find her alive now. I just want to know what happened to her. I need an end to her story. And I owe it to her family too.'

Molly nibbled at the salted pretzels served with their order. 'I've been thinking about what you said about how the ordinary Germans couldn't have stopped this happening. When I talk to them, I'm going to ask them *why* they think it all happened. I mean, what got into people's minds, for God's sake? When did such cruelty and disregard for human life become so acceptable?'

'Good idea. It's not enough for the guards to say they were just following orders. In many instances they decided for themselves to carry out deliberately cruel acts of violence and degradation. Some even clearly enjoyed it.' Sylvia remembered that flicker of a smile when she had questioned Boemelburg. She knew for certain that he had taken pleasure in his work.

'You think they didn't have to act that way? That the whole set-up encouraged them to be vicious and brutal?'

'It would seem so. The whole system encouraged the worst inhumanity.'

Molly looked thoughtful. 'You know, when our guys got to Dachau, they were battle-hardened, fighting men, but they said the sights at that camp gave the war a whole new meaning. They said it made them realise they weren't just fighting an enemy, they were fighting evil itself.'

'Well, I think they were right. And I suppose that's why one of your American officers that day lost control, when some German soldiers came out of the nearby woods holding up a white handkerchief.'

'Yeah. He shot them and then his men finished them off. He was just overcome with anger at what had happened here.'

Both women were quiet for a moment, thinking about what they had heard of the camp's liberation and what they had now seen for themselves. Then Sylvia said, 'You know, I sometimes wonder how I'll react when I finally find out what happened to Phyllis. Will I want to take matters into my own hands? I certainly couldn't blame your American officer for his response in that particular moment.'

'But isn't it better to make sure charges are brought and that all the facts are out in the open? I know there have already been a lot of trials, but we can't let any of those brutes go free. We've got to round them all up and make them face the music.'

'In theory, yes. But I suppose what I've also been afraid of on my quest is finding out that what Phyllis experienced was more terrible than I could ever imagine. And if I'm right, how could I ever let her family know how much she had suffered?'

'Oh, you mustn't think that. You shouldn't torture yourself.'

'But I can't help it. She was young and innocent. I recruited her, supervised her training and, when she was ready, I saw her off. I will always feel that whatever happened was my fault.'

'This is the time we need another Martini,' Molly said, flicking her fingers in the direction of the bar. 'You know what they say. One Martini is good, two are too many and three are not enough.'

Sylvia laughed. 'Then we should stop at two. But they are delicious and just what we needed after today.'

'So, after this, would you say you've reached a dead end?'

'Maybe not entirely. A contact who was in Dachau, who was badly treated herself, gave me a name. She was pretty sure of the identity of the guard who was mostly responsible for Phyllis. There will be a record somewhere, I'm sure.'

'And he hasn't come up in any of the trials?'

'Not this particular man. But the system was very efficient. It might mean doing a lot of paperwork, but I'll see what I can dig up. There might well be a record of his home town, date of birth, that kind of thing.'

'You really think he'd have just gone home? Not tried to hide away?' Molly looked incredulous. 'Didn't they all know they'd committed the most terrible crimes?'

Sylvia shook her head. 'They were just following orders, or so they said. And look at how many of them did slink back home. They could be all around us still.'

Molly looked over her shoulder towards the bar. 'It gives me the creeps just thinking that any of them here could be Nazis.' She shuddered.

'The rats may have left the sinking ship, but loads of them managed to get ashore,' Sylvia said, also looking around the bar. 'So, I worry that the man I want to meet may have slipped back unnoticed into civilian life and I'll never find him.'

'Give me his name,' Molly said, reaching in her bag for her notebook and a pen. 'And let me take a copy of that photo. I'm an investigative reporter, goddammit! I can ask questions and dig around.'

Sylvia laughed, but she said, 'His name was Klaus Schäfer. But that's probably a common name. And you're welcome to take that print of Phyllis. I have plenty.' She knocked back the dregs of her Martini. 'What the hell? Let's throw caution to the wind and go for three!'

'You're on, lady,' Molly said, slamming her glass down on the table. 'Here's to catching the bastards any way we can.'

September 1950

Dear Miss Benson,

I have now completed my National Service, which fortunately saw me posted to Germany. Whenever I was on leave I did my best to visit the prisons and camps where my sister may have been held. I was not able to turn up any information about her fate, so I want to know if you have any more news for me. I really do think you owe it to my family to let us know what happened to Phyllis. I am realistic enough, after seeing those places for myself, to realise that she could never have survived, but I do feel we deserve to know exactly how and when she died. After all, if it hadn't been for you she would never have had the nerve to undertake such dangerous work in the first place.

I am about to take up my university place, where I shall be studying modern languages, including German. I should be grateful if you could contact me at the enclosed address.

Yours sincerely,

Humphrey Lane

FORTY-THREE

THE SILVER SCREEN

I've always enjoyed going to the pictures and seeing a film on a big screen. It's simply not the same watching a film at home on the telly now, is it? But out where Sylvia lived, we didn't have a cinema nearby, so it meant going to an afternoon performance in the nearest big town and a long drive back in the dark. But then a community group started showing films in the village hall once a month. We both liked that as it was cheaper and easier to get to. You didn't get popcorn or tubs of ice cream of course, but they had an interval with biscuits and cups of tea, so that was very nice.

We went quite a few times and saw some good films over the years. There was *Chariots of Fire*, I remember, oh and *A Room With a View*. That was lovely, as I've never been to Florence and am never likely to either. The seats in the hall weren't very comfortable though and I think in the end that was why we stopped going. Sylvia's back was getting quite bad by then. She'd definitely got osteoporosis and, even if we took a cushion to soften the chair, she couldn't bear to sit there for the whole length of most films.

So, then I had the idea that sometimes we'd watch a film at

home on TV and pretend we were in the cinema. I'd get us little bowls of popcorn, a chocolate or two and maybe a fizzy drink with a straw. Sylvia quite liked that for a while. I can't remember all the old films we saw that way, but often on a Saturday or Sunday afternoon, when everyone else was football mad, we'd watch an old film. *Gone With the Wind* was one of them, I think, and certainly *Great Expectations*, the really scary one with Abel Magwitch.

It worked all right for a while, but she was never that keen on films to do with the war. You'd have thought that with all her background in war work she'd have been interested, but she was quite funny about it. 'Huh, what do they know?' she'd say, getting all huffy about films like *The Great Escape* and *The Bridge on the River Kwai*. 'It was far worse than they could possibly imagine.' I quite enjoyed that kind of film as it showed another side of what had been going on. I mean, I'd been stuck underground all that time, making all sorts of bits and pieces, with no clue what my thingummyjigs were being used for, so I rather liked seeing what had been happening in other parts of the war. My war was just get up, go to work, trot down below and try and keep out of Lugg's dirty, groping hands.

Anyway, it was quite a nice habit we got into. Me bringing in our snacks and dimming the light and us both sitting there munching away, glued to the box. It was best if it was on the BBC channels because we didn't like being interrupted by commercial breaks. That's always so annoying if you're in the middle of a good bit.

It was all very well until one particular weekend, when Sylvia got really upset. She'd often moaned that the war films didn't show that women had had an important role to play too. So that Saturday, I thought she'd be pleased to know that a film about the sort of girls she'd worked with was showing. It was called *Carve Her Name With Pride* and was about a brave agent who'd eventually been caught and sadly got shot. I know it wasn't a happy ending, but it was meant to be a very good film, so I thought she'd like it.

Well, we sat down, all ready to enjoy ourselves, and we'd been watching for about half an hour when Sylvia suddenly stood up and turned the TV off. 'What are you doing?' I remember saying. 'I was just getting interested.'

'I can't watch it,' Sylvia said. 'It's too upsetting... My poor girls...' and she went upstairs and shut herself in her bedroom.

Quite honestly, I thought she was overreacting, so I turned it back on again and watched the whole thing. I know that sounds harsh, but I'd been looking forward to watching it and I was getting fed up with her frequent moods. I was all settled in my armchair with snacks and a drink, so I didn't see why I should give in to her.

But I kept the sound down low – well, as low as I could manage with my hearing, so it didn't disturb Sylvia. I assumed she was reading a book or having an afternoon nap, all the time she was up there. Well, in the end it was very upsetting, seeing the poor young female agent in it being killed in one of the concentration camps, but it was a very good film all the same.

When it finished, I called up the stairs to Sylvia and told her I'd make tea, just like we always had in the afternoon. I think we had a lemon drizzle cake that afternoon. One of the church ladies makes them all the time and sells them in aid of a refugee centre or something.

By the time she came down, I'd had one cup of tea and was starting to wonder whether I'd allow myself a second slice of cake. 'You took your time,' I said. 'Did you doze off?'

She just stared at me, then sat down. 'You've no idea,' she said. 'Those dreadful places. Nothing like that film, nothing at all.' She wouldn't touch the cake and barely sipped her tea. 'I've seen them,' she said. 'I went there.'

I looked at her. She was talking like I didn't know anything about those terrible places and the bodies, but I did. 'We all saw the newsreels, about Belsen and that,' I said. 'I know the camps were awful, I'm not ignorant.'

She stood up to leave the table. 'My poor girls. They should have been prisoners of war, not sent to one of those dreadful camps.'

I hadn't meant to upset her. I suppose I could never really understand. And I didn't know anyone who'd been in one of those places, while she had. We didn't do home cinema after that. It was a shame, because I'd quite enjoyed it.

FORTY-FOUR

PROOF OF IDENTITY

Where would I have started to look without the legendary German efficiency? Sylvia thought, as she sifted through the documentation retrieved from Dachau. Most of the prisoner files had been destroyed by the SS before liberation, along with police records, but she continued to work through the information until she came to the personnel section. Card after card contained the same kind of details. Date of birth, date of recruitment by the Party, official rank and a standard black and white photograph, unsmiling, eyes straight ahead.

One after another they stared at her with their cold, hard eyes, ready to do their duty. But did some do it more enthusiastically and willingly than others? Surely they couldn't all be war criminals? There must have been some who were there because they couldn't escape, because they were cowed, or simply because they kept their heads down and refused to notice the chaos and cruelty all around them.

And finally, she found him. There he was. A filed card for Klaus Schäfer, Gauleiter. Was his expression harder than the others'? Did his mouth look meaner? It was impossible to tell just from this single photograph, taken before it all began. In this picture he was young, light-haired, a good-looking boy who'd make any mother proud. And if his parents believed the myth that Dachau was a legitimate prison for political prisoners, then maybe he really had made his mother proud. With his Aryan looks he was an ideal example of the model young German man, moulded by the Hitler Youth to serve his country without question.

Sylvia studied the registration card and made notes that might lead her to his current whereabouts. He was born in Buchhorn, a small town near Heilbronn in the Baden-Württemberg region. Like many towns and villages throughout that area and indeed much of Bavaria, the resident population had largely supported the expulsion of Jews from their communities, starting with Kristallnacht, in November, 1938, when Jewish businesses and homes were attacked. Sylvia knew this meant that Schäfer, with his biased upbringing and education, would never have questioned the existence of concentration camps and would have considered them to be justifiable institutions. But what had made him so particularly cruel? Surely not everyone who had been brought up on a farm would treat human beings as less worthy of life than the animals they bred, nourished and slaughtered?

Sylvia studied the card she held, willing it to tell her more. Her contacts hadn't yet traced him. Maybe he had changed his appearance and his name, or had died in the upheaval that accompanied the advance of the Allies victory. But, she thought, the only way to learn more was to visit the area and see if she could find the farm where he had been born and to which he had possibly returned. Maybe that way, even if she couldn't actually find this man, she would gain some insight and know what she had to do next.

· · ·

The train from Munich travelled through gloriously green countryside where farms and vineyards flourished on the sunny slopes of the valleys. When she'd told Charles she was visiting the region, he'd said, 'Be sure to try the Trollinger-Lemberger wine while you are there, if you can. Most wine drinkers think Germany only has white wines and beer, but that region's red wine is outstanding.'

Sylvia made a mental note to bring back a bottle or two if she could, assuming the area was still capable of production after the travails of the last few years. On arriving at Heilbronn, she walked around the town to get her bearings. Like many other German cities and towns, there was considerable bomb damage, but remnants of the city's former grandeur were still in evidence. An ancient church boasted a fine octagonal tower and, at the town hall, workers were busy restoring the gilded astronomical clock above the imposing front entrance.

Many shops and businesses were still clearly struggling to get back on their feet, but Sylvia found the Ratskeller restaurant was open and welcoming visitors. It boasted of a fine selection of wines from its 700-year-old cellars. Sylvia thought they'd be lucky if the Allied forces had left them a decent stock in their cellar, but decided to have coffee rather than wine anyway as it was early in the day.

When the waiter took her order, she said, 'Do you know how I could get to the village of Buchhorn? There's a farm I want to visit out there.'

He shrugged and shook his head. 'Try the station. Get a taxi maybe.'

'The farm belongs to the Schäfer family. Do you know that name, by any chance?'

Again he shook his head. 'The driver might know, you will have to ask.'

Sylvia sipped her coffee and wondered what was the likelihood that she would discover anything at all. Perhaps this was the wrong way to uncover information about the man she was seeking, a man who might not want to be found. Better perhaps to see what help she could gain from the Americans now controlling the area and running the refugee camps they had set up nearby in two former German barracks, with the help of the United Nations Relief and Rehabilitation Administration.

After a short taxi ride, she arrived at Priesterwald, a temporary home to over three thousand displaced Polish people, all longing for visas to transport them to America or Canada rather than back to villages and towns that were now under Russian control. In the central administration office, she was welcomed and offered a tour of the facilities by the American woman in charge. 'Thanks, but what I think I need most,' Sylvia said, not wishing to seem ungrateful for her friendly offer, 'is some answers to my questions.'

'Fire away,' said the coordinator, who introduced herself as Ellen. 'I've been here since the end of last summer and it's a lot better now than it was, I can tell you for sure.' She offered Sylvia a seat in her office and poured them both coffee from a percolator bubbling on a camp stove beneath a framed picture of President Truman.

'I've come out here today because I have reason to believe that a guard who ill-treated one of my agents in Dachau may have returned to this area. He was born around here and his family had a farm in the region, possibly out at Buchhorn.'

'It's beautiful out there. Very good farming country, but some of the farmers are struggling to get going again as they've lost so many able men from their workforce.'

'I suppose it must be the same everywhere. So, I assume a fit young man would be welcomed back with open arms?' Sylvia unwrapped the Hershey bar Ellen had placed alongside her cup of coffee and took a small bite.

'They sure would. The farms round here are extremely productive, but only if they've got the manpower. They can grow just about everything and they're known for their wine too.'

'So I've heard.' Sylvia smiled. 'I'm hoping to take some back with me. I haven't tasted any yet, but I hear it's excellent.'

'It sure is. You must get some if you can. Our boys haven't quite drunk it all yet.' Ellen laughed, then said, 'You might not want to go out there alone though.'

'Really? I was hoping I might be able to borrow a car or get a lift out there. Do you think that would be a problem?'

'Not especially, but I'm guessing you haven't had much contact with ordinary Germans around here.'

'I suppose that's true. I've mostly been dealing with the authorities and any contacts they've found for me.' Sylvia was curious. Why was Ellen urging caution?

'Look, we all know that ordinary folk didn't always know what was really going on with the camps, however much they may have supported the expulsion of Jews from their communities. But much of the civilian population has suffered too. Their towns have been bombed, they've lost members of their own families and times are hard.' Ellen frowned. 'And now they're seeing all these displaced foreigners, the former camp prisoners and slave workers, who've been released and helped. They resent Ausländer, as they call them, being given better food rations than they're getting themselves. There's a lot of ill feeling when ordinary German families are struggling to feed their children.'

'I hadn't really thought about it like that. Is that giving you a lot of problems?'

Ellen looked weary and shook her head. 'It certainly doesn't help matters. Our residents here, at both this barracks and our other one, suffered terribly and blame and despise all Germans. That's quite understandable. Many of them were slave workers, who've lost their homes and families and were torn from their homelands. But because they were deprived for so long and were treated so badly, some of them have formed small gangs and gone out pilfering and dealing in the black market. It really doesn't help to calm the situation down.'

'I see. But I'm not one of the refugees, so why would I have trouble?'

'There's a whole lot of suspicion out there.' Ellen sighed. 'Families whose sons have returned are hardly going to welcome anyone who turns up to question them. People are feeling very uncomfortable. They've had a lot to put up with during the war years and now representatives of the occupying forces and aid agencies are coming along and asking them what they actually knew and what part they might have played in the atrocities.'

'I see what you mean. So, they're not going to be particularly pleased if I start wandering around, asking about a man who was a guard at Dachau, who I'm pretty sure is guilty of war crimes.'

Ellen shook her head. 'You're certainly not going to get them to cooperate. If he's crept back home to his family farm, they'll want to keep him hidden there, working. And if he hasn't made it home, they still won't help you. They'll say he was just a good boy, doing his duty and following orders. You won't get anywhere.'

Sylvia sighed and her shoulders sagged. 'It's beginning to look like a fruitless search, isn't it? Then I don't know how I'm ever going to find him.'

'It sounds like this really means something to you. Is it personal?'

'In a way. We lost someone and I feel it was down to me. In fact, we lost several and I know that one of my female agents ended up at Dachau. Every one of them matters, of course they do, but this girl in particular was really special. She was the youngest.'

Sylvia pulled the dog-eared photograph of Phyllis from her pocket. 'She was extremely capable and I blame myself and others in our organisation for her fate. I'm pretty sure she lost her life in the camp after brutal treatment from the man I'm seeking.'

'Sadly, many did. So many lives were tragically lost.'

Sylvia gazed at the creased image of Phyllis. Why did she matter so much to her? It seemed to her that this one girl was a distillation of all those who had sacrificed their lives to help the war effort. 'All the deaths are terrible, of course. But I'm pretty sure that this girl didn't die of starvation or disease. From what I've been told, I believe she died at the hands of this man, Klaus Schäfer.' Sylvia produced a copy of the identity card she had found on file.

'A nice-looking Aryan boy. So many of them were.' Ellen took in the image, shaking her head in disbelief. 'What on earth got into them? They weren't brought up to hate and kill, were they?'

'But they were brought up to think they were better,' Sylvia said. 'They believed in their superiority and their right to crush lesser beings.' She took in Schäfer's blank stare with those cold, hard eyes, twisting the empty Hershey bar wrapper in her fingers as if she was strangling his throat with her bare hands.

Ellen continued studying the two photographs: Phyllis with her optimistic smile and Schäfer with his icy glare. 'You mustn't give up,' she said. 'Tell you what, I've got some free time this afternoon. I'll give you a ride out to the farm. I think I know where it is. You might not find him, but it might help you feel you've covered every avenue.'

'Thank you,' Sylvia said. 'I'd kick myself if I didn't follow up every lead.' Yet again, she was thankful for American optimism. She knew there was only a slim chance, but it felt good to be doing all she could.

SPECIAL OPERATIONS EXECUTIVE MANUAL

COVER

1. DEFINITION

Your cover is the life that you outwardly lead in order to conceal the real purpose of your presence and the explanation that you give of your past and present.

N.B. Application of disguise is dealt with in a special lecture.

FORTY-FIVE

EVERYTHING BUT THE SQUEAL
SPRING 1947

After a simple lunch of fresh bread from the refugee centre's own bakery, with wholesome cabbage and potato soup that was far more nourishing than the thin gruel that had been dished out to the slave labourers for many years, Sylvia and Ellen set off by jeep into the surrounding countryside.

'Thanks for being so helpful,' Sylvia said as they drove towards the green hills, scattered with grazing dairy cattle.

'It makes a change to get away from the barracks. Maybe we'll pick up some fresh sausage or ham. The farmer's wives all do their own out here.' Ellen waved her hand towards the well-ordered farmsteads they passed on the road.

Soon they arrived at a property that looked a little more run-down than the others. Perhaps this was to be expected with a reduced manpower, Sylvia thought as they both jumped out of the jeep. She looked around, wondering where they should start and hoping she could keep her feelings under control if they found her man. If he turned up, she knew it would be best to leave his arrest to her contacts. Neither she nor Ellen was carrying a gun, although both were authorised to do so.

'I guess this is it,' Ellen said. 'As far as I know, this is the old Schäfer farm. Let's wander round and see who's at home.'

They started heading for the farmhouse, but then they heard a high-pitched scream that made both their heads whip round towards the barn. The squealing suddenly stopped and they saw a woman hanging a small pig from a hook in the barn doorway. As they watched, she slid a knife into its chest and a rivulet of blood spilled out and into a bucket below.

The two women stopped in their tracks. 'She's holding a knife,' Sylvia said. 'Maybe we should wait a minute.' Then a young girl emerged from the darkness of the barn with another large bucket and held it underneath the carcass, and the woman slid her knife into the animal's belly. With a helping hand, glistening guts slid out and into the container the girl was holding steady.

The woman turned to stare at her visitors. She bent down and cleaned her bloodied knife on a tussock of grass, slid it into her belt, then wiped her stained hands with her coarse, heavy apron. She turned to say a few words to the girl, who retreated into the barn with her bowl of intestines and offal, then took a couple of steps towards the outsiders. 'Was willst du?' she asked, not even bothering to use the polite form of the question.

'Frau Schäfer?' asked Ellen. 'Is Ihr Sohn Klaus zu Hause?'

Sylvia noticed how the woman's eyes narrowed and her right hand twitched towards her knife at the question about her son. 'Ask her if we can speak to him.'

Ellen took a breath to speak, but the woman was next. 'Klaus starb im Krieg. Hier sind keine Männer.'

'It's all right, I know what she's saying,' Sylvia said in a low voice. 'He's dead and there aren't any men here.'

'I told you they wouldn't be pleased to see us,' Ellen said. 'I think we'd better apologise for intruding on them and leave.' She spoke again in German, saying they were sorry for Frau Schäfer's loss and for the intrusion. The woman nodded but didn't smile, as she stood in front of the suspended carcass still slowly dripping blood into the bucket. The young girl came back out to stand by her mother's side but this time she was accompanied by another, taller and heftier girl holding a pitchfork like a pikestaff. The young girl had blonde hair braided into two long plaits, while the older one wore a kerchief that covered her head, almost down to her eyebrows. They were clearly related, all with the same unflinching expression that Sylvia recognised from the identity card she had discovered.

Sylvia took a few steps towards the jeep, but after a moment turned back to take another look at this family without men. The youngest girl was holding the pig's emptied intestines, which she was rinsing in water, presumably to use as sausage skins. But the older sister was standing to attention, on guard, glaring as they departed.

Ellen noticed too. 'A little more unfriendly than I'd expected,' she said. 'Usually the farms round here are keen to sell us some of their produce. And that was Spanferkel they were preparing. Suckling pig. They usually only do that for a celebration. Or maybe they'll offer it on the black market – they'd get a fair price for it at present.'

A celebration? What was there to celebrate? Or was a suckling pig the German equivalent of the fatted calf? A special meal to welcome home an errant son? Sylvia couldn't resist a final glance at the barn and the house as they pulled away. Who had they really just met? A tall, broad-shouldered daughter or a young man in disguise?

'What do you mean there's only one daughter?' Sylvia was frustrated by Charles's news when he phoned her at her hotel in Munich the following day.

'We met the mother and a young girl, but there was no sign of an older daughter. Frau Schäfer said her eldest girl, Lotte, had to go and look after an elderly aunt in the town. She gave us an address, but it turned out to be incorrect.'

'You mean they deliberately gave you false information?'

'Possibly. We couldn't find the place. It doesn't exist or no longer exists. Perhaps there was something before the war. I don't know.'

'So, if that was him in disguise, he's now gone?'

'I'm afraid so. No trace. And she still stuck to her original story, that she lost her son in the war.'

'Well, she would do, wouldn't she? If she was smart enough to hide him once he was home, she's not going to give him up now, is she?'

'I'm sorry to disappoint you, Sylvia. We'll keep an eye on the farm, in case he comes back, but he may well decide to stay clear for quite a while if that was indeed him.'

'Well, keep an eye out for a tall well-built blonde, will you? It would be funny if he felt he had to keep up his disguise. How would the girl-beater feel about that, eh?'

She could hear Charles laughing on the other end of the phone. 'All right. We're on the alert for a large badly dressed blonde with a red face. That could apply to half the hausfraus we come across! Look, we won't give up on this, but there are so many villains skulking around still, we may not be able to give it as much time as you'd like.'

'Thanks anyway. I just wish I'd realised when we were there, but it wasn't an easy situation and I wouldn't have wanted to put Ellen in an awkward position.'

As Charles rang off, Sylvia thought back to the moment it had occurred to her. If that really had been Klaus Schäfer, she and Ellen could easily have been skewered with his pitchfork. And as for his mother... she was still holding the knife that had killed and gutted the suckling pig.

June 1953

Dear Miss Benson,

I have now graduated in modern languages, including German, and am taking up a post with the diplomatic corps in Germany. I feel that this opportunity may bring me closer to finding out what actually happened to my sister Phyllis.

I am very disappointed that you have failed to keep me informed of any further searches you have undertaken. I assume you have continued to seek information and have not given up on trying to find the truth about my sister's fate. If it were in my power, I would expect you to continue your enquiries as a priority. After all, Phyllis would never have taken up that dangerous position if you had not persuaded her, so I hold you entirely responsible for the fact that she never returned to her family when the war ended.

I trust that the minute you have any fragment of news you will contact me. I shall not cease seeking information myself.

Yours sincerely,

Humphrey Lane

FORTY-SIX

IT'S ONLY THE POSTMAN

Oh my goodness, you wouldn't believe how jumpy Sylvia was as she got older. You'd have thought her hearing would have got less sharp, like mine, but she seemed to start at every bump and rattle. Gawd knows how many times she cried out to me in the dark because she thought she'd heard something. I never heard a thing, of course – I slept like a log every night. The great storm of 1987? Never heard it. Got up in the morning and couldn't believe my eyes. Rubbish thrown all over the streets, trees down in the park, a right mess.

So, really it was lucky that my ears were tuned in to Sylvia's cries for help. A bit like they say a mother is with a baby, I suppose, though she was an old lady and not a little mite. Oh yes, she was jumpy all right. Though I could never really understand why. I mean, there was two of us in the place and the cottage was all locked and barred. No one could get in at night. I was more worried that in an emergency, we'd have trouble getting out! What if there'd been a fire? We'd have had a right old time getting out of the cottage in a hurry with all those bolts and whatnot.

When I first started staying there, Sylvia was in the habit of taking the keys out of the doors when she locked up at night. I soon stopped that all right. I said, 'We can't go rummaging around in the dark for the right key if we need to get out in a hurry. You should leave them in the doors so we can unlock them quickly.'

She got quite huffy with me that time. 'How do you know someone won't try to fish the key out?' she said, with that look of hers. 'I've managed very well here so far on my own.'

But I got my way in the end, saying I couldn't be expected to know which key was which in an emergency and I think she saw sense then so I felt much more comfortable after that.

Now, where was I? Oh yes, her being jumpy and all that. I used to think, if you're going to take fright at every little noise, why come and live out here on your own in the first place? To my mind, she'd have been better off in a quiet town surrounded by neighbours who would look out for her. Out here in the countryside, well, the gamekeeper was her nearest neighbour, but he wasn't near enough to hear her scream now, was he? Anyway, half the time he's out with his dogs patrolling the pheasant pens in the summer, then letting them out for the shoots in the autumn, when he has to go out with the posh people who pay a fortune to come down here and dress up in their fancy tweeds and go off shooting.

We hear the guns sometimes in the season, from November to February, but it's quite distant and that never set Sylvia off. You'd have thought if someone was really nervous like that they'd be bothered by the sound of shooting, but it never seemed to upset her. It was always little things, like the postman. Sometimes if our regular postie had to knock at the door with a larger package, she'd look like she was having a heart attack. Nearly jumped out of her chair, she did.

I'd calm her down, of course. 'It's only the postman,' I'd say.

'Stay there, I'll go and see what he's got this time.' But she didn't seem to like regular post that got pushed through the letterbox either. Not that there was ever very much of it. She never got what I call ordinary post from friends and family. Oh, there were official brown envelopes from the electricity (she didn't have gas this far out in the countryside) and white ones from the council about this and that, but she never got what I'd call friendly, happy, normal post like most of us get. No cards on her birthday, no Christmas cards, no postcards even.

On the rare occasion when she did get a personal letter, it was always from London, handwritten, and she'd go quite pale. She'd snatch it from my hand just as I'd picked it all up the off the doormat and was putting it on the side table in the hall. She never said who it was from either. She'd turn away, go and sit in her little office at her desk and be very quiet for a bit.

I never saw her open those letters. She must have done it when I was busy in the kitchen or had popped out. So, I never saw what was in the envelopes. Could have been from an old boyfriend, for all I knew.

Thinking about it now, she was often a bit quieter than usual on a day when she'd had one of those letters. And she'd quite often go into one of her funny moods, staring out the window or muttering like she often did. Then every now and then, if it was daytime, she'd run out into the garden, trying to catch the pigeons that were always after the bird seed we put out. She'd bend low with her hands outstretched, but she'd never catch them. She'd mutter about carrier pigeons and messages, but anyone could see these birds were just a nuisance. They weren't trained pigeons, like my Uncle Jim had in cages in his backyard. He used to race them, so I should know.

I suppose I could have asked her who the letters were from, but she'd always get touchy if I asked personal stuff like that. And I respected her privacy, so I never questioned it. I might have had a sneaky look at the postmark now and then though, if she wasn't right by my side when the post arrived. The ones I was able to have a close look at showed they'd been posted in London, so that didn't mean anything, and I was still no clearer what it was all about. Maybe it was an old colleague from her working days. Or maybe an old flame, as I say. I'd like to think someone else cared for her and that I wasn't all she had.

4. CARRIER PIGEONS AND PHOTOGRAPHY

Pigeons offer a very useful method of communication; in conjunction with miniature or micro-photography very long messages can be sent by a single bird.

FORTY-SEVEN

WHAT'S IN THE POST?

How many dogs he'd acquired over the years she couldn't begin to guess. But they were always the same. Always a replica of Prinz, the gentle, faithful Great Dane she had known when she first met Charles, whom she came to know and love as Charlie.

By now, she was working for a trade delegation that made frequent trips to Germany and she always found time to see him in the restaurant he had established in the revived and thriving resort of Baden-Baden. 'Do you ever think we got them all, Charlie?' she said as they chatted over a gin and tonic, the latest incarnation of Prinz lounging at their feet in a grey velvet sprawl.

'I doubt it, my love. I think we only ever managed to pick up a fraction of the bastards. Just think of the thousands employed in the camps. Slippery buggers sloped back to their homes and their former jobs, half of them. The big fish got out of the country with their gains if they could. But we taught them a lesson when they saw what happened to those we caught. I'd like to think that none of them could ever rest easy in their beds for the rest of their lives, knowing what could happen if someone talked. I hope it gave them nightmares to the end of their days.'

'And what about those who did receive sentences?'

'It still sticks in my craw to think how some of them spent hardly any time in jail. Not much of a price to pay for what those sods inflicted on their prisoners.'

Sylvia emitted a despairing sigh. 'I feel the same way. All trying to cover themselves by claiming they were following orders. All excusing themselves and saying they didn't know the half of it. I can't bear it. I wish you'd been able to find more of them and dealt with it yourselves.'

Charlie raised an eyebrow as he said, 'We did our best. Still do, as a matter of fact. These days if I pick up a tip I liaise with the National Office for the Investigation of National Socialist Crimes. They're very thorough and legitimate. However, time will run out for their organisation one day as witnesses grow older. But they're determined to keep on going if they can, until the last war criminal and the last survivor have gone. They don't care how old or how frail the bastards are. If they can pin one on them, they'll prosecute. Even if it's a minor war crime compared to some of those brutes, it still reminds the world what that terrible regime organised and authorised.'

'But time will run out in the end, won't it? You and I might peg it before the last one is caught. And to think I once thought we had all the time in the world to put these things right.'

'You've got to live each day as if it's your last, my love.' Charles ran the tips of his fingers up the back of her neck and into her hair. 'I'd say you've made a pretty good fist of it so far.' He tilted the little diamond bird brooch pinned to the lapel of her grey suit so it flashed rainbow glints of fire. 'Little swift,' he said. 'I should call you Little Swift for that daring quicksilver mind of yours.'

She nuzzled her head back against his hand. It was so delicious returning to Baden-Baden, where Charlie was just the same as when she'd left his bed all those years ago. He had married, divorced and married again since she'd left, while she'd enjoyed hopping from bed to bed and never settled. 'I'm not staying for long this time,' she said, 'but there's something I'd like you to look into with your contacts, if you can.'

'Of course, my love. Anything for you. Someone you want me to track down?'

'The Magnet Men are still active, aren't they? You haven't lost interest, all of you?'

'Not at all. In fact, we've acquired a couple more members. Guys who've been fired up by knowing what happened to their relatives during those years of terror. You know how it is. For years there seems to be a dead end and then suddenly it's all there in front of you. It never ceases to shock and disturb me and my friends.'

The replacement for the original Prinz yawned and looked up at his master. 'My boy needs to stretch his legs for a bit,' Charles said. 'Let's do the same. We can carry on talking outside.'

They left their quiet table and strolled through the gardens in the glowing evening light. A deep red sunset was spreading beyond the forests, touching the iced mountain tops with a tint of rose. 'It's niggled me for years,' Sylvia said, snuggling her chin into the fur collar of her thick coat, 'that there was one last guard who dealt with Phyllis who I couldn't find. I had information that he was responsible for her care, or lack of it rather, in her last few weeks, but I've never been able to find him. I thought I'd tracked him to his family's farm, but that turned out to be a dead end. I can't believe he had the contacts or the means to slip out of the country and disappear, so I have to assume that he sneaked back into anonymity somewhere and is still in Germany.'

'Like many of the buggers did. Was that the one whose farm we checked out years ago? Up near Heilbronn?'

'That's right. Karl Schäfer, but he wasn't there. His mother claimed he'd died in the war, but I never found a record of that. He was a Gauleiter at Dachau, but so far I've never managed to pick up any more details.'

'I remember. The farm was being run by a woman and her daughters. His mother and sisters presumably. They'd restricted themselves to what they could manage without farmhands. A few dairy cattle and pigs. But by the time we got there, we could only find the one daughter.'

'I thought one of the girls we met the day I went there might have been Klaus if he'd been disguised.'

Charlie laughed. 'I remember now. You asked us to look out for a large, badly dressed blonde!'

'Yes, and I remember the pig,' Sylvia said, picturing the woman wiping her stained hands on her apron.

'What's that?'

'When I arrived there, they'd just slaughtered a suckling pig.'

'Aah yes, I think I remember you saying that at the time. A bit extravagant for a small household, I thought. But I seem to recall the woman saying they'd had a black-market order. Who could blame them? Times were still very hard back then.'

'I always wondered if I should have gone back there and tried again.'

'Probably best you didn't, my love. The locals could be very touchy in those days. There was a lot of resentment.'

Sylvia sighed. 'I know and then I couldn't stay any longer – I had to get back. But I've always wondered if she was telling the truth. It was the way she looked at us. She was so guarded and the fact that the older daughter had disappeared by the time you got there was suspicious.'

'Look, I can still ask around. We have links to a few Dachau witnesses. They keep their ears open too. And they're not choosy.'

'You mean they aren't particular about the consequences of their tip-offs?'

'Oh, they're particular all right. They particularly want to see those bastards getting their just deserts. And they don't much care what form it takes. It's always better of course if it's official and out in the open, because as time goes on people forget and start to doubt that hell ever happened. But if the course of justice doesn't run smooth, then they don't care as long as the culprits get punished somehow in the end.'

'How I love you, Charlie,' Sylvia said, clutching his arm and pressing herself against his firm, warm body, wrapped in thick sheepskin.

'Don't get too excited. I can't promise we'll get a result, but we'll certainly try. If you're sure he's still on your list, we'll take on the case.' He put his arm round her as they followed Prinz, who was trotting along the path dividing the frosty lawns. 'And may I ask why now? You've known about this guy for a long time, I assume?'

'I suppose I have. I just kept thinking another clue would crop up some time. I mean, I attended so many of the trials, read all the reports and I've spoken to many witnesses and staff from that ghastly place, so I suppose I always thought he'd turn up again.'

'But something's prompted you to try harder all of a sudden?'

Sylvia gave a little muffled laugh and nudged Charles with her elbow. 'You know me only too well.'

'I should hope so. How long has it been now? Twenty years?'

'We met in the winter of '46, so yes, nearly twenty years, Charlie, and you are still as handsome and charming as ever. It's only Prinz who's changed, although this one looks pretty damn close to the dog you had when we first met.'

'I stick to what I know and like, my lovely, you should know that. But don't change the subject. You're on a mission with this one, aren't you?'

Sylvia sighed and her breath clouded in the frosty evening air. 'She was always special. They all were, but Phyllis was exceptional. Talented, quick to learn, fearless and beautiful. And we let her down. That's what really sticks with me: we let her down badly.'

'I remember you saying. What did you call it at the time?'

'Probably departmental shenanigans, or something even less complimentary. Harrington and his cronies seemed to forget they were dealing with real live human beings, shuffling them around like chess pieces for their gratification.'

Charles hugged her tight. 'Some hurt more than others, don't they? But you mustn't blame yourself. There were others who made that call as well, weren't there?'

She hugged him back. He'd lost close friends. Actually seen them die. Been imprisoned and seen men beaten and shot in front of him. Everyone who'd fought and lived through the war had their ghosts. 'We're never going to be able to leave it behind us, are we?'

'Impossible to. But we can make the most of the time we have left.' He wrapped her in his arms and kissed her left ear, his breath warming and tickling her. 'We should go back, Prinz will start hunting for his supper soon. You can tell me more over dinner.'

Charles's efficient but expressionless maître'd took their order and left them to sip chilled Gewürztraminer while they waited for their food. 'Now come on,' Charles said. 'You haven't finished telling me what's really going on. I can tell something else is bugging you.'

Her fingertip traced the condensation on the side of the

cold glass. 'I've been getting letters and they're making me feel uneasy.'

'From whom?'

'Phyllis's younger brother. He came to see me once before the office finally closed. That was shortly after you and I first met. By then I knew it was unlikely there'd ever be any good news about her.'

'And you're telling me you're still getting letters after all this time?'

'Yes. He's been sending them for years. I get unsigned ones too. But I can tell they're still from him.'

'Saying what exactly? Are they threatening?'

She shook her head. 'No, not specifically. They all make out that I'm to blame for Phyllis never being found. Well, to be more accurate, he blames me for encouraging her to join us and go out to France in the first place.'

'But she was a willing adult. She was fully prepared.'

'I know, but that doesn't stop him or anyone else from thinking that she was put under pressure to sign up and wasn't told exactly how dangerous it would be.'

'And he holds you responsible?'

'It would seem so. He says she was only convinced she could do the job because of me. I have a feeling she may have told him more about me than she should have done.'

'Well, you are a very persuasive woman, Sylvia.' Charles poured more of their wine and slipped the bottle back into the ice bucket.

'No, please don't joke about it, Charlie. You don't know how guilty I feel. When I stop to think about it, I really do wonder if she only went because I made her think she'd be invincible.'

'Can't you just ignore these letters?'

She frowned. 'They've got under my skin. He keeps pointing out what she has missed by losing her life so young. They imply she was sacrificed.'

Charles clasped her hand. 'You mustn't worry about it. That sounds like crank stuff. We only did what we had to do. Those were desperate times, remember.'

'But it's true, Charlie, I do feel as if she was sacrificed.' Sylvia bit her lip. 'I really do feel guilty.'

'You mustn't, darling, you were following orders and she was a volunteer. What happened was way beyond your control.'

She sighed. 'Oh, I know. If anybody's to blame, it's Harrington. And it's too late to point the finger at him.' Sylvia hadn't mourned his passing, five years after the war ended, but she bitterly regretted him not being castigated for his calculating manipulation of agents, which increased the risk and definitely sent many to their deaths.

'But you did your duty, Sylvia. And you did it well.'

'Huh, that doesn't make me feel any better, Charlie. Like the brutes I'm trying to seek, we can all claim we were only following orders. That doesn't sit very well with me.'

Plates of sizzling, golden Wienerschnitzel, served with creamy potato salad, were slid in front of them. Charles attacked his veal cutlet with enthusiasm, but Sylvia stared at her food, thinking that she had little appetite now.

SPECIAL OPERATIONS EXECUTIVE MANUAL
COUNTER-MEASURES

B) DURING QUESTIONING

xv) Beware of apparently foolish interrogator of whom you may think you have got the better. This may be a trap to tempt you to boast of your cleverness in circumstances where your boastings will be reported.

FORTY-EIGHT

AFFAIRS OF STATE

Once Sylvia had to be moved into the hospice I visited her every day, of course. I'd hoped she could stay in the cottage right to the end, but her doctor said it really wasn't suitable. I'd been doing my best, trying to give her a bed bath and deal with all the necessary and that, but it's very difficult when someone becomes more or less bedbound. I was up and down those stairs umpteen times a day and it was very awkward for the bathroom, of course.

I should know, because I looked after Harry for as long as I could, until he had to go into hospital. That was nowhere near as calm as the hospice though. In hospitals they can't keep the noise down – there's always people running around, other patients buzzing and calling out and all sorts every hour of the day and night. And you don't want that kind of disturbance in your final days, do you? Peace and quiet is what you need, so we decided that was what Sylvia should have.

She had to be taken there by ambulance, because she couldn't manage to walk more than a couple of steps by then. I followed in the car so I could come back here again afterwards. And she was soon settled in her room – a lovely room it was too

– overlooking the garden of the hospice, with the last of the dahlias brightening up the flowerbeds. Then, once she was comfortable and tucked up in her bed, she grabbed my wrist and said, 'My affairs, Peg. You've got to sort out my affairs. I can't leave things the way they are.'

'But you're all sorted, aren't you? With the solicitor and that?' I knew everything was in order, because her solicitor, a lovely girl called Jane something, had been to the cottage weeks before to get Sylvia to sign over power of attorney to me. I didn't want to do it really, but Jane said Sylv had to do it while she could and it was better that someone who knew her really well had the job. So that all got signed and her will was handed over so she couldn't make any more changes to it, at least I think that's what it was. So, as far as I was concerned, her affairs already were in order.

'You don't need to worry about this, Sylv,' I said. 'You did all that when Jane came to the cottage, remember? There's nothing more to be done, dear.'

'Of course I remember her coming,' she snapped at me. 'My body may be falling apart, but not my mind.' She was often a bit tetchy towards the end, but I always ignored it because she couldn't help being irritable because of the pain and so on. Then she said, 'There are lots of other important things Jane has had nothing whatsoever to do with. All my letters and papers. You're not to look at them, but I want you to destroy the whole lot of them.'

'And where will I find all of this, Sylv?'

'In my office of course, darling. You know, where all my files are.'

Well, I knew about those, obviously, but I'd hardly call it an office. It was more like a dingy cubbyhole under the stairs and it was chock-full of stuff. I think I sighed and rolled my eyes and said, 'What, you mean you want me to deal with all of that?'

'Yes, all of it, darling. I don't want anyone seeing any of it.

Not a single word.' She gave me such a look when she said that. Really fierce, her blue eyes looking almost more blue than they ever had.

'Are you quite sure, Sylv? Why don't I bring all that stuff here so you can check it over first?' She'd never let me touch her files before, so I wanted to be sure she wasn't going to change her mind all over again and get upset with me.

'I'm absolutely sure about this, Peg. I'm not going to be around for very much longer, darling, and it would be a great help to me if you would deal with all of it. I can't trust anyone else.'

'So, you're saying I've got to get rid of all your files and all the papers in your bureau? You've got an awful lot piled up in there and I can't exactly go having a bonfire, can I?'

We both knew that the insurance for the cottage didn't let you have a bonfire in the garden because of the thatched roof. Barry was always saying it would be all right, because he'd keep a close eye on the fire. He was quite miffed that he couldn't burn all the leaves he had to sweep up around the place. They either had to go on the compost heap or be packed in black bags to break down for leaf litter he could use a year or so later on the garden. But Sylvia was very firm with him and said there was no way he was going to go lighting bonfires while she was around. I half wondered if I could leave the files and that until she'd passed away, and ask Barry to do it all for me, but then I thought that wouldn't be right because she'd said no one else should see any of these papers.

'Well then, you'll just have to have a big fire indoors, darling. You're very good at lighting fires, aren't you?' Sylvia laid her head back on the big, propped-up pillows, closed her eyes and in a weary voice, as if she no longer had the energy to argue, said, 'Oh, just do it for me, Peg, darling, do it for my peace of mind.'

How could I refuse? She seemed so certain it should be

done that I said, 'Of course I will, dear. I'll have a lovely big fire tonight and see how much I can get rid of. It will keep me nice and warm.' The nights had started to turn colder and we had a fire every night anyway.

So that evening I laid the fire as usual and lit it, then sat down beside it in the armchair with a small glass of sherry. It didn't seem as cosy as it usually did, without Sylvia there beside me talking nonsense. Even in the last few days, when she was bedridden, I'd sit upstairs in her room with her and we'd have our evening drink. I sipped my sherry, then remembered I was meant to be burning her papers, not knocking back the Amontillado. The fire was going well, so I thought I'd let it burn for a bit while I enjoyed my drink and then I'd start doing as she'd asked.

After a while I went across to her bureau, pulled down the lid and rested it on the wooden props that slide out alongside the drawers. *Oh my goodness*, I thought, seeing the amount of paper stuffed into every cubbyhole. *There's tons of it. I'm not going to get all this, and the files as well, burned up in one night. I'm going to be at it for days.*

I knew it was going to take quite a while to get the job done, because Sylvia had always said she'd been told that you mustn't burn huge amounts of paper on a fire in a thatched cottage. 'Fragments of paper can fly up the chimney,' she said. 'They can settle on the thatch and start a fire. You have to do it little by little.' She said that every Christmas after we'd unwrapped our presents and wanted to get rid of the gift wrap. 'Not too much at a time, Peg,' she'd always say, as I was pushing starry paper into the flames.

And so I remembered that and thought I'd take just one bundle of papers out of the desk to start with and begin putting them on the fire. I could see straight away that they were all those handwritten letters she used to get, opened but still in their envelopes, and, although she'd said I wasn't to read anything, I couldn't resist taking a little peek.

I mean, she wasn't going to know, was she? But I rather wish I hadn't. I suppose I thought they might have been love letters. Naughty of me, I know, but it would have been nice to know she'd had some fun in her life. So, I took out the first letter and I could see it was fairly recent. I was pretty sure it was one of the letters she always grabbed from me and scuttled away with when they came. And oh, my goodness, it was nasty. Really nasty. *Poor Sylvia*, I thought, *you didn't deserve this in your condition*. The writer obviously had no idea she was so poorly. I felt so sorry for Sylvia, having to read this sort of thing at her time of life.

And having opened one of them, well I couldn't stop there, could I? Such spite, every single one of them, one after another. *Poor Sylvia*, I thought. *You poor girl, to be so hated, when all you'd tried to do was your duty*. They were mostly all from the same man and I could see that even the unsigned ones were from him, because of the handwriting.

I felt quite shaky when I'd finished opening them all, sitting there with the letters in my lap, wondering if I should still burn them. It was criminal, I thought, these horrible letters accusing her of causing this girl Phyllis's death. Really awful. How could someone be so disgusting, hounding a woman of Sylvia's age?

I half wondered whether to ring Jane, her solicitor, in the morning and ask whether there were grounds for prosecution. But then I stopped myself. *Peg*, I thought, *you've had your instructions from Sylvia. She said no one was to read her papers. So, you must do as you're told. Put them on the fire.* So, I did, one by one, I watched them all catch alight, curl and blacken.

And soon those wicked words were ash.

July 1969

Dear Miss Benson,

I wonder if you found that the moon landing provoked thoughts similar to the ones I experienced on hearing this momentous news? I watched the television broadcast and my thoughts turned to my darling sister Phyllis. I then went outside that night to gaze upon the moon and wondered how the spacecraft could have landed when it was a waxing moon and only a sliver of light was visible from Earth.

And then that sight reminded me that you sent Phyllis off on a night of the full moon. She would have seen that silver disc in the sky as she flew away from us forever. Was she frightened then, or thrilled by the idea of the adventure you had sold her? And if she was still alive, what would she have thought of this tremendous news of man's achievement? Would she have even recognised it as an achievement at all, when she risked her life to end a war yet war is still all around us? I know the current conflict in Vietnam would have saddened her deeply, she was such a sensitive, kind girl.

So more than ever it feels to me that she was sacrificed in vain. You sent her to do an impossible job she could never have accomplished, however well you thought you had trained her and however much she tried. How can you live with yourself, knowing that she was sacrificed?

Yours sincerely,

Humphrey Lane

FORTY-NINE
A WATCHER
NOVEMBER 1965

Sylvia woke to the sound of Prinz the fourth or fifth scratching at the bedroom door. She slid out of bed to let him in, wondering if she would be the one to take him out for his morning walk, just as she had done with Charlie's original dog all those years ago.

Prinz padded over to the bed and nudged his master's elbow with his wet nose. Charles was startled into waking. He fondled the giant dog's ears. 'What time it is?' He yawned and stretched.

'Breakfast time, I should think,' Sylvia said. 'At least Prinz seems to think so. Do you want me to take him out?'

'No, I'd better go. I promised Gregor I'd look in first thing at the restaurant this morning. I can grab toast and coffee there. Will you be around later?'

'I'm not leaving till tomorrow. But you don't have to keep the evening free for me again tonight.'

He grabbed her wrist and pulled her towards him, so she lost her balance and landed on the bed in his arms. 'We must continue our conversation. And I want you to enjoy your dinner tonight. Promise me you'll join me again in the restaurant.'

She knew Charles had noticed she couldn't enjoy her food the night before. And she usually had such a good appetite – for all things. 'I'll be there,' she said, spinning away from him and into the bathroom.

That evening, Charles looked unusually serious. 'I've been thinking about what you said last night. About the letters and so on.'

Sylvia shrugged. 'Oh, forget it. I shouldn't have told you. It's just silly nonsense.'

'No, it's not. Anything that unsettles you bothers me. Even if there's no foundation to it, these letters are making you nervous. I can see that. Anyone would feel unnerved getting stuff like that. You get them at the office, I take it?'

'Well, yes, but...'

'But what? Your home address?'

She nodded. 'The office has moved around for a start, but it's not surprising that letters to my old work address would eventually find me there. However, I'm not at all happy about receiving such letters at home. I don't know how he's managed to get hold of my addresses.'

'You mean you've moved house and this brother has still found you?'

'Letters signed by him are forwarded through the office. It's the unsigned ones that go to my home address and I've moved three times.'

'That does it. You're being stalked, Sylvia. I've been thinking about it all day, but this is even more worrying than I thought. Have you ever noticed anyone hanging around or following you?'

She playfully tapped his hand. 'I get followed all the time, even at my age, Charlie!'

He grasped her hand and held it tight. 'This isn't a joke, my love. I'm being serious here. This doesn't feel right.'

'Well, no, I haven't noticed anyone, as a matter of fact.' She let him keep her hand in his. 'I used to have men following me all the time, but maybe I'm no longer attractive.'

He shook his head, then kissed her cheek. 'You'll never stop being gorgeous, my love.'

'But seriously, when I've moved house I've been very careful only to leave the office as a forwarding address. I use that for most of my post too and I have a poste restante for other items from time to time. I'm well aware of tradecraft, Charlie, and I haven't forgotten how to throw someone off the scent.'

'But this person or persons isn't being put off, are they? And it's making you jittery, isn't it?'

'Yes, it is rather. But I didn't come here to talk about this. I'd rather concentrate on getting a lead on my elusive Schäfer.'

'I'll come to him in a minute. In the meantime, when you get back to the UK I will put you in touch with a very good friend of mine. I want you to have some protection.'

'Oh, Charlie dear, are you getting a dog for me? I couldn't possibly. I'm out all day, the poor thing would pine.' She knew this wasn't his meaning, but she wanted to lighten the tone and thought it might amuse him.

'No, I'm thinking of a bodyguard, at least a part-time one. And I won't take no for an answer.'

'Very well. If it makes you happy.'

'It does. And now for your Herr Schäfer.' Charles brought out a notebook. 'I've a name and address here for you. This fellow says he knew of him.' He ripped out a page. 'This is where you can find him. I could follow it up for you, if you like, but I thought you might like to do it yourself as this task is some-what personal for you.'

Sylvia stared at the single name and address scribbled on the paper. Personal? It was utterly tragic, that was what it amounted to. Such a waste of a vibrant life. She thought of Phyllis every time she used her powder compact. She sometimes wondered if she should have handed it over to the girl's brother as part of her personal effects, but she liked to think it was a connection with her, both of them glancing into that round bevelled mirror every time they powdered their noses or reapplied their lipstick.

'Interesting,' she said. 'He's based in Reutlingen. I think I could arrange to meet my trade contacts in Stuttgart to justify an extra couple of days.'

'Would you like me to come with you?' His hand, lightly squeezing her arm, implied that he'd happily slip away for a day or two if she was booking a hotel.

'I'll be fine on my own, Charlie. I can drive there. It won't take more than an hour and a half. Besides, isn't it about time you caught up with your wife?' Sylvia laughed, wagging her finger at him. 'You haven't been home since I arrived, have you?'

He pulled a comical face. 'Guess I'd better. I can't afford another divorce.'

The next day Sylvia parked in the centre of Reutlingen, near to where her contact lived. The town had been largely rebuilt after the war and had little of the charm of nearby Tübingen, a university town that had retained many of its fifteenth-century buildings. Knocking on the door of the address on the slip of paper Charles had handed to her, she prepared herself for an inconclusive dead end. There had been so many over the years and the chances were that this would be yet another one.

The door was answered by a bent, grey-haired man, his face etched with lines. This was her contact, Stefan Schmidt. 'You are the Englishwoman?' His voice was whispery, as if it hadn't been used in a while. 'You will come in, please?'

Sylvia entered the dim, sparsely furnished flat; the warmth

was stifling and it smelt as if the dust of many years had collected in the air, alongside the smoke of many cigarettes. Stefan led the way towards a crumpled, stained sofa and an armchair from which he removed a stack of newspapers. She opted for the armchair.

'Thank you for agreeing to see me,' she said. 'I really appreciate your help and I'm sorry to have to ask you questions about your time in prison. I mean, in Dachau.'

'It wasn't a prison, it was hell. For all of us. Sometimes I think I was unlucky to survive.'

'Why do you say that, Stefan?'

'Because I am still alive, I have to remember that time. I can never forget. It lives with me every day.' He bared his arm to show her the indelible numbers inked onto his skin. His wrinkled flesh still showed the mark with clarity and, as he pulled the sleeve of his stained and pilled sweater back down, Sylvia thought he looked as crumpled as his sofa, slumping into the sagging cushions.

'How old were you when you went there?'

'Twenty-three. I was an engineer. But they didn't like the look of me or my friends.' He reached for a pack of cigarettes, his hands trembling.

Sylvia did a quick calculation and was shocked. He was only forty-seven years of age; he looked so very much older. The punishing conditions of the camp had done their worst to him, she supposed. And one day he and other witnesses to the horrors would be no more. She was lucky Charlie's network had tracked down this witness for her.

'I've been told that you might remember a guard from that time. I believe he went by the name of Schäfer.'

Stefan seemed to wince at the sound of the name. 'Your friends were asking about him. I knew him all right but I wish I'd never met him.'

'Did you ever learn anything about him? His family? His

home town?' She willed him to remember, much as he wanted to forget.

'Nasty piece of work, he was. All I learnt about him was that he was the cruellest bastard there and that's saying something, given they were all merciless.' He took short, nervous puffs of his cigarette, then remembered to hold the pack out to Sylvia.

Sylvia waived his offer and wondered whether this was the moment for her to produce her photo of Phyllis. Was there a chance that a studio portrait of a beautiful girl might prompt his memory? By the time she was taken to that notorious camp she must have been filthy, starved and beaten. She might have borne no resemblance to her picture.

'I'm trying to find out what happened to one of my special recruits,' she said. 'Her name was Phyllis, but she might still have been calling herself Simone at that time. She should have been treated as a prisoner of war, but that never happened to any of our secret agents. And I'm fairly certain she ended up in the camp around the time you were there. Schäfer's name has already been mentioned to me in connection with her, so if you know anything about him it might help.'

'Poor girl. If she ended up in his hands, she didn't stand much chance.' Stefan stubbed his cigarette out in the overflowing ashtray, pushed himself out of the collapsed cushions and shuffled towards the little kitchen area. He busied himself for a few minutes, crockery chinking, then returned with two cups of coffee and set one down in front of Sylvia, after sweeping the low table's litter of circulars and magazines onto the floor.

She sipped the tepid grey liquid, just to buy a few minutes while he settled himself again. After a moment, she said, 'Did you ever see him ill-treating prisoners?'

He cradled the cup in his hands. She noticed his nails and cuticles were bitten down. 'I can show you a picture of the girl

I'm interested in,' she went on. 'But I know she probably looked very unlike this by the time she reached the camp.' She slid the photograph onto the table between them and turned it the right way round so Phyllis could beam her enchanting smile upon this broken man.

Stefan put down his cup, stared at the image and sighed. 'I never saw anything as beautiful as her in all my time there. We didn't see many women in my section, so I'm sure I would have noticed her, even though women were not for me.'

Sylvia caught his hint. So that was why he was sent to Dachau. 'I'm sorry. I realise that she would have been much changed by the time she was transferred there.' She left the print in front of him for a few moments longer, then slid it back towards herself. As she picked it up to return it to her file, she heard a slight sucking, tearing sound as it peeled away from the table's sticky surface.

'He had it in for everyone, Schäfer did, no matter who they were, especially men like me. Your girl's beauty wouldn't have stopped him, if she even still had it by then. If she'd been attractive, he would have enjoyed ruining her looks.'

Sylvia felt a shudder run down her spine. She wanted answers, but she knew she would never be happy with what she heard. 'I'd like to find him if I can. Do you have any ideas? Can you offer me any clues?'

'I believe he was a country boy. From a farming family, somewhere not too far away.'

'Is that all you can tell me?'

'He bragged about how he liked working in the slaughter-house and how good he was at castrating lambs and pigs. It was his speciality.'

Stefan's face twisted and Sylvia thought she could guess what he was about to say and almost couldn't bear to hear him say it. 'So, is that what he did to you?'

He nodded, twisting his hands and reaching for another

cigarette. 'He boasted about it. He said he had special tools on the farm but, failing that, a few kicks in the right direction with his steel-capped boots would do the trick in the camp. He said my kind deserved it. He enjoyed destroying men's power to be proper men, but knowing his talent for cruelty I should think he was quite capable of destroying women too.'

Sylvia closed her eyes for a moment, trying to dispel the image of Phyllis being kicked by this sadist. 'You've been most helpful. Is there anything else you can remember that might help me find this brute?'

Stefan shook another cigarette from the crumpled pack. 'There was one thing. It was odd for a man of his character and background. He liked Black Russian cigarettes. The expensive ones. You could smell them on him. Strange, that.'

FIFTY

SMOKESCREEN

I know loads of people who've never managed to kick their smoking habit, but honestly, once there started to be health warnings about cigarettes, I couldn't touch them any more. The thought of slowly killing myself put me right off, which I suppose was the whole point really. Not that I'd ever smoked much, mind. It was only ever the odd one, now and then. But it was quite a nice way to relax, in my armchair after work, with a cuppa and a copy of *Woman's Realm*.

Sylvia and I smoked our first fags when we were quite young. I should think we were around eleven or so. Everyone who could afford to smoked in those days. It was just about the most popular pastime there was, apart from you-know-what.

As my parents had the sweetshop, which also sold tobacco and ciggies, I'd nicked some cigarette papers, and me and Sylv would roll them up with various fillings and pretend we were smoking. We had a go with dried grass first, but that just burst into flames and we nearly burned our fingers. We had more success with raspberry leaves, but we knew we were just posing and it wasn't the real thing. Then, when my old dad found out what we'd been doing, he said, 'If you really want to smoke, don't mess about like that, have a proper cigarette. Here, have a Woodbine.' So, I tried it and didn't really like it.

I'd say that Sylv probably smoked more than I ever did, later on when we were working. She said it was because of her job and that everyone around her smoked. Well, I think everyone around me smoked too, but because we were on the machines all the time in the factory, we could hardly chain-smoke like she maybe could. We could only do it in our breaks, which weren't often enough for my liking. And we never smoked anything fancy, it was Woodbines mostly, same as our fellas got in their army rations. Quite a few of the girls went on to roll-ups as it was cheaper, but I always preferred taking a clean fag out of a packet. That whole business of rolling your own never seemed very ladylike to me.

And talking of ladies, Sylv was a one, she really was. One time, in her early or mid-teens it must have been, she turned up with a cigarette holder. I ask you! We didn't see many of those round Ilford and Gants Hill. I reckon she must have pinched it from her mother. It was a very theatrical thing and, her being on the stage and all that, I think that's where it must have come from.

And another time she turned up with Sobranie Black Russians and those she did admit she'd nicked from the theatre, from someone she said was making a nuisance of himself. Whether he was pestering her or her mother, I couldn't quite work out, but we both enjoyed posing with our smelly black cigarettes, until we realised our fingers were turning green with the paper. My mum complained about the smell too, saying it was like a damp bonfire, but me and Sylv both thought they smelt lovely, like a mixture of treacle and Bourneville dark chocolate.

Oh, we thought we were being so clever, but the best time

was when Sylv came round to mine one Christmas with the prettiest box of coloured cigarettes. I'd never seen anything so beautiful before, these slender gold-tipped ciggies in brilliant turquoise, pink and mauve. I remember asking her, 'Can we really smoke them?' We'd never ever had anything glamorous like that in my mum and dad's shop.

'Oh yes,' she said. 'They're still proper cigarettes. Mother's new boyfriend gave them to her for Christmas, but he's given her loads of other stuff too, so she'll never miss these. Mother says they're cocktail cigarettes. She smokes this sort when she's having drinks with her friends. Anyway, she's got to cut down on smoking now. The director says her voice is soon going to be too deep and husky to ever play Ophelia again.'

I didn't really know then what she was talking about, but I loved taking one of those pretty cigarettes between my fingers and pretending I was an elegant lady. I was far from that though, with my bitten nails and rough skin, ingrained with dirt from sweeping up in the shop. They were much worse later of course, when I was handling oily machinery all day long at Plesseys. Looked like a garage mechanic I did, especially when I came home from the factory, my hair tied up in a scarf, wearing grubby overalls. I don't think even a fancy, coloured cigarette and a cocktail could have made me look sophisticated then.

But Sylv was always sophisticated, right up to the end. And I think sometimes she remembered those days when we put on airs and pretended to be grown up. Perhaps she always was. Funny the things you remember. Only last Christmas, which turned out to be her last, in fact, she suddenly said, 'Ooh, Peg, let's put Sobranie on our delivery order. You'd like that, wouldn't you? It would be like old times.'

I was lost there for a minute. 'Sobranie? What's that when he's at home?'

'Cigarettes, darling. You remember, the lovely coloured ones with gold tips we had when we were young.'

In the end, she couldn't get them on her supermarket order and after moaning about it for a few days, she forgot all about it. But I hadn't forgotten and I looked in the shops in the nearest town, but couldn't find them there either. So, one day when Barry came round to clear out the gutters, I asked him while he was up the ladder, 'Where do you think I could get Sobranie cigarettes? Sylvia would love to smoke them again, just for old times' sake.'

'I'll ask around,' he said. 'I've got a mate who can get hold of anything. If he can't find it in this country, he knows a bloke who drives a lorry.'

And would you believe it, a few days before Christmas that year, he sneaked his head round the kitchen door one morning and said, 'You're in luck. How many d'you want?'

'How many what?' I said, because I couldn't think what he was on about and I was busy washing up the pans from the night before. I always leave them in to soak till the morning. I'd burned the custard, so that pan needed a good old soak.

'Your foreign fags,' he said, with a rather leery wink. 'How many?'

'Oh, just one pack will do. Your mate managed to get some then?'

'Yeah, he's given me a whole box. But don't worry, I can sell the rest down the pub. They're not available over here now. Come all the way from the Ukraine, these have.'

I peeled off my rubber gloves and wiped my hands on a tea towel and slipped outside with him. I didn't want Sylvia seeing because I wanted to give her them as a surprise for Christmas, see, so I slipped down the path to Barry's car with him. His car is the one thing he keeps really clean. Always surprises me, but it's his pride and joy.

'There you are,' he said, peeling back the cellophane on the big package. I stared at the packs inside. 'But they're not coloured,' I said.

'Yes, they are,' he said. 'They're black and gold.'

'Couldn't he get the pretty ones in different colours?'

'Well, you should have said, shouldn't you? All I heard you say was Sobranie and these are Sobranie Black Russian. These are really special. You can't get them over here now. Do you want them or don't you?'

I hesitated a moment, but then I remembered the lovely smell of the Black Russians me and Sylv had smoked in her bedroom all those years ago. 'Oh, go on then, I'll take them,' I said. 'In fact, I'll take two packs.' I can't quite remember what they cost, but I think it was an arm and a leg compared to ordinary Player's or what-have-you.

I was quite pleased with myself that Christmas, thinking it would be a nice surprise for Sylvia. I wrapped them in paper covered in stars and tied a red ribbon round the package. But when she opened it, she stared at them as if she didn't understand what they were.

'I thought as we couldn't get the coloured ones, we'd have these,' I said, hastily trying to make it all right. 'You remember. We smoked these once up in your bedroom, back in Ilford years ago.'

She picked one out of the box and sniffed it, wrinkling her nose. I thought she'd remember the smell if nothing else. 'I'll get the table lighter,' I said. She had this rather grand Wedgwood cigarette lighter that was kept in a china cabinet. It was very pretty, being that special pale blue with white decoration, like an iced cake. It still worked, though I wasn't sure at first as it hadn't been used in goodness knows how long. So, I flicked it and the flame perked up so she could lean forward and light her cigarette.

I lit one too, just for old times' sake, though I knew I wasn't going to try to inhale it. Soon the room was filled with that very strange strong smell and I thought what we needed was a little drink to go with it. So, I said, 'Do you fancy a little glass of some-thing, Sylv, to celebrate?'

'What are we celebrating?'

'Years of friendship,' I said. 'Think how long ago it was that we first tried to smoke Black Russians. And I've got a treat for us too. We won't have sherry like we always do, I thought we'd have gin and Dubonnet, just like the Queen Mother does. You stay right there and I'll be back in a tick.'

I had to go back out to the kitchen, because Sylvia's never had a drinks cabinet in the sitting room. The drinks bottles are all lined up at the back of the worktop, along with orange squash and Robinson's Barley Water. I mixed our drinks and went back in to give a glass to her. But honestly, when I saw what she was doing, I nearly dropped it, I was that shocked. There she was, staring at the glowing end of her Black Russian, with her left hand held out. And as I watched, she brought the burning cigarette close to her hand, holding it about an inch above her skin.

'Sylv, whatever are you doing?' I said. 'For goodness' sake, be careful. You don't want to burn yourself, you silly thing.'

I remember her staring at me, still holding the cigarette in her hand and saying, 'He smoked these. And he burned her. I was wondering how much it would hurt.'

'Well, I don't want you burning yourself now, do I? If you're not going to smoke it properly, you'd better stub it out.'

She stared at it again and I could see she couldn't decide what to do with it. So, I thought I couldn't hang about waiting until she made up her mind and I snatched it away from her and threw it in the fire. Then I noticed that mine was still burning in the glass ashtray where I'd left it when I'd gone to get the drinks, so I threw that on the fire as well. I wasn't taking any more chances. I thought I'd better chuck the rest of the packs later when she wasn't looking.

'Cheers,' I said. 'Let's toast the Queen and the Queen Mum,' and I gave her the glass.

Sylvia sipped it cautiously, then took a larger sip and a smile slowly spread. 'Delicious, darling. Good old Queen Mum,' she said. 'Cin-cin.'

SPECIAL OPERATIONS EXECUTIVE MANUAL

SURVEILLANCE

A. INTRODUCTION

Surveillance is the keeping of someone under observation
without his knowledge.

FIFTY-ONE
HAVING A BUTCHER'S
AUTUMN 1972

'Good news,' Charlie said when Sylvia answered the phone in London. 'We think we've finally found him. We've tracked down your man at last. What do you want us to do?'

'You mean Schäfer? How can you be quite so sure it's him?' Sylvia felt her heart skip a beat at the news. After all this time? Really? At last, a chance to avenge the lovely Phyllis?

'It seems he's been hiding in plain sight all these years. Never even changed his name or his profession. He's still Schäfer and he's still in the meat trade. And he never went back to the family farm either. At least he may have done so at first, but he's got a high-class butcher's shop now. Supplies all the good hotels and restaurants around Tübingen.'

'So, he's not going to suddenly do a flit then?'

'No, he's making a good living for himself, so I think you can rest assured that he's not going anywhere. Do you want us to deal with it or do you want to come out and see him for yourself?'

'And you're quite sure it's him?'

'Absolutely. He hasn't exactly kept quiet about his achievements. He's proud of them, in fact. Been heard boasting to his cronies in his favourite local bar about his way with female prisoners when he was younger.'

Sylvia paused for a moment, gathering her thoughts about how unsullied and excited Phyllis had been at the moment of her departure all those years before. 'I'll fly out soon,' she said. 'In about a week. Shall we go into his shop and place an order, tell him he's mincemeat once I've finished with him?'

She knew that would make him chuckle. She heard it in his rich voice as he replied, 'We could ask for a kilo of tripe maybe, or some brawn.'

'We'll see what he has to offer,' she said. 'I'd like to see him squirm first.'

'Me too. I'll meet you at the airport.'

As their call finished, Sylvia wondered about the man she had sought for so long and was going to meet at last. And she couldn't stop herself thinking, once a butcher, always a butcher.

Ten days later, Charlie drove Sylvia to Tübingen. The latest Prinz sat on the rear seat of the Audi, his head hanging out of the open window, long ears blowing back in the breeze.

'Do you think Prinz would like to come with us and ask for some bones from our friend the butcher?' Sylvia said. 'My aunt always gave her dogs raw bones to chew. She thought it was good for their teeth.'

'My boy comes everywhere with me at all times,' Charlie said. 'Don't you, boy?' At which point Prinz pulled his head back inside the car and rested it on his master's shoulder, licking his ear.

Charlie flicked the dog's muzzle away with his hand and Prinz resumed his vigil at the breezy window. 'I suggest we take it slowly. Don't want to alarm the man at this stage. Besides, he may have an assistant in the shop and butchers are known for being handy with their cleavers.'

'Mmm, I can still picture his mother with her knife even after all these years.' Sylvia cast her mind back to that unnerving day at the farm. 'And now we've found him at last, I wouldn't want to scare him away. But once we're sure of him, do you think your men could move in quickly?'

'Not a problem,' Charlie said as he let the car roll to a halt near the shops in the centre of the town. 'But this is just a recce, remember?'

Sylvia knew that the man she was about to confront would have no idea who she was, but she wrapped her head in a scarf tied under her chin and donned dark glasses all the same. He might recognise her later, but for now she wanted to appear anonymous.

They strolled along the street past various shops until they came to his premises. A sign in green and gold boldly proclaimed the butcher's name and his calling. The gleaming words FLEISCHEREI SCHÄFER were prominent above the window displaying trays of pork chops, steaks, veal cutlets and whole game birds. Now it was autumn, unplucked pheasants and haunches of venison also hung from hooks above the trimmed cuts of meat and charcuterie.

Through the glass they could see two men in white coats and dark aprons behind the counter, serving customers. At the back of the shop an assistant was operating a machine that oozed minced meat into a large metal bowl. 'That's him on the left,' Charlie said. 'The large one with the moustache.'

Sylvia peered into the shop to catch a glimpse of her target. It was hard to tell if it was the same man she had seen pictured on the small identity card when he was young and a new recruit. 'We'd better go inside. It will look very odd if we're seen staring at the staff and not so much at their goods. What do you fancy getting? We can't cook raw meat back at the hotel, so do you fancy any of these cured meats?'

'I think Prinz would appreciate some Weisswurst,' Charlie

said. And as if he'd heard those inviting words, the huge dog put his front paws onto the windowsill, stood on his hind legs looking at the display and gave an appreciative whimper. 'Right, white sausages it is then,' Charlie said, telling Prinz to stay outside while the two of them entered the shop.

Sylvia decided to keep quiet and let Charlie do the talking. Behind her dark glasses she just wanted to observe and take in every detail of the man she believed had tortured and finally killed her lovely Phyllis. He had probably always been well built, but now, in middle age, he had run to fat, his belly swelling his apron, his chins in rows beneath his full lips and drooping handlebar moustache, linked to his balding head by bristling muttonchop whiskers. There was only the faintest resemblance now to the photographic image she had held in her mind for so many years. His voice was gruff, with a regional accent.

'Half a kilo of your finest Weisswurst and do you think you'd like anything else, darling?' Charlie said, turning to Sylvia.

She shook her head. She could not drag her eyes away from the meaty hand, with fingers the size of chipolatas, grabbing the white sausages from the pallid pile that looked so like severed male members. Combined with the underlying smell of blood and flesh that pervaded the shop, the sight sent a shiver creeping down her neck. She could not bear the thought that those coarse, fat fingers had touched dear Phyllis.

The stained fingers of the groping hand also told her something else quite significant: he was a smoker. That fitted in with what she had heard about one of his favourite methods of abuse in his former life. And she noted another significant detail: the index and middle fingers of one hand were stained a blackish-green. She lowered her sunglasses so she could be sure. It wasn't a stain from offal or any of the cuts of meat in his shop, it was the highly distinctive mark left by Sobranie Black Russian cigarettes, identifying him as a frequent and extravagant smoker, indulging in this expensive brand. An odd choice for a man like him, she thought, remembering Stefan Schmidt's comment from years before. And if Schäfer had indeed stubbed these special cigarettes out on Phyllis's tender flesh, then the stain they had left on his skin had marked him out for the whole of his life.

As they left the shop and walked away, Prinz nuzzling Charlie's leg and trying to sniff the parcel of sausages, Sylvia said, 'What else have you found out about him?'

'He often plays cards with one of the restaurant owners late at night, after service has finished. His debts have built up and he'll be in dire trouble soon.'

'Where do they do that?'

'There's a little bar in a backstreet. And I have it on good authority that he staggers home on his own after a few drinks.'

'Do you think we should go there?'

'Mmm, probably not. It's not a respectable establishment. If you're hoping to get a closer look before we grab him, I don't think it would be a wise move. Better that my boys move in on him while he's alone.'

'Then do you think you can pick him up there tonight?'

Charlie laughed. 'My, aren't we eager? You might have to wait twenty-four hours, my love. And where would you then like us to take him?'

'Somewhere I can safely meet him and ask a few questions. Is that possible?'

'Easy. We'll stay in Stuttgart and wait for news. You won't be disappointed, he'll soon be all yours.'

Sylvia smiled to herself. It would give her plenty of time to find her target's favourite cigarettes.

FIFTY-TWO

INTO THE WOODS

Charlie's contacts were certainly men of their word, Sylvia thought. How many other isolated shacks, barns and cowsheds did they know of, tucked away in the forests of Germany, places where they could conduct their secret business without questions being asked?

She peered into the darkness and saw a sliver of light filtering through the trees as Charlie's car rolled to a halt and he switched off the headlights. 'Are you sure this is the right place?'

'This is where I was told to bring you. Our butcher might not be expecting us, but he's waiting here for something to happen all right.' Charlie turned off the engine and all was still and dark around them.

Sylvia shivered, pulling her sheepskin coat closer, as they left the car and slipped through the trees to the wooden cabin hidden in the forest. Their feet made barely any noise on the soft carpet of pine needles, so unlike the crisp autumn leaves of deciduous trees. As they crept to their rendezvous, their breath clouding in the chill, she heard a pheasant's harsh cry and saw a deer slipping away in the moonlight. A hint of pine resin and woodsmoke hung in the air and she could see a spiral of smoke curling up from the shack's chimney. Under any other circumstances, this forest cabin would have been perfect for a romantic assignation, rather than a scene of interrogation.

Charlie rapped his knuckles on the heavy wooden door, which opened a crack after the pause of a moment. On recognising him, the man inside stepped away and slipped his pistol back into the holster strapped across his chest. 'Good to see you both. Your guest has been getting rather impatient, awaiting your arrival,' he said, tilting his head towards the large figure tied to a chair. Schäfer was jerking his body against the ropes binding him. The gag prevented him from speaking, but Sylvia could hear his angry growls of frustration.

'Well done, Otto,' Charlie said. 'Has he given you much trouble?'

'Not as much as some,' Otto said with a laugh, 'though Hermann here got a bruised rib or two in the process.'

Sylvia heard the soft shuffle of a second man slipping in through the door behind them. He must have been keeping watch outside behind the trees, waiting for their arrival.

'Our friend is not as nimble as he might have been in his youth,' Hermann said, laying down his shotgun on the plain wooden table. 'He's let himself get out of condition.'

'But we're delighted that he could join us all the same,' Charlie said, pulling off his soft leather gloves and hanging their coats over the back of a chair. 'So why don't we all make ourselves comfortable?' He offered Sylvia a seat facing her man and took one to the side for himself. For once, he was unaccompanied by Prinz. He'd told her before they left that they'd have enough assistance that evening.

Schäfer had quietened down and was staring at both of them, a few strands of greasy hair falling over his eyes. His nose had bled a little, but otherwise he appeared to be totally unharmed. The cabin was warmed by a glowing pot-bellied iron stove and droplets of sweat, whether from the heat or sheer terror, beaded his forehead.

'You can relax now,' Charlie said. 'We just want to ask you a few questions.'

Otto leant across the table with glasses of steaming glüh-wein that were releasing the scent of cinnamon and cloves. Salted pretzels and nuts were set out on a plate.

'Perhaps Herr Schäfer would like to join us,' Sylvia said. 'Hermann, can you remove the gag so our guest can enjoy a drink with us?'

As soon as the obstruction was removed from his mouth, Schäfer bellowed, 'How dare you treat me like this! I am an honest businessman. If this is anything to do with the gambling debt I owe my friend, this is not the best way to go about settling it.'

Otto bent over Schäfer, holding the glass of fragrant wine close to his lips, but he jerked his head away, so the glühwein splashed across his chin and clothes.

Sylvia raised her eyebrows in slight disappointment. She took a couple of slow, appreciative sips of the warm wine, then said, 'We hear you enjoy talking about your wartime exploits, Herr Schäfer, or may I call you Klaus?'

'Englisch? You are Englisch?' He stared at her and then a flit of recognition sparked in his eyes. 'You came into my shop yesterday.'

'Yes, I did. And so did my friend here. Your sausages were excellent.' She inclined her head towards Charlie, who was enjoying the pretzels and wine. 'I am English and Charles has spent a lot of time in my country. And I believe you may have met some of my other friends during the war. What do you have to say to that?'

His eyes narrowed, as did his mouth. 'You won't find anyone of my age who didn't have a part to play in those years. What of it?'

Sylvia took another sip. 'I'm not here to trick you, Klaus. I just thought we could have a nice little chat about that time. I mean, I feel like we're already old friends, because it was you I saw years ago, at your family's farm, wasn't it?'

She registered the frown that creased his brow. Was he remembering her now from that time? 'You looked very fetching in your dress and kerchief. Did you enjoy dressing like your sister? You almost had me fooled that day.'

All the other men in the room laughed and Charlie said, 'I expect he still likes dressing up after a hard day's butchering. I should think it really suits him.'

Klaus's face reddened even further and his brows knitted, so Sylvia could tell he was getting annoyed. 'Ignore them,' she said. 'Why don't you just drink this lovely wine, relax and talk to me just like you chat with your friends in your favourite bar about old times?'

He gave a scoffing laugh at that point, then began coughing a phlegmy cough, the legacy of his long smoking habit. Otto stepped forward again and this time Klaus drank some of the wine. 'Why would I want to talk to a woman the way I talk with my drinking companions?'

'I'm all ears, Klaus. We've got all night and all tomorrow as well if you want. But why wouldn't you be happy talking to a woman?'

He cleared his throat, turned his head slightly to the side, then spat on the wooden floor. 'War's no place for women. Should've stayed home.'

'Did you resent those women who were involved in the war?'

He stared at her, sniffed, then spoke. 'Men can't be blamed if women get in the way. Orders had to be followed and tempers ran high.'

Sylvia could see he wasn't going to freely repeat the boastful remarks he'd been so fond of handing out in his regular haunt.

She turned to Charlie and the other two men. 'What was it that Klaus was heard telling his friends? He seems to have forgotten. Can you remind him?'

Otto sat down, crossing his legs and cupping the warm wine with both hands. 'Aah, yes. Let me see, he likes to talk about how he was in charge of the women and especially the English woman. Apparently, he says he liked to teach them a lesson before they died.'

'All of them or just the one?'

'Oh, he was very fair. He claimed to have given them all special treatment, but he had a favourite, didn't you, Klaus?'

Sylvia could see the beginnings of a smirk lifting the corners of the butcher's mouth. Even here, even under duress, he was sickeningly proud of himself. She despised him with all her heart. 'Do you remember the English prisoner now, Klaus? Is it all coming back to you?'

He lifted his head and looked her straight in the eyes. 'You women are all the same. So superior. Especially that English woman. I was only doing my job, I just followed orders.'

'Please try to remember everything, Klaus. I really want you to remember for me.' Sylvia reached into her deep coat pocket and pulled out a photograph. Her old print had become so creased and dog-eared, she'd had a new copy printed. 'I thought this might help you. But perhaps you never saw her looking quite as lovely as this.'

The men and the cabin seemed to hold their breath as she stood up and held the photo out before him. Klaus stared at it and then smiled, a sneery leer of a smile. 'She didn't look anything like that when she came to us,' he scoffed. 'She was a mess by the time I met her. Filthy bitch.'

'It's such a shame you never met her when she looked like this. You'd think she was a film star, wouldn't you?' Sylvia snatched the picture away, laid it flat on the table, then reached into her pocket and brought out the pack of Sobranie Black Russian cigarettes.

She sat down again and opened the pack, taking one for herself. 'Oh sorry, how rude of me. Would you like one?'

His left eyebrow twitched as he said, 'You smoke my favourite brand. I've smoked them for years.'

'You have expensive tastes. But I must say they are rather special. Otto, could you light one for our guest and perhaps hold it so he can enjoy it?'

Otto took a cigarette from the pack, lit Sylvia's first and then lit the second, taking a couple of short drags to ensure it was alight. He held it to Schäfer's lips and he drew on the black and gold cigarette, making the tip glow bright red, closing his eyes as he inhaled the smoke.

'There, that's better, isn't it? I can see you're feeling much more relaxed now. A cigarette can do that for you, can't it? Just marvellous. Did you offer them to your beautiful English prisoner? And by the way, did you know her real name was Phyllis?'

He inhaled again and, as the smoke slowly escaped, he gave a lazy smile. 'I never wasted expensive cigarettes like these on filth like her, but she felt the effect of a cigarette all right.'

'Did you find it useful to use them as persuasion?'

'Huh, that one couldn't be persuaded to do or say anything. Stubborn bitch. We knew she was English but she wouldn't admit it. Still pretended to be French.'

'And did that annoy you?'

'What was the point? She'd nothing to gain by then. I tried to make her talk but she wouldn't. Stupid cow. Kept saying her name was Simone.'

Sylvia drained her glass of wine. The dregs had grown quite cool. Otto stepped forward to offer her more, but she waved him away. She held the black and gold cigarette to her lips. The chocolatey scent of the tobacco mingled with the spice of the mulled wine and she briefly remembered the first time she had smoked Black Russians with Peg. A time of innocence and friendship, just like Phyllis might have enjoyed with her own school friends in a golden time before all the horror. 'I wonder why you hated her so much? She was such a lovely girl. So loyal, so brave.'

Schäfer glared. 'She was a spy. We were told to treat her as a dangerous prisoner. If she'd been in army uniform, she'd have had military status, even though she was a woman. And she'd have been treated as a prisoner of war. But no, she was a damned liar, an underhand filthy spy.'

'Gosh, you really didn't like her very much, did you? What a shame you, and your colleagues who'd beaten her up before she got to you, hadn't ever known her at her best.' Sylvia picked up the photo again, looked at it with fondness, then turned it towards Schäfer. 'Such a pity. She really was the most marvellous girl.'

And then she saw that smirk again. Just before he bent his head to take another drag on the cigarette held out for him. He let the smoke curl out of his bulbous nose above that bristling moustache, then said, 'She wasn't much by the end. I could barely bring myself to touch her.'

Sylvia had to take a breath to calm herself before she could speak without trembling with disgust. 'And did you touch her, Klaus? Did you touch her in a special way?'

'I let her know the power of a real man before she died. Bitch had never done it with anyone before me. At least I did that for her. She didn't die a virgin.' He winked at Sylvia. 'Me and the lads performed that service for all your female spies. It was the least we could do before we got rid of them.'

He leant towards the cigarette again, but Otto pulled it away. Schäfer stared for a moment and then gave a careless shrug, despite the restraints around his body.

Sylvia couldn't bear his cruel arrogance. She looked at this bloated, whiskery brute and hated his very being. Taking a calm drag on her cigarette, she turned to the others and said, 'I think we've got a rapist here, who liked to beat up young girls and burn them with cigarettes.'

'If you want it done, he's the man to do it,' Charlie said with a curl of his lip that demonstrated his revulsion for Schäfer.

Sylvia stared straight at this coarse, bound man, trying to decide what to do next. And then he made up her mind for her. He chuckled and he winked. It may well have been nerves, but it seemed to her like arrogant insolence. And she couldn't help herself. She snapped. She marched across to him and stubbed her glowing cigarette out on his cheek. 'That's for Phyllis, you vile pig.'

He screamed, trying to jerk his head away from the burning tip as she ground it into his skin, just as she imagined he had done to her lovely Phyllis.

'He's all yours,' she said to Hermann and Otto, who were both silent. 'You can do whatever you like with him. Feed him to the pigs he butchers if you want. That's the only kind of justice he deserves.'

The two men moved towards him, but Sylvia didn't want to wait and see what happened next. She pulled her coat around her and Charlie followed her out into the cold, still forest. As they reached the car, they heard a single shot.

'It's all over,' Charlie said. 'Are you quite sure that's what you really wanted?'

'We made it too easy for him,' she said in a weary voice. 'But at least it's finished now. Just drive, will you?'

As the car rolled away into the dark night, Sylvia felt ashamed of her loss of control. She prided herself on remaining aloof but that wink had been the final straw. And she didn't regret leaving him to the mercy of Otto and Hermann, who would dispose of the body in the vast, empty forest.

Despite having Charlie by her side, Sylvia felt alone with

her thoughts, staring into the blank darkness. Although a public trial would have brought Schäfer's cruelty to the attention of a court, exposing the camp system and its perpetrators yet again in all its horror, his crimes would have become public knowledge and she couldn't bear for Phyllis's younger brother to hear what had been inflicted on his beautiful sister. It was bad enough to know that she had been beaten without hearing that she had been defiled as well.

If she had been dispatched with a clean shot to the back of the neck, a Genickschuss, as the guards used to call them, then perhaps he could have faced charges. But not this, not this filthy, humiliating act of degradation. Phyllis's brother didn't need to hear that described in court. And he would never hear it from Sylvia either. Whatever nightmares he suffered already would be a thousand times worse if he found out that the only man his sister had ever known was a brutal pig, who had beaten and burned her, then forced himself upon her.

2. Digging should be done under cover.

The spot for burial should be chosen in a wood and as remote as possible from big trees because roots are a serious handicap to quick and silent digging.

FIFTY-THREE
THE FIRE IS OUT AT LAST

It didn't half take a long time for me to get rid of all those files, you know. All that cardboard and tons and tons of paper. I could only burn a little bit at a time in the fireplace. Some of it was official-looking stuff, all typed out properly, but a lot of it was Sylvia's handwritten notes. I read everything, of course. I know she said not to, but in the end, I felt I had to. It seemed it was the only way I could ever begin to fully understand what she'd gone through and why she was so strange in later years.

Those poor girls. No wonder Sylv was always going on about her brave girls and worrying so. She was responsible for them right from the moment they signed up. And what happened? They managed to get a few messages sent out and then that was it, that was the end of their war work. Imprisoned, tortured, then killed, some of them.

And to think how Sylv had kept it quiet all these years too. She could have shared it with me, but I realise now that she felt so guilty that it was hard for her to ever talk about it. She'd told these girls she'd train them and look after them and in the end she couldn't do a damn thing to save them.

From all the notes in the files, I now understand how hard

Sylvia had tried to track them all down. That must have been so soul-destroying for her, because she must have known she was never going to find all of them and that it was only ever going to be bad news. And the places she'd had to visit...! I knew she'd travelled a bit after the war, but I had no idea she'd had to go to all those dreadful prisons and Dachau. No wonder her mind was filled with nightmares about the plight of those poor girls.

I nearly wept reading her notes on what she eventually discovered. Such dreadful treatment for those young women. She'd finally found that three of them weren't even shot, but were injected with poison and then cremated. Honestly, everything about that time was worse than I could ever imagine and then poor Phyllis was abused like that on top of everything else. I'm not surprised how it all ended up preying on Sylvia's mind.

There were photos of them in the files as well. Such beautiful young girls, all of them. They could have been models or film stars, they were so attractive. Especially Phyllis. I could see why she was so special. Her photo was quite dog-eared, as if it had been handled and looked at many, many times.

And when I'd finished burning all the papers and the photos, it really struck me that Sylvia had been doing such important work in the war and afterwards too, when she tried to trace her agents. I know she'd always fobbed me off, saying she just did a lot of filing, but it was so much more than that, even though she did leave me a lot of files to deal with.

And although she'd told me a little bit more that time the journalist came to interview her, I couldn't quite understand why she didn't end up telling me everything then. But I think she'd had it drummed into her so much that this was all secret work that she could never have broken the habit of keeping schtum. I found a copy of the little booklet of rules her department gave all the agents and right at the beginning, it said they could never disclose anything about their training so she could never talk about it, could she?

And then another thought came to me as well. Me and Sylv, we'd both done important war work in our way. I'd had a dreary job making thingummybobs for goodness knows how many gadgets and so on, while she was training people to go out there to undermine the enemy. But, I told myself, all I did was make parts that were meant to help us fight the war, while she sent those girls out to an almost certain death. At least my job didn't directly kill any beautiful young women, as far as I know.

The letters Sylvia received were still nasty and frightening though. I can sort of understand why Phyllis's brother wrote them and probably wrote the anonymous ones as well. He'd wanted to protect his big sister but was too young to intervene. It was just his way of trying to show that he could still fight for her. But it was mean and unkind all the same, scaring poor Sylv like it did. No wonder she always hated the post and wanted to hide away here in the countryside where no one knew what she had done before.

Dealing with all of this since the funeral has given me plenty of time to think about what I need to do next too. At first, with Sylvia gone, I was all for selling the thatched cottage and moving back home, but I'm having second thoughts now. You see, I'd started looking into it and had a couple of estate agents over to give me a price for the cottage and I told them I'd be moving back to London. Then one of them said, Hackney, eh? That's quite an up-and-coming area these days. So, I thought I might as well find out what I'd get for my house there. Could have knocked me down with a feather, you could. It's worth way more than the cottage, so I can afford to stay here and get the roof rethatched as well if I want.

I went over the figures a couple of times, I was that shocked. But I've decided it suits me being out here. It's like me and Sylvia are still together. I've got to learn how to use a computer so I can do grocery orders and so on, but a lovely young man from the village is coming in to show me what to do. He says I'll be silver-surfing and wondering how I ever managed without it in no time. I'm not sure quite what he means, but if I can get all the heavy shopping delivered here, I'll be quite happy.

I'm thinking of getting a dog again and that means bags of biscuit and tins of food, so I won't want to be dashing down to Sainsbury's for that every five minutes. And it would be nice to have a companion on my daily walks, now Sylvia's gone. Something small that doesn't eat much would suit me, not one of those huge dogs she liked so much. Maybe I'll call it Fergus in memory of her.

Barry's been very kind too. He says he'll do any little jobs around the place as well as the garden. He suggested I might want a lift down to the pub now and then, and I might well take him up on it. He's smartened himself up a bit and his car would be handy if I ever have trouble driving myself.

I also half wondered about selling some of Sylvia's things, once I'd sorted out her belongings. I've kept a lot of her clothes, because she had some very good-quality bits and pieces and they more or less fit me, so they'll see me out, I should think. Most of it was hung with dust covers and mothballs in her wardrobe, but there was a suitcase under her bed as well. I pulled it out, thinking it was going to be more clothes, but it turned out to be a uniform, which I think she must have worn back in the war. I wouldn't know what to do with a thing like that, so I pushed it back under the bed, along with all the fluff balls and cobwebs.

I was tempted to sell some of her better jewellery, but it reminds me so much of her, I think I should keep it. Besides, it's all a part of her life. That compact that had belonged to Phyllis, for example – I can't go selling that. And then there's her little diamond bird brooch she was so fond of.

Well, I found out where that came from in the end. She still had the original jeweller's box it came in and tucked under the velvet lining was a little note. It was from an old boyfriend, just like I'd always thought. I'd spotted the name a few times in the files. Campbell. She never mentioned him, but I know how fond she was of that brooch. I wondered at first if it was him I'd seen at the funeral with the dog, but after reading through her notes, I reckon that was Charles Muller. He was the one for dogs. Sylvia had asked me to put an announcement in the obituary columns of *The Times* and the *Daily Telegraph*, when the time came, so he could have found out that way.

Phyllis's brother must have heard the news too, because there haven't been any more letters since Sylvia died. I wonder how he feels now, not being able to vent his frustration any more? Does he feel guilty about threatening an old woman, or is he still blaming Sylvia? Part of me feels sorry for him, never knowing exactly what happened to his sister. But I have to say, I'm in agreement with Sylv. He wouldn't have benefited from knowing exactly what happened to Phyllis. His nightmares would likely have become worse, it was so awful. So I think, in the end, Sylvia did the right thing, however much pain it gave her to keep it all to herself. Poor girls, poor Sylvia.

It's very foggy here today. It often is in the autumn. But I don't mind it. I know there's no one hiding out there in the thick mist that clouds the fields. There's nothing to be afraid of. So, I've decided to stay put right here. I'll stay on in the thatched cottage with my memories of her. Me and my friend Sylvia. We'll be quite content, talking about old times, drinking sherry by the fire in the evenings. Oh, and did I tell you? There was a gun in that suitcase I found under the bed. It doesn't surprise me Sylv had one tucked away. I probably won't ever use it, but it could see off a burglar one day, couldn't it?

The Thatched Cottage,
Bourne Lane,
Little Bourne-Hardy

November 1999

Dear Mr Lane,

You don't know me, but I was Sylvia Benson's best friend and companion for over eighty years. So, if anyone should know what she was really like, it's me. And I want you to know that she was the most loyal and decent person I've ever known.

I found your address on your most recent letter to her, shortly before she died. I can understand why you were very upset not knowing what had happened to your poor sister during the war, but I don't think you should have sent all those letters blaming Sylvia for your sister's disappearance.

I know exactly what sort of nasty things you kept on saying, because Sylvia left it to me to sort out her affairs and I've read all of your very unpleasant letters. Why she saved them, I can't think, but at least it gave me a chance to understand why she was so afraid of the post arriving.

If you could have seen the effect your letters used to have on Sylvia, maybe you'd have thought twice about blaming her so much. They really upset her, so you should be ashamed of yourself. She did her best to look after her agents during the war and afterwards she spent years trying to work out what had happened.

I think you must know that Sylvia passed away recently as there haven't been any more of your letters since the notice appeared in the paper. So, I hope that is the end of it and you can stop being bitter. There were many casualties in the war and sadly your sister was just one of them. I know Sylvia fretted about all the agents who were lost and not just Phyllis. My friend felt guilty to the end of her days and, if she could have ever given you some good news, I know she would have done.

At Sylvia's request I have destroyed all of her personal papers, but among her effects I came across a sealed envelope addressed to you. I wasn't sure at first whether to send it, but I suppose she wrote it for you so there you go. I have no idea what it might say, but hope it might bring you some consolation. I am also enclosing an old photograph of your sister that Sylvia had kept all these years. It's a bit creased, but you might as well have it.

I hope you can find some peace of mind now that there is no longer anyone to blame.

Yours sincerely,

Peggy Wilson

A LETTER FROM SUZANNE

Thank you so much for choosing to read *The Girl Who Never Came Back*. If you did enjoy it, and want to keep up to date with all my latest releases, just sign up at the following link. Your email address will never be shared and you can unsubscribe at any time.

www.bookouture.com/suzanne-goldring

I hope you enjoyed *The Girl Who Never Came Back* and, if you did, I would be very grateful if you could write a review. I'd love to hear what you think and it makes such a difference helping new readers to discover one of my books for the first time.

I really appreciate hearing from my readers – you can get in touch through my Facebook page, through Twitter or my Wordpress website.

www.suzannegoldring.wordpress.com

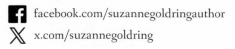

facebook.com/suzannegoldringauthor

x.com/suzannegoldring

AUTHOR'S NOTE

I always think that the best historical novels consist of a gripping story based on a framework of facts. They shouldn't try to bombard the reader with lengthy information dumps but should dress the underlying scaffold of dates and actual events with a hefty dollop of 'yes, but what if?' to create the most riveting plot and convincing characters.

Any reader who, after reading *The Girl Who Never Came Back*, wants to know precisely what happened in the Special Operations Executive, and specifically what fate awaited some of its courageous agents, should study the reference sources listed below. In particular I cannot recommend Sarah Helm's brilliant account of the work undertaken by Vera Atkins highly enough. It is an astonishingly detailed account of this extraordinary woman's work and life. Not only did Vera Atkins select and equip these agents for their dangerous missions, but she also tirelessly devoted herself to establishing the facts about the demise of the twelve young women who failed to return home.

Under the guise of 'what if', I found myself asking how it must have felt preparing these girls for such perilous work and how it felt knowing they had suffered terribly in prisons and concentration camps. Would the person responsible for their recruitment and training experience extreme remorse or guilt? And did the families of these young women ever question whether their training had fully prepared them for the dangers they faced and hold the recruiters and trainers responsible?

I found myself imagining a somewhat less efficient, less sympathetic, misogynistic SOE, a world in which the suspicions of lower ranks, particularly women, were not always taken seriously. And with that in mind I developed a story in which the challenges undertaken by an SOE recruitment officer lead to a lifetime of blame, both by herself and by a close relative of one particular agent.

In doing so, I hope I have not downplayed the importance of the real SOE and its personnel and especially the remarkable Vera Atkins. Her extraordinary search for the truth is utterly inspiring and I have shamelessly followed in her footsteps to convey my character's harrowing journey through post-war France and Germany. But other than the names of certain real German characters and locations, the details like Sylvia's love of men, alcohol and desire for revenge are entirely the product of my imagination. However, I have not invented the terrible cruelties inflicted on the lost SOE agents, nor have I exaggerated the length of time for which they suffered. These brave young women were said to have even greater powers of endurance than the men who experienced brutal interrogation in similar circumstances. And meanwhile, on the home front, women like Peggy applied themselves to jobs that had not been available to them before, making a vital contribution to the war effort. My grandmother worked for the Plessey factory during the war and for many years afterwards, but I don't ever remember her talking about her work, only about the camaraderie she experienced. Nor did she ever talk to me about her days in the adapted tube train tunnel, but I like to think that her underground experience was, in its own way, as important as the undercover work of the SOE.

I can't know to what degree Vera Atkins may have collaborated with men like those I have created in the Magnet Men, but she certainly met members of the Haystack group, which was involved in similar work rooting out cowardly Nazis. She would also have met a man who loved Great Danes, but whether she had an affair with him, like Sylvia, I really couldn't say. But she may have appreciated the dog more than the man, so I felt obliged to feature the elegant grey Prinz in my story.

REFERENCES

Special Operations Executive Manual: How To Be An Agent in Occupied Europe. London: William Collins, 2014.

Bailey, Roderick. *Forgotten Voices of the Secret War.* London: Ebury, 2009.

Crowdy, Terry. *SOE Agent – Churchill's Secret Warriors.* Oxford: Osprey Publishing, 2008.

Escott, Beryl. *The Heroines of SOE: Britain's Secret Women in France: F Section.* Cheltenham: The History Press, 2010.

Helm, Sarah. *A Life in Secrets: Vera Atkins and the Lost Agents of SOE.* London: Abacus, 2006.

Milton, Giles. *Churchill's Ministry of Ungentlemanly Warfare.* London: John Murray, 2016.

Minney, R.J. *Carve Her Name with Pride.* Barnsley: Pen & Sword, 2006.

Nicholas, Elizabeth. *Death Be Not Proud.* Cresset Press, 1958.

Overton Fuller, Jean. *Madeleine.* Omega Publications, 2019.

Stevenson, William. *Spymistress.* Arcade Publishing, 2011.

Verity, Hugh. *We Landed by Moonlight.* Shepperton: Ian Allan, 1979.

Walters, Guy. *Hunting Evil.* Bantam Books, 2010.

ACKNOWLEDGEMENTS

Firstly, I must thank HarperCollins for granting permission for me to quote from the *Special Operations Executive Manual*, the handbook for all SOE agents. As I was reading the manual and deciding which lines I would like to include in my novel, I felt a strong sense of the vulnerability of the young men and women whose lives depended on these instructions.

Secondly, I am immensely grateful for the encouragement of writing friends and colleagues, particularly the Vesta girls, Carol, Denise and Gail. I was also spurred on by the Elstead Writers Group and the Ark Writers, who are all happy to share their honest opinions of my work.

I greatly appreciate the enthusiastic support of my editor Lydia Vassar-Smith, who encourages me to undertake exciting journeys. I am so grateful for her confidence that I will develop strong characters and a gripping story. I must also thank my agent Heather Holden-Brown for her calming reassurance whenever I feel I am getting lost. And lastly, thanks are due to the entire Bookouture team, who make my books happen and ensure I complete the journey from idle thought to publication.

Made in the USA
Columbia, SC
25 May 2024

36183741R00214